HAVE YOU READ THEM ALL?

Discover the entire Robert Hunter series ...

'Carter is now in the Jeffery Deaver class'
Daily Mail

THE CRUCIFIX KILLER

A body is found with a strange double cross carved
into the neck: the signature of a psychopath known as
the Crucifix Killer. But Detective Robert Hunter
knows that's impossible. Because two years ago
the Crucifix Killer was caught. Wasn't he?

THE EXECUTIONER

Inside a Los Angeles church lies the blood-soaked
body of a priest, the figure 3 scrawled in blood on his
chest. At first, Robert Hunter believes that this is
a ritualistic killing. But as more bodies
surface, he is forced to reassess.

THE NIGHT STALKER

When an unidentified victim is discovered on a
slab in an abandoned butcher's shop, the cause of death
is unclear. Her body bears no marks; but her lips have
been carefully stitched shut. It is only when the full
autopsy gets underway that Robert Hunter
discovers the true horror.

THE DEATH SCULPTOR

A student nurse has the shock of her life when she discovers her patient, prosecutor Derek Nicholson, brutally murdered in his bed. But what shocks Detective Robert Hunter the most is the calling card the killer left behind.

ONE BY ONE

Detective Robert Hunter receives an anonymous call asking him to go to a specific web address – a private broadcast. Hunter logs on and a horrific show devised for his eyes only immediately begins.

AN EVIL MIND

A freak accident leads to the arrest of a man, but further investigations suggest a much more horrifying discovery – a serial killer who has been kidnapping, torturing and mutilating victims all over the United States for at least twenty-five years. And he will now only speak to Robert Hunter.

I AM DEATH

Seven days after being abducted, the body of a twenty-year-old woman is found. Detective Robert Hunter is assigned the case and almost immediately a second body turns up. Hunter knows he has to be quick, for he is chasing a monster.

THE CALLER

Be careful before answering your next call. It could be the beginning of a nightmare, as Robert Hunter discovers as he chases a killer who stalks victims on social media.

GALLERY OF THE DEAD

Robert Hunter arrives at one of the most shocking
crime scenes he has ever attended. Soon, he joins forces
with the FBI to track down a serial killer who sees
murder as more than just killing – it's an art form.

HUNTING EVIL

Lucien Folter, the most dangerous serial killer the FBI has
ever known, has just escaped. Now, he's hunting for Detective
Robert Hunter – and he's going to make him pay . . .

WRITTEN IN BLOOD

When Angela Wood gains possession of a book
containing horrific descriptions of multiple murders, it
becomes clear that a serial killer is on the loose – and even
Robert Hunter might not be able to stop him.

GENESIS

Robert Hunter is on the trail of the most vicious
and disciplined serial killer he has ever encountered.
Their crimes have only one disturbing link – pieces of
a poem, left inside the victims' bodies.

CHRIS CARTER

THE
DEATH
WATCHER

SIMON &
SCHUSTER

London · New York · Sydney · Toronto · New Delhi

First published in Great Britain by Simon & Schuster UK Ltd, 2024

Copyright © Chris Carter, 2024

The right of Chris Carter to be identified as author of this work has been
asserted in accordance with the Copyright, Designs and Patents Act, 1988.

1 3 5 7 9 10 8 6 4 2

Simon & Schuster UK Ltd
1st Floor
222 Gray's Inn Road
London WC1X 8HB

Simon & Schuster: Celebrating 100 Years of Publishing in 2024

Simon & Schuster Australia, Sydney
Simon & Schuster India, New Delhi

www.simonandschuster.co.uk
www.simonandschuster.com.au
www.simonandschuster.co.in

A CIP catalogue record for this book is available from the British Library

Hardback ISBN: 978-1-4711-9761-1
Trade Paperback ISBN: 978-1-4711-9762-8
eBook ISBN: 978-1-4711-9763-5
Audio ISBN: 978-1-3985-2879-6

Typeset in the UK by M Rules
Printed and Bound in the UK using 100% Renewable Electricity
at CPI Group (UK) Ltd

MIX
Paper | Supporting
responsible forestry
FSC
www.fsc.org
FSC® C171272

Dedication

I would like to dedicate this novel to all the readers out there who for the past fifteen years have shown me the most incredible support and love. I have been privileged enough to have met so many of you throughout my career, and I'm always humbled by how amazing, kind and patient you all are.

You are the reason I do what I do. You are the reason I'm still here. From the bottom of my heart, thank you all so much for keeping me and my dream alive.

See you on a book tour sometime soon.

This story was inspired by real events

One

Consciousness returned to Shaun Daniels in unsteady waves. First came a heavy flutter of the eyelids, quickly followed by a desperate, gasping breath. The little air that he managed to breathe in felt musty, leaden, with an odd mixture of smells he couldn't quite identify. He swallowed the few drops of saliva that his glands were able to produce, but as he did he felt his throat scrape and burn, as if he had gulped at a bowl of crushed chili, garnished with broken glass. The pain made him wince and hold his breath for a couple of seconds. His eyes, lost and out of focus, instinctively moved left then right.

Nothing.

Shaun could see nothing other than darkness.

'What the hell?' The words dripped out of his dried lips in a slumber, his eyelids feeling too tired to blink fully open. *Have I passed out again after another heavy night of drinking?*

The thought didn't surprise him and the headache that had just exploded inside his skull surely did feel like the mother of all hangovers.

'Urgh,' he grunted, as he took another lungful of stale air. He tried to swallow some more saliva, but instead he ended up coughing, which triggered the burning pain in his throat to join forces with his headache, making his whole face throb.

'Fuck,' Shaun whispered, as he exhaled another drowsy breath. 'What the hell did I drink last night ... gasoline?'

It was then that he realized he was lying flat on his back, against some not-very-comfortable surface. This certainly wasn't his bed.

Where the fuck am I? The kitchen floor? The thought came with another tired breath. *I guess I better get up. I don't even know what time it is.*

But as Shaun tried to move, nothing happened.

'What the fuck?'

He tried moving again.

Absolutely nothing – his toes, his feet, his legs, his arms, his hands, his fingers, his neck ... nothing moved.

'What the hell is going on?'

That was when Shaun heard an odd sound coming from somewhere to his right. It sounded like someone shifting their weight on a chair.

Shaun's eyes immediately moved in that direction, but there was nothing for him to see.

'Hello? Who's there?' he tried calling out, but his throat was too dry ... his vocal cords too weak to produce any sounds louder than a whisper. Still, he carried on. 'Please, can you help me? I can't move.'

Shaun got no reply.

'Hello?' he tried again. 'Is anyone there?'

Silence.

What the fuck is happening? Is this a dream? Why can't I move?

Shaun squeezed his eyes shut as tight as he could before blinking them open again. It didn't feel like a dream. Everything was still there – the darkness, the throbbing headache, the burning throat, the stale air ... and he still couldn't move. He felt desperation quickly settling in.

'Good. You're awake.'

The flat and smoky male voice Shaun heard came from his right.

He tried as hard as he could to turn his head in that direction, but his neck muscles simply didn't respond. His eyes, on the other hand, moved as far right as they possibly could.

'Who's there?' Shaun asked, his words sounding strangled. 'Can you help me, please? I'm not sure what happened, but I can't move.'

'Yes. I know,' the man calmly replied, as he flicked on the light switch.

Directly above Shaun, a light bulb inside a heavy-duty metal mesh box flickered a couple of times before engaging, bathing the room in so much brightness, it burned at Shaun's retinas. Instinctively, he once again squeezed his eyes shut, but since the back of his head was flat against whatever uncomfortable surface he was lying on and he couldn't move his neck, he had no real way of escaping the bright glare that hit him like a sucker punch. Despite having his eyes shut, the light was still strong enough to travel past his eyelids and through the optical nerve to collide with his already unbearable headache. Right then, his brain felt as if it were about to melt.

'Urgh,' he moaned, his breath catching on his throat. 'That's so goddamn bright.'

'Give it a minute,' the man said, his tone placid. 'Your eyes will get used to it.'

'What's going on?' Shaun asked, his tone gaining a desperate edge. 'Where am I? Why can't I move? Who are you?'

'You're in my OR,' the man replied. 'On my operating table.'

'Operating table?' Shaun shot back, his eyes blinking open for a split second before he squinted, the light still too strong for him to be able to fully open them. 'This is a hospital? Was I in some sort of . . .' his voice croaked at the implications '. . . accident? Oh God, what happened? Please tell me that I'm not paralyzed . . . please.'

The man paused, as if pondering what to say. He decided to go with a question instead of an answer. 'What's the last thing you remember, Mr. Daniels?'

Shaun heard the man's footsteps go around him to the other side.

'Umm . . .' He tried to think, but his headache seemed to have built a fortress around his memory. 'I . . . I can't really recall. My head is pounding so much it feels like it's going to blow.'

'Take your time,' the man said, his voice now coming from Shaun's left. 'You've been sedated. The headache, the dried throat, the numbness, the blurred memory . . . it's all quite normal.'

Right then, Shaun heard a new sound, something like metal clunking against metal. He breathed out and blinked again, his eyes finally calming into the brightness enough for him to be able to semi-open them. As soon as he did, they immediately moved from right to left, trying to take in as much as he could.

Due to his inability to turn his neck and the position of his head – its back lying flat against the operating table – Shaun wasn't able to see much.

The ceiling was painted all in white. The walls were tiled, also in white, and, from what Shaun could see, they looked to be squeaky clean. The smells that he couldn't quite identify earlier began making a little more sense then – cleaning agents, antiseptics, disinfectants . . . the typical odd combination of scents that usually came with every hospital.

'Umm . . .' Shaun closed his eyes and tried pushing his memory again. The headache was proving to be a very worthy opponent. 'My head is a mess . . . and it hurts like hell. Could I maybe get something for the pain?'

'That wouldn't be a good idea,' the man replied. 'Painkillers don't work well with the sedative you were given. Please, just try your best.'

What do you think I'm doing? Shaun thought, his eyes shooting left. *Singing 'Mambo Number 5' in my head? I'm doing what I can here, buddy.* He took a deep breath and fought through the headache until flashes of something began coming back to him, but they didn't amount to much.

'My memory is as hazy as a meth hooker,' he said, once again blinking against the bright light. 'But I . . . kind of remember going down to my local bar for a couple of drinks.'

'Where's that?' the man asked. 'Do you remember the name of the bar? Do you remember where you live?'

Shaun hesitated for a quick moment, his memory misfiring like an old engine.

'Umm . . . I live in South LA.'

The man waited but Shaun offered nothing else.

'Can you be a little more specific?' the man pushed. 'Can you remember the neighborhood in South LA you live in?'

A single-second pause.

'Yeah,' Shaun replied, as things finally started taking shape inside his head. 'I live in Lomita – at the corner of Eshelman Avenue and 250th Street.'

'That's very good, Mr. Daniels,' the man said, finally stepping close enough for Shaun to be able to see him for the first time.

The man towered over the operating table, but from a lying-down position and with the light shining down straight into his eyes, it was impossible for Shaun to even guess how tall he really was. The man's hair, if he had any, was completely tucked under a teal-colored scrub cap. His nose, mouth and chin were also hidden behind a standard-issue surgical mask. All Shaun could really see were the man's eyes – dark and deep-set behind a pair of operating goggles.

'Anything else you can remember?'

Shaun pushed his memory a little more.

'Umm . . . I think that I was having a chat with someone. But I can't remember who.'

'In the bar?'

'I think so, yes.'

'Good. Can you remember anything else?'

Shaun tried, but his memory was just a puddle of mud.

'No, nothing,' he replied, his eyes filling up with tears. 'Please tell me, what happened to me? How come I'm here? How come I can't move? How come I can barely remember anything?'

The man stepped back from the operating table, disappearing from Shaun's line of sight for a quick moment.

'That's totally fine, Mr. Daniels. No need to worry. To be completely honest, memories can't exactly be trusted, did you know that? Especially the ones that are formed directly following a traumatic event. They warp, they shatter, and then, as we try to recollect, memories are put back together in ways that look nothing like the original. And that's when the problems really start. People put so much faith in what they supposedly remember, thinking of it as a verbatim record of what happened. But that's rarely the case. Where there are gaps in our memories, the brain takes a best guess, filling those gaps with whatever it thinks fits. Important details that can't be remembered get substituted by imagination. Can you see how problematic that can get?'

Shaun didn't know that.

'Too many people take memories as fact,' the man continued. 'But they simply don't work like that. They are more a perception of what happened than actual reality.'

'So . . .' Shaun hesitated, tears gathering at his lower eyelids. 'Are you telling me that I might never remember what happened to me?'

'No, not at all. That much I can tell you. You went drinking at your local bar, Mr. Daniels, and while doing so, you ran into some trouble.'

Once again, Shaun heard what sounded like metal clunking against metal. Not a heavy sound – more like instruments being placed on a metal tray.

'Trouble?' Shaun queried, his tone hesitant and worried in equal measure. 'What do you mean? What sort of trouble?' A tear ran down the side of his face.

The man stepped back into Shaun's line of sight. This time, he brought an instruments cart with him.

'You were chatting to someone at the bar, Mr. Daniels,' he replied. 'And that someone was trouble.'

'What?' Shaun asked, yet again squinting at the harsh light, trying hard to remember.

Had he been in a fight? Had he been stabbed ... or shot? Did this someone who he was chatting to at the bar somehow damage his spine? Was this why he couldn't move? Was that what the doctor was trying to tell him.

Among all those questions, a new thought rushed to the top of the pile, bothering Shaun. He tried to focus on the man's face.

'I don't understand. How do you know that the person who I was talking to at the bar was trouble?'

The man chuckled, holding the suspense for a couple of extra seconds. 'Because that man was me.'

Shaun frowned at him. 'What?'

The man reached for something on the instruments tray to his right. 'I have a question for you ... *Shaun*.'

The change in how the man addressed Shaun had clearly been deliberate. From the instruments tray, he retrieved a small hammer and something that looked like a chisel with a thick, round end, instead of a pointy one.

'For breaking bones,' the man asked, 'do you think this sort of chisel will do, or should I go for something a little heavier ... perhaps sharper?'

'*What?*' Shaun's eyes moved to the hammer and chisel for a second before refocusing on the man's face.

'I don't want to break skin,' the man explained. 'I want to fracture the bone, but I don't want to make any cuts to the skin or flesh.' He shrugged. 'Hematomas and bruises are fine, obviously. It's hard to break bones without any bruising, right?'

Shaun's heart stuttered. 'I . . . I don't understand.'

'Oh, sorry,' the man said, placing both the hammer and the chisel back on the instruments tray. 'Please allow me to clarify. Back at the bar, last night, I spiked your drink.'

This time, Shaun simply squinted at him, trying to figure out if he was joking or not.

'It was about a quarter past eleven,' the man continued. 'That was when you told me that you had to go. I offered to buy us one more round – for the road, you know? I knew that you wouldn't say no to another whiskey, so, while you went for a piss, I drugged your drink.'

'Is . . . this a joke?'

The man broadly gestured to the room they were in. 'Clearly not.'

Shaun blinked and a new tear ran down the side of his face.

'I've done the "drink spiking" thing quite a few times before,' the man carried on. 'And I can say that I've got my technique and timings down to perfection. We had already finished our drinks and were just exiting the bar when the drug started to take effect. By the time it rendered you unconscious, we were right by your car. No witnesses. Getting you inside was a piece of cake.'

'I . . . I don't understand.' Fear had clearly taken over Shaun's tone of voice. 'Why? Why are you doing this?'

'The short answer?' the man replied. 'Because I'm going to hurt you, Shaun. A lot.' There was no play in his voice.

Shaun tried moving again, but no muscle in his body responded.

'And this is the great thing about the state you are in, Shaun,' the man explained. 'No matter what I do to you – shatter bones, rip your toenails out, crush one of your testicles, whatever . . . you won't feel a thing.' There was a deliberate pause. 'For now . . . but the neuromuscular blocking agent that I've administered, which has paralyzed you from the neck down, will wear off in . . .' The man checked his watch. 'About an hour and fifteen minutes. Then, the pain *will* come . . . mild at first, as your nervous system slowly regains its sensibility. It will probably start with muscle aches, which will gradually turn into spasms. Then, your joints will feel like they've been ripped out and replaced with shards of broken glass.'

Shaun's petrified eyes were on the man, who was once again towering over the operating table.

'Next . . .' The man clearly wasn't done. 'Your stomach will fill with bile and you're going to vomit. There's nothing you can do about that, but vomiting will feel like someone is ramming a burning fist down your esophagus, scorching and tearing at its walls, sending blood dripping down the back of your throat, which will choke and gag you, making you feel like you're drowning. The more your nervous system awakens, the more pain signals it will send to your brain . . . the more pain signals your brain receives, the more you'll vomit because the pain will be unbearable, I'll make sure of that. But in your case, I've got a real cool surprise for the grand finale.'

Shaun felt as if the air around him had become heavier . . . harder to breathe.

The man once again reached for the hammer and chisel on the instruments cart. Even though his nose and mouth were covered by his surgical mask, Shaun could tell that he had a smile on his face.

'I'm sure that you've realized this by now,' the man said. 'But you're not really in a hospital. And I'm not really a doctor, but I'll do my best.' He turned and consulted a piece of paper on the instruments cart. 'OK, shall we start?'

'Please . . .' Shaun begged, his voice strangled by tears. 'Whatever you're thinking about doing . . . please don't. I don't have much money, but you can have whatever I've got. Please don't do this. Please . . . just let me go.'

'Shhhhh,' the man breathed out, as he placed the chisel against Shaun's right thigh and lifted the hammer high in the air. 'Don't close your eyes.' He nodded. 'Watch this.'

Two

Thirty-two days later

Located on the fifth level of the famous Police Administration Building in Downtown LA, the LAPD's Ultra Violent Crimes Unit's office sat at the far end of the Robbery Homicide Division's floor. Even though it was named a 'unit', Ultra Violent Crimes was composed of only two detectives: Robert Hunter – the head of the unit – and his partner, Carlos Garcia. They were both just about to exit their office when Barbara Blake, the division's captain, appeared at their door.

'Going somewhere?' she asked. Her long jet-black hair was elegantly styled into a bun, pinned in place by a pair of metal chopsticks. She wore a silky white blouse, tucked into a well-cut, navy-blue pencil skirt. Her flat-heel shoes were black and shiny, with a silver detail at their tip.

'Just about to go grab some lunch,' Garcia replied, instinctively checking his watch. It was a quarter past two in the afternoon. 'Why, Captain? What's up?' he asked, quickly noticing the yellow folder that Captain Blake had with her. Usually, investigations assigned to the UVC Unit came either in a black or dark-gray folder.

'I wanted you two to have a quick look at something for me,' the captain replied, stepping into the office and closing the door behind her.

'Sure,' Hunter said, standing up to meet her. 'What is it?'

'It's an autopsy report,' Captain Blake explained, handing a copy of the report to each detective.

'Linked to which case?' Hunter asked.

'At the moment, to a traffic incident,' the captain replied.

Hunter and Garcia both frowned at her.

'About forty-five minutes ago,' Captain Blake clarified, 'I got a call from Dr. Hove. She had just finished a post-mortem examination on a Shaun Daniels, forty-six years old and a resident in Lomita. His body was found by the side of Lake Hughes Road in the Sierra Pelona Mountains, victim of an apparent hit-and-run.'

'A hit-and-run?' Garcia asked, flipping open the report. Hunter did the same.

'An *apparent* hit-and-run.' Captain Blake re-emphasized the word as she nodded at the files in their hands. 'Just have a look at it and tell me what you think.'

'Well,' Garcia said, even before he started reading the file. 'If the LA County Chief Medical Examiner called the LAPD Robbery Homicide Division's captain with an *apparent* hit-and-run, something clearly didn't sit right with her at the autopsy.'

Captain Blake lifted her hands in a surrender gesture. 'Like I've said – have a look at it and let me know what you think.' She pulled a chair in front of Hunter's desk and took a seat.

Garcia's eyes widened at her. 'What, like right now?'

Silence.

'But lunch . . .'

Captain Blake sat back on her chair, crossed one leg over the other, and calmly rested her hands on her knees before glaring back at Garcia.

'. . . can clearly wait.' He finished his sentence, leaning back against the edge of his desk. His tone carried no enthusiasm.

Hunter had already begun reading the file, which started with an occurrence sheet from the LAPD Valley Traffic Division.

The body had been discovered four days ago, in the early hours of the morning, by Marcus Stamford and his son Julian as they drove up Lake Hughes Road in the direction of their favorite fishing spot in the Castaic Lake. At around 5:10 a.m., about 150 yards past the entrance to the community church, heading north, both father and son spotted what looked to be a body by the side of the road – one that didn't look like an animal. Concerned, Mr. Stamford stopped the car and went to check. That was when he discovered the lifeless body of an adult male, who looked to have been run over by a vehicle. Mr. Stamford then proceeded to call 911.

The LA County Sheriff's Department was first at the scene, quickly followed by an ambulance and Detective William Sharp, from the LAPD Valley Traffic Division.

Hunter flipped a page on the report and studied the scene photographs. There were twenty-six in total. The first eight were of the body in full, taken from various angles. The next twelve were close-up shots, detailing the severity of the injuries that the body had sustained. There was an exposed fracture to the right wrist and one to the right tibia, where the bone had even protruded through the fabric of his black trousers. His left shoulder and clavicle were visibly dislocated and broken, and there were lacerations to his face, head, arms, legs and hands, with the skin having been scraped at places.

The final six photographs showed the road, mainly concentrating on the tire skid marks that were clearly visible against the asphalt. There were four of them, with all four showing just as prominently. That, together with the gap between the front and the rear skid marks, indicated that the vehicle that had hit Shaun Daniels had almost certainly been a four-wheel-drive pickup truck. One of the photographs showed measurements done against the skid marks – the ones created by the front wheels were both around four and a half feet long, the rear ones just a couple of inches shorter.

According to Detective Sharp, the position and the distance of the body in relation to the skid marks was consistent with a hit-and-run accident where the victim was struck by a vehicle traveling at a speed somewhere between forty and fifty miles per hour. The brakes seemed to have been initiated just a fraction of a second before the fatal collision, indicating that the vehicle's driver did not see the pedestrian until it was way too late. Upon impact, the victim was thrown over the vehicle's hood, made contact with the windshield and was projected forward and to the right, landing back on the road.

'My first question here is,' Garcia said, flipping back and forth on the report for an instant. 'What was the victim doing up in the mountains at that time in the morning?'

'Fishing, maybe?' Captain Blake speculated. 'Hiking?'

'You would've thought so, right?' Garcia came back. 'But there's no mention, or photos, of anything else found by the side of the road – no backpack, no bag, no cases, no fishing rod ... nothing.' He shrugged. 'Yes, there are quite a few fishing spots around where the body was found – near the picnic area. But even if he was there hiking, fishing, or having a lonely picnic in the dark, what was he doing crossing the road all the way at the top? What I mean is – the picnic areas and the fishing spots are well away from Lake Hughes Road.'

'Good question,' Captain Blake agreed.

'His station wagon was found parked down a dirt road, not that far from where the body was found,' Hunter said, reading from the report. 'It doesn't say anything about a picnic basket, a bag, a backpack, a fishing rod ... nothing.'

'Was his cellphone found?' Garcia queried.

Hunter flipped back and forth on the report for a moment. 'There's no mention of it, so probably not.'

'So the theory here would be what?' Garcia asked. 'He drives up there, parks his car, goes for a stroll and gets hit by a truck, which then flees the scene?' His eyebrows arched at Captain Blake.

'Suicide?' she asked, but her tone carried no conviction.

'No.' Garcia shook his head, a gesture that was reciprocated by Hunter. 'He lived in Lomita, Captain. If the plan had been to kill himself by stepping in front of oncoming traffic, then why drive all the way to a quiet road up in the Sierra Pelona Mountains, when he had the super-busy Pacific Coast Highway right at his doorstep. This wasn't suicide; if it was, it wasn't a planned one, that's for sure.'

Captain Blake agreed with a nod. 'I just wanted to make sure that we had covered as many possibilities as we could—'

'Before suggesting murder,' Hunter said, anticipating where the captain was going.

The captain angled her head slightly left, as her perfectly drawn eyebrows arched at her detectives. 'Please, read on.'

Hunter and Garcia both moved on to the autopsy report. In it, Dr. Hove had confirmed that most of the injuries to the body, especially the exposed fractures to the right wrist and lower right leg, were consistent with a pedestrian being struck by a moving vehicle at speed.

Hunter paused for a moment and quickly went back to the photos of the body in full. One of them had been taken from a distance, where the body and all four skid marks were visible. Something in that image got the gears in his brain turning just a little faster, but his thought process was quickly interrupted by Garcia, who had jumped straight to the final page of the report to check on the cause of death.

'What? Is this right?'

His eyes shot to Captain Blake.

'COD?' she asked.

Garcia nodded.

'Dr. Hove was one hundred percent certain,' the captain confirmed.

Hunter flipped over to the last page and paused. '*Hypothermia?*' Doubt coated the word as it came out of his lips. 'Are you telling me that this guy froze to death?'

'Not me,' Captain Blake replied. 'The report is.'

'In California?' Garcia asked. 'In June? It's about seventy-three degrees outside.'

The captain saw a sparkle light up in Hunter's eyes. He looked over at his partner.

Garcia knew that look well enough. He gave Hunter a shrug. 'I'm a sucker for a mystery, you know that.'

Without saying a word, Captain Blake stood up and left the UVC Unit's office.

She didn't collect the files.

Three

Seconds after Captain Blake had left their office, Hunter called the Chief Medical Examiner for the LA County – Dr. Carolyn Hove. At the time of the call, Dr. Hove was just about to start a new post-mortem examination, but she explained that she would be free to talk in about an hour's time, so straight after lunch, Hunter and Garcia took a quick trip to the Department of Medical Examiner-Coroner in North Mission Road.

After making their way up the lavish steps that led to the main entrance of the impressive old hospital-turned-morgue, they entered the lobby and approached the reception counter. The attendant, a kind-faced, African American woman in her mid-fifties, greeted them with a very well-rehearsed, courteous smile.

'Good afternoon, Detectives.'

'Good afternoon, Sandra,' Hunter and Garcia replied at the same time, both of them returning the smile.

Sandra had been with the Department of Medical Examiner for over thirteen years.

'How are you doing today?' Hunter asked.

'I'm OK, thank you.'

Hunter knew that the question wouldn't be returned. None of the department receptionists ever asked anyone entering the morgue how *they* were doing, regardless of who they were.

'Here to see Dr. Hove?' Sandra asked, already checking her computer screen.

'That's right,' Hunter replied, quickly consulting his watch. 'She told us that she'd probably be free around this time.'

Sandra gave both detectives a renewed smile. 'Perfect timing. She just finished an autopsy about five minutes ago. I'll buzz her for you.'

Hunter and Garcia waited while Sandra had a quick ten-second conversation on the phone.

'Dr. Hove will meet you in Autopsy Theater Four,' she said, as she instinctively indicated the double swinging doors to the right of the reception counter.

Hunter and Garcia thanked her, pushed through the doors and carried on down the long, squeaky-clean, white corridor. At the end of it, they turned right into a shorter corridor, where two empty gurneys were pushed up against the left wall.

Hunter pretended to be scratching his nose, but what he was really doing was cupping his hand over it, as the smell of those corridors got to him every time. It was like a smell with a hidden punch – and that hidden punch packed some serious power. Hunter didn't mind it at first, many years ago, but the more he visited the morgue, the more he noticed it . . . and the more he noticed it, the more it bothered him because, no matter what, that smell could only be associated with one thing – death.

As they walked past the gurneys, they turned right again. Autopsy Theater Four was the first set of double doors on the right. Hunter pushed them open and he and Garcia stepped inside a room that was chilled to a few degrees below comfortable. This was a small autopsy theater when compared to theaters one, two and three, with only one stainless-steel examination table that sprang out of a long counter that ran along the east wall. On the ceiling, directly above the examination table, there was a large, circular, surgical light, which was already turned on, bathing the room in warm brightness. The west wall was completely made of cold metal storage crypts, which looked more like large filing cabinets with bulky handles than anything else. The interesting fact was that the strong smell from the corridors was a little less intrusive inside the autopsy theater.

Tall and slim, with penetrating green eyes and in her traditional long, white lab overcoat, Dr. Hove stood at the other side of the empty examination table. Her long chestnut hair was rolled up into a simple bun at the top of her head.

'Robert, Carlos.' She greeted each detective with a subtle nod. 'I'm guessing you're here about the file I sent Barbara early today, right? Male victim, found up in the Sierra Pelona Mountains?'

'You knew that Captain Blake would come to us with that file, didn't you, Doc?' Garcia asked, a quirky smile on his lips.

Dr. Hove replied with an eyebrow-lift. 'I admit that this victim doesn't exactly fall under the category of ultra-violent crimes, but it's certainly a very intriguing case, and I know that the two of you like "intriguing", so yes, I was pretty sure that Barbara would take the file to you first.'

'Well,' Garcia said, as he and Hunter approached the autopsy table. 'The COD was definitely something different.'

'Yes, it was,' Dr. Hove agreed. 'That and a few minor details that just didn't sit right, you know?'

'Really?' Hunter asked. 'Like what else?'

'Here,' she said, her head tilting in the direction of the metal crypts. 'Let me show you.'

Hunter and Garcia followed Dr. Hove over to the theater's west wall and waited while she opened the door to compartment 3C, before rolling out the body stored inside it. It lay inside a white, plastic body bag. Dr. Hove pulled the zipper from head to toe, splitting the bag open to reveal the body in its entirety. Shaun

Daniels had been an average man in height, but a little slight in weight.

Live and up close, his facial lacerations were even more shocking than how the pictures that Hunter and Garcia had looked at just over an hour ago had shown. The body's left eye socket seemed to be out of level with its right one – a little deeper and certainly fractured. His nose, completely twisted out of shape and scraped down, had also clearly been broken. Despite the body having been found days ago, his face, hands and feet still showed signs of swelling. His skin looked rubbery and porous, but instead of ghostly white, it had taken on an odd shade of purple, which made it harder to see the large number of bruises that graced most of his body.

'I wasn't supposed to have been the ME in this post-mortem,' Dr. Hove explained. 'Seemingly apparent CODs, like hit-and-runs, bullet to the head, suicide and so on, are always assigned to one of the several advanced classes we run in conjunction with UCLA forensic pathology degrees. These types of corpses often go to students, but due to some paperwork error at the university, it ended up here. I was supposed to have been in a meeting all morning today, but the meeting got canceled. To help out with the backlog of autopsies, I took a couple on this morning.' She nodded at the body on the slab. 'This was the second one.'

Dr. Hove stayed quiet for a moment, allowing both detectives to quickly study the body in front of them. Hunter was the first to pick up on something odd.

'He's missing four of his toenails on his left foot,' he said, frowning at the doctor, who smiled back at him.

'Good eye, Robert,' she said, with a nod. 'That was one of the clues that something about this hit-and-run didn't feel quite right.'

Garcia, who was still studying the victim's facial lacerations, quickly moved his attention to the corpse's feet. 'What the hell?'

Hunter thought back to the photos that he and Garcia had looked at in their office. It took him just a second to remember.

'He was wearing sneakers,' he said, his gaze settling on Dr. Hove. 'On the photos in the file you sent us, Doc, he was wearing sneakers.'

Dr. Hove nodded in silence.

'Do you have them?'

'In the storage room,' she confirmed. 'His nails weren't inside it, if that's why you're asking.'

'This can't be a consequence of being hit by a car, Robert.' Garcia shook his head.

'I know,' Hunter accepted. 'The reason I asked is because there's no way that he was walking around wearing sneakers, with no toenails on his left foot. Too painful.'

'He wasn't,' Dr. Hove confirmed. 'He was dead before he got to the spot where he was found.'

Hunter scratched his chin. 'How long before? What's the time of death?'

The doctor quickly reached for her notes. 'According to the traffic incident report, his body was discovered by the side of the road at around 5:10 a.m., on Sunday, June 16th. That's four days ago.'

'That's correct,' Hunter confirmed.

'Well,' Dr. Hove continued. 'He was dead at least six to eight hours before that time, but not longer than eighteen.'

'So he died sometime on Saturday afternoon/evening,' Garcia queried, 'not on Sunday morning?'

'That's right.'

A couple of silent seconds followed the doctor's revelation.

'But according to the LAPD Traffic Division,' Garcia again, '*and* your autopsy report, his injuries are consistent with a pedestrian being run over by a car at speed.'

'They are indeed.' The doctor nodded at the detectives.

'OK,' Garcia countered. 'But there's no way that he was run over by a car sometime on Saturday evening and no one saw the body lying there, by the side of the road, until 5:10 a.m. on Sunday morning. Lake Hughes Road might not be the busiest of roads, but it's busy enough. It links Santa Clarita to Lancaster through the Sierra Pelona Mountains. Traffic might die down late at night and in the early hours of the morning, but you would still get cars crossing over every couple of minutes or so.'

'Like I said,' Dr. Hove insisted. 'The compound fractures, together with all the bruising, the damage to the cranium, the scraped skin and the torn clothing, are all consistent with him being struck by a car at speed, but . . .' Her eyebrows arched again.

'But the accident could've been staged to mask the state that the body was already in.' Hunter completed the unfinished sentence. 'And by "staged" I mean – there was no accident at all. The perp could've easily created the skid marks on the road, using his truck, and simply left the body there.'

'Very much so,' Dr. Hove agreed. 'The assumption of a hit-and-run accident here was purely circumstantial – the body was found on the road, at a location that showed some pretty hard-braking skid marks against the asphalt. The distance between the body and the skid marks were consistent with the pedestrian being hit by a vehicle traveling at around fifty miles per hour—'

'But that can be easily calculated.' Garcia, this time.

'Correct again,' the doctor confirmed. 'There was nothing at the scene that indicated foul play, so very understandably, anyone wouldn't really think twice before assuming that the body on the road was there due to a hit-and-run accident.'

Hunter shifted his attention back to the body's feet. 'You said that the missing toenails were *one* of the clues to the fact that something about this hit-and-run didn't feel right. What were the others? The skin color?'

'That was another, for sure,' the doctor replied. 'This purply shade that his skin has taken on can be caused by a number of different factors – loss of body heat is one of them. His face, hands and feet also show signs of swelling, but not as a consequence of a fracture, which is odd.' Her head bowed in the direction of the body. 'But the main clues here are the comminuted open fractures – both of them.'

Hunter and Garcia studied the fractures for several long seconds.

'There's a lack of ecchymosis.' Hunter spoke first.

'Bang on the money,' Dr. Hove agreed. 'There's no bruising . . . no hematomas directly around the wound, where blood vessels were clearly severed from such severe trauma. If his blood circulation was normal at the time those fractures occurred, ecchymosis would've appeared all around the wound, like you can see around the nail plates on his toes.'

'So what you're really saying here is,' Garcia shot back first, 'that he was alive when he lost his toenails, but already dead by the time he fractured his wrist and leg?'

'That's what the necropsy evidence is showing us, yes,' the doctor agreed. 'Which indicates that the perp didn't just create the tire skid marks on the road, and simply leave the body there, like Robert suggested.'

'He actually ran him over,' Hunter corrected himself. 'Causing the compound fractures . . . but that happened way after he was already dead.'

Dr. Hove nodded. 'That's why the lack of ecchymosis. But that's not all. He also has three fractured ribs, six broken fingers, three on each hand, and a fractured eye socket – the left one. Those, on the other hand, occurred while he was alive.'

Hunter once again studied the victim's feet before moving over to his hands. Most of the nails on all of his fingers, including his thumbs, were either chipped or broken. Despite the purple hue that the victim's skin had taken on, Hunter saw no indications of frostbite, nor on his toes or on his fingers, but he also knew that frostbite wasn't a prerequisite for hypothermia, which could also occur in temperatures that weren't considered *bitterly* cold. That was usually due to the person being wet, sweaty, trapped in cold water, lacking any kind of unnatural body-heat insulation (clothes) or a combination of those. The fact that Shaun Daniels's body fat seemed to be on the low side would've also slightly accelerated the hypothermic process. All in all, there were indeed some indicators to hypothermia, but Hunter knew that Dr. Hove would've needed something a lot more concrete to justify her findings.

'So what led you to conclude that the ultimate cause of death was hypothermia, Doc?' he asked.

'Good question, Robert,' the doctor replied, her head angling slightly left. 'Because that was where things got a little trickier.'

'Why is that?' Garcia, this time.

'Well, the identification of hypothermia as a COD has always been somewhat problematic in the field of forensic pathology. In the majority of cases, our biggest indication to hypothermia comes from circumstantial evidence – the person is found in the snow, or submerged in freezing water, etcetera. It was precisely the lack of evidence that got me looking for different possibilities. The purpling of the skin, together with the swelling of the face, hands and feet, can indeed be caused by hypothermia, but it can also be caused by—'

'Poisoning.' Hunter beat her to the punch.

'Exactly,' the doctor agreed, her index finger pointing at him. 'Which sounded like a much more plausible alternative for a COD, given that we are in California and right at the beginning of summer.'

'Poisoning sounds fair,' Garcia commented.

'That was what I was looking for,' Dr. Hove continued. 'Signs of poisoning, when I discovered multiple black spots in his gastric mucosa.'

'Are you talking about Wischnewski spots?' Hunter asked.

'The one and the same.'

Garcia chuckled. 'I'm not even surprised that you know what they call black spots in someone's gastric mucosa, what boggles my mind is that you actually know how to pronounce that.'

Hunter shrugged. 'I read a lot.'

'And there it is,' Garcia's hand came up in a 'what can you do?' gesture.

'Wischnewski spots are considered one of the most reliable and important features in identifying hypothermia,' Dr. Hove carried on. 'I was very surprised to find them, which obviously prompted me to search for supportive links to fatal hypothermia – hemorrhages into the synovial membrane, bloody discoloration of synovial fluid of the knee . . . and other details.'

'And they were all present?' Hunter asked.

'All of them.' The answer came with a firm nod before she, once again, indicated the body. 'Ultimately, his heart gave up, but I have no doubt that the reason behind his heart failing was hypothermia.' Dr. Hove slipped off her latex gloves and threw them in the disposing container. 'So yes, as crazy as this might sound, this man has frozen to death . . . in Los Angeles . . . in mid-June.'

Four

Outside, the temperature had just hit 65°F, with the sun high on a bright-blue and completely cloudless sky. It hadn't rained in Los Angeles for over two weeks, which had already prompted a barrage of TV, radio and Internet adverts warning everyone about the risks of people inadvertently starting wildfires – something that, unfortunately, tended to hit the City of Angels almost every year during the summer months, causing tremendous destruction, death and loss.

As Hunter and Garcia stepped outside the reception lobby, they both reached for their sunglasses. Garcia's shades were squared, while Hunter's were classic aviators.

'You look like an FBI agent,' Garcia said, looking Hunter up and down.

'Really?' Hunter smiled back at him, as he quickly rechecked his attire. 'Is it the old T-shirt, the faded black jeans or the biker boots that gave you that impression?' He didn't wait for a reply. Instead, he removed his sunglasses and used his index finger to point to his right eye. 'Look into my eye.' Those words were delivered in an overly deep tone of voice.

'What the hell was that?' Garcia asked. There was no play in his tone.

'Me sounding like an FBI agent.'

'Are you . . . serious?'

'Yeah. It's a line from an old movie.'

Garcia's jaw dropped open. 'You're kidding, right? That line is from *Aliens*, Robert. Absolutely nothing to do with the FBI. And the sergeant uses his middle finger to point to his eye, not his index one. In other words – he's flipping the bird at the marine. Like this.' He used his middle finger to slightly pull his lower-right eyelid down. 'Look into my eye.'

Hunter frowned at him. 'Are you sure that's from *Aliens*?'

'Yes, I'm sure. You *are* hopeless, you know that?'

'I don't watch a lot of films.'

'You don't say.'

They got to Garcia's car.

Garcia unlocked his door and got behind the steering wheel. 'I have to admit that this whole thing is sounding weirder by the minute.'

Hunter took the passenger seat, but stayed quiet, the look on his face pensive.

'The speculation right now is that we have a victim,' Garcia continued, throwing his thumb over his shoulder to indicate the building behind them, 'who died somewhere else, potentially murdered, but someone, potentially the killer, or killers, took him way up the mountains, just to make it look like he was run over by a truck.'

'That pretty much sums it up, yes,' Hunter agreed.

Garcia sat back on his seat and chuckled. 'I am made of questions right about now.'

'OK, I'll bite. What's the first question that pops into your head? Right now.'

Behind his shades, Garcia's eyes narrowed at his partner.

'Don't think,' Hunter prodded. 'Just ask. What comes to mind first?' He quickly lifted a hand at Garcia. 'Don't go with the obvious "why was he murdered". Let's skip that one for now.'

'OK,' Garcia said, giving Hunter a single-shoulder shrug. 'Why the hell was he tortured?'

Hunter nodded, accepting that that was a good start.

'Because that's what really happened before he died. He was tortured, Robert. For how long, we have no idea, but he was definitely tortured. Someone ripped his toenails off, one by one. Someone broke six of his fingers, three of his ribs and his left eye socket before sticking him into a freezer ... while he was still alive ... because there's no other reasonable explanation to how he froze to death in the middle of June in LA. And did you notice that he had no ligature marks?'

Hunter nodded. 'Not on his wrists, nor on his ankles.'

'Exactly,' Garcia agreed. 'It doesn't look like he was restrained at all. His fingernails were all chipped and broken. His fingertips all scratched to shit because he clearly tried clawing his way out of somewhere – probably the freezer that he was locked in. Now ... how do you torture someone without restraining them?'

'Simple. You sedate them.'

Garcia drummed his fingers on the steering wheel. 'What fucked-up kind of torture is that, where the person doing the torture sedates the victim first?'

'The pretty horrible kind. Think about it – the victim feels nothing at first. Maybe they are even conscious and can see the perp inflicting the damage – ripping his toenails out, snapping his fingers, all of it – no pain, but the sedation wears off eventually ... and that's when the pain starts ... slowly ... gradually ... and it just keeps on coming, from everywhere – feet, hands, arms, legs, face, head, torso – getting stronger and stronger by the second. The perp could torture him an injury at a time, or all at once. It's a horrible way to inflict pain.'

'That's just fucking insane.' Garcia shook his head. 'And that takes me back to my question – why was he tortured like that?'

Hunter moved his shades up to his head. 'Textbook answer to why someone is tortured.' He used his fingers to count. 'To obtain information; to force the victim to do something the victim didn't want to do; as payback for something; as punishment for something; to extract money; or pure and simple sadism – to fulfill the killer's morbid desire to inflict pain. Some killers get off on that.'

'Don't I know it?' Garcia dipped his chin to look at Hunter over the rim of his glasses. 'But the ones who get off on that kind of crap can never limit themselves to a single victim, right? They all ultimately become serial killers because they simply can't stop themselves. They're never completely fulfilled, no matter how many they kill.'

Hunter stayed quiet.

'But I have no reason to believe that that's the case here. Do you? It just doesn't feel like the work of a serial murderer.'

'No, it doesn't.'

'But all the other options you mentioned are a real possibility,' Garcia continued. 'We know nothing about who Shaun Daniels really was. He could've been a drug dealer, a loan shark, a thief, a business owner . . . whatever.' He shrugged. 'Or the other way around – he could've owed money to the wrong person, or have slept with the wrong person's wife, or have told on the wrong person . . . you know – shit like that can easily get you tortured and killed, especially in a city like LA.'

'Research is already collecting all they can on him,' Hunter told him. 'We should have some sort of file on Mr. Daniels by tonight – tomorrow morning, latest – including credit card activity and phone records.'

'There's something else,' Garcia said. 'Something that's been bothering me since I read the traffic accident report.'

Hunter studied Garcia's expression for a couple of seconds. 'How come his car was found up there?'

Garcia's index finger pointed at his partner. 'Precisely. He didn't drive it up there, that's for sure. If he'd been shot, beaten to a pulp, strangled, whatever . . . even really run over by a truck, him having driven up there would've been a possibility.'

'But the victim died from hypothermia,' Hunter said, leaning against the passenger door.

'That's the wrench in the works,' Garcia agreed. 'He froze to death hours before he was found, which means – it didn't happen up in the Sierra Pelona Mountains. He didn't drive up there with a lover, or for a drug deal or whatever, and something went wrong. He didn't get ambushed up there either . . . and he sure as shit didn't freeze his ass to death while walking around Lake Hughes Road.'

'And yet,' Hunter commented, 'his car was parked up there.'

'Which means that someone else drove it up there. Probably the killer . . . or killers, but even if it wasn't, I'd really like to have a word with whoever it was.'

Hunter nodded as he slid his shades back up his nose. 'Yeah, me too.'

Five

To Hunter and Garcia the thought was simple and logical – Shaun Daniels couldn't have driven his car up to the Sierra Pelona Mountains and parked it down a dirt road because he was already dead by then, so someone else had to have. That someone else could very easily have left some sort of forensics evidence behind – on the seat, on the steering wheel, on the carpets, on the door handles, on the gearshift . . . somewhere. They just needed to find it.

From outside the LA County Department of Medical Examiner-Coroner, Hunter placed a call to Detective Sharp of the LAPD Valley Traffic Division, who told him that Shaun Daniels's car had been towed to the San Fernando Valley Police parking garage for storage. The problem was – since Detective Sharp hadn't suspected any foul play when he studied the 'accident' scene, four days ago – Shaun Daniels's vehicle wasn't treated as evidence, or a potential hub for it. The tow-truck driver and the car handlers at the police parking garage had probably completely contaminated the vehicle, and there was simply nothing that Hunter and Garcia could do about that now, except hope for the best . . . but the best wasn't exactly what they got.

It took Garcia just a little under an hour to drive to the other side of Hollywood Hills and on to San Fernando Valley. At the LAPD storage garage, they talked to one of the officers at the front gate. The officer handed Hunter the car keys, which had been found inside Shaun Daniels's trouser pocket at the 'accident' site, and directed them to the lot where the vehicle was parked.

'There it is,' Hunter said, indicating a white Volvo VX70 parked next to a VW Golf on the east wing of the large parking lot.

'That's the one,' Garcia agreed, checking the license-plate number.

He and Hunter gloved up, approached the vehicle, and had a quick peek through the driver's window.

'You have got to be shitting me!' Garcia said, his face almost melting into a question mark. 'How old was this guy? Six?'

'Damn!'

It looked like a bomb had gone off inside that car, but instead of explosives, the bomb was filled with trash. There was stuff everywhere – on the passenger seat, on the floor, on the dashboard, by the gearshift, stuffed into the door pockets . . . everywhere – wrappers, empty cans of soft and energy drinks, plastic bottles, paper cups, boxes, empty cigarette packs . . . it was just a mess.

'I don't think this car has ever been cleaned,' Garcia said, rounding the vehicle to look through the back window.

'You might be right,' Hunter agreed.

The back seat had been folded down to create more carrying space, which was packed with a ladder, PVC and copper pipes, rolls of white sealing tape, connectors, wires, a toolbox, buckets, and more.

'Was he a plumber?' Garcia asked. 'There's a lot of plumbing material in the back here . . . tools and all.'

'Maybe,' Hunter replied with a nod.

'Why would someone want to torture a plumber in the way that he was tortured? Bad pipework?'

'That's the million-dollar question.'

'Like I said,' Garcia breathed out. 'This case keeps on getting weirder by the minute.' He paused and straightened his body. 'Shall we call forensics and tell them not to bother? There's no way they'll be able to process all this crap. It will take them weeks and it will no doubt turn out to be a waste of time. There's probably a wrapper from every junk-food joint in the city in there.'

From Garcia's car, on their way there, Hunter had called Dr. Susan Slater, one of the best lead forensics agents California had to offer. She and her team had worked together with the UVC Unit on innumerable cases before. In the call, Hunter quickly explained what they had so far before asking Dr. Slater if she could dispatch a couple of agents to the police garage in San Fernando Valley to process Shaun Daniels's car. She'd replied that she wouldn't have anyone available until the morning, but that she would have it done by lunchtime tomorrow.

'You're right,' Hunter said. 'The trash in there will give us nothing, but we do need them here.' He moved over to the passenger side. 'They can concentrate their efforts on the door handles – inside and outside – steering wheel, gearshift, trunk handle and the center-console controls – radio, aircon and whatever else. Who knows? We might get lucky with something.' Hunter pressed the button on the key fob to unlock the doors.

Garcia took a step back. 'You're a brave man. The floor in there must be like the ground in the Amazon rainforest, you know what I'm saying? A breeding ground for insect species not yet known to man – like mosquitos with teeth, or something.'

'I'm not really getting inside.'

Hunter pulled the passenger door open and some of the trash that was wedged between the seat and door dropped to the ground.

Garcia joined Hunter and immediately cupped his hand over his nose. 'Jesus! I think the heat has cooked some of the leftover food in there from at least five years ago. It smells of puke and cigarettes.'

Hunter too cupped his left hand over his nose and used his right one to open the glove compartment – more trash, a set of screwdrivers and the vehicle's user manual. He moved some of the trash out of the way, pausing at times to study some of the wrappers a little more closely.

'Looking for anything in particular?' Garcia queried.

'Any kind of drug paraphernalia,' Hunter replied. 'Burned tinfoil, needles, glass pipes, cut water bottles, that sort of thing.' He moved some of the trash from the passenger seat, before doing the same to the junk on the floor.

Back at the morgue, Dr. Hove had told them that she had found no track marks on Shaun Daniels's arms, but most addicts were experts in hiding their track marks by using different veins around their bodies to shoot up – veins that could've been easily hidden by the large number of bruises to his body.

Hunter found nothing to indicate that Shaun Daniels was a user. Not even an old prescription bottle. He tried the center-console compartment – a pack of cigarettes, two unopened packs of gum and a set of keys.

Hunter reached for the keys.

Garcia looked over his partner's shoulder.

'House keys?'

'I'm guessing so, yes.'

'His home address is in the file,' Garcia said, his head angling left. 'In the car.'

Hunter nodded and checked his watch – 5:38 p.m. 'Let's hope that his house isn't the same kind of train crash his car is.'

Six

Shaun Daniels lived in a small, one-bedroom apartment on the second floor of a two-story building, right on the corner of Eshelman Avenue and 250th Street, in Lomita – part of the Metropolitan Area of Los Angeles. The building itself was nothing more than a dilapidated, rectangular structure, painted avocado green, with a front yard that was in much need of some attention. Two concrete staircases – one at each end of the building – led to the exposed upper deck, with a rusty, vertical, iron-bar rail running the length of the whole deck. In all honesty, the building looked more like one of those cheap, old, side-of-the-road motels than a residential building.

At 6:31 p.m., the street wasn't exactly busy, which allowed Garcia to park directly across the road.

Three kids, none of them older than twelve, were hanging out on the sidewalk by the street corner. Two of them watched, while the third one was trying hard, and failing, to do a kickflip on a battered skateboard.

As he and Hunter stepped out of the car, Garcia indicated a baby-blue door on the upper deck. The first door if they took the staircase at the left end of the building. 'Apartment twenty-one.'

'Yeah, I see it.' Hunter nodded.

They crossed the road and took the stairs up to the second floor. The curtains on both windows to the right of the door were drawn shut. Both detectives gloved up before Hunter used the keys he'd found in Shaun's car – first on the metal security grill gate, then on the actual apartment door, which opened with some resistance, not much, and a high-pitched squeak at the hinges.

As Hunter pushed the door ajar, he and Garcia were met by a heavy breath of warm and stale air. Not really surprising, given that the building faced west, therefore getting the sun pounding on the apartment's front door and windows for the entire afternoon. What was disconcerting was the scent that accompanied that warm breath. It was as if the smell that they had gotten from Shaun's car had acquired a new overpowering kind of punch-to-the-gut that brought tears to the eyes.

'Jesus!' Garcia said, reaching into his pocket and retrieving two teal-colored surgical masks. 'After the storage garage, I had a feeling that we'd be needing these.'

Hunter took the mask from Garcia and put it on before pushing the door fully open.

Despite the sun still being high in the sky, the apartment looked somberly dark. Hunter reached for the light switch on the wall to the left and flicked it on.

The front door opened directly into Shaun's living room/ kitchen space, which was a restrained and sparsely decorated room. The living room area had an old sofa, a mismatching armchair, and a wooden TV module pushed up against one of the walls. The kitchen area, which was accessible via a large opening on the wall to the right, had an old fridge, a stove unit, a microwave that sat on the counter and a small Formica table at its south corner. The sink was piled high with dirty dishes.

The air inside the apartment was saturated with the smell of mold and food gone bad. It was so heavy that, even with their masks on, Hunter and Garcia cringed as they stepped into the apartment.

Hunter checked behind the door. The reason for the subtle resistance was a small pile of unopened mail.

'It looks like he hasn't been home for a lot longer than just four or five days,' Hunter said, as he picked up the mail from the floor.

Garcia walked past him to look around the living room.

On the floor, next to the armchair, there were several empty bottles of beer, a few mugs and three plates with food leftovers that had long hardened onto the porcelain. A few flies were hard at work, trying to feed on the leftovers, but even they seemed to be struggling with it. On the Formica table, there was a small mountain of empty microwavable dinner boxes and takeout food containers – mainly Chinese and pizza – with even more flies buzzing around everything.

'How can someone be such a slob?' Garcia asked, staying well away from the table. 'I'm actually scared of opening that fridge and that trashcan.' He gestured toward the kitchen.

Hunter was still looking through the mail.

'He obviously wasn't married,' Garcia continued. 'Or had a girlfriend, a partner ... whatever. At least not a live-in one.'

'According to the file we have,' Hunter asked, 'his body was discovered four days ago, right – June 16th?'

'That's correct,' Garcia confirmed, turning to face Hunter. 'Why? What have you got?'

'Just bills and junk mail,' Hunter explained. 'Nothing of any real interest, but the earliest of these, according to the postal stamp, is the electricity bill. It's dated May 18th.'

Garcia frowned. 'It's June 20th today. So he's been missing for almost a month?'

'Something like that,' Hunter confirmed. 'It's been over four weeks since this bill was delivered. Gas and electricity bills are usually delivered the day after they've been posted. He could've been missing for longer than that.' He chose one of the envelopes and ripped it open.

'What's that?' Garcia asked.

'His cellphone bill.' Hunter quickly checked the front of the envelope. 'It was posted to him at the end of last month – May 31st.'

'And?'

'And his last communication using his cellphone was also made on May 18th.' Hunter met Garcia's stare. 'That's it. Absolutely nothing after that – no calls, no texts.'

'So he *has* been missing for about a month.'

'It looks that way, yes,' Hunter agreed.

'And no one has reported him missing?' Garcia's head tilted to one side. 'A friend? His boss? The neighbor? No one?'

'I don't think he's got a boss,' Hunter said, flipping back through the pile of envelopes in his hands. 'A few of these are addressed to "Daniels Plumbing Ltd". He worked for himself.' His eyebrows lifted at Garcia. 'But we don't know if he was reported missing or not. We haven't checked yet.'

'Say no more,' Garcia said, reaching for his cellphone and stepping outside the apartment for a moment.

Hunter returned the pile of envelopes to the floor and took a moment to look around the rest of the living room.

'Nope,' Garcia informed Hunter, as he re-entered the apartment. 'Shaun Daniels was never reported missing.'

'Yeah,' Hunter said back, his eyes circling the room. 'I'm not exactly surprised. He was a loner. Probably not that in touch with his family either.'

'How do you know that?'

'Look around,' Hunter replied. 'There's not a photo frame or photo in sight. Nothing here in the living room, though there are plenty of spaces on the TV module . . .' He gestured toward the kitchen area. 'And nothing stuck to the fridge either. I haven't checked the rest of the apartment yet, but I'm willing to bet that we won't find any kind of photos – not of him alone, not of him with his parents, or family, or partner . . . or anything. He lived alone. He worked alone.' He indicated the takeout and microwavable dinner boxes on the table. 'He ate alone. He probably went out alone too.'

'Well, you don't really have any photos displayed in your apartment,' Garcia volleyed back. 'Except for that one of you and your dad.'

Hunter looked back at him with a look that simply said: '*Think about it.*'

'OK.' Garcia lifted his hands in surrender. 'Point taken. You *are* a loner, but you've got good, solid friends – me, Anna, Captain Blake.' He shrugged. 'You wouldn't go missing for more than a couple of days before one of us reported you missing.'

'All of the close, solid friends you've mentioned, I've acquired because of my job, which is not a lonely job.' Hunter shook his head. 'This isn't the case with Shaun Daniels. He was a plumber, working for himself. My guess is that he tended to take on smaller, one-man jobs most of the time. I'm sure he had friends . . . maybe even family around, but it doesn't seem that he was close to anyone.'

Garcia checked the drawers on the TV module – nothing but a few local takeout menus, a tax-invoice book registered to Daniels Plumbing Ltd, a lighter and a bunch of old receipts. 'This is just so fucked up, Robert.'

'What is?'

'The fact that he's been missing for almost a month,' Garcia replied, pausing to look back at his partner. 'Because if we use logic, we have to assume the most probable sequence of events here, which is that he was taken around May 18th – when all of his cellphone communications ceased, right?'

Hunter nodded.

'But according to Dr. Hove,' Garcia continued, 'he only died of hypothermia at least six to eight hours before he was found, which only happened four days ago, in the very early hours of Sunday, June 16th – meaning that he died on Saturday. Logical conclusion is that he was probably tortured for almost a month, Robert.' He broadly gestured at the entire living room. 'Look at this place. It's a mess. The guy was a slob. He was a plumber. Not a drug dealer, not a millionaire, not a spy, not a scientist on the verge of some magnificent discovery . . . and I'm pretty sure that he wasn't the keeper of some major government secret – so why torture him like that? What *did* he do?'

'I really don't know, Carlos.' Hunter let go of a worried breath. 'But it tells us something very specific about our perp.'

Garcia massaged the back of his neck. 'That he might not be a serial killer, but he's definitely a psychopath – someone capable of not only imprisoning another human being for about thirty days, but also capable of purposely inflicting tremendous pain on his victim . . . day, after day, after day.'

'Which indicates rage toward Mr. Daniels,' Hunter added. 'A lot of it.'

'So we're talking about someone he knew,' Garcia concluded. 'This wasn't someone who he might've had some silly altercation with in a bar or something . . . someone he met on the night. This was someone who truly hated him.'

Another nod from Hunter, who entered the kitchen, where the stench of rancid food gained a new, moldy dimension.

Garcia followed him.

'Wow!' he said, grimacing as he cupped a hand over his nose mask. 'Something is definitely very funky in here. Probably that bread.' He indicated a loaf of bread at the far end of the counter that had molded days ago. 'That thing's got a beard now.' He hung back, while Hunter had a quick look around.

The wall cabinets were mostly empty, with the exception of a few plates, cups and mugs, and a small variety of canned food. The ones under the sink housed a few cleaning products, together with a bucket, some pans, and not much else. In the drawers, Hunter found some sparse cutlery, some matches, a few local takeout menus and several leaflets advertising Shaun's plumbing business. His tagline was: *No job too small.*

As Hunter reached for the fridge handle, Garcia took another step back.

'Careful,' he said. 'Something might jump out from in there.'

Hunter pulled the door open.

Nothing jumped out, mainly because there was barely anything in the fridge – a few bottles of beer, a tub of butter, a half-empty water container, four eggs and an opened milk carton. Hunter didn't have to check to know that the milk had curdled.

In the living room, directly across from the apartment front door, a very short corridor led first to the bathroom, on the right. It was small and tiled all in white. Inside the mirror cabinet, other than razors and shaving cream, Hunter and Garcia found a half-full bottle of Percocet – one of the brand names that the combination of the opioid oxycodone with paracetamol was sold under. It was used to treat moderate to severe pain.

Garcia twisted his lips to one side, while his stare moved to Hunter.

Hunter shook his head. 'No. No one gets into a life-threatening debt over Percocet.'

They exited the bathroom and reached the end of the short corridor. As Hunter pushed open the door to the only bedroom in the apartment, the smell that came from inside hit them like a baseball swing to the head, making both detectives bring a hand up, as if to defend their faces.

'Damn!' Garcia cringed. The smell was so strong it made his left eye water a little. 'This can't be good.'

Hunter hit the lights.

Nothing.

He flipped the switch off then on again. This time, the lights flickered once before bathing the room in celluloid orange.

Hunter and Garcia both saw it at the exact same time.

'Oh fffffuck!'

Seven

Terry Wilford watched as the brown-haired, well-built and sharply dressed man entered The Varnish, one of the most famous speakeasy-themed cocktail lounges in Downtown LA, and took a seat at the bar. As the man sat down, he took off his glasses, closed his eyes, placed both elbows on the bar counter, and used the tips of his fingers to slowly massage his eyelids.

Terry, who had just started mixing a couple of cocktails for table seven, lifted a quick finger at the man. 'I'll be right with you, sir.'

That Thursday night, Terry was working the bar alone.

'There's no rush,' the man replied, still massaging his eyelids. His voice sounded tired and rough. 'Take your time. I won't be going anywhere for a while.'

Terry had been working as a bartender at The Varnish for just over four years now. During that time, he'd seen more than his share of similar-looking customers – pristine haircut with manicured nails, dressed in perfectly fitted, overpriced suits, smelling of expensive cologne, and looking like the world was just about to cave in on them.

Terry wasn't really surprised by how distraught the man looked. The Varnish was located slap bang in the middle of the Los Angeles Financial District and since it first opened its doors back in 2009, it had become one of LA's favorite drinking dens for the entire financial sector. Terry had been behind the bar during some of the most lavish of celebrations, where $10,000 bottles of champagne were being handed out as if they were wine coolers and cocaine was being passed around as if it was a bag of Skittles. On the flip side, Terry had also witnessed some of the most depressing and embarrassing scenes he'd ever seen – desperate grown men on their knees, bawling their eyes out, asking their bosses for forgiveness. Once, right there at the far end of his bar, Terry saw a man empty a bottle of sleeping pills into his mouth and swig down a full glass of whiskey. If not for Terry's sharp eyes and fast reaction in immediately compressing the man's stomach until he vomited, that man would've probably ended his life right there at The Varnish, and that was never good for business.

Terry finished mixing two traditional Sidecar cocktails, placed them on the waitress's tray, and approached the man sitting at the bar. From the troubled look on the man's face, together with the way in which he kept on slightly shaking his head disapprovingly, Terry guessed that he had probably lost a considerable amount of money that afternoon.

'Good evening, sir,' Terry said, placing a coaster on the bar in front of the man. 'What can I get you tonight?'

The man finally stopped massaging his eyes and reached for his glasses. 'What would you say is the strongest cocktail you . . .' The man paused, his uncertain eyes resting on Terry. 'Don't I know you from somewhere?'

The main reason why Terry knew very few of his customers by name was because the daily customer flow at The Varnish was truly overwhelming, but he could still recognize a great number of returning patrons from looks alone, and Terry was very certain that he had never seen that man before.

'I don't think so,' Terry replied, his head shaking just a touch.

The man's eyes narrowed, as he studied Terry's face for a couple more seconds. 'Are you sure? You do look rather familiar.

Did you ever work in Santa Monica Pier, or in any of the bars at the promenade? I used to go there a lot.'

'No, never,' Terry lied. 'All the bars I've worked in until now have been here ... in Downtown.' He didn't allow the silence to stretch. 'But people say that I have one of those faces.'

Physically, Terry, who was forty-three years old, was a slight man. An inch under six-foot, with a thin, ascetic body, helped by a daily exercise routine and a diet that stopped him from having sweets and ice creams, which he secretly adored. His longish black hair was pulled back into a messy manbun, and his three o'clock shadow contoured a pretty average jawline.

'One of those faces?' the man asked.

'The plain, average-looking face,' Terry explained. 'The one that looks like a million other faces.' He gave the man a single-shoulder shrug. 'Every now and then I catch people squinting at me from afar, clearly trying to place me against some old memory because my face looks vaguely familiar.' He pointed to his hair. 'Even with the manbun.'

'Yeah ... maybe,' the man accepted. 'But if you've always worked in busy bars and lounges like this one, they probably *have* seen you before somewhere. That's why I asked about Santa Monica.'

'Yeah, that's true.'

It was Terry's turn to quickly study the man sitting at the bar in front of him. He looked to be in his early to mid-thirties, with shaggy brown hair that fell over deep-brown eyes. His beard was long enough to cover his jawline. He was slender, but not thin, with enough muscle to add plenty of power to his frame. The bones on his face were delicate, which only added to his somewhat attractive looks. If Terry had seen him before, he was sure that he would've remembered.

'So,' Terry said, going back to his original question. 'What can I get you tonight?'

The man let out a deep breath before his expression turned serious. 'What would you say is the strongest drink you can make?'

'That depends,' Terry replied, handing the man a cocktail menu. 'Strong as in . . .?'

'As in obliterating brain cells,' the man answered, before sniggering. 'Not that I seem to have that many left, anyway.'

'That bad of a day, huh?' Terry asked.

The man once again took off his glasses, but this time he didn't place them on the counter, he just used his thumb and index finger to pinch the bridge of his nose, as if trying to halt a headache that was already lurking behind his eyelids. 'I'm Liam,' the man said after a couple of seconds, offering his hand.

'Terry.' The bartender shook it.

'Well, Terry . . . on a scale from one to ten – ten being the worst day possible – I'd say that today was a seven-point-five million.'

Terry almost choked.

When the man returned the glasses to his face, the bartender was looking back at him wide-eyed.

'That's a hell of a lot of bad,' Terry said, his chin angling forward as he nodded.

'You don't say,' Liam agreed, his voice sounding as defeated as he looked. 'So . . . if by any chance you've got any sort of poison behind that bar, Terry, just pour it and I'll drink it. Neat. No ice.'

'No poison,' Terry replied with a sarcastic, disappointed look. 'But I can mix you up something that'll hit like a heavyweight champ.'

Liam smiled a smile that was small and tense . . . and it didn't linger. 'Sounds like it's just what I need . . . times a whole bunch.'

Terry nodded. 'Any drinks or flavors I should steer away from?'

Liam tried to chuckle, but it came out more like a cough. 'Right now, my friend, I'll drink dirty water from the devil's barrel . . . I don't much care. Just pour it.'

If I'd just lost seven and a half million dollars in one day, Terry thought, as he reached for the cocktail shaker, *I wouldn't much care what I was drinking either.*

'Heavyweight champ knockout coming right over, buddy,' Terry announced, as he slid a few cubes of ice into a tall glass.

Liam didn't look to see what spirits Terry was pouring into the mixer. Instead, he turned and allowed his gaze to move around the cozily lit drinking lounge.

At 9:55 p.m. on a Thursday evening, The Varnish was busy and getting busier. Two very attractive waitresses, dressed in sexy secretary outfits, took orders from customers sitting at the old-fashioned dinner booths scattered around the bar floor. As Liam observed one of the waitresses, a medium-height, short-haired man, also dressed in an expensive-looking pinstriped suit, entered The Varnish, walked over to the bar and indicated the stool to Liam's right.

'Is this seat taken, buddy?' he asked.

Liam's stare moved to him but he stayed quiet.

The man's eyebrows lifted, inquisitively.

'No,' Liam finally replied. 'I don't think so.'

The man smiled and took the seat just as Terry placed a glass containing a dark-colored cocktail on the bar in front of Liam.

'Hey, Terry,' the new arrival said, with a nod.

Terry reciprocated the gesture. 'Hey, Ken, what can I get you tonight?'

Ken eyed Liam's glass. 'What is that?' He frowned at Terry.

'I call it Amnesia,' Terry said. His smile was aimed more at Liam than at Ken. 'It makes you forget things for a while ... a lot of things.'

'Interesting,' Ken nodded. 'What's in it?'

Liam lifted a hand at Terry. 'I actually don't want to know.'

Terry's attention moved to Ken. 'Neither do you, Ken. Believe me.'

Liam reached for the glass and had a healthy sip. As the drink cleared his throat, on its way to his stomach, his cheeks puffed up with air and his eyes seemed like they were about to melt on his face.

'Damn,' Liam said, as he took a deep breath. 'This thing could degrease engines.'

Terry nodded his agreement. 'And then some.'

'Yep,' Ken said, his hands up in the air. 'I'll pass.' He thought about it for an extra second. 'For now, at least.'

'Ken,' Terry said, as he introduced the two men at the bar. 'This is Liam.'

Liam and Ken shook hands.

'I'll have a beer with a chaser, please, Terry,' Ken said, placing a hundred-dollar bill on the counter. 'And just keep them coming, will you?'

As Terry turned away to fetch Ken's order, Ken turned to face Liam. 'It must've been a particularly bad day, if you chose to drink engine degreaser.'

Liam had another sip of his cocktail ... or at least he pretended to.

'I think you could say that.'

'Are you in finance?' Ken asked.

Liam nodded once. 'Isn't everyone in here?'

'Most of them, yes,' Ken replied, looking left then right. 'And don't worry, we all have similar bad days every now and then. It's the nature of our business. I'm sure you know that, but the good thing is – it's never *our* money that we lose.' Ken winked at Liam. 'So who really cares, right?'

Liam looked down at Ken's shiny Italian-leather shoes. They looked like they had been polished just seconds before he entered the bar.

'The customers care,' Liam replied, returning to his drink. 'Very much, actually.'

Ken laughed a little harder than Liam expected. 'Investment, stock market, finance ... all of those are risky businesses, my friend. The customers know that. They knew that before they decided to invest. Don't beat yourself up about it.'

'Too late,' Liam whispered, just as Terry placed a bottle of beer and a whiskey shot on the bar in front of Ken.

'Thanks, Terry.' Ken reached for the shot and lifted it at Liam. 'To better days, my friend. To better days.'

Liam nodded as he brought his glass to his lips, but once again, he simply pretended to have a sip. He really wasn't there to get drunk.

Eight

The Varnish closed its doors at 1:00 a.m. every morning. After closing, while the waitresses collected all the glasses and cleaned up the tables, Terry would cash up and do a stock check before wiping down the bar and mopping its floor to the point of shining. All that done, Terry, the waitresses and the management would sometimes grab a beer together at the bar and shoot the breeze for a while before finally heading home. That night, though, only Terry and Sabrina, one of the two cocktail waitresses that had been working the floor that Thursday, were in the mood for a beer.

Terry lived alone in a small one-bedroom apartment in East LA, about seven miles from Downtown, which in a city as large as Los Angeles was considered to be 'just around the corner'. At that time in the morning, it would take him less than twenty minutes to drive home. But Terry wasn't exactly ready to call it a night yet.

Back inside The Varnish, as Terry and Sabrina worked through a bottle of Bud and a chaser each, they shared a couple of lines of cocaine in the bathroom.

Terry and Sabrina weren't a couple, but they had slept together plenty of times before, mainly when they were both drunk and high. The fact that they only had sex when they were a little off their heads had never really bothered either of them. Casual, drunken-and-wasted sex was a thing in LA. But that night, even though Terry did make a move as they shared their second line of coke, Sabrina politely declined, saying that she had a dentist's appointment in the morning, which was actually true.

'Are you sure I can't come over for a little while?' Terry tried again, as he and Sabrina emerged from The Varnish. 'I'll be quick. I promise.' A devilish smile on his lips.

Sabrina walked up to him, stretched her body onto her tiptoes, and gave him a friendly peck on the lips. 'You know that "quick" is never the case with you, Terry.'

Terry chuckled. 'You're making it sound like that's a bad thing.'

'Definitely not.' As she came back to a flat-foot position, Sabrina purposely allowed her hand to gently brush against Terry's groin. 'Wow!' She smiled an even more devilish smile than Terry's. Her eyes moved down to where her hand was. 'I can feel and see how much you'd really like to come over.'

'Uh-huh.' Terry nodded. 'You know that's right, baby.'

Sabrina kept her hand right where it was for another second before stepping back. Her eyebrows pointed inward and down, creating a sad expression. 'Pity that tonight really is a "no-no" for me.'

'Ohhh, that's so cold.' Terry looked down at the volume in his pants. 'Are you really just gonna leave me hanging here like a dog with blue balls?'

'I'm sure that you can take care of that yourself,' Sabrina said, as she waved Terry goodbye. 'You've got big hands, big boy.'

'Damn, girl, that's freezing cold. I ain't getting nothing?'

'You've got tomorrow off, right?' Sabrina asked.

'That's right. We can party all night.'

'No, I'm good. I'll see you on Saturday.'

'Don't you even want a ride?' Terry tried one last shot. 'We could fool around in the car.'

'Nope, I'm good. I've got my bike.'

Still not quite believing that Sabrina had simply left him there, Terry watched her disappear around the corner.

'Damn!' he whispered to himself, reaching into his pocket for his car keys. 'And now I'm horny.'

Inside his pocket, his fingertips brushed against the small cellophane bag filled with cocaine that he and Sabrina had shared moments earlier.

'Umm . . .' Terry bit his bottom lip while he thought about it for an instant.

On the weekends, instead of going straight home after his shifts, Terry would sometimes go to an underground club – the kind that stayed open until the break of dawn . . . the kind where he could easily get his kicks – and in LA, the weekend started on Wednesday.

Terry crossed the road and turned the corner to get to where his car was parked. The street was almost empty, with the exception of his blue Chevy Cruze and a dark-colored pickup truck that was parked to its left. Leaning against the side of the truck, facing the opposite direction, a tall man was smoking a cigarette. It was only when Terry got to about five feet from his car that he recognized who the man was.

'Liam?' Terry frowned, pausing by his driver's door.

Liam turned on the balls of his feet. 'Hey, Terry.' He nodded before flicking what was still left of his cigarette over the truck to the other side. 'Just finished work?'

'Umm . . . yeah.' Terry subtly shook his head, as if trying to wake up from a quick nap. 'What are you doing out here?'

'I was smoking a cigarette.'

Terry frowned again. A little harder this time. 'No . . . I mean . . . I thought you'd be home by now. You left about an hour ago.'

'I did,' Liam agreed, rounding the truck to get a little closer to Terry. 'I needed to get some fresh air.'

'I'm not surprised,' Terry said, sounding impressed. 'You managed to down two of those Amnesia cocktails. Those puppies were strong, man. I know. I mixed them.'

Liam dismissed the feat with a careless shrug. Once the bar got busier, it had been easy for him to keep on tipping some of his drink into glasses left at the bar without anyone noticing it.

'Is this your truck?' Terry asked.

Liam nodded. 'Yep.'

'Are you sure you're OK to drive? Do you want me to call you a cab?'

'No, I'm good,' Liam replied, tucking his left hand deep into his jacket pocket. 'But I wanted to show you something that is a bit shocking, if you don't mind.' He took two steps forward to be within an arm's reach of Terry.

'Shocking.' Terry craned his neck forward. 'What is it?'

Liam smiled, and in one very fast move pulled a Taser out of his pocket and brought it to Terry's neck. One effortless click of the trigger and fifty thousand volts were discharged throughout the bartender's body, immediately causing neuromuscular incapacitation. Terry's eyes disappeared into his head, while his whole body shook uncontrollably for about three seconds before his legs gave way and he collapsed. Liam was ready for it and grabbed Terry before his head hit the ground.

'I wanted to show you something that's a bit shocking,' Liam chuckled to himself, as he dropped the tailgate on his truck and dragged an unconscious Terry into the truck's cargo bed. 'What a fantastic joke.'

Nine

In the morning, Hunter and Garcia had been at their desks for less than half an hour when Captain Blake appeared at their door.

'So what happened yesterday?' she asked. Captain Blake wasn't one to beat around the bush. 'What do we have?'

Garcia indicated the picture board pushed up against their office's south wall. On it, he and Hunter had already pinned the few photos they had taken inside Shaun Daniels's apartment and of his station wagon, together with the autopsy shots.

'Not a lot,' he replied, with a shake of the head. 'Except for us confirming what we already knew.'

'That he wasn't killed in a pedestrian/vehicle traffic accident,' Captain Blake said, stepping closer to the board.

'No chance of that,' Garcia confirmed. 'The accident was staged.' He had just begun explaining what he and Hunter had found out from Dr. Hove the day before, when the captain paused him with a hand gesture.

'Whoa! Hold on just a second.' Her stare was fixed on a particular photo on the board. 'What the hell is this?'

'Once we made it to his apartment,' Hunter said, getting up from his desk. 'We were able to check his mail, including his last cellphone bill. From it, we have reason to believe that Mr. Daniels had been missing for almost thirty days before his body was discovered five days ago.'

Captain Blake turned to face him. 'Thirty days? Has there been a Missing Persons Report?'

'No.' Garcia, this time. 'We've checked it. No MPR.'

'Mr. Daniels lived alone in a one-bedroom apartment in Lomita,' Hunter explained. 'No indications of a partner. Once he was gone, the apartment was left completely empty.' He indicated the same photo that Captain Blake had been looking at just moments earlier. 'No one to attend to anything.'

'Fuck!' the captain breathed out the word. Her attention returned to the board and to the photo that Hunter had indicated. It showed three dead birds inside a large birdcage. Their bodies were already in the very late stages of decomposition, with maggots about halfway through their morbid feasting.

'The poor things had no food or water for a month?' she asked.

'No, not exactly,' Hunter explained. 'They probably only ran out of food and water just about a week ago. Give or take a day.'

The captain's eyes narrowed.

'Birds have a very fast metabolism,' Hunter clarified. 'Especially small birds. They store almost no fat. That's why they're constantly feeding and hydrating. If they completely run out of food and water, due to their low fat reserves, they won't last more than four or five days, if they're lucky. Once they're dead, the process is pretty identical to that of a human body – blow-flies ... eggs ... maggots ... the body gets eaten. Tiny little bodies like those,' he said, indicating the photo once again, 'would be devoured in less than twenty-four hours. If those birds had died just after Mr. Daniels went missing, about a month ago, there'd be nothing but bones left.'

'We were very unlucky.' Garcia took over. 'Those birds only died about a day or two ago.'

'So are you saying that you think somebody fed them after the victim went missing?' Captain Blake pushed.

'There is that possibility,' Garcia replied. 'But we found no evidence inside his apartment that anyone else had been there other than us. The most probable explanation is that Mr. Daniels left enough seeds and water to last his birds quite a few days.'

The captain thought about it for a millisecond. 'So you think he knew that he'd be taken?'

'I don't think he did.' The answer came from Hunter. 'If he suspected that he was in danger, especially mortal danger, why didn't he run? You know ... disappear. Birds do have a very fast metabolism, Captain, but they also don't exactly overeat or drink. Many bird owners overfill their feeders out of convenience. Mr. Daniels lived alone and ran his own one-man plumbing business, which clearly meant irregular hours. Overfilling his bird feeders might be something that he'd always done.'

'Poor little things,' the captain commented, as her stare moved on to the next few photographs. 'So, you were saying?' she addressed Garcia, who once again started from the beginning, explaining what they had found out from Dr. Hove. Just like both detectives had been, Captain Blake was very surprised when Garcia told her that the victim seemed to have been tortured for days.

'Days?' she questioned, her gaze bouncing from Hunter to Garcia, then back to Hunter.

'Dr. Hove explained that due to him being run over by a truck,' Hunter said, 'an exact timeframe for his injuries is practically impossible, but she was positive that all of the hidden injuries she found were sustained over a period of time that spanned days, not hours.'

'Which kind of explains why he was only found twenty-nine days after he went missing,' Garcia added. 'The bogus hit-and-run accident was used to mask the torture injuries.'

Captain Blake spent a moment studying the injury photos on the board. 'So who *is* this guy? And why would anyone want to torture him like this?'

'That's what we've been asking ourselves since we got his file from Research earlier today,' Garcia replied, reaching for a print-out on his desk. 'Full name – Shaun Frederic Daniels, forty-six years old. Like Robert said, Mr. Daniels was a plumber, who ran his own small business out of his apartment in Lomita – Daniels Plumbing Ltd. He was born in Seattle, but moved to LA with his mother when he was nine years old, after his parents divorced. Mr. Daniels and his mother lived in El Segundo, where Mr. Daniels went to school, both primary and high school. He never went to university. After graduating from high school he began working construction, which he did for several years, before specializing in plumbing. He started his own business about nine years ago.'

'Parents?' Captain Blake asked.

'Both deceased.'

'Was he married?'

'Nope,' Garcia replied. 'Never been married . . . no kids, either.'

Captain Blake faced Hunter. 'And you said that he had no girlfriend . . . boyfriend . . . nothing?'

Hunter's head tilted sideways as he shrugged. 'In his apartment we found no indications that he was dating anyone. Everyone we asked said that they'd never seen him with anyone.'

'Everyone like who?'

'The neighbors.'

'OK.' Captain Blake nodded at Garcia. 'Let's skip the yadda, yadda for now. Any known connections to anything that could've earned him weeks of torture? Drugs, gangs, crime . . . anything?'

'Not exactly,' Garcia replied. 'He did have a record. Been arrested three times for disorderly conduct and twice for DUI.'

'Did he do any time?'

Garcia searched the printout. 'No. Just a couple of fines and six months of community service.'

Captain Blake nodded before addressing Hunter. 'You said you talked to the neighbors, right?

'Last night,' Hunter confirmed.

'Anybody had anything else to say other than Mr. Daniels didn't seem to be dating anyone?'

'Well . . .' The reply came from Garcia. 'Despite him residing in the same address for almost six years, no one really seemed to know Mr. Daniels well enough to be able to express an opinion on his character. Most of the neighbors said that every now and then they would see him leaving his apartment early in the morning then coming back in the evening . . . sometimes late evenings, but nothing really out of the ordinary. They all said that he was always polite enough every time they crossed paths – good morning, good evening, good night, that kind of polite – but that was about it. He didn't talk much and no one seemed to have ever really engaged him in a long conversation. According to everyone we spoke to, and this includes his landlord, Mr. Daniels was a good and quiet resident – no loud music, no parties, no noise . . . nothing. And no one remembers ever seeing any visitors coming or going from his apartment.'

'Your perfect inconspicuous resident,' Captain Blake commented.

'Pretty much,' Garcia agreed. 'Which in itself makes him conspicuous.'

'The lady who lives in the apartment directly under his,' Hunter added, 'Mrs. Cross, said that Mr. Daniels was a kind man.'

'Kind as in?'

'He fixed a couple of leaks in her bathroom and sorted out her kitchen plumbing free of charge.'

'That's nice of him,' Captain Blake commented. 'Were they sleeping together, maybe? Could that have been a factor?'

'No.' Hunter and Garcia shook their heads at the same time.

'Mrs. Cross is eighty-one years old,' Hunter clarified. 'She said that he told her that she reminded him of his mother.'

Captain Blake raised both of her hands to halt her detectives.

'So, according to his file – no drugs, no theft, no gambling . . . nothing except a few fights here and there and driving under the influence?'

Garcia nodded.

'How about any gang affiliations? Maybe something from earlier in his life?'

'Nothing in the file,' Hunter replied.

Captain Blake faced the picture board once again. 'Any chance of him being a low-maintenance gambler, or an occasional drug user – you know, something that ran just under the radar?' Her eyebrows lifted at Hunter. 'Because we all know that in America, especially in LA, people will still get whacked for owing a hundred bucks just the same as they would for owing millions.'

'Maybe so,' Hunter agreed. 'But he wasn't just murdered, Captain. He was tortured . . . for a month. People just don't go through that much effort for small debts.'

'That's true.'

'Or maybe it could be something else entirely.' Garcia jumped in.

'Like what else?' the captain pushed.

'Money laundering. People can definitely get whacked for money laundering.'

Hunter nodded. 'There is that possibility.'

'We're having Special Crimes take a look at his company's books and bank accounts,' Garcia continued. 'A lot of these "one-man companies" are used for money laundering for smaller criminals. The "one-man" company takes on a big job, which really isn't big at all, overcharges, takes a nice cut, and returns the rest to the client via some other bogus transaction.'

Captain Blake turned to look at the photos on the board one last time. 'Well, if it turns out that he was involved with some sort of organized crime, doing some of their money laundering for them, we're turning this over to the FBI in a heartbeat. That's not our fight. If you find out that he was linked to drugs and that what happened to him was some sort of payback due to a drug debt, no matter how small . . .' Captain Blake shrugged. 'Also not our fight. His file goes straight to the DEA. We're not taking on other agencies' investigations.'

Neither detective objected to Captain Blake's decision.

'But until then,' she continued. 'What do we have to go on?'

'Not much,' Hunter informed her. 'But his last credit card transaction dates back to the evening of May 18th – same date as his last cellphone communication.'

'And where did it flag up?'

'A drinking den in Lomita called O'Hearn's Bar and Grill,' Hunter replied. 'Not that far from his apartment. His last transaction came at 10:41 p.m.' Hunter returned to his desk and picked up a copy of Shaun Daniels's credit card statement. 'The good thing here is that Mr. Daniels had recurring transactions at that same bar several times during that week and practically every week prior to it.'

'So that was his local wet hole,' Captain Blake concluded.

'It appears so, yes,' Hunter confirmed. 'Which means that hopefully the bartenders . . . maybe even other customers, might know a little bit more about our mysterious Mr. Daniels.'

'It's a start,' Captain Blake agreed.

'They open at midday,' Hunter said, instinctively checking his watch – 9:33 a.m. 'We'll drop by in the afternoon and see if we can find anything else.'

'Last night we also placed a request for his cellphone records,' Garcia added. 'Hopefully we'll have something by tomorrow.'

'All right.' The captain nodded as she made her way to the door. 'Keep me in the loop whatever happens, because there's something very fishy here. We've all been in this game for long enough to know that if somebody wanted him dead because of a debt, they'd just shoot him in the head and move on. If somebody wanted him punished, they'd beat him up, break his legs and walk away, but instead, somebody went through great lengths to torture and *stage* the death of a, so far, on paper, very average man. That only happens in films, not in real life.'

As Captain Blake closed the door behind her, Hunter and Garcia turned to face the board. They both knew that she was right – there was definitely something very wrong with that entire scenario.

Ten

The San Andreas Fault line was one of the longest fault lines on the planet, running approximately 800 miles. It essentially sliced California into two halves. At its southern end, the line crossed Los Angeles County right along the north side of the San Gabriel Mountains, and it had the potential of causing earthquakes as powerful as a magnitude eight. That fault line was the main reason why the Los Angeles Metro line was so limited, servicing only a very small portion of such a large city. Underground digging in Los Angeles was extremely restricted and it had to follow an immense list of rules and guidelines because if an earthquake hit, and one could at any minute, subterranean tunnels would collapse like a house of cards in front of a wind turbine and the loss of life could be catastrophic.

It was for that same reason that underground parking in Los Angeles barely existed and very few homes in the whole of California had basements or cellars. But this one, located in Hollywood Hills, did.

The house belonged to the man who, at The Varnish, called himself Liam. His parents had purchased it in the early 1980s and they got it for an absolute bargain. The house had been the former home of Todd Meier, a 1970s-era cardiovascular surgeon, who fell from grace in quite a spectacular way for the time.

Despite being a talented doctor, Meier also owned a couple of popular nightclubs on Hollywood Boulevard, and in his clubs, other than just selling alcohol, he also trafficked in prescription drugs.

In the 1960s and 70s, hallucinogens like LSD, mescaline, psilocybin and PCP became enormously popular, as did opioid-based painkillers. Dr. Meier kept the LAPD well greased and in the space of just a few years, his side business had made him a very wealthy man, until his whole life fell apart sometime in the mid-70s, when he began taking too many of his own pills. One morning, right after a heavy night of booze and drugs, Dr. Meier killed a patient on the operating table after slicing through the wrong artery. The long investigation that followed led to a number of wrongful-death suits and, ultimately, criminal charges, but Dr. Meier never went to prison. He chose to take his own life a week before his trial was due to start.

In California, real-estate agents are obliged by law to disclose not only the history, but also any relevant incidents that might've happened inside a property that could potentially influence the buyer in one direction or another.

Unfortunately, Dr. Meier had chosen to end his life with a gunshot to the temple inside his own living room. That information, when revealed, served as a huge sale-deterrent for almost seven years, until Liam's parents, who couldn't have cared less who the previous owner had been, finally purchased the large, two-story house in the summer of 1984 – five years before Liam was born.

The house's cellar – or, better yet, secret cellar – never appeared in the house's floor plan because no one, other than Dr. Todd Meier and the few people he had used to build it, knew about it. That secret lasted until 1988, when Liam's father decided that it was time to finally get rid of those old, chunky and ugly cupboards down in the kitchen. But Liam's father was a man's man. He would've never hired a company, or someone else, to do a job that he could do himself.

It was right on the first day of work, as Liam's father was trying to remove the first of five cupboards on the kitchen's south wall, that he came across a secret lever hidden behind a false panel at the back of the cupboard. He hesitated for a moment before he flipped the lever. As he did, he heard a noise come from somewhere behind him. It took him a few minutes to discover that the noise had come from inside another cupboard, this one under the kitchen sink. In there, another false panel had sprung open, revealing a round, metal button. This time, there was no hesitation. Liam's father immediately reached for the button and pressed it. What he heard next was the thump of a lock opening under the floorboards.

On their first visit to the house, four years earlier, Liam's parents were readily impressed by the Italian-style, Nero Marquina and Bianco Carrara marble replica flooring in the large kitchen. What was different about it was that the squares on the black-and-white checkered floor were of various different sizes and orientation, creating a somewhat disturbing psychedelic effect, something that wouldn't be to everyone's taste; but Liam's parents liked odd and unconventional things.

As Liam's father looked in the direction of the thump he'd just heard, he finally understood the reason for the psychedelic floor design; it perfectly hid a Murphy door – a concealed door designed to blend seamlessly into an existing room. It was impossible to see it, unless the hidden button had been pressed.

The door led down to an enormous secret space – as vast as the property's entire ground floor – which consisted of an entry lobby, a large living room that linked to a comfortable dining room, a spacious study and an ample kitchen with an attached laundry room that offered more than enough storage space.

Part of that secret basement had been decked out like a medical examiner's office, 1970s style. There were two stainless-steel examination tables – both with drains – white metal cabinets with glass doors, surgical lights on the ceiling and two fully equipped instrument carts. The floor and walls had been tiled all in white for easy cleaning. A large sink with an extendable hose tap hugged one of the walls. Clearly Dr. Meier kept his drugs stash down there, but the examination tables and the instruments carts were a surprise.

What else had Dr. Meier been into?

Liam's father was both amazed and shocked in equal measure, but right then he knew that, by pure luck, he had stumbled across the perfect house.

Liam had known about the secret basement since he was a little kid, when his father had shown it to him. After his parents were gone, Liam inherited the property and decided that he needed to renovate his secret cellar.

Due to all the underground work restrictions in California, Liam decided to work alone, using every spare minute he could get. He kept the medical examiner's room just as it was, but he made much better use of all the extra space that surrounded it. And he had loads of it. He learned how to brick-lay, how to wood-cut, how to reinforce walls and doors, how to wire walls, floors and ceilings, how to professionally soundproof a room so that no sound could get out or in . . . whatever he needed to learn to achieve what he had set out to achieve. The job took him over five years to complete, but in the end, Liam had the perfect cellar. The perfect secret underground prison, torture chamber and surgical room, all rolled up into one. A place no one could escape from.

And it was in exactly that secret underground prison that Terry Wilford woke up just a few hours after he'd been Tasered outside The Varnish cocktail bar. He was lying on a shabby mattress that had been pushed up against a solid wall. The mattress smelled of vomit, blood, sweat and urine, but, to his surprise, Terry hadn't been shackled, tied up or gagged, although his whole body hurt as if he'd been used as a punch bag by a gang of heavyweights.

It was dark in the room where Terry was being held. So dark that it seemed that there was no sound, no light, no reality beyond the frantic beating of his own heart.

Slowly and through the pain, he pushed himself into a sitting position and used his hand to feel around. Past the mattress, all he could feel was the coldness of a concrete floor.

His mouth felt dry . . . so dry that he almost believed that if he coughed, a mist of dry powder would fly up in the air.

He desperately needed a drink of water.

'Hello?' he tried calling out, but his vocal cords were so weak, so dried up, that all he got was a meager whisper.

He tried feeling around once again. Nothing. No water. No food.

Terry brought both of his hands to his face. His lips were chipped and cracked . . . his skin dry and rough . . . his eyes tender to the touch.

'What the fuck is going on?' he whispered to himself, allowing his hands to drop down to his thighs like dead weights. 'Where the fuck am I?'

That was when fear truly took over, crawling into the hollows of his body and pressing outward until he could feel his organs, his bones, his spine shaking inside of him.

Terry wasn't expecting an answer to his question – *Where the fuck am I?* – but an answer was exactly what he got, because he wasn't alone in that room.

Coming from the darkness just behind him, a guttural voice whispered the words.

'In Hell!'

Eleven

In Lomita, O'Hearn's Bar and Grill was located right on the Pacific Coast Highway, which was the longest state route in California, running along most of the state's Pacific coastline. Since it was located on a state highway, parking would've proved to be not only impossible, but also illegal, if not for the fact that the Irish-themed bar was positioned directly next door to a small shopping mall, with plenty of off-street parking spaces to accommodate both establishments.

At 3:36 p.m., Garcia parked his car at the south corner of the parking lot, right next to a wild-cherry Mustang Mach 1. As he stepped out of his Honda Civic, he paused for a second.

'You should get one of these,' he told Hunter, nodding at the Mustang. 'You need to retire that bathtub on wheels that you call a car, and this would be the perfect substitute.'

Hunter chuckled. 'Really?' He too eyed the car parked next to Garcia's. 'Do you have any idea how much one of these costs?'

'Quite a bit, I'd imagine,' Garcia replied with a shrug.

'Well, let me add a tag end to your answer,' Hunter came back. 'Quite a bit . . . *more than I can afford.*'

Garcia made a face at Hunter, as if he didn't really believe his partner.

'What?' Hunter challenged. 'Can you afford a car like this?'

'Probably not.'

Hunter smiled back. 'I rest my case.'

On the inside, O'Hearn's did resemble a typical Irish pub, with a few added features to create a sports bar atmosphere.

At that time in the afternoon, the place wasn't exactly busy. On the main floor, only three out of their fifteen tables were taken. At the large bar, which was located across the floor from the entrance door, three men sat alone at the stools, an empty seat in between each of them. Two of the men were busy with their cellphones and the third one was watching a basketball game re-run on one of the four large flatscreen TVs high on the back wall.

There was only one bartender – a tall, skinny man with a bushy goatee and a LA Lakers cap. He was standing at the far-right end of the bar, polishing glasses with a dishcloth.

Hunter and Garcia approached him.

The bartender put down the dishcloth and turned to face the two new arrivals.

'Top of the morning to ya both,' he said, placing both hands on the bar counter and leaning forward slightly. His Irish accent was very pronounced. 'What can I get you fel . . .' He paused, and as his stare bounced from Hunter to Garcia, his left eye narrowed just a touch. He leaned back from the bar, his expression a lot less relaxed than a second ago. 'Yer five-o, right?'

The American slang sounded strange in an Irish accent.

'Is it that obvious?' Garcia asked, looking at his and Hunter's attire.

'Aye.' The bartender nodded at Garcia's waist. 'It is when yer gun is showing, like.'

Garcia looked at Hunter, as he adjusted his jacket over his waist. 'My bad.'

Hunter immediately noticed that the bartender had kept his voice quiet enough not to be heard by any of the other customers. That clearly indicated that this wasn't the bartender's first rodeo. Hunter expertly positioned himself with his back toward the three customers sitting at the bar, before quickly showing the bartender his credentials.

'I'm Detective Hunter and this is Detective Garcia – LAPD Robbery Homicide.'

Garcia followed suit.

The bartender acknowledged with a nod. 'I'm Conor. What can I do ya for?'

'We were just wondering if you've ever seen this man.' Hunter reached into his jacket pocket and retrieved a photo of Shaun Daniels, placing it on the counter in front of the bartender.

Conor's eyes moved to it for just a second before returning to Hunter.

'It's hard to say, like,' he replied. 'A lot of people come in here for a pint. We're a busy bar, ya know?'

Garcia turned to look back at the empty tables just behind them. He didn't say anything, but when he looked back at the bartender, it was as if the Irishman could read the words – *you could've fooled me here* – written on the detective's forehead.

'Nights are a lot busier than the days,' he said, offering an explanation.

When the bartender glanced at the photo on the counter, Hunter had kept his eyes on him. The 'it's hard to say' answer had come too fast. Not enough time for the human conscious mind to take in any details and match them against a memory; but Hunter wasn't really surprised. He and Garcia were both very used to those sorts of replies – '*I'm not sure . . . it's hard to say . . . it doesn't ring a bell . . .*' and so on. That usually happened because a great number of civilians tended to retreat into a shell of doubt when confronted with police badges and then asked about a person in a photograph. They usually did it not exactly because they had something to hide, or they didn't want to help, but because they had recognized the person in the photo and they didn't know what sort of trouble that person was in. They simply

didn't want to 'rat' on someone they knew, even if they didn't
know them that well.

'Please, have another look,' Hunter insisted, tapping the photo
with his index finger. His tone was calm and non-threatening. 'He
was a regular at this bar – two or three nights a week, at least.'

Conor's eyes returned to the photo. This time, it stayed on it
for a couple of seconds.

'Aye,' he finally accepted, nodding sideways at the photograph.
'I think I've seen him around a few times, like.'

Once again, Hunter had studied the bartender's expression and
eye movement. His reply had, yet again, been too quick for the
human brain to identify and place a total stranger. The only way
that the human brain could've recognized someone that fast, was
if the brain didn't have to do too much searching. That meant that
Shaun Daniels wasn't exactly a stranger to Conor.

Hunter needed to level with him.

'You probably already know this,' he said, meeting the bartender's stare. 'But his name is Shaun Daniels.'

Conor replied with an almost imperceptible nod. 'Aye.'

'The last time that he was in here, at O'Hearn's,' Hunter
continued, 'was a month ago, on May 18th. His last ever credit
card transaction came at 10:41 p.m. on that night, registered to
this bar.'

Hunter saw the bartender blink then frown.

'Last *ever* credit card transaction? What do you mean?'

Garcia nodded. 'Mr. Daniels was abducted. Very possibly on
that same night, after he left here.'

Conor's head jerked back slightly. 'Abducted?'

A confirmation nod from Garcia.

'Yer codding me, right?'

Garcia's eyebrows arched at the bartender. 'I'm not exactly
sure I know what that means, but I'm quite certain that I'm not
"codding" you.'

Conor looked at Hunter, who subtly shook his head at him.

'We believe that Mr. Daniels was abducted just after he left your bar on the night of May 18th,' Garcia continued. 'Which makes O'Hearn's the last traceable location for Mr. Daniels.' He paused, giving Conor a few seconds to process the severity of his words. 'So, what we're really wondering is – on the nights that he came into O'Hearn's, did Mr. Daniels use to drink with someone else? Did he have any beer buddies ... any of the regulars we can talk to? Does anyone remember seeing him here on the night of May 18th? Did he have company that night? Anything that can maybe help us put together what might've happened to Mr. Daniels once he left this bar.'

Conor pinched his lower lip with his left thumb and index finger. His expression turned thoughtful for an instant. 'I thought that that was odd, like – not seeing Shaun in here for a while. Especially on Saturdays. He was always here on Saturdays.' He shook his head. 'So Shaun's been missing for a month?'

Hunter and Garcia exchanged a deliberating look.

'He's not missing,' Hunter said.

Conor's gaze once again bounced between both detectives, this time for a couple of hesitant seconds. 'Wha ... what ya saying?'

'His body was found five days ago,' Garcia informed the bartender. 'He's been murdered.'

'Go way outta that.' Conor took a step back, his eyes wide open.

Hunter and Garcia gave him a moment.

'Were you friends?' Hunter finally asked.

Conor shrugged. 'Not exactly. We weren't mates or anything like that, but like you've said, he did use to come in here quite often. I work most nights, so every now and then we'd chat, ya know? Mostly about sports, like.'

'Were you working on the night of May 18th?' Garcia asked.

'I couldn't say off the top of my head, but I have a feeling that I might've been. Like I said, I work most nights.' Conor lifted a finger at both detectives, while retrieving his cellphone from his back pocket. 'But if ya give us a second, like, I'll find out.'

Hunter and Garcia waited while the bartender tapped through a couple of screens before scrolling through his calendar app.

'Aye,' Conor said with a firm nod. 'May 18th – it was a Saturday, like. I was working the bar.'

'I know that this is a big ask,' Hunter said, knowing how unreliable human memory really was, especially when trying to remember a not-very-memorable event. 'But can you remember seeing Shaun Daniels here that night? Did he seem different at all to you? Nervous? Agitated? Concerned? Anything out of the ordinary? Anything you can remember?'

Conor once again pinched his bottom lip. His eyes narrowed for a long moment, as he looked down at the floor.

'I can't be certain if it was the 18th or not,' he began. 'But it could've well been because it's the last time I remember seeing Shaun in here. It was a busy night. The Lakers were playing, if my memory serves me right. They were sitting at that table right over there.' Conor pointed to one of the empty tables on the floor.

'They?' Garcia asked.

Conor nodded. 'Aye. He was here with a mate that night. I remember it because he usually comes in by himself. He's the quiet type, ya know? Usually prefers to sit here at the end of the bar.' He indicated the stool between Hunter and Garcia.

Hunter had already clocked the three CCTV cameras inside O'Hearn's – one at the entry door and two on the bar wall, just between the flatscreen TVs. He indicated the ones between the TVs. 'Do those work?'

Conor chuckled. 'Aye, but you've got no chance if you think we'll have a recording from a month ago. We only keep them for a few days. There's no point in saving them if the tills cash out properly and there was no trouble in here.'

That reply didn't surprise either detective.

'This mate of his,' Garcia asked. 'Is he a regular? Have you seen him here before?'

'Nah, I don't remember ever seeing the likes of him before, or since.'

'Did they come in together that night?' Hunter asked. 'Do you remember?'

The bartender thought about it for a few seconds, his tongue poking on the inside of his left cheek. 'Nah, I can't remember if they did, but in all fairness, probably.'

'And why do you think that?' Garcia pushed.

'Like I said, I never seen the likes of his mate here before and Shaun was the pretty quiet type. He wouldn't be the one to start a conversation with many folks, let alone a stranger, so aye, they probably knew each other from before and chances are that they did come in together that night.'

The customer sitting at the opposite end of the bar from where they were signaled the bartender for a new pint of Guinness.

'I won't be but a minute,' Conor said, as he poured the customer a brand-new pint of the black stuff.

'Can you remember any other time that you saw Mr. Daniels here with a friend?' Hunter asked, as Conor returned to their end of the bar.

The bartender paused again and the lip pinching came back. 'Nah,' he finally said after a few long seconds. 'I actually can't remember ever seeing him in here with a mate. He really was the quiet and lonely type.'

'Lonely?' Hunter prodded.

'Aye.' Conor's nod was firm. 'He usually came in, sat at the bar, had a few beers . . . a couple of shots of whiskey sometimes, then he'd be on his merry way. Always by himself. No mates. No ladies. Nothing. Sure,' the bartender gave the detectives a careless shrug, 'sometimes he would get fluthered, we all do, but even then, he wasn't one to make a fuss, like. He would just stagger out and that was that.'

'This friend of Mr. Daniels,' Hunter asked. 'How was he dressed?'

Conor frowned at the detective.

'What I mean is,' Hunter explained, 'Mr. Daniels was a plumber. Did this friend of his look like he was a plumber as well? Or a builder, or something like that? Could they have been on a job together before coming in for a drink at the end of their work day?'

'Umm . . .' Conor paused, yet again. 'There's no way I can be sure. We're talking a month ago here, but I don't think that either of them was dressed in their work clothes, to be fair.'

'Do you think that you'd be able to describe what Mr. Daniels's drinking partner looked like?' Garcia asked.

The bartender took no time in shaking his head. 'Nah, I barely looked at the fella. Like I said, I only really remember it because Shaun never comes in with a mate and he never takes a table. Always sits at the bar.'

'Do you remember if they seemed to be arguing at all?' Garcia asked.

'I can't really say, but if they were, it wasn't anything serious or loud.'

'I take it that they left together?' Hunter, this time.

'Can't say for sure again, but probably. I don't remember serving the fella on his own, or seeing him here by himself.'

Garcia quickly peeked at Hunter in a peculiar way. The look was almost code for *I think that we're done here.*

Hunter reached into his pocket for a card and handed it to Conor. 'If you remember anything else, or if, by any chance, you happen to see the person that was sitting with Mr. Daniels that night in here again, or anywhere else for that matter, please, contact me straight away. No matter the time. That person is probably the last person to have seen Mr. Daniels before he disappeared ... probably the last person to have seen him alive too. We need to find him.'

'Aye, no bother,' the bartender said, taking the card. 'If I see him again I'll get in touch.'

As Hunter and Garcia turned to leave, Conor halted them.

'There was this one night, like. He said something ... odd.'

Both detectives exchanged a quick glance before returning to the bar.

'I'm not quite sure exactly when this happened,' the bartender began. 'But I'm pretty certain that it wasn't too long before the last time I saw Shaun in here. It was also one of the nights that he got pretty ossified, like.'

'He got what like?' Garcia asked.

'Umm ... quite drunk,' Conor replied before continuing. 'So that night we got chatting here at the bar. It was a slow weeknight. No games on TV or nothing.' He threw his thumb over his shoulder to indicate the TVs high on the wall behind him. 'So I'm guessing it was probably a Monday or a Tuesday.' He shrugged. 'Anyway, we're chatting about something or other and somehow the conversation turned to "feck-ups".'

Garcia's eyes narrowed. 'What do you mean?'

'Ya know, life feck-ups – I should've done better with my life, but I fecked up and everything went arseways. Ya know what I mean, right?'

'Yeah, sure,' Hunter replied. 'So what happened?'

'Well ...' Conor pressed his lips together and subtly shook his head. 'I think that it was Shaun who mentioned something about being a feck-up and that his whole life was a feck-up. So I said something back like – we've all fecked up in life one time or another, ya know ... we just gotta carry on ... that's what's important. I fecked up plenty in mine, I told him.'

'OK ... ?' Garcia nodded him along.

'I remember that when I said that,' Conor explained, 'Shaun looked at me with this terribly sad look in his eyes, finished his pint, downed a shot of whiskey, and just before he walked off he said – and these were his words – "Not in the way I have, Conor. Not in the way I have."'

Twelve

Hunter sat quietly at his desk, eyes closed, mind plowing through the little they had so far, trying hard to understand what sequence of events could've led to Shaun Daniels being tortured for days before being murdered, but there were too many missing pieces ... too many unanswered questions for any sort of workable image to materialize.

Back at O'Hearn's Bar and Grill, Hunter had asked the bartender if he'd ever asked Shaun what he'd really meant when he mentioned that he had fucked up in life. Conor said that he never did. From experience, he said, he knew that comments like Shaun's were better left alone. The more you prodded, the more it stunk.

Hunter couldn't really argue with that logic. Conor wasn't exactly Shaun Daniels's best friend, or his analyst. He was just a bartender in Shaun's local bar. There was no reason for him to go snooping around in Shaun's personal life.

Right then, a 'ping' came from the computer on Hunter's desk, announcing the arrival of a new email. His eyes blinked open and his attention moved to his screen. The email was from Dr. Slater and it contained some of the forensics results from the analysis her team had conducted on Shaun's car. The report wasn't very long. The team had managed to retrieve several full and a few partial fingerprints from the external and internal door handles on all four doors, the steering wheel, the dashboard and the car's trunk lid. They had also recovered a few strands of hair from the driver and passenger seats.

No luck.

All lifted fingerprints, together with all recovered hair strands, belonged either to Shaun Daniels himself, or to one of the car handlers at the police parking garage in San Fernando Valley.

That result didn't really surprise Hunter. In fact, it stood to reason. If somebody had gone through the trouble of abducting, torturing and freezing Shaun Daniels to death, before trying to cover it all up by staging a fake hit-and-run accident, that someone wouldn't be the one to make a silly mistake like forgetting to wear gloves and some sort of hairnet while driving Shaun's car.

Hunter finished reading the report before getting to his feet and approaching the picture board, but his attention didn't go to any of the photographs. It moved to the map of the Sierra Pelona Mountains that he had pinned to the top right-hand corner of the board.

'Looking for anything in particular?' Garcia asked. He too had just finished reading the vehicle forensics report.

'Not exactly,' Hunter replied. 'Just having a look at the routes to and from the mountains.'

Garcia joined Hunter by the board. 'How did Shaun's car get there, right?' He indicated a photo on the board.

Hunter nodded.

'I was wondering the exact same thing,' Garcia began, pointing to the area on the map where Shaun's body was discovered. 'And the options are – the killer either had help, or he did a hell of a round trip, because to stage a hit-and-run accident, he needed two cars up there.'

Another nod from Hunter. 'Shaun's station wagon, parked down the dirt track to add authenticity to the fake hit-and-run, and the pickup truck that had supposedly run Shaun over. The same pickup truck that created the brake marks on the road.'

'Exactly,' Garcia agreed. 'With help, that's an easy trip – the killer drives one car and the help drives the other. They park Shaun's station wagon down the dirt road, stage the fake hit-and-run, then they both jump back into the truck and *hasta lasagna, amigos*.' Garcia gave Hunter a sarcastic salute.

Hunter carried on studying the map.

'But if the killer acted alone,' Garcia continued, his head shaking at his partner, 'then we're talking at least a couple of trips up and down those mountains.'

'First car up,' Hunter said in agreement, indicating on the map. 'Parks, then back down, picks up the second car – presumably the one that carried the body – back up the mountain, stages the hit-and-run, and finally back down again.'

'Easily doable,' Garcia said. 'But damn risky, not to mention time-consuming. And . . .' He lifted a finger at Hunter. 'How do you think that he got back down after driving the first car up?' He indicated on the map. 'That must be at least two, two-and-a-half miles, down to the bottom of Lake Hughes Road. And that is assuming that the second car was parked somewhere there, which it probably wasn't. So what did he do? Walked all the way back to where the second car was parked? Called a cab? Waited for the bus? What?'

Hunter's attention stayed on the map for a couple more seconds. 'What would you have done?'

Garcia shrugged. 'Picked a different location to dump the body. That's what I would've done.'

'Maybe,' Hunter agreed. 'But that's not an option. This is what we have.' His chin jerked in the direction of the map. 'So if you had to do this two-vehicle up-and-down, up-and-down trip all by yourself, how would you have done it?'

'Do I need to consider least amount of time possible, or what?' Garcia asked.

'I don't think it matters, but the day that the trip was done does.'

The answer surprised Garcia.

It took an instant for the penny to drop.

'His body was discovered in the early hours of a Sunday morning,' he said, sure that he had picked up on Hunter's line of thought. 'In an area that's packed full of fishing spots and picnic areas.'

Hunter nodded.

'Clever fuck,' Garcia said with a chuckle. 'A lot of people who go fishing tend to camp overnight. They'll spend the whole week-end up there. The killer could've driven Shaun's station wagon up the mountains the day before, on Saturday.'

'At any time,' Hunter agreed. 'He could've parked there in the morning, had a picnic, and then taken his time to make his way back down. He could've walked down, taken the bus, hitched a ride . . . it doesn't matter because he wouldn't care if he were seen or not. He wasn't doing anything wrong.'

Garcia ran the palms of both hands over his pulled-back hair before retightening his ponytail. 'That answers the question, doesn't it? Why was the body dumped in such an awkward location?'

'At first,' Hunter explained. 'I thought that it was simply due to how isolated that spot on Lake Hughes Road was.' Once again, he indicated on the map. 'No cameras anywhere around this whole area, and that's why it's a very popular location with young cou-ples and whoever else might be looking for some privacy in their cars. Lots of trees and dirt tracks, loads of little hideout places . . . but if we're talking about the killer acting alone, then I don't think that was the real reason why that spot was picked. It was chosen because it gave the killer the entire weekend to roll out his plan. No need to rush. No need to worry about anyone spotting the first car parked up there overnight. No need to worry about anyone spotting him either. It's the perfect location.'

Garcia puffed his cheeks before breathing out slowly.

'But we're not discarding any possibilities just yet,' Hunter was quick to add. 'The likelihood that this killer had help is still very high on the list.'

'Fine,' Garcia said, leaning back against the edge of his desk and folding his arms in front of his chest. 'Maybe we've figured out why the odd location, but what keeps on bothering me is the victim, Robert. Let's stick with the "one-killer" theory for now, OK? Let's say that he had no help. Let's say that he did drive the first car up that mountain sometime on Saturday before returning in the early hours of Sunday morning to stage the hit-and-run.'

Hunter could already tell where his partner was going. 'Why go through all that effort, right?'

Garcia agreed with a shrug. 'To disguise the murder of someone who, so far, seems to be no one special. He was just a plumber, Robert. That doesn't make sense. I accept, we still haven't checked his financial records. Who knows? Maybe all his money is tucked away in the Bahamas.' The sentence was delivered with an over-sarcastic look. 'But we've seen his car, we've been to his apartment . . . if Shaun Daniels was laundering money – or involved in any sort of illicit financial transaction where he was supposed to be taking a cut – he was being conned. That man did not live a life of luxury. It doesn't even look like he had a stable financial life.'

'No, it doesn't,' Hunter agreed.

'So this cannot have been about money, Robert. We both have seen it many times before. If this was about Shaun Daniels ripping someone off in any sort of way, he would've just been shot in the face, or chopped to pieces and that would be that. There'd be none of this hit-and-run staging crap. Loan sharks, gangsters, gang bangers, drug pushers, whoever . . . they won't torture a person for dimes, you know that. They'd have to have been ripped off big time, and even when they do torture somebody . . .' Garcia gave

Hunter a despondent headshake. 'They do it to set an example . . . to send out a message. They'd want others to know that they did it, so no one else would be getting any more funny ideas. They wouldn't have tried to cover anything up with a fake accident.'

Hunter said nothing back because he got the exact same feeling – whatever Shaun Daniels had meant when he told the bartender at O'Hearn's that he had fucked up, it couldn't have been about money.

Thirteen

Ten days after Terry Wilford's abduction

Monday 1 July

The waters of the world-famous Los Angeles River, historically known as the Porciúncula River, began their nearly 51-mile journey in Canoga Park. From there, they traveled south through the San Fernando Valley and into the City of Angels before finding their way to Long Beach – where they finally flowed into San Pedro Bay. Unlike most natural rivers, as it passed through Downtown LA, the LA River flowed through a man-made concrete channel on a fixed course, which was only built after a series of devastating floods hit Los Angeles in the early twentieth century. But its worldwide fame went much deeper than its waters and the destructive floods of the last century. In fact, it went all the way down to its man-made concrete channel.

During winter and spring, the river was fed primarily by rainwater and snowmelt, but during summer and fall, when temperatures in southern California could get up to 80°F and the entire state could experience months without a drop of rainfall, long stretches of the river's concrete channel would practically dry up – and that was why the LA River became so famous.

When dried of water, the man-made concrete channel became,

in essence, a freeway. During the Second World War, for example, trucks sped loads of munitions and war materials down the paved river to the harbor – but war didn't bring fame to the Los Angeles River ... Hollywood did, thanks to some of the most iconic scenes shot down at the concrete freeway for blockbusters such as *Grease*, *The Dark Knight Rises*, *Terminator 2*, *Drive*, *Point Blank*, *All Quiet on the Western Front* and *To Live and Die in LA*.

Despite its fame, the LA River freeway did have one major drawback. In the summer, when it didn't rain, the freeway didn't just run dry. At certain specific spots, it was fed wastewater discharged from three distinct treatment plants – Burbank, Glendale and the City of Los Angeles. Whenever that happened, the concrete channel needed to be cleaned, a job that fell to the LA Sanitation & Environment Division (LASAN), and there was no job that LASAN employees Luis Toledo and Randy Douglas hated more than cleaning and sanitizing the LA River freeway. Unfortunately for them, they'd been assigned to LA River sanitation duty for that entire week's nightshift, starting that Monday evening.

'Look at all this shit,' Luis said, gesturing at the amount of wastewater that he and Randy were looking at. His Mexican accent was mild, but still clearly noticeable.

'Literally,' Randy replied, crinkling his nose before hooking the wings of his P3 disposable mask behind his ears and handing one to Luis.

They were both sitting inside the cabin of their LASAN vacuum sweeper truck. Even with the windows shut the smell from the wastewater was still strong enough to itch the inside of their nostrils.

'This will take us all night ... every night,' Luis said, putting on his mask before slumping back against the driver's seat.

'Well, it's not like we haven't done it before,' Randy

commented, his mouth twisting left behind his mask.

'My point exactly.' Luis did nothing to cover the annoyance in his tone. 'I mean – we got assigned to night*shit* duty every goddamn year for the past seven years. They could've given us a break this year. Let some other *cholos* clean it for once.'

'I've only done four out of the past seven,' Randy reminded Luis. 'But you're right, they could've assigned this crap to a different team this year.'

Luis had parked the vacuum sweeper truck directly under the East 7th Street Bridge, one of the 136 bridges that provided some sort of crossing over the LA River. He checked his watch before letting go of a deep breath. It was just past eight in the evening, and their shift ran from 8:00 p.m. to 6:00 a.m.

'I guess we better get started,' Luis said, nodding at Randy, before pausing and quickly studying the stretch of concrete in front of their truck. 'The right side looks heavier with wastewater, but not as bad as last year.'

'Yeah, I noticed that too.' Randy nodded. 'So let's start with the right side. I'd rather get through the heavier stuff first.'

'Yeah, me too, but since the whole stretch doesn't look as heavy as last year, I'm thinking that maybe we can cover one hundred yards at a time, instead of only fifty. What do you think?'

Randy's bottom lip pursed forward as he nodded. 'Yeah, I think that's doable. We're cleaning all the way up to the next bridge and then back, right?'

'That's right.' Luis nodded.

'OK, let's get this party going.'

Luis shook his head at Randy. 'You and I have very different ideas of what a party is, *cholo*.'

There was no specific procedure that a team had to follow when cleaning the LA River concrete channel. It was all a question of preference, which was left to the team itself. The way Luis and Randy went about it was a simple and efficient one, but certainly laborious.

First, they would divide the channel into two halves – right and left side. Then they'd use the truck to sweep the bulk of the wastewater toward the edges, where drainage gutters ran for almost fifty miles. After that, came the hardest part – they needed to manually sweep the leftover water and waste from the main concrete body to the side gutters, picking up any large debris they might find, so as not to clog up the gutters. Due to how wide the channel was – equivalent to about four freeway lanes – they had to repeat that entire process four times – twice on the left . . . twice on the right.

Luis started the truck and activated the sweeping blades together with the wind turbines before driving south, in the direction of the 6th Street Viaduct, which was the next bridge along. They drove for about one hundred yards before stopping the truck and switching off the blades and the turbines.

'Ready?' Luis asked, as they both jumped out of the truck and collected their equipment from the back.

'As I'll ever be,' Randy replied, breathing out through his mask.

The driving part usually took them around five minutes to complete, but the manual sweeping, depending on what sort of grime they encountered along the way, could take them anywhere between fifteen and twenty-five minutes per hundred-yard section. Once that was done, the process repeated itself for the next hundred yards, until they got to the 6th Street Viaduct, which they did at around 10:30 p.m.

'Do you want to take a break now?' Luis asked, using his sleeve to mop the sweat from his forehead. 'Or when we make it back to the 7th Street Bridge?'

'I'm all right,' Randy replied. 'I can wait until we get back, if you want.'

'Let's do that then,' Luis agreed.

They both got back into the truck, moved it one lane to the

right, closer to the gutter, and began their first of two return journeys back from the 6th Street Viaduct to the 7th Street Bridge, but they never finished the job.

It was Luis who spotted it first, just a couple of minutes past midnight, during their last hundred-yard manual sweeping job before they got to the bridge. When they were just about seventy yards away from it, as he swept another rake full of dirty water toward the side gutter, his wandering stare moved up to meet the bridge. He didn't see it at first, but as his gaze was coming back to his rake, he spotted something – a silhouette, it seemed – just by the second lamppost up on the bridge. The only one out of four that was faulty.

As his eyes clocked the silhouette, Luis did a double-take before pausing.

'What the fuck?' he said, squinting, trying to sharpen his focus.

'What the fuck what?' Randy asked, looking in the same general direction as Luis, but failing to spot anything.

'Up there.' Luis raised his right arm to indicate. 'On the bridge. By the second lamppost from the right. The one that's busted.'

It took Randy a second, but he finally spotted it too, his neck craning forward. 'Is that someone up there?'

'I think it is, yeah,' Luis replied before he realized what was just about to happen. His eyes widened as he let go of his rake. 'Jesus Christ, I think the dude's gonna jump.'

Randy's mouth dropped open. Luis was right. The man on the bridge looked like he was about to leap to his death.

'HEY!' Luis yelled at the top of his voice, waving his arms in the air frantically. 'HEY . . . STOP!'

The man didn't look back at him. His head stayed low, with his chin almost touching his chest, and as Luis began a mad sprint in the direction of the bridge, the man simply stepped off its edge.

Luis was still too far away to make it there in time.

Horrified, all he could do was watch the man's body slice

through the air, gaining speed as it did, before splattering itself against the concrete channel down below. Even from a distance, as the body hit the ground hard, Luis could hear a sickening cracking noise, as the man's bones fractured on impact – some rupturing through muscle and skin to protrude out of his arms, legs and shoulders. His head also hit the ground with tremendous momentum, the collision hard enough to shatter his cranium, making it cave in and deforming his whole face out of shape.

Luis didn't stop running until he got to the bridge ... his breathing labored, his body shaking, tears already welling up in his eyes.

'What the fuck?' he called out, desperately bringing both hands to his head. His gaze moved to the mangled body on the ground and the pool of blood that was slowly forming around it. 'Jesus Christ, man!'

Randy, on the other hand, stood exactly where he was, about seventy yards away. His eyes were still squinting, trying hard to sharpen their focus and see through the darkness, but he wasn't looking at the man on the ground or at a freaked-out Luis Toledo. No, Randy's eyes were still squinting at the bridge ... because what he actually saw, couldn't really be possible ... could it?

Fourteen

Hunter and Garcia were right – Shaun Daniels's murder couldn't have been about money.

Eleven days after they visited O'Hearn's Bar and Grill, they finally received a report from Financial Forensics. An expert forensics accountant had spent days digging through Shaun Daniels's personal and business accounts. The accountant had checked everything on record and followed every electronic and paper trail that Shaun had left behind. There was nothing there – no large deposits or withdrawals, no steady money drip, no offshore accounts, no investment bouncing, no obscure transactions ... nothing. On the contrary, Shaun and his limited company – Daniels Plumbing Ltd – were barely managing to keep afloat. In fact, in the past twelve months, he'd been in the red with his personal account more times than a traffic light, surviving mainly on bank overdrafts and small credit card loans.

The forensics accountant had also looked into Shaun's credit card accounts. He had three of them – two personal ones and one registered to his limited company. They weren't maxed out but, just like his bank accounts, all three credit cards were in the red. It seemed that most of the time, Shaun Daniels got by through mainly paying only the interest that he was being charged every month. Every now and then, he was able to pay a little more, making a small dent into his debt, but soon enough he would overspend on one thing or another and that debt would either grow, or be right back to where it was before.

When Financial Forensics examined Daniels Plumbing Ltd's invoice books, they did find a few discrepancies, but nothing that truly worried anyone. The discrepancies came in the form of inflated invoices for small jobs, just like Garcia had suggested, but definitely not on the same scale. Every once in a while, Shaun Daniels would overcharge a client by as much as $450, depending on the job – hardly a money-laundering operation. Shaun would then create two invoices – an inflated one for the client and a 'real' one that he would bundle together with several other invoices and file as a single accumulated bill with the IRS.

According to the forensics accountant, that was the most used trick by small businesses. As long as they kept the overcharge under $500 and bundled them into an accumulated bill, detection was practically impossible. They'd have to be properly audited to fall into the IRS net and the IRS simply wouldn't waste time and resources going after such small fish.

All in all, the conclusion of the forensics accountant was that Shaun Daniels wasn't exactly a crook. He didn't really swindle the system. He simply did what he had to do to get by ... the American way.

Fifteen

One week later. Monday 8 July

Ronald Reagan Medical Center
UCLA, Westwood

While most of the students in the advanced Autopsy and Frozen Section class hung out in their usual groups, scattered around the large pathology theater, waiting for their professor to arrive, Carol Sixtree sat alone at the far back of the class. Like always, she had at least two books open in front of her, her gaze bouncing like a ping-pong ball from one to the other, while at the same time she sped-typed notes into her laptop, which, funnily enough, was sitting on her lap.

Carol, or Kay, as her friends called her, was the best student in that class by a long shot – she knew it . . . her professor knew it . . . and every student in her class knew it too. In fact, Kay Sixtree had been the best student in her class since her freshman year in high school, where her grade-point average never once dropped below 3.8. Once she entered university, almost eight years ago, that GPA increased to 4.0, all year round . . . every year.

For as long as she could remember, Kay Sixtree had always wanted to be a doctor. Her ambition had started sometime when she was around ten years old, but not even she could pinpoint how it exactly began. The story that she always told everyone was that it was due to that old buzzing game – Operation. Maybe it did have something to do with it. She did love playing it when she was a kid, but Kay didn't really believe that something so silly – a simple game of steady hand – had been 'ground zero' for what had become her lifelong obsession.

With a high school GPA of 3.8 or higher and an almost perfect score in her SAT exams, it was no surprise that after her graduation Kay got to have her pick of colleges to go to, with almost all of them offering her a full scholarship. For a while, she did consider going to Harvard or Yale – both world-famous and ranked in the top ten best medical schools in the USA, also known as the Ivy League – with Harvard holding the top spot. But Harvard was located in Boston, Massachusetts, and Yale in New Haven, Connecticut, both on the very east coast of America. For Kay Sixtree, that did constitute a problem.

Kay was born and bred in Los Angeles, California – the very west coast of America. Her father was a school janitor by day and an office cleaner at night. Her mother did clothes repairs out of their front room for a living. Even with her father working two jobs, her parents' combined income wasn't quite enough to breach the line between 'poor' and 'working class', but they did all they could. What they lacked in dollars, Kay's parents more than made up for with love.

Not once had either her father or her mother raised their voices with Kay, or her older brother, Nathan. Any problems in their household were always fixed through dialogue. No shouting, no running away from it ... and no physical violence, not under any circumstances. The result was a family that loved, trusted and respected each other in a way that was rarely seen in today's modern society. And it was that love and respect that most influenced Kay in her decision of where to go to college.

Kay and her family lived in Lynwood, an underprivileged

neighborhood in South LA, where crime and gang violence used to be a common occurrence. Almost nine years ago, when Kay was just about to start her senior year in high school, her brother Nathan, who was two years her senior, was shot through the heart during a store robbery gone very wrong. He was not part of the robbery. He was just unlucky. The proverbial 'in the wrong place at the wrong time' – shot by accident as the storeowner, a sixty-five-year-old African American man who went by the name of Joe, reached for the loaded shotgun that he kept behind the counter when he saw two masked men enter his shop. They were carrying two Smith & Wesson revolvers, which they made no effort in concealing. What ensued was a Wild West gunfight. Nathan, who hadn't seen the gunmen, had just reached the counter to pay for his groceries at the exact moment that Joe opened fire. As the gunmen retaliated, one of their 357 Magnum rounds perforated Nathan's chest and sliced right through his heart, rupturing the aortic and pulmonary valves, severing the right ventricle and obliterating the left and right atriums. He died right there on the store floor.

Nathan's death devastated the Sixtree family. Both of Kay's parents slumped into a spiral of deep depression, something neither had ever managed to fully recover from.

Graduating from high school just a year after her brother's death, Kay just didn't have the courage to leave her broken-hearted parents alone and move across America all the way to the west coast. Who cared if Harvard and Yale were two of the top medical schools in the country? Despite not being considered Ivy League, UCLA was still a great university with a fantastic medical program, and Kay Sixtree was an outstanding student. There was no way that she could go wrong with that combination, but most important of all, Westwood and UCLA were just a couple of short bus rides away from Lynwood and her parents' home.

A week after she graduated, Kay Sixtree accepted a full

scholarship from the University of California Los Angeles and began her journey to becoming a doctor.

On average, in the USA, the education and training needed to become a specialized medical doctor will require at least eleven years of education, including four years of college, four years of medical school and three to four years of residency at a teaching hospital.

It was during her very first year of medical school that Kay decided that she wanted to become a forensic pathologist. The reason for that was simple – she loved the quiet and tranquil feel of an autopsy theater. There was no rush, no time challenge to try to save a life, no mess, no mental and physical exhaustion at the end of a procedure . . . and no room full of other doctors and nurses. It was just her, the body and maybe an assistant. Plus, Kay felt a lot more comfortable among the dead than she did with the living.

After eight years of university, Kay was now just about to graduate from medical school and she was looking forward to a residency at the Los Angeles County Medical Examiner-Coroner – a position that she had been offered at the end of her third year of medical school by the LA Chief Medical Examiner herself, Dr. Carolyn Hove – who just happened to be the UCLA professor teaching the class that morning.

'Good morning, everyone,' Dr. Hove said as she entered the pathology theater. 'I hope you all had a good weekend and are all rested and ready to start cutting.' She followed her greeting with a smile.

'Always, Doc,' Kenny said, returning the smile, as he reached for a scalpel from an instruments tray and lifted it up in the air. 'Just point me to the body.'

The comment got laughs from everyone in the class, except for Kay Sixtree.

Kenny was a tall and muscular student, with fair hair and a

nose that seemed to have been sculpted by Michelangelo. He was both the hunk and the joke maker in that class.

'Put the knife down, bad boy,' Dr. Hove said back, her tone dismissive. 'Before you cut your finger like last time.'

More laughs, this time harder and accompanied by a few 'woo-woos'.

'The scalpel slipped, Doc,' Kenny came back, a little embarrassed, as he returned the sharp blade to the instruments tray.

'Yeah, yeah, yeah,' another student commented from across the room. 'Of course it did.'

'OK, everyone, settle down,' Dr. Hove said, lifting a hand at her students. 'We need to get started. Today, we're going to have a hands-on, long-procedural class, so time is very important here, as it will be when you're out in the real world. Let's see what you can accomplish in just over two hours and, yes, what you accomplish here today will certainly count toward your final grade.'

Every student in that class knew full well that Dr. Hove didn't quite subscribe to what was considered a conventional, end-of-term exam. She would never gather all of her students inside a classroom, sit them down and hand everyone an exam paper. That wasn't how the real world functioned. Instead, Dr. Hove was known for springing what she liked to call a 'procedural' class onto her students. Those were classes without a lecture ... without her helping them at all. Yes, they could use each other, just like in the real world, but procedural classes didn't require the use of textbooks, so conventional 'cheating' didn't really take place. Procedural classes were always hands on – just the students and a body.

Dr. Hove quickly did a headcount. All fifteen students in her advanced Autopsy and Frozen Section class were present.

'Perfect,' she said, giving everyone one of her famous enigmatic smiles. 'Fifteen students and five bodies to work on. Please get yourselves into groups of three. C'mon, let's go.'

Voices echoed through the autopsy theater, while everyone quickly organized themselves into their favorite 'buddy' groups, except for Kay Sixtree. Instead, she slowly closed the two books on her desk before putting away her laptop. She would group up with whoever was left behind, as she always did.

If they had a choice, no student in any of Kay's classes would ever be paired or grouped up with her. She was too knowledgeable, too serious . . . and way ahead of everyone in every discipline. No one liked to be second best but, truthfully, the main reason why most of the other students disliked her was because Kay didn't hold back if another student in her group made, or was about to make, a mistake at the autopsy or operation table.

'Oh, I sure wouldn't do that,' was her favorite phrase to stop a fellow student from cutting in the wrong place or making a mistake that would've cost a patient's life had they been inside a real operating room. It annoyed the hell out of the other students, but the fact of the matter was that Kay was almost always right . . . almost.

It took less than half a minute for the students to organize themselves into four groups of three. The two students left without a group were Myeong Jang Bo, a petite exchange student from Seoul in South Korea, and Tullik Bryant, a twenty-eight-year-old African American student from Mississippi, who had the big hazel eyes of a baby deer and the ego of a narcissist. Tullik and Myeong exchanged a dispirited look before they approached Kay.

'I guess you're with us then,' Bambi-eyed Tullik said, the expression on his face matching his total lack of excitement.

'I guess that's a question of perspective, isn't it?' Kay had bit back on the cutting sarcasm that was her initial reaction, but it still came out meaner than what she had intended.

'Are we all sorted?' the doctor asked.

A choir of 'Yep' and nods followed.

'OK,' Dr. Hove began. 'Like I said earlier, we've got five bodies to work on today. All five of them were victims of suicide. The suicide method used will be quite obvious with most of them.' She paused to make sure that she had everyone's attention on her. 'Regardless of how obvious that method was, I want indisputable confirmation of the COD.'

Dr. Hove watched as all fifteen students in her class nodded back at her in silence.

'Now, that is the easy part,' she continued.

Most of the other students shifted on their feet, uncomfortably. They all knew that Dr. Hove always liked to add something else on top of the obvious. Kay Sixtree, on the other hand, pressed her lips together tightly to keep herself from smiling. That 'something else on top of the obvious' was what she lived for, so to speak. To her, the obvious was nothing more than just that – the obvious. It was the details that made all the difference.

'Almost every dead body hides a secret,' Dr. Hove clarified, guiding the groups toward the bodies on the five autopsy tables. 'So, other than indisputable confirmation of the COD, I want you to find and catalogue whichever details of that person's life you might find – surgeries, accidents, bone breaks, wound scars . . . anything – and if possible, I'd like time frames. If you come across an old surgery, I want to know how long ago that surgery took place. Same with everything else – accidents, bone breaks, scars . . . whatever you find.'

'Are we doing a brain autopsy as well?' Kay asked, her dark eyes showing the excitement that her expression managed to hide.

'If you deem it necessary – by all means,' Dr. Hove replied, as her gaze strayed to her students. 'Like I said, almost every body hides a secret, and that secret can be hidden just about anywhere, and those are the sort of details that can easily shine light on an investigation going dark. Today, I'll be walking around and checking on your progress, but I'll not be helping in any way. Use your group members for that – ask for opinions . . . bounce ideas ... you know what to do.' Her head tilted slightly to one side in a doubtful gesture. 'I know that many of you are only here today courtesy of a few very well glamorized TV series.' She indicated the bodies on the autopsy tables. 'You wanted forensics CSI? You wanted to be the heroes and solve the case for the police?' She gave her students a subtle wink. 'Well, this is it, ladies and gentlemen. Let's see how closely you can listen to what the body is trying to tell you.'

Sixteen

Completely covered by long, teal-colored surgical sheets, the five bodies inside the pathology theater at the Ronald Reagan Medical Center in UCLA were lying on wide, stainless-steel autopsy tables. A green folder sat on top of the instruments tray, by every table. It contained the official police report and some background information on the body, but the students weren't allowed to look at it until Dr. Hove gave them the green light.

'OK,' she said, as she gestured toward the autopsy tables. 'We have three male bodies and two female ones. They were brought into the theater earlier this morning and, to be honest with you, I really don't know which one is which. I haven't looked.'

'Can we choose?' a tall and slim student asked. Her long, barley-colored hair was clipped at the top by a claw-clip.

'Will you be able to choose in real life?' Dr. Hove challenged her.

'I guess that if you're the chief medical examiner you could have your pick.' The reply came from Kenny, which once again got him a few scattered laughs.

'Wow,' the doctor chuckled. 'Four to five years still to go and you're already gunning for my job? Good luck. Just try to keep all your fingers attached to your hands before graduation day, all right?'

This time, even Kay had to laugh. She really didn't like Kenny.

'OK, everyone.' Dr. Hove's tone was back to serious. 'Get your groups by an examination table. No peeking.'

She waited until every group had paired itself up with a body.

'Are we all set?' she asked, her stare moving slowly from group to group.

Another united chorus of agreement.

'I'm giving you all a total of two hours and fifteen minutes,' Dr. Hove announced, indicating the clock high on the theater's back wall. 'So each member in the group will have forty-five minutes as the head pathologist.' This time, her stare found and settled on Kay Sixtree. 'The head pathologist is allowed to do whatever he/she wants. The other two members of the group – the *assistants* . . .' The pause that came after the word was deliberate. 'May observe and perhaps suggest something, *if . . . and only if . . .*' Another pause, this one accentuated by the doctor's index finger up in the air. 'The head pathologist asks for advice, otherwise keep your opinions to yourself. Is that understood?'

While all the other students nodded and muttered their agreement, Tullik and Myeong both turned to look at Kay, their eyebrows arching, silently asking her the exact same question Dr. Hove had posed to the class.

Kay crossed her arms in front of her chest as she shrugged. 'I won't say a word. Do what you must.'

'All right,' Dr. Hove said, her gaze once again finding the clock on the wall. 'Have all of you decided on who is head pathologist first?'

Murmurs took over the theater again.

Tullik and Myeong's eyes returned to Kay, who stood still, her poker face giving nothing away.

'I can go first,' Myeong said. Her voice was naturally quiet and so sweet, sometimes Kay believed that she could get a cavity just by listening to Myeong talk.

'I'll go second then,' Tullik was fast to suggest, as his attention returned to Kay. 'If you don't mind.'

Kay knew exactly why they wanted to go before her. She wasn't only the best student in her class. She was also very fast and precise with a scalpel. If she went first, she could easily cover more ground in her forty-five minutes than Tullik and Myeong could in their combined hour and a half. Once she was done, there probably wouldn't be that much left for the two of them to examine. Plus, if Kay went last, it meant that she would probably have a chance to do the brain autopsy.

'I don't mind,' Kay said, the corners of her lips stretching, but not into a smile. It was more like a mouth shrug. 'I can go last if you guys want to go first.'

'Great,' Tullik said, while Myeong repositioned herself around the autopsy table, moving closer to the instruments tray.

'We're all ready, then?' Dr. Hove asked one last time.

Everyone in the class nodded.

'OK, your time starts . . . now.' The doctor finally gave everyone the go-ahead as she clicked a button on her wristwatch. 'I'll give you all a heads-up when you're ten minutes from time . . . then again at five minutes. And remember – treat the body with respect. They deserve it just as much as the living.'

More, even, Kay thought, but kept it to herself.

Kay, Tullik and Myeong had chosen the third autopsy table – the one right in the center. As Dr. Hove finally gave everyone the go-ahead, Tullik pulled the surgical sheet away, revealing a tall, white, male subject. The subject looked to have been in his early to mid-fifties when he died, but Kay, Tullik and Myeong all knew that with death, human skin would quickly acquire a different tone, dehydrate, lose elasticity and wrinkle. Add that to days spent in cold storage and correctly guessing someone's age at the autopsy table became a magic trick that very few got right.

The body had already been stripped naked and the injuries to it made all three of them cringe – his right leg was twisted out of shape, with his ankle completely bent backward, showing a comminuted open fracture. His left leg didn't look broken, but it was cruelly bruised. There were three other exposed fractures – right forearm and elbow, and right shoulder – while his left wrist and shoulder looked visibly dislocated. His torso was covered by different-sized hematomas, which were a sign of at least two broken ribs, but it was his head that made even Kay Sixtree shiver in place. The right side of his face was damaged beyond recognition – cheekbone and jaw broken, with the skin and flesh lacerated. On his skull, just above his right ear, there was an impact dent so severe that they could see the fracture to his cranium, leading all the way to his gray matter. Kay didn't need to do a brain autopsy to know that bone fragments from his skull had broken inward and perforated his brain.

'Jesus!' Tullik said, taking a step back, unable to peel his eyes from the body. 'What happened to him?'

'This is a suicide victim?' Myeong asked. 'What did he do, jump into a meat grinder?'

'He probably either stepped in front of high-speed incoming traffic,' Kay replied, reaching for the file on the instruments tray. 'Or he jumped from a building ... a bridge ... some place high off the ground.' She nodded at the body. 'Those are high-impact fractures and lesions.'

'Poor guy,' Myeong said as she exhaled. 'I wonder what he must've been going through to believe that he had no other way out other than to do this to himself.'

'That's a cardinal sin if you're a forensic pathologist,' Kay said, as she flipped open the file in her hands.

'I know,' Myeong replied, lifting a hand in an apologetic gesture. 'I'm not getting personal with the body. I've just always been fascinated by the kind of darkness that can lead a person to end his or her life with extreme prejudice like this. Especially so late in life.'

'How old would you say he was when he died?' Tullik asked.

Myeong shrugged. 'Somewhere in his fifties ... sixties, possibly?'

Tullik nodded, signaling his agreement.

'Even if you knew what had led him to this,' Kay offered, 'chances are it wouldn't make too much sense to you. But it did to him. He simply had had enough.' She once again indicated the body. 'Are you ready to start? Your time is ticking.'

'I am.' Myeong took a second to recompose herself.

The autopsy body-block had already been put in place. This was a thick block made of rubber that was placed under the body's back to make the chest protrude forward, so that the arms and neck fell back, making cutting a lot easier.

Finally ready, Myeong nodded at Tullik, who started the digital recording.

Myeong began by giving a detailed description of the body's appearance, including ethnicity, gender, and hair and eye color, but when Myeong pulled open the body's eyelids to register his eye color, Kay frowned.

'That's odd,' she said, stepping closer and bending over to get a better look.

'What is?' Myeong asked.

'Just around his bottom eyelid,' Kay replied, and used her index fingers to pull down the body's right and left lower eyelids. 'Here, can you see it?'

There was an odd color change right on the inside edge of both eyelids.

'Yeah, so?' Tullik challenged, his tone already dismissive. 'Skin discoloration happens after death, you know?'

'That's not post-mortem discoloration,' Kay told him.

'Oh really?' Tullik pushed. 'So what is it then?'

'I don't know.' Kay was still analyzing the subject's lower eyelids. 'Some sort of burn mark or skin irritation, for sure. We'd need a biopsy to properly determine what this is.'

'No, it isn't,' Tullik disagreed, also stepping a little closer to have a better look. 'And no, we don't need a biopsy, Kay. That's post-mortem discoloration, pure and simple.' He paused and looked at Myeong. 'What do you think?'

'I'm not really sure either,' Myeong replied, giving them a shy shrug. 'I think that the best we can do right now is describe it as part of the external examination, noting your observation that a biopsy could be needed.' She addressed Kay. 'How does that sound?'

Kay was about to say something, but Tullik saw it coming and halted her with a look. 'No butting in until it's your turn, Kay, remember? You agreed. Myeong is right – the best we can do right now is to describe it as part of the external examination.'

Kay accepted it with a nod before positioning herself at one end of the autopsy table, by the body's feet. Her eyes moved down to the file that she had with her and she was immediately surprised to find out that the man they were looking at was not in his fifties or sixties like Myeong and Tullik had initially thought. Not even close. His name was Terry Wilford and he was only forty-three years old at the time of his death.

In the police report, Kay found out that Mr. Wilford's body had been found a week ago by two LA Sanitation & Environment Division employees, as they cleaned the LA River concrete channel during their nightshift. Terry Wilford had jumped off the 7th Street Bridge.

Kay returned the file to the instruments tray and allowed her attention to go back to the body. When Myeong spread the body's legs just a couple of inches to get a better look at the inner thighs, Kay caught a glimpse of something else that immediately intrigued her.

'Myeong,' Kay said, grabbing her colleague's attention. 'Have you seen this?' She indicated the body's right foot.

Myeong and Tullik joined Kay at the far end of the examination table.

'What am I looking at?' Myeong asked.

'Right there,' Kay said, as she indicated. 'In between the big toe and the pointer one.'

Myeong used both of her index fingers to spread the two toes apart. There was something that looked like some sort of lesion on the soft flesh between those two toes.

'So he suffered from athlete's foot,' Tullik said, after looking at the lesion for a mere second.

'I don't think that's athlete's foot,' Myeong said, as she looked between all the other toes.

Just like the color change in his eyelids isn't post-mortem discoloration, Kay thought, but kept it to herself.

'Why not?' Tullik disputed.

'Athlete's foot is a fungus infection,' Myeong replied. 'It's caused by damp socks or shoes together with warm and humid conditions—'

Tullik chuckled, as he cut Myeong short. 'Well, you just described LA's yearlong weather. All he needed to do was go for a long run and step into a puddle right at the beginning of the run. Keep the wet shoes and socks on for longer than necessary and bingo, bango, bongo.' He pointed to the body's right foot. 'Athlete's foot.'

'True,' Myeong agreed. 'But you didn't let me finish – because it's a fungus infection, it's practically impossible to develop it in between only two toes. Inside a close and tight environment like a shoe, it would've spread like butter.' She finished checking the rest of the body's right foot. 'But we don't have that here.' She indicated, so that Tullik could have a look. 'All his other toes look healthy.'

Kay quickly checked the body's left foot, where she found a very similar lesion, once again, only between the big and the pointer toes. 'And he's got the exact same thing on his left foot.'

'OK,' Tullik lifted his hands in a tentative surrender gesture. 'So it's not athlete's foot, but it's clearly just some other skin condition.'

'Like what?' It was Kay's turn to challenge him.

'It could be one of many different types of eczema,' Tullik offered, while reaching for the file that Kay had returned to the instruments cart. 'Or even psoriasis. With his skin in the condition that it is now, we'd need a full lab analysis to know for sure.'

That paused Kay for an instant. Tullik did have a point. The lesion between the toes could be psoriasis.

'Regardless of what that really is . . .' He pointed at the body's feet before turning to face Myeong. 'I can tell you what it's not.'

Myeong's eyebrows lifted at him.

'That's not the COD,' Tullik continued. 'Which is what we're supposed to be identifying here. It's also none of the other things that Dr. Hove asked us to unearth – old surgeries, bone breaks . . . whatever. If you want to spend any more of your "fast running out" forty-five minutes on some "who gives a damn" toe infection, go right ahead. I'm sure that Kay would love you to do so, but when my turn comes, I'm cutting right into him because that's what great pathologists do.'

Tullik delivered those words in such a way that Myeong looked at Kay a little sideways, as if the lesions on the body's toes had been some sort of expert ploy from Kay to make the other two group members waste their time as the head pathologist.

Myeong took in a deep breath before addressing Kay. 'Tullik is right. I've already wasted way too much time here. Whatever that is, it isn't important. I'll describe it for the benefit of the recording once again, like I did with the eyelid discoloration, but the decision is mine and I'm moving on.'

Myeong quickly completed the external examination while her 'assistants' collected samples of hair and debris from under his fingernails for lab analysis, if needed.

'I'm ready to start,' Myeong announced.

Kay and Tullik stepped closer.

Myeong retrieved a long scalpel from the instruments tray, stepped up to the body and started the famous 'Y' incision, cutting from both shoulders to the lower end of the sternum and then downward, in a straight line, over the abdomen to the pubis.

'I'm going to need a little help with the pulling,' Myeong said, her gaze moving from Kay to Tullik.

'We're on it,' Tullik replied.

Kay and Tullik used special scissors and toothed forceps to peel back skin and soft tissue, pulling the chest flap over the body's face to expose the ribcage and neck muscles.

'Oh, Jesus!' Myeong said, indicating two clearly visible severe fractures to the ribcage – frontal, right side – ribs four and five. 'Very big contenders for the COD, right here.'

With both fractures, the ribs had broken completely free from the cage and, in both cases, perforated the subject's right lung.

'He wouldn't have survived this,' Myeong announced. 'Not without immediate assistance.'

'Definitely not,' Tullik agreed, but Kay stayed quiet.

The injury was real. Kay could clearly see that, but she could also clearly see that something didn't seem right. She bent over the body to have a closer look.

'You look doubtful, Kay,' Myeong said. 'Don't you agree with my assessment?'

'I'm not doubtful about the injury,' Kay replied, using her left hand to gently move one of the ribs that had implanted itself into the subject's lung. 'This would've definitely been life-threatening, but . . .' Instead of finishing her sentence, Kay studied the perforations to the lung a little more closely.

'But what, Dr. House?' Tullik asked, sarcastically referring to Kay's favorite medical TV drama series.

'Don't you think that there's a lack of internal hemorrhaging?' Kay asked, indicating the area next to the lung. 'There should've been more blood everywhere around here.' Using her left hand, she applied a little pressure to the lung, in a squeezing motion. 'There should've been a lot more blood inside his lung too.'

'You can't really tell if there is or not with a simple hand-pressure exam,' Tullik countered. 'Not to mention the fact that he died a week ago and has spent the last few days lying in cold storage. To confirm the hemorrhaging, the lung has to be removed and autopsied, which is what we're about to do . . . if we're allowed to.'

'Also,' Myeong offered, her sweet voice doing its best to sound authoritative, 'like I've said, this is just a contender for the COD, but let's be honest here – his body is pretty mangled – and we just barely opened him up. A double-punctured lung isn't the only life-threatening injury we're going to find. I'm one hundred percent sure of that.'

Kay tilted her head, opened her mouth, then closed it again. She'd been about to raise a different point, but in the end, all she did was smile and nod.

Discussion over, Myeong used a bone saw to cut and remove the ribcage. Without its protection, extracting the larynx, the esophagus, arteries and ligaments was easy work.

Kay had to admit that she was quite impressed by how precise Myeong was with every autopsy cutting instrument she had reached for, but that precision came at a cost – time. By the time that she had finished severing all the attachments to the spinal cord and removing the internal organs as an entire set, Myeong's time as the head pathologist was over.

Tullik was quick to step into his new role and, as he did, he looked Kay straight in her eyes. 'Not a peep from you from now on. This is my show now.'

Seventeen

'So how are we doing here?' Dr. Hove asked, walking up to Kay, Myeong and Tullik's group to check on their progress, just as the first forty-five minutes were over.

'We're OK, I guess,' Myeong replied, her head angling slightly to one side, showing uncertainty. 'I wish I could've covered a little more ground.' Halfway through her sentence, Myeong's stare moved to Kay and stayed on her until seconds after she had delivered the last word. 'But things didn't run as smoothly as they could've done.'

Kay's eyes widened at Myeong. 'Not quite like that,' she said, not so much in an effort to defend herself, but more to try to grab Dr. Hove's curiosity. 'Straight from the external and preliminary exams, Doc, a couple of things just didn't look quite right. Here, have a look . . .' Kay tried, pointing at the body's eyes, but before she could say or do anything, Dr. Hove paused her with a subtle hand gesture.

'It doesn't look like it's your turn, Kay.'

'Damn straight,' Tullik said, repositioning himself at the head of the examination table.

Dr. Hove knew how dedicated Kay Sixtree was. After all, she had already offered Kay a residency at the Department of Medical Examiner-Coroner. Kay would be an exceptional medical examiner someday, but her enthusiasm did get the best of her most of the time. That was something Dr. Hove also knew would eventually die down naturally, but as a student, Kay wanted what every other forensics pathology student wanted – to be the hero . . . to find that one thing that no one else saw . . . that one thing that was overlooked by everyone . . . that one thing that so happened to solve the whole mystery, if there was one.

Tullik reached for the body block and moved it from under the body's back to under the body's neck, like a pillow.

'What are you doing?' Kay asked, her eyes narrowing at Tullik's action.

'What do you think I'm doing,' Tullik replied, unconcerned, as he reached for the electric hair clippers on the instruments tray.

'You're going to autopsy the brain?' Kay stepped closer. 'Right now?'

'Wow, you're definitely with it today, Dr. House,' Tullik said back, as he started shaving the body's head. 'Another excellent spotting job.'

'But what about the rest of the body,' Kay tried to argue. 'All the exposed fractures? The bone breaks? All of it. You're not going to look into that?'

Tullik turned off the clippers for an instant and faced Kay. 'The assignment is to supply Dr. Hove with indisputable confirmation of the COD.' His gaze moved to their professor. 'In my professional opinion as the *head* pathologist, following an expertly detailed external examination by Dr. Myeong . . .' A quick glance at Myeong followed by a single nod. 'The cause of death will, most certainly, be linked to the extensive blunt trauma to the subject's head. I'm going to obtain that indisputable confirmation first.' He quickly checked his watch. 'If time allows, I'll then dig into everything else, if not, then you can do it when your forty-five minutes come up.'

Before Kay had a chance to voice the rebuff, which Dr. Hove knew was coming, she stepped in. 'Tullik is right, Kay. He's the head pathologist. Once all the internal organs have been removed, it's his decision where to start.' The nod that she gave Tullik was a confident one. 'I'll also admit that his call on the probable COD looks to be right on the money here. If this was my session, I'd start with a brain autopsy as well.' She softened her words with a smile. 'As I'm sure would you and Myeong, if she had more time.'

Kay had no returning argument because Dr. Hove was right. If she were going second, she too would've opted to start with a brain autopsy.

As Dr. Hove left their group to go check on the next group along, Tullik restarted the clippers and picked up from where he'd left off. A minute and a half later, their autopsy subject had a fully shaved head and that was when Kay noticed something else that nagged at her senses – something that once again, just didn't seem right – but this time, when neither Tullik nor Myeong seemed to have noticed the same thing as Kay did, Kay decided to stay quiet. She knew that if she said anything, even if she was right, Tullik wouldn't care for her opinion. All he would do would be to tell her to shut the hell up. Kay decided that her best move would be to just wait until her turn came up.

With the subject's head fully shaved, Tullik reached for a scalpel and made a deep cut from behind the left ear, across the forehead, and over to the right side.

'Lift, please,' he called for his assistants' help.

Kay and Myeong carefully lifted the head off the body block so that Tullik could finish the cut around the back of his head, creating a full 360-degree incision.

As Kay and Myeong returned the subject's head to the body block, Tullik swapped the scalpel for an electric saw. The smile he gave Kay just before he brought blade to bone almost made her sick.

'Now watch and learn, people.'

Despite his arrogance, Kay couldn't argue that Tullik wasn't just fast with his cutting – he was also millimeter-perfect. Less than two minutes later, he popped off the top of the subject's skull like a cap, exposing his brain.

'Wow,' Tullik said, moving his head from left to right, as he studied what they could see of the subject's gray matter. 'We don't even need to extract the brain to identify the cause of death. Look at this.'

Kay and Myeong stepped closer.

Tullik used a scalpel to indicate an area of the subject's brain that sat just a little above his right ear, where tiny skull fragments could be seen embedded into the brain.

'The head impact with the ground was so severe,' Tullik explained, 'that his skull didn't just splinter-fracture. It caved in. The sharp bone edges sliced off a portion of his gray matter. Can you see here? There are pieces missing.'

'Yeah,' Myeong replied first. 'I see it.'

'This,' Tullik continued, 'hands down, trumps a perforated and collapsed lung.' He nodded at Kay.

Kay accepted it with a head gesture, but her attention was already on something else.

How can they not be seeing this? The thought exploded inside her head. *Am I overthinking things?* She once again waited for a heartbeat, but no one said a word. *If I am, it doesn't feel like I am.*

They removed and weighed the brain and before Tullik's forty-five minutes were over, he had confidently established the COD – blunt trauma to the skull, caused by the head impacting the ground at high speed due to a fall, where the skull splinter-fractured and caved inward, not only perforating the brain, but also slicing off and extracting a portion of the right temporal lobe. The injury would've caused immediate ceasing of brain functions, resulting in instant death.

By the time Kay Sixtree assumed the role of head pathologist, there was very little else left to do other than examine the many fractures and bone breaks around the subject's body. And that was exactly what she did.

Tullik wasn't the only one who was fast and precise with the autopsy instruments. Kay worked her way around every fracture in the subject's battered body with so much pace and dexterity that even Tullik found himself pursing his lips and nodding at every cut she made. But with every fracture and bone break that she cut around, the odd feeling she had inside that something just wasn't quite right with the information they had on the subject's death grew. Every time she exposed the muscles and ligaments around a new fracture, she would pause and look at the other two members in her group, waiting for them to notice some of the same things that she was noticing, but neither one said a word about any of it.

'OK, everyone,' Dr. Hove called, lifting a hand to get everyone's attention. 'Time's up. Please cover the subjects back up, leave the recordings as they are and go scrub down. I'm sure that you all did great. Meanwhile, I'll do my best to get through all of the recordings by the end of the weekend.'

While everyone noisily exited the theater, discussing what they all had just done, Kay stayed behind – her gloves still on, her mask hanging around her neck, her surgical cap still covering her raven-black hair.

'Kay,' Dr. Hove called, gathering a few files from her desk and placing them inside her brown leather briefcase. 'We're done here. You've done great. Go scrub down and celebrate. You're all going to graduate in less than three weeks. Enjoy the moment.'

'Doctor, can I show you something?' Kay said, once again, uncovering the body on the autopsy table in front of her.

Dr. Hove didn't even glance back at her student as she sighed. 'No, Kay. Like I've said, we're done here. Class is over. Semester is over. Year is over. Med school is over. You've done it. All the years of hard work have paid off. All you need is a few more years of residency and you'll be a fully accredited forensics pathologist. Seriously, go celebrate, girl.'

'Doctor,' Kay insisted, her tone just as serious as ever. 'I really think that you'd want to see this.'

'Kay,' Dr. Hove said, finally locking eyes with her student. 'You know that your residency is already guaranteed, right? You don't have to try to impress me anymore. Plus . . .' She paused, an affectionate smile evident in the curve of her words. 'If you can get that excited with a suicide victim, I can't wait until you're face to face with some of the real, open homicide investigations we get.'

'That's the problem here, Doctor,' Kay said back, not allowing the doctor's stare to run away from her. 'I don't think that this is a suicide case. He didn't die on impact.'

Those words certainly managed to halt Dr. Hove.

'What do you mean? That he was dead before he hit the ground?' There was a shrug in the doctor's voice. 'It's not uncommon, Kay. It sometimes happens.'

'No, Doctor.' Kay's eyebrows arched as she shook her head. 'I'm not saying that he was dead before he hit the ground. I'm saying that he was dead before he jumped . . . he was dead before he even got to that bridge.'

Eighteen

At a quarter past seven in the evening, Hunter was just about to power down his computer and call it a day, when the phone on his desk rang.

Garcia, who was just about to do the same, paused. His gaze skittered over to Hunter, as if waiting for confirmation that their workday was truly over.

'Ultra Violent Crimes Unit,' Hunter said, as he brought the receiver to his ear. 'Detective Hunter speaking.'

'*Robert.*' The female voice at the other end of the line was calm and composed. '*It's Carolyn Hove at the ME Department.*'

'Oh, hello, Doc,' Hunter said back. His eyes quickly moved to his watch before he looked back at Garcia for a split second. Hunter and Dr. Hove had been friends for many years, but if this was a friendly call, Hunter knew that she would've called him on his private cellphone, not on the UVC Unit's landline. 'How can I help?'

Garcia rounded his desk and paused by Hunter's.

'*Do you remember that odd case I sent your way about eighteen days ago, on June 20th?*' Dr. Hove asked. '*Shaun Daniels? Supposed hit-and-run, but my conclusion was that he died from hypothermia?*'

'Shaun Daniels.' Hunter repeated the name, as he switched the call to speakerphone. 'Yes, of course I remember.' His tone gained a somewhat disappointed and frustrated edge.

'Did you manage to get anywhere with that? Any leads at all?'

Garcia's eyes narrowed first at the phone, then at Hunter. Dr. Hove had always been the epitome of professionalism. She never got emotional ... she never allowed herself to get personally involved with any of her cases either, and the reason for that was simple: being too close to an investigation had the magic power of amplifying every blind spot – and when that happened, important details tended to get overlooked. Unless the detectives, or anyone else linked to the investigation, came back to her with more queries, once a body left her examination table, that subject was history. Only in a few truly bizarre cases, for the benefit of knowledge, in case she encountered something similar in the future, did Dr. Hove ever ask Hunter and Garcia about their progress in any given investigation.

'Nothing that could really lead us anywhere, Doc.' The answer came from Garcia. 'We've been hitting dead ends everywhere we've looked. We hoped that his financial records would maybe give us something to go on, but that too went cold just a few days ago. But why the question, Doc? Did anything else relating to Shaun Daniels come up?'

'Umm ...' Hunter and Garcia could practically hear Dr. Hove scrunching her nose. *'Not exactly?'*

The two detectives exchanged a questioning look. They both also knew that Dr. Hove loved to solve enigmas, not create them.

'We're a little unclear as to what that really means, Doc,' Garcia said, shrugging at Hunter. 'Can you help us out?'

'Well,' Dr. Hove said, before pausing for a second. *'I think that we've got another body.'*

The room seemed to inhale.

'What do you mean, another body, Doc?' Hunter stepped in. 'Another body in relation to what?'

'Another body that was dead before being dead, if you get what I'm saying.'

The room exhaled.

'Wait a second.' Garcia leaned a little closer to the phone on Hunter's desk. 'Are you saying that you've got another person who died of hypothermia, but came to you as a hit-and-run?'

'No,' Dr. Hove replied. *'The body came to us as a jumping suicide.'*

Hunter and Garcia exchanged another concerned look.

'But we can prove that he was dead way before he jumped.'

'Hypothermia?'

'Not this time, but there are other similarities to Shaun Daniels's case.'

'And where's that body now, Doc?' Hunter asked.

'Right in front of me.'

'Are you at the morgue?'

'No, I'm at the Ronald Reagan UCLA Medical Center in Westwood – Main Pathology Theater.'

Hunter reached for his jacket.

'We're on our way.'

Nineteen

The Ronald Reagan UCLA Medical Center in Westwood wasn't just a fully functional teaching hospital. It was also ranked the fifth best hospital in the whole United States, providing students and the community with research centers covering nearly all major specialties of medicine and nursing, as well as dentistry. It was located in the southwest quadrant of the UCLA campus, just by Westwood Village, which was about fifteen miles away from the Police Administration Building.

Garcia took a parking space by a black Mercedes Benz, on the second floor of the visitors' multi-story car park.

The main entry lobby to the Ronald Reagan Medical Center was so spacious it looked like a Vegas hotel reception foyer, minus the slot machines. It was brightly lit and airy, with the floors decked out in two-tone marble and the walls in white polished granite, giving the entire hall a very clean, welcoming and comforting feel.

The main pathology theater was located right at the end of the ground-floor concourse, just past a large auditorium.

'Doctor?' Hunter called, as he pulled open the door so that he and Garcia could step inside a very spacious, conference-type classroom.

'In here.' They heard Dr. Hove's voice call from around the corner, just past a wall of wheeled hospital-style partitions.

A second later, her head popped out from behind the last of those partitions. 'In here,' she said again, this time with a head gesture.

Hunter and Garcia rounded the partitions to find themselves in what they knew looked exactly like an autopsy room, just four times bigger. The five autopsy tables from Dr. Hove's class earlier that day had been wheeled away, with the exception of one. The body on it had, once again, been covered up by a teal-colored medical sheet. Standing by the examination table were Dr. Hove and a second woman, who was as tall as the doctor herself, but at least twenty-five years her junior. She wore a conventional coroner's coverall, the same as Dr. Hove, and a pair of typical surgical clogs. Her black hair was tied back into a short ponytail, but had it been loose, it would've fallen to just above her shoulders, framing a delicate and attractive face.

'Robert, Carlos,' Dr. Hove said, as she introduced them. 'This is Carol Sixtree, one of my top students.'

Kay chuckled as her gaze skipped from Hunter to Garcia, then to Dr. Hove. 'What the doctor really means is – "I'm her top student". And please, call me Kay.'

'She's also very modest,' Dr. Hove added. 'As you can tell.'

Hunter stepped forward to offer his hand, but Kay halted him by lifting her gloved ones. 'I was just working on the body. I don't really think that you want to shake these.' She wiggled her fingers.

'I suppose not,' Hunter said, taking back his hand.

'But it's a pleasure to meet you both,' Kay added.

'Likewise,' Hunter said back.

Garcia simply greeted Kay with a nod.

'Kay was the one who discovered all the inconsistencies between the body's injuries and the information that we were given,' Dr. Hove explained, handing Hunter the occurrence report.

'OK.' Hunter flipped open the folder.

Garcia stepped closer to have a look.

'Terry Wilford.' He read the name at the top of the file before his and Hunter's eyes scanned the rest of the report, which wasn't longer than just a couple of pages.

'And what sort of inconsistencies are we talking about here, Doc?' Hunter asked, handing the folder over to Garcia.

Dr. Hove nodded at her student. 'I'd better let Kay explain. Like I said, she was the one who discovered them all.'

Kay took in a proud breath of air and positioned herself across the examination table from the two detectives. 'I'll try to go over everything slowly, but if I go too fast, or you guys fall behind on any explanation and can't keep up, just stop me at any time, OK?'

From the corner of his eye, Hunter saw Dr. Hove press her lips tightly together, trying to suppress the smile that was visibly threatening to erupt. He also saw Garcia frown at Kay. He was clearly trying to figure out if the Advanced Pathology student was being sarcastic or not.

She wasn't.

Kay pulled the surgical sheet from over the subject. As she did, Garcia's eyes widened at the state of the male body on the table in front of them. The 'Y' incision hadn't been stitched back up yet. In fact, the chest flaps were still pulled back over the sides of his torso and neck, revealing a somewhat hollow thorax, as none of the removed internal organs, or the ribcage, had been put back in place. The top half of his skull, on the other hand, was exactly where it was supposed to be, but it hadn't been stitched back up either.

'Wow,' Garcia commented, once again flipping open the folder in his hands. 'Where did he jump from again?'

'Allegedly—' Hunter tried to correct his partner before he was corrected by Kay.

'He didn't jump,' she said. Her tone was confident, leaving no room for argument. Her stare moved to Hunter. 'Not even allegedly. He couldn't have, but he fell from the 7th Street Bridge.'

Garcia nodded, as he found that same confirmation in the report. 'That is a nasty fall. It explains the awful state of his limbs.' He nodded at a couple of the exposed fractures on the body's right leg and arm.

'It does,' Kay agreed. 'And to be honest, it is because of those fractures that I know that this man didn't jump to his death from the 7th Street Bridge a week ago.'

'How so?' Hunter asked.

'Here,' Kay said, guiding their attention to the two exposed fractures on the subject's right arm. 'Let me show you.'

As part of the full post-mortem examination, Kay and Dr. Hove had already cut open all the skin, flesh, muscle tissue and ligaments surrounding the wounds to better expose the fractures.

'Bones are composed,' Kay started, indicating the fracture on the forearm, 'of both organic and inorganic material, each of which contribute to the biomechanical properties of the bones.'

'Kay,' Dr. Hove interrupted her student, her chin dipping down, her eyes looking at Kay over the rim of her glasses. 'Unclench. This is what we call a "post-mortem briefing", not a pathology class. Stick to the facts in plain English, pure and simple. No need to complicate anything with in-depth explanations in anatomy, biology, physiology … any of it. If they need details, they'll ask you for them. Trust me, they've done this before.'

Kay paused and looked at the two detectives across the table from her. Both of them looked relaxed. Hunter had his arms loosely by his sides, while his eyes were on Kay. The look in them was friendly, as if seconding what Dr. Hove had just said.

Garcia had his arms folded over his chest, with his left one bent upward at the elbow and his chin resting on the knuckles of his left hand. His eyes were also on Kay, with a sympathetic smile showing at the corner of his lips.

'OK,' Kay said, as she clearly began rethinking her words. A second later, her shoulders seemed to relax a little. 'If a fracture is sustained while the subject is still alive,' she began again, 'or at the moment of death, which should've been the case here because most of these fractures came as a result of the impact between his body and the ground, when he fell from the 7th Street Bridge, hemorrhage would've been very easily identifiable in the surrounding soft tissue.' She indicated with the tip of the scalpel. 'That's because until the moment of death, blood would've been flowing normally throughout his body.'

'But we've got none there,' Hunter said, his eyes narrowing at the tissue surrounding the wound that Kay had indicated.

'Not only here,' Kay confirmed, redirecting their attention to the exposed fracture on the subject's right elbow. 'We've got none here either.' Then again to the fracture in the subject's right leg. 'Or here.' Collarbone. 'Or here . . . or pretty much anywhere else. Can you see that?' She gave everyone a couple of seconds. 'That's because at the moment of impact between his body and the ground, his heart wasn't pumping blood through his veins anymore. No blood, no hemorrhage . . . it's that simple.'

Garcia's gaze moved from wound to wound. There really was no sign of any hemorrhage in any of the surrounding soft tissue. 'You're not wrong.'

'I rarely am,' Kay replied.

This time, while Dr. Hove allowed her head to drop, as if she had given up hope, Hunter and Garcia didn't disguise the smiles that bloomed on their lips.

'Ooh, I like her,' Garcia said, nodding at the doctor.

Kay turned and pointed in the direction of the stainless-steel counter that hugged the east wall, where the subject's internal organs lay inside separate containers filled with formalin. 'The impact also fractured a few of his ribs, two of them so severely that they broke loose from the ribcage and perforated his right lung.' She paused for effect. 'That perforation should've, in theory, done two things.'

'Caused the lung to collapse,' Hunter offered. 'And filled it with blood from the tissue tear.'

Kay looked back at Hunter with surprised eyes.

'I read a lot,' Hunter explained.

'Good for you,' Kay replied, without missing a beat. 'Well, Detectives, neither of those things happened. We autopsied the lung. There was no sign of any internal hemorrhaging. No trauma to the tissue surrounding the tear either.' She paused again, this time to allow the severity of what she had just said to sink in for a second.

'That was a major discovery,' Dr. Hove explained, 'because it tells us that he'd been dead for well over twenty-four hours before the injury to his lung took place ... before he fell from that bridge.'

Concern showed on both detectives' faces.

'There's more,' Kay said, once again redirecting everyone's attention, this time to the subject's head and skull.

'There always is,' Garcia replied, giving Kay a single nod.

Kay looked back at Dr. Hove.

'Ooh, I like him,' she said, in the same tone that Garcia had used just a moment ago.

Garcia laughed.

'As you can see here ...' Kay got serious again, indicating the severe wound to the subject's skull. 'Most of the impact was absorbed by his right side. His head hit the ground heavy, like a dead weight, causing extensive trauma to his skull. If he was alive, this should've been the end-of-life injury.' She used both hands to remove the top of the skull and expose the brain. 'Epidural and subdural hematomas should've been clearly visible here. With epidural hematomas, blood accumulates outside the dura – the lining of the brain.' She indicated as she explained. 'Subdural hematomas are injuries to the veins in the brain itself. Blood then leaks to the space just below the dura.'

'But we've got neither,' Hunter commented.

Dr. Hove shook her head. 'No blood. No hematomas. No hemorrhaging of the brain, which clearly confirms our theory that this man was dead way before he even got to that bridge.' There was a heavy, anxious pause. 'Someone dragged this guy's dead body to the 7th Street Bridge and then threw him off.'

Kay returned the top of the skull to the subject's head. 'Whoever killed him was obviously trying to mask the murder as a suicide.'

'And he would've gotten away with it,' Dr. Hove added. 'If not for the fact that, unfortunately for him, Kay's Advanced Pathology group picked this subject, by chance, for today's exam. I'm not sure that if this subject had gone to a different group of students, all these details would've been properly picked up.'

'The other members of my group failed to notice the obvious.' There was a proud air about Kay as she delivered that sentence.

'I've got a question,' Hunter said, lifting his right hand, his gaze on Kay. 'When you began, you said that *most* of these fractures came as a result of the impact between his body and the ground. What did you mean by that? Are there other fractures that didn't come as a result of the impact?'

Garcia nodded. 'I was about to ask the same thing.'

'Great question,' Kay said. 'It means you were both paying attention, and the answer is – yes – there are other fractures that didn't come as a result of the impact. Have a look at this.'

From the instruments cart, by the head of the examination table, Kay retrieved a couple of X-ray sheets before leading everyone to the X-ray viewer mounted on one of the classroom walls. She switched on the light and clipped the sheets onto it.

'Here,' she said, indicating on the sheets. 'This is his left forearm and this is his right one.'

Hunter and Garcia got close to examine the X-rays.

'Are those spiral fractures?' Hunter asked, his forehead creasing as he looked back at Dr. Hove.

'I'm impressed,' Kay said, nodding at Hunter. 'That's exactly what they are.'

'Spiral fracture?' Garcia asked, his eyes moving from Hunter, to Dr. Hove, then finally to Kay.

'It's like the way a stick would break,' Hunter explained, using his hands to demonstrate the movement. 'If you twisted it like you were wringing water from a dishrag.'

'Very good analogy,' Kay admitted before addressing Garcia, as she indicated on the X-ray. 'Here, you see? You get this S-shaped crack in the bone as it gives way.'

'And how do you get those?' Garcia asked.

'Someone, or something, has to twist your arm,' Hunter replied. 'Like a dishrag. Either slowly or in a sudden, jerk-type movement. You don't get those from an impact fall.'

'No, you don't,' Kay agreed again. 'But here's the thing – those fractures are also fresh. There's still considerable bruising to the surrounding soft tissue, which means that they happened recently.'

'What Kay means by *recently*,' Dr. Hove explained. 'Is about three or four days before his supposed suicide.'

Hunter and Garcia carried on studying the X-ray sheets.

'So what you're telling us,' Garcia asked, 'is that somebody broke both of his arms just a few days before actually killing him and throwing his body from the bridge?'

'That's what the body tells us,' Kay replied. 'And bodies don't lie.' Her proud eyes darted to Dr. Hove for an instant. 'Bodies don't lie' was Dr. Hove's catchphrase.

'Those fractures also indicate something else,' Dr. Hove added.

Hunter and Garcia turned to face her.

'The spiral fractures in both of his arms run counterclockwise,' the doctor explained. 'If the perpetrator used his hands to cause those fractures—'

'It means that he's left-handed,' Hunter said.

Dr. Hove and Kay both nodded.

'If the perpetrator used his hands to cause those fractures,' Garcia added, 'it means that he's one strong motherfucker. Mr. Wilford here wasn't exactly frail.'

'That too,' Kay agreed. 'But we're not done yet. There's more.' She directed everyone back to the body on the examination table. 'Let me start with the eyes.'

Hunter and Garcia repositioned themselves by the head of the table.

'Have a look at this,' Kay said, as she used the tips of her fingers to pull down the body's right-lower eyelid. 'See this odd discoloration right at the edge of the eyelid?'

Both detectives got closer for a better look.

'Uh-hum,' Garcia nodded.

'It repeats itself on the other eye.' Kay showed them. 'But the mark pattern is different, as you can see.'

'OK.'

'That's not post-mortem discoloration,' Kay explained.

'OK, so what are they?' Garcia asked.

Kay took a second, as if she needed to prepare herself for the answer. 'Those are chemical burn marks.'

Garcia's jaw tightened. 'Hold on. Are you saying that someone used some kind of acidic chemical as eye drops on him?'

Kay peeked at Dr. Hove before responding. 'That's what it looks like, but to know exactly what caused those burns, we would need to biopsy some of the eyelid tissue. Right now, all we can offer is an educated guess.'

Both detectives questioned with a look.

'Definitely not something as strong as acid. That would've blinded him straight away. Our best guess is that whoever did this used something a little milder ... something like diluted toilet bleach, or diluted methanol, or some kind of soft detergent – something that would've caused considerable pain, but not blindness.'

Hunter looked at Dr. Hove, who nodded.

'Still, there's more.' Kay then guided their attention to the body's feet. 'Here.' She used both hands to spread the subject's big toe from the pointer one. 'See this mark?'

Two seconds of silence.

'Another burn mark.' Hunter didn't phrase it as a question.

'Yes, but not acidic this time.'

Hunter had seen similar marks a few times before. Despite the after-death deterioration of the skin, he was still able to identify it.

'Cigarette burns,' he said.

Once again, Kay looked impressed. 'Very good. And due to the not-exactly-circular pattern of the mark, I'd say that he was burned repeatedly over the same spot.'

Garcia cringed.

'And that's why I've called you here today,' Dr. Hove said. 'This man was tortured for days before he died. After his death, like Kay explained earlier, someone tried to mask his murder as a jumping suicide. Sound familiar?'

'Familiar?' Kay was unable to hide the excitement in her voice. 'There's been a similar case before?'

Dr. Hove's gaze bounced over to Hunter for a second, who signaled no objection. 'There are similarities to a body I examined just over two weeks ago,' the doctor confirmed.

'Tortured then a faked death?' Kay pushed.

Dr. Hove voiced no reply, but Kay read her expression.

A moment of absolute silence followed, where Hunter and Garcia were clearly trying to get their thoughts in order.

'So what was the actual cause of death?' Garcia asked. 'On the phone you said that it wasn't hypothermia.'

'Hypothermia?' Kay questioned, wide-eyed. 'In California ... in June?' A quick, unsure pause. 'Was that the previous victim's

COD? Hypothermia? Really?' Her stare moved from person to person, but all she got was a quick shake of the head from her professor before Dr. Hove handed Hunter and Garcia her autopsy report.

'The cause of death, once again, was heart failure. It gave away under the stress of the torture he suffered.'

Hunter looked down at the report in his hands before allowing his stare to return to the body. 'Can you please send us everything you have on him, Doc?'

'Of course.'

'We'll also need the biopsy result for his eyelid burns,' Garcia added. 'And a full toxicology report.'

'I can email his files to you tonight,' Dr. Hove replied. 'The eyelid biopsy and the toxicology report will take a few days, as you well know.'

As Hunter and Garcia exited the pathology theater, Kay smiled proudly at Dr. Hove. She didn't need any confirmation to know that, even before graduating, she had just stumbled upon her very first serial murder case.

Twenty

By the time Hunter got to his office at 8:00 a.m. the next day, Garcia was already pinning photos to their picture board. He had divided the board in two halves. The left side belonged to Shaun Daniels, while Terry Wilford's photos occupied most of the opposite half.

'Good morning,' Hunter said, as he placed his jacket on the back of his chair and instinctively checked his watch. 'What time did you get in?'

'Not that long ago,' Garcia replied, before driving Hunter's attention to the last two photos he had pinned to the board. The first was a portrait of Terry Wilford – film casting style – the second was a full body shot of Terry in his bartender uniform – white, pristine long-sleeved shirt with a classic bowtie that matched his dark waistcoat. 'OK, so Research has managed to expand a little on the basic report that Dr. Hove had received on Mr. Wilford.' He grabbed a printout from his desk. 'It's still not a lot of info, but it will give us a start.'

'OK.' Hunter fired up his computer. 'So what did they manage to come up with so far?'

'Full name – Terry B. Wilford,' Garcia read from the printout. 'No one knows what the B. stands for. Born in Phoenix, Arizona, on November 1st, 1980, where he lived until the age of thirty-eight. That was when he moved to Los Angeles, where he'd been living for the past five years. His last listed address is an apartment in East LA – Wellington Heights.'

'Married . . . girlfriend . . . partner?' Hunter asked, as he keyed in his computer password.

Garcia's eyes quickly scanned the printout. 'Nothing about a present girlfriend or partner,' he replied. 'But back in Arizona he *was* married for sixteen years to a Joana Suarez, who became Joana Wilford. She died five years ago – cancer.'

'Is that why he moved to LA?' Hunter asked, meeting Garcia's stare. 'Because his wife passed?'

Garcia searched the printout again. 'Nothing on the report, but I'd say that the dates are a pretty good match. Mrs. Wilford died in March 2019. Five months later, in September that same year, Mr. Wilford relocated to LA.'

'Any kids?'

'One,' Garcia nodded. 'Joseph Thomas Wilford.'

'Is he also in LA?' Hunter asked.

Garcia flipped back a page then forward a page. 'Again, it doesn't say, but if he is, he didn't live with his father.'

Hunter's eyebrows rose at his partner.

'According to this,' Garcia clarified, 'Terry Wilford lived alone in Wellington Heights.'

'Was there a Missing Persons Report?' Hunter queried. 'Was Terry Wilford ever reported missing?'

'Yep.' A firm nod from Garcia. 'He was. The report was filed just over two weeks ago – on Monday, June 24th, by a Sabrina Davis, who works as a waitress in the same cocktail lounge that Mr. Wilford used to work.' He instinctively pointed at the window. 'The Varnish cocktail bar, which is less than a mile from here.'

'Yeah, I know the place,' Hunter said. 'He worked at The Varnish?'

Garcia nodded. 'For the past four years. He was the head bartender. Have you been there lately?'

'Not for at least three or four years,' Hunter replied, approaching the picture board. As he studied Terry Wilford's portrait photo, he found it hard to find any resemblance between the carefree face on that picture – with his messy manbun, his well-cared-for stubble and his cheeky smile – and the completely disfigured face and body that he and Garcia had seen lying on the autopsy table back at the Ronald Reagan UCLA Medical Center the night before. 'The Varnish is big with the financial sector crowd – white-collar people with a lot of money. Not really the kind of crowd I mingle with.'

Garcia laughed. 'You don't really mingle with any crowd, Robert, but I know what you mean.' He flipped a page on the report. 'Before The Varnish, Mr. Wilford worked at a place in Santa Monica beach – Bar Chloe. He was a bartender there for almost a year.'

'I know it as well,' Hunter said. 'Quite a trendy place. Just off Santa Monica Boulevard.'

'If you say so,' Garcia replied. 'I'm not that familiar with the cocktail bars in Santa Monica.'

'Who was handling the Missing Persons investigation?' Hunter asked.

'The report was filed with the Central Bureau,' Garcia read from the file. 'Before being allocated to Detective Graham Cohen with the MPU.' Reflexively, his index finger pointed up. The Missing Persons Unit of the LAPD Detective Support and Vice Division was located on the seventh floor of the Police Administration Building – two stories above their office. 'Do you know him?'

Hunter shook his head. 'Not exactly, but I think I know who he is – stumpy guy, balding, drives an old Volvo ... but I never really interacted with him.'

'Yeah, me neither.' Garcia nodded once.

Despite knowing that the Missing Persons investigating team

would no doubt have conducted interviews with a plethora of people, Hunter and Garcia would still want to conduct their own interviews, at least with some of the people that MPU had already talked to.

Hunter had a gift when it came to observing people and he and Garcia worked as one, seamlessly. While Garcia asked most of the questions – applying pressure and easing off at key moments – Hunter simply listened and watched. But he didn't listen only to the words that people spoke. He listened to their silences ... to the pauses between their words ... to their breathing. He watched their eye movements, their mannerisms, the crossing and uncrossing of their legs, the way in which they scratched their noses ... everything. So often, people's silences and movements spoke volumes, giving away a secret that their words were trying so hard to hide.

'So what else do we have?' Hunter asked.

Garcia flipped a page on the printout. 'Well, Mr. Wilford was an only child – no brothers or sisters. His father passed away when he was nineteen years old – heart attack. His mother is still alive and lives in a nursing home back in Phoenix. She's seventy-one.'

'Has she been notified of her son's death?' Hunter asked. 'Has his kid?'

'No mention of it in the report,' Garcia clarified. 'But Mr. Wilford's body was discovered eight days ago, on July 1st. The news of his death has certainly been reported to the MPU and Detective Cohen. They would've notified the next of kin.'

Another nod from Hunter.

'Now here comes the intriguing part,' Garcia said, indicating the left half of the picture board. 'Just like Shaun Daniels, Mr. Wilford had a sheet, which, funnily enough, isn't too dissimilar.'

Hunter paused and looked back at his partner. 'Really?'

'A bunch of offences but no major convictions,' Garcia explained. 'Check this out though.' He indicated on the printout.

'Just like Shaun Daniels, Terry Wilford was also arrested three times for disorderly conduct – bar fighting.'

'Here in LA?

'Nope. All three arrests happened back in Arizona. He was also taken into custody four times throughout his sixteen years of marriage for domestic violence, but in all four occasions, the charges were dropped.'

'So our victim had a temper,' Hunter concluded.

'It looks that way,' Garcia agreed.

Hunter craned his neck to have a better look at the printout in Garcia's hands.

'Nothing since he relocated to LA?' he asked.

'Absolutely nothing,' Garcia confirmed. 'Not even a parking ticket. Who knows? Maybe it was his New Year's resolution – new town . . . new beginning . . . new Terry.'

'Maybe,' Hunter agreed.

Garcia's stare returned to the printout and he paused. 'Hold on a second.' He reread the paragraph just to be sure.

'What?' Hunter asked, once again craning his neck to look at the printout.

'According to the police report,' Garcia explained. 'There were two witnesses to Mr. Wilford's jumping suicide.'

'Witnesses?' Hunter's widened eyes searched the page.

'Right here,' Garcia indicated. 'It says that Luis Toledo and Randy Douglas, both employees of the Sanitation and Environment Division, actually *witnessed* Mr. Wilford jump from the 7th Street Bridge.' Garcia blinked at the page. 'How is this even possible when, according to Dr. Hove, Terry Wilford was dead way before he got to that bridge? How could they have seen him jump?'

'I guess we better go ask them.'

'No doubt,' Garcia agreed, flipping back and forth on the printout one last time, searching for anything else that they might've missed. There was nothing else. 'That's pretty much all we have.'

Hunter nodded.

Garcia turned to face the board again. 'So where do you want to start?'

Hunter checked his watch. 'Too early to drop by The Varnish or go talk to the two employees from the S&E Division.'

'Yeah, but Missing Persons should be alive and kicking by now.'

'Yep,' Hunter agreed. 'Let's go talk to Detective Cohen and see how far his investigation has taken him. We'll move on from there.'

'I'm right behind you.'

Twenty-One

The LAPD Missing Persons Unit, located on the seventh floor of the Police Administration Building, looked nothing like the Robbery Homicide floor, despite covering a pretty similar-sized area. Classic floor screen partitions separated the investigators' desks in a confusing and chaotic way, creating a crazy labyrinth of uneven corridors that few outside the MP Unit could successfully navigate. The entire north wall was one huge photo board, displaying portraits of at least three hundred individuals whose investigation was still ongoing. The board had been split into two – children and adults. The children's side clearly overwhelmed the adults' one.

The large number of ongoing investigations did not surprise either Hunter or Garcia. Out of the fifty American states, California topped the charts with the largest number of reported missing person cases per year – over three thousand. In California, Los Angeles took the second spot on the list of counties with the highest ratios of people going missing, never to be found – behind only Humboldt County, a densely forested, mountainous and rural county, with about 110 miles of coastline. Their reported number of missing persons who were never found was so staggering that it had been dubbed 'the black hole county'.

Hunter and Garcia didn't visit the Missing Persons Unit's floor very often, but every time they did they were mesmerized by the fact that every single person on that floor always seemed to be either navigating through the chaotic labyrinth of desks, or on their phones. And the conversations weren't exactly hushed. The place sounded and looked like a distressed beehive.

Just a couple of paces in front of both detectives, a short and slender man ended the phone conversation that he was having, reached for the empty mug by his computer screen, and quickly got up from his desk. Garcia seized the opportunity before he could step away.

'Excuse me, could you please direct us to Detective Cohen?'

The man barely lost a beat, turning to face the rest of the floor. 'Cohen,' he shouted. 'Where you at?'

Hunter's and Garcia's eyes widened at him.

'I could've done that myself,' Garcia whispered through the edge of his mouth.

About halfway down the detective's floor, just by the large photo board, Detective Graham Cohen stood up and craned his neck to look over his desk partition. 'I'm at my desk. What's up?'

'Right over there,' the short and slender man indicated before veering left and disappearing into the labyrinth.

Hunter and Garcia began zigzagging their way toward Detective Cohen.

'If someone gets to the Robbery Homicide floor,' Garcia said, in a hushed voice, 'and just shouts a name from the door like he did, he'd probably get shot.'

'Several times,' Hunter agreed.

'Detective Hunter . . . Detective Garcia,' Cohen said, extending his hand as the UVC detectives got to his desk.

'Have we met before?' Garcia asked, as he shook Cohen's hand.

Hunter had remembered correctly: Detective Cohen really was a stumpy man. He looked to be in his mid-forties, with two graying islands of hair just above each ear. The rest of his smooth head glimmered under the strong halogen lights that lined the ceiling. His dark, beady eyes sat behind thick glasses, his teeth were lightly stained from years of smoking, and his blue suit was ill-fitting, mainly because his stomach protruded forward just enough to make his trousers slip down below the pouch of his belly.

'No, never,' Cohen replied, addressing both detectives. 'But from reputation, we all know who you are.'

Hunter and Garcia did know about their reputation. Inside the police headquarters and throughout the entire police department, many referred to the Ultra Violent Crimes Unit as the 'Hell-No Unit' – the only detective unit inside the LAPD that no detective wanted to join.

'Please, have a seat.' Cohen indicated the two chairs squashed between the floor partition and his desk, a desk that seemed too small for the mountain of folders and paperwork scattered all over it.

Hunter took the seat on the right, while Garcia had to reposition the chair on the left so that his legs could fit.

'So how can I help?' Cohen asked, sitting back on his chair. The movement almost made him disappear behind a pile of blue folders.

'Terry Wilford,' Garcia began, handing Cohen a printout of Terry's portrait and a copy of the Missing Persons Report. 'You were the lead detective on his MP investigation. He was reported missing just over two weeks ago – June 24th.'

Cohen looked at the portrait for just a second. 'Yes of course, I remember this case.' He pushed his glasses up on his bulbous nose. 'But this case was closed just over a week ago. Mr. Wilford was never found, until he jumped to his death from the 7th Street Bridge on . . .' He began typing something onto his keyboard.

'July 1st,' Garcia helped him.

Cohen's attention moved from his screen to Garcia. 'Yes, that's correct – on the evening of July 1st. Apparently there were two witnesses to it.' He returned both pieces of paper to Garcia. 'Whatever reason he had to disappear seemed to have finally taken its toll on him.' He shrugged as he nodded. 'Unfortunately, missing-person suicides happen quite a lot.'

'Could I ask you,' Garcia said, taking back the documents, 'how far did you get with the MP investigation? Any leads as to where he might've been, or gone? Anyone he might've been with?'

Cohen's eyes returned to his computer screen for a moment before he shook his head. 'Nothing. We got absolutely nowhere.'

'No leads at all?' Garcia pushed.

Cohen's head angled slightly to the right. 'We took every path available to us. Since Mr. Wilford only moved to LA five years ago, one of the first things we did was get in touch with Phoenix PD in Arizona for some help. As you know, that's where he's originally from, and since he still has friends and family back there, it stood to reason that he could've decided to take a trip back to Arizona without informing anyone.' Cohen shook his head. 'Phoenix PD got in touch with everyone they could. Apparently none of Mr. Wilford's old friends have heard from him since he left Phoenix. His father passed a few years back, but his mother resides in a nursing home, paid for by her social security and a private pension scheme from a job she held for thirty-odd years. They tried talking to her, but they got nowhere. Mrs. Wilford suffers from late-stage dementia. She couldn't even remember that she had a son.'

'Did any of the staff at the nursing home know Mr. Wilford?' Hunter asked. 'Did he visit his mother often?'

'They never met him,' Cohen replied, his lips forming a thin line. 'According to the nursing home records, he never visited her. Not even once.'

'How about his kid, Joseph,' Garcia, this time. 'Does he still live back in Phoenix? Anybody talked to him?'

Cohen scrolled down on the page on his screen. 'Oh yeah, now

I remember. No, he doesn't. He now lives in Chandler, and he was a hard one to get in touch with.'

'How so?' Garcia prodded.

'First of all, he doesn't go by Joseph Thomas Wilford anymore. He dropped his father's name and now uses his mother's maiden name – Suarez.'

'Joseph Thomas Suarez?' Garcia asked.

Cohen half-nodded. 'And he hates being called Joseph.'

'So what is it? Joe?' Garcia again.

'Yep,' Cohen confirmed. 'Joe Thomas Suarez. That name change added at least a couple of days to the process of tracking him down. He had also relocated from Phoenix to Chandler around the same time that Mr. Wilford relocated here.'

'Just after his mother passed?'

'Yep.'

'But he was sixteen at that time,' Hunter commented. 'Isn't that right?'

'Yep.'

Hunter and Garcia's expression asked the same silent question.

'I don't really know the ins-and-outs of what happened,' Cohen explained. 'Not my place to ask, but one thing is for sure – Joe and his father *did not* get along.'

'Is that what he told you?'

'He didn't have to say it.' Once again, Cohen clicked and scrolled on his computer screen. 'At least not in so many words.' He found what he was looking for and adjusted himself on his chair. 'I was the one who spoke with him on the phone, after leaving him countless messages. He finally called me back the day before his father committed suicide, on June 30th, days after we left him the first message explaining that his dad had gone missing.'

'He didn't seem to care?' Garcia asked.

Cohen chuckled before explaining. 'I started recording the

conversation after we'd already exchanged a few sentences, but I'm sure you'll get the gist.' He used his left hand to gesture Hunter and Garcia closer. 'You'll need to move closer to hear it. This is a loud floor.'

'We've noticed,' Garcia came back, as he and Hunter leaned forward, placed their elbows onto Cohen's desk, and craned their ears closer to the computer speakers.

On his screen, Cohen clicked 'play'.

'Listen, like I just told you,' Joe Thomas Suarez's voice came through the small desktop speakers. He sounded annoyed. *'I don't care if my father is missing. I haven't seen or spoken to him in five years and truthfully, I hope I never will again, so please, stop calling me and leaving messages.'*

'So he hasn't tried to contact you in the past few days?' Cohen's voice came through in the recording.

'Jesus, man. Why the hell did you call me if you're not going to listen to what I tell you? I'm not sure how I can make this any clearer – I haven't SEEN or SPOKEN to my father in five years, since my mother died, OK? Even if he tried to contact me, I wouldn't talk to him. I've got nothing to say to that man. I don't care if he's missing. I don't care if he turns up dead in a ditch. I don't care about him and he doesn't care about me. Now please, stop calling me, OK?'

The line went dead.

Hunter peeked at Garcia. The reference to Terry Wilford turning up dead in a ditch was clearly concerning.

'Like I've said,' Cohen commented. 'Joe and his father did not get along.'

'Was he informed of his father's death?' Hunter asked. 'Was Mr. Wilford's mother?'

'We left messages,' Cohen said, his stare crawling over to the UVC detectives. He gave them a one-shoulder shrug. 'Like I've explained, his mother can't even remember that she had a son.

Informing her directly would make no difference, but we did notify the nursing home. In the case of his son . . .' Cohen's eyebrows arched. He used both index fingers to point at his screen. 'You heard the phone conversation I had with him, right? He couldn't give a monkey's piss for his father, but yes, I did call him. Of course, he didn't pick up, so I left a message. That's the best I could do. He never called back.'

Hunter and Garcia nodded their understanding.

Cohen clicked his mouse twice then scrolled down on his screen. 'Over here in LA, we talked to everyone we could – work colleagues, neighbors, friends . . . nothing. We couldn't even pinpoint the exact day that he went missing.'

'Really?' Garcia asked.

'Terry Wilford was last seen in the early hours of Friday morning, June 21st, after finishing his Thursday night shift at The Varnish,' Cohen began. 'The place closes at 1:00 a.m. every morning. That same Friday evening – June 21st – he was off work. He was only expected back on Saturday at 5:00 p.m.'

'And he never turned up.' Garcia stated rather than questioned.

'No, he didn't,' Cohen confirmed. 'Then he didn't turn up for his shift on Sunday either. On Monday morning, June 24th, he was reported missing by a Sabrina Davis, who also works at The Varnish.'

'But according to these records,' Garcia interjected, 'the investigation didn't really start until the next day, Tuesday, June 25th.'

'And there's a reason for that,' Cohen explained. 'The number of times that people try to report an independent adult as missing, only to have that person safely reappear two or three days later, would blow your mind.' He shrugged. 'People do stupid things, especially over a weekend – they binge-drink and pass out somewhere . . . get high on acid, Xanax, opioids, whatever, and zone out for days. Sometimes they disappear with a lover that no one knew about . . . or simply have had enough and decide to clock off for a while without telling anyone. Things like that happen . . . *a lot*. We just can't afford to allocate people or resources every time somebody *thinks* someone has gone missing. That's why we waited one more day.'

Hunter and Garcia both nodded.

'At The Varnish,' Cohen continued. 'I was told that Mr. Wilford was friendly enough with everyone, including the customers, without ever stepping over the too-friendly line. I got the same response from all the neighbors I talked to. No one seemed to dislike him.'

'Miss Davis,' Hunter asked. 'The waitress who reported Terry Wilford as missing, did she seem to know Mr. Wilford well?'

'Better than anyone else we've spoken to,' Cohen confirmed. 'Not only did they work together at The Varnish most nights, but they also spent time together outside work.'

'Time together as friends or as a couple?' Garcia asked.

'According to Sabrina Davis, they were *not* a couple. But she did admit that they slept together sporadically – sometimes at her place, sometimes at his. She also told me that they were working together on the night of Thursday, June 20th – his last ever shift at The Varnish – and that Terry had suggested that they spend the night together, but Miss Davis declined. The subject's last sighting time was around a quarter to two in the morning.'

'A quarter to two?' Hunter asked.

Cohen clarified that despite The Varnish closing at 1:00 a.m. every morning, it was common practice for the staff to share a beer or two after hours, but that night, out of the five-strong staff, only Sabrina and Terry had stayed behind.

'And that sighting was done by Miss Davis?' Hunter asked.

'Correct. She also told us that Mr. Wilford was his normal self that night and that he didn't seem concerned, or troubled, or anything at all. She said that she had no reason to worry.'

'Did she know if he went straight home that night?' Garcia tried.

'We did ask her exactly that,' Cohen confirmed, his attention pinging to his screen for a moment. 'She said that she had no idea, but she did tell us that sometimes, after a shift, instead of going home, Mr. Wilford would go to one of two underground drinking dens – The Hole in the Ground, in the Fashion District, or Bottoms Up, in the Art District.'

'I've never heard of them.' Garcia frowned first at Cohen then at Hunter.

'I'm not surprised,' Cohen agreed. 'I didn't know about them either because these aren't well known or popular places. They don't even advertise.' He sat back on his chair and crossed his left leg over his right one. 'Apparently, cocktail bartenders don't really like to go drinking in the same kind of places they work at. They have their own "special hangouts", just like us cops do. Drinks are considerably cheaper than on the high street and they stay open until quite late.'

Hunter nodded. 'They don't advertise because they don't really cater for the open public – industry people only. I've heard of such places. For you to get in you need to show them your work ID at the door.'

'That's right,' Cohen confirmed. 'Though your LAPD badge will also get you in.' His lips stretched into a humorless smile. 'We checked both places. Talked to everyone we could.' A despondent shake of the head. 'People certainly knew who Terry Wilford was. He was a regular at both places, but no one remembered seeing him on the night in question, and before you ask, no, neither place had CCTV going. We asked, and probed, and dug just about everywhere we could . . . nothing. Our disappearance window never narrowed.'

'And that window is between a quarter to two in the morning on Friday, June 21st, and his work shift starting time the next day – Saturday, June 22nd, 5:00 p.m.' Garcia said.

'That's it,' Cohen confirmed. 'None of his neighbors could recall seeing him either, neither that Friday nor Saturday, which wasn't unusual. People who work night shifts tend to sleep throughout most of the next day.'

'How did he usually get home at that time in the morning?' Hunter again. 'Cab?'

'No, he drove a beat-up 2008 Buick LaCrosse.'

'They're good cars,' Hunter commented.

Cohen's eyes moved to him and he frowned. 'No, they aren't.'

Garcia half-coughed a laugh.

Hunter knew that there was no point in arguing. 'Was the car ever found?'

'It was,' Cohen told them. 'But not until the night that he jumped from the 7th Street Bridge.'

'Let me guess,' Garcia interrupted. 'Parked on the bridge?'

'No, but very close. His car was parked on the corner of South Mission Road and East 7th Place – less than two hundred yards from the bridge.'

'Was there a note found?' Hunter again. 'Either on him or in his car?'

'Nope. Nothing. But that isn't unusual. Especially with loners like Terry Wilford. People like that simply don't feel the need to explain their decision.' Cohen shrugged. 'To whom would they be explaining it, anyway? Many of these lone suiciders feel that no one really cares. In many cases, that's the reason why they're doing it.' Cohen swiveled his chair around to face the north-wall photo board. 'Unfortunately, Detectives, the ugly truth about so many of these people – so many of these faces you can see here – is that they've gone missing out of their own choice. They don't wanna be found.'

Hunter and Garcia didn't object because they both knew that Detective Cohen was right. They understood that not only in the USA, but all around the world, so many of those who disappeared – who seemingly went missing – did so because they wanted to, not because they were taken. It happened on a daily basis.

'And that's pretty much all we had, Detectives,' Cohen added, using his left hand to massage his neck, while at the same time stretching back his shoulders – classic body language that he was ready to end that meeting. 'A pieceless puzzle – no leads ... no clues ... nothing. Terry Wilford had simply vanished without a trace until the case solved itself when he ended his own life eight days ago.' Once again, he lifted his hand, anticipating the question that he was sure was about to come. 'Everyone we've spoken to said that, no, Terry Wilford did not appear depressed ... he did not look like he was about to do what he did, but so many of them never do. I'm sure that you're aware of that.'

Hunter had picked up on Cohen's 'we're done here' body language, but he wasn't quite through yet. 'Any indications that he was struggling financially?'

'None whatsoever. We checked his bank account and all transactions going back a whole year. He wasn't a big spender.' Cohen checked his watch before opening his top-left drawer and reaching for the packet of cigarettes inside it. 'Like I've said, whatever was troubling Terry Wilford, unfortunately became too much for him to handle and he gave up.' He got to his feet and searched his pockets for a lighter.

Hunter and Garcia also got up from their chairs.

'We appreciate you giving us your time, Detective Cohen,' Hunter said. 'It was a great help. Could we maybe get a copy of all those files?'

'Absolutely.' Cohen nodded at both detectives, reaching for the keyboard on his desk. 'I can do it now.' He clicked a couple of times, typed, then clicked again. 'Done.'

'Very much appreciated,' Garcia said, as they turned to leave.

'Detectives.' Cohen paused them just as they were about to

re-enter the partition labyrinth. 'Can I ask – what's the interest in Mr. Wilford? Was he linked to a UVC case?'

Hunter and Garcia exchanged a quick look.

'Not exactly,' Garcia replied. 'He *is* the case.'

Twenty-Two

Back in their office, Hunter and Garcia spent the rest of their morning going over the Missing Persons investigation file that Detective Cohen had sent them. They read through every interview transcript, every report, every note. They studied every photograph attached to the file. Cohen's summation of the MP investigation into Terry Wilford's disappearance had been right on the money – there really didn't seem to be anything there that could point anyone in any sort of direction – no clues, no leads, no witnesses, no motive for an abduction . . . no apparent reason for a disappearance, let alone a suicide.

Hunter and Garcia agreed that from the list of people who Missing Persons had already talked to, they would try to revisit as many as they could – not to re-interview everyone, as from the transcripts it was clear that that would be a waste of time. What they wanted to do was show them all a photo of Shaun Daniels. It was a very long shot but, as they had found out, Shaun liked drinking almost every night, and with Terry being a career bartender, there was a possibility, however small, that they had crossed paths at some point. If they were lucky, maybe another bartender, one of the waitresses, or even a regular customer at one of the places that Terry had worked at might remember seeing him and Shaun together at the bar.

The only person who Hunter and Garcia believed was worth

re-interviewing was Sabrina Davis. Not because they thought Missing Persons had done a bad job with her interview, but because she seemed to be the only person to have known Terry Wilford at a more personal level, and they needed to know what she knew.

They also needed to have a look inside Terry Wilford's apartment in East LA, but after five attempts, neither Hunter nor Garcia had managed to get hold of Mr. Aldridge, Terry Wilford's landlord – the only person in possession of a key – since no keys were found on Terry Wilford's body, or inside his car. Despite leaving messages, they decided to delegate the task to their Research team. If Research failed to get in touch with Mr. Aldridge in the next twenty-four hours, they'd use a warrant and enter the property without needing anyone's permission . . . or key.

'So who do you want to go see first?' Garcia asked, sitting back on his chair and readjusting his ponytail.

'It's still too early to drop by The Varnish, or Bar Chloe in Santa Monica,' Hunter said, checking his watch. It was coming up to 2:00 p.m.

'It's been over four years since Terry Wilford worked at Bar Chloe,' Garcia said. 'Do you think there'll be someone there who'd still remember him?' He quickly lifted a hand at Hunter before explaining. 'The reason I ask is because in general, bar staff turnover, especially in hip places like Santa Monica, is a constant – six months to a year, max. Hence Mr. Wilford only being there for less than a year. Those kind of trendy places don't pay well, Robert, and the bulk of their customers are usually tourists, who aren't used to tipping in the same way Americans do.'

Hunter's question was a silent one, asked with a simple eyebrow-lift.

'What?' Garcia came back. 'You never worked in a bar when you were younger?'

'Have you?'

'Of course. Both of my spring and summer breaks during junior and senior years – plus a few months after I graduated, before joining the academy. Back then, bartending was an easy job. Cocktail making wasn't exactly the art that it is today.'

'How old were you?'

'Under the legal age, if that's what you're asking, but I was already around six-foot back then. I didn't really look like a high school student. And since when did being under the legal drinking age stop bars from hiring students, especially during spring and summer breaks? Cheap labor for them. They pay low, but they pay cash and no one is supposed to drink on the job, anyway.' Garcia smiled. 'But there are ways around that.'

'I'm pretty sure there are.'

'Just out of curiosity,' Garcia asked, resting his elbows on his chair's armrests and interlacing his fingers together, 'what did you do during your spring and summer breaks?'

'I tutored other kids,' Hunter replied. 'Helped the ones who were lagging behind with their class work.'

Garcia chuckled. 'Are you telling me that during your school and college breaks you taught summer school to other kids?'

'Well, privately, yeah.' Hunter nodded.

'I should've known.'

'Easy money.' Hunter shrugged at Garcia. 'Students' parents pay well when their kids are flunking.'

'I'm sure they do, Professor Hunter.' Garcia laughed. 'Anyway, back to my question – do you really think that there might be someone who's been working at Bar Chloe for the past five years? Someone who might remember Terry Wilford from all those years ago?'

'It's a long shot,' Hunter admitted. 'But Bar Chloe isn't exactly your regular Santa Monica tourist dive bar.'

'What do you mean?'

'Bar Chloe is actually part of a hotel. Hotel Carmel, if I

remember right. Same building, but it has its own separate entrance. Also, it's not a dive bar. It's more of an "upper class, elegant" cocktail lounge. Very different clientele to the bars down at the pier, and I'd be surprised if they paid their staff that badly. But since it actually belongs to a hotel, there's also a chance that some hotel employees might remember him.'

'Well, there's no harm in dropping by later on,' Garcia agreed.

'So for now,' Hunter continued, quickly checking the time again, 'all we've got left are the two employees from the LA Sanitation and Environment Division – Luis Toledo and Randy Douglas.'

'We're splitting them up, right?' Garcia asked.

'Of course.'

Hunter and Garcia both knew that there had to be something wrong with what Randy and Luis had told the police officer who took their witness testimonies at the 'suicide' scene because, according to Dr. Hove, there was no suicide. So what did they actually see?

From experience, Hunter and Garcia knew that when two witnesses were interviewed together, it wasn't uncommon for one of their testimonies to drastically overpower or influence the other. If one of the witnesses, let's say Luis Toledo, had sounded overly confident about what he had seen, the second witness, Randy Douglas, if just a little unsure about what he had actually seen, could very easily modify his account to better match Luis's version of events. In a court of law, this was referred to as 'peer testimony adjustment', and it could totally change the outcome of a trial.

'OK,' Garcia said, reaching for the phone on his desk. 'Let's give LASAN a call then, shall we?'

Twenty-Three

It took Garcia just a couple of phone calls to find out that Tuesdays were Randy Douglas's day off and that he was spending the day with his wife and kid at home, in Green Meadows – the most densely populated neighborhood in South Los Angeles. One extra phone call and Garcia was informed that that afternoon, Luis Toledo was part of a cleaning team working the sewer system in South Gate – an incorporated city of Los Angeles County, located seven miles southeast of Downtown LA.

Since the plan was to split up the two witnesses and chance had already placed them in different parts of town, Hunter and Garcia decided to also split the workload for the rest of the day. Hunter would first visit Randy in Green Meadows before heading west to Santa Monica and trying his luck with the staff at Bar Chloe and Hotel Carmel. Garcia would start with Luis in South Gate and on his way back he would drop by The Varnish to talk to Sabrina Davis and whoever else was working that evening. If time allowed, they were to meet back at the UVC Unit's office once they were both done.

Hunter was the first to get back.

Garcia arrived just ten minutes after his partner, bringing with him a very colorful bunch of flowers.

'Should I ask?' Hunter said, nodding at the bouquet.

'It's Tuesday, remember?' Garcia replied, matter-of-factly, placing the flowers on his desk.

'Oh yeah.'

'What about Tuesday?' The question came from Captain Blake, who was standing at the door to their office. Her head jerked back slightly, as her stare landed on the flowers. Her lips stretched into a dubious smile. 'OK, so what have you done now?'

'Absolutely nothing,' Garcia replied.

'Really?' From her tone, it was clear that she wasn't buying what her detective was selling.

Hunter gave his partner a subtle nod. 'Tell her the story. It's a cool story.'

'Story?' the captain asked, closing the door behind her.

'It's nothing much,' Garcia explained. 'Our first date, Anna and me, was on a Tuesday, May 28th – junior year in high school. On that first date, I bought her flowers and Anna, being the way Anna is, said, "I wonder if you'll still buy me flowers after we've been dating for a while?"' Garcia shrugged. 'Challenge accepted. Since then, I've bought her flowers every two weeks, without fail.'

'Every two weeks?' Captain Blake queried. 'How long have you two been together?'

'We've been married for seventeen years, but we dated for a year and a half prior to that.'

'And you've bought her flowers every two weeks for almost nineteen years?'

This time, even Hunter nodded.

'Without fail,' Garcia confirmed. 'I have an alarm set up on my phone and all. I usually get them on my way home, but right next door to The Varnish there was a florist, and I thought that this was a nice bunch.' He nodded at the flowers.

'It's a beautiful bouquet,' Captain Blake agreed. 'And I didn't know that we had such a romantic in our midst. Not many of those around.' She turned to face the picture board. 'But I didn't come here to talk flowers. I just got back from another ridiculously long and equally pointless budget meeting to a message from Carolyn. She came across a second body that was dead before being dead? What the hell is going on?'

'Terry Wilford,' Garcia confirmed, guiding the captain's attention to Terry's portrait on the board before quickly summarizing everything that Dr. Hove and her student had found out.

Captain Blake listened to everything without interrupting. When Garcia was done, she adjusted her glasses up the bridge of her nose and leaned against the edge of Hunter's desk. 'So what you are telling me here is – I seem to have some deranged psycho loose in my city, who abducts people before torturing them for days ...' Her gaze moved to Hunter. 'Then fakes their deaths to dispose of their bodies.'

'That seems to be the case, Captain, yes,' Garcia agreed.

'And we have absolutely no idea how long this has been going on for, or how many victims he's already claimed?'

'Not even a ballpark figure,' Garcia said, before clarifying. 'As you well know, we've only come across our first victim, Shaun Daniels, by pure chance – an autopsy that was supposed to have gone to advanced forensic pathology students ended up on Dr. Hove's examination table. Our second victim, Terry Wilford, like I've explained, was a similar case. His body did go to students, but fortunately for us, it ended up on the slab of one of Dr. Hove's most gifted and stubborn students. She was the one who recognized the inconsistencies.'

Captain Blake approached the board and took her time studying all the new photographs.

'So in truth,' she said, 'this could be going back years ... decades, even. We could be talking about tens of victims here.'

'Theoretically, yes.' Hunter, this time. 'There's no real way of knowing.'

'How is this even possible?'

'Because whoever is doing this,' Hunter explained, 'isn't stupid, Captain. He figured out a loophole that would've kept him unnoticed for years.' He shrugged. 'With a bit of luck . . . for ever.'

'A loophole?' Captain Blake queried. 'Explain, Robert.'

Hunter broadly gestured at the board. 'When a body is brought into the LA morgue, with a clear, seemingly "apparent" cause of death – hit-and-runs, suicides, car crashes and so on – unless there's some sort of request from a law enforcement agency, that body goes straight to the back of the autopsy pile. Their priority is as low as it gets. If that body goes unclaimed for more than just one to two weeks and a post-mortem examination still hasn't been performed, that body will inevitably end up being donated to estate universities for medical studies. Out of those, only a small number end up with the pathology department. Out of that small number, only some end up getting a full autopsy examination instead of being dissected for other purposes, and those post-mortems are performed by students, not senior doctors.'

'Are pathology students that clueless that they won't pick up on these types of inconsistencies?' the captain asked.

'That's not it, Captain,' Hunter came back. 'There are two main factors that you need to consider here. One: with these bodies, the cause of death is already as evident as it can be. The exercise is usually to simply confirm it, not go on a fishing expedition around the body to try to disprove the apparent COD.'

'Don't forget that the students are also on a clock,' Garcia added. 'Few will be willing to waste time going off on a tangent when their grades are at stake.'

Hunter nodded before continuing. 'And two: the sort of inconsistencies that we're talking about here, Captain, can easily be overlooked, even by career pathologists, because they very closely match injuries that could occur had the faked deaths been real – fractured bones, punctured lungs, dislocated joints and what-have-you – those do happen when someone jumps from a bridge, or is run over by a truck.'

'If Dr. Hove hadn't been the one who had discovered the inconsistencies with Shaun Daniels's hit-and-run death less than a month ago,' Garcia pointed out, 'she would've discarded her student's findings as overthinking – just a student trying to impress her teacher. Something that happens in every class.'

'And at first,' Hunter took over again, 'that's exactly what she did – discarded the findings as overthinking – until her student told her that Terry Wilford couldn't have jumped off the 7th Street Bridge that night because he was already dead way before he got there. That kind of coincidence was too much for Dr. Hove to ignore – two victims who were apparently dead before being dead in the space of just a few weeks?' Hunter shook his head.

'In short,' Garcia again, 'we were lucky, Captain. The minor inconsistencies with Terry Wilford's jumping suicide could've easily been overlooked. But fortunately, like Robert explained – this Kay Sixtree girl is pretty stubborn . . .' He smiled to himself. 'And smart.'

There was a silent moment before Captain Blake spoke again. 'So what's the theory here?' Her gaze settled on Hunter. 'Do we think that this killer could be a medical professional in some capacity? Or was? Maybe even a medical student? How does one figure out a loophole like this one?'

'Of course there's that possibility,' Hunter confirmed. 'But to be honest, Captain, none of that information is really hard to come by. All it takes is a bit of research over the Internet and maybe a couple of phone calls, that's all.'

'But even if he is,' Garcia interjected, 'or was a medical professional, a student or whatever . . . we have absolutely no way of finding out who he is simply because he figured out a way to operate under the radar. All that the loophole really tells us, Captain, is that he's very clever.'

Hunter glanced at the board. 'Maybe that's not all it can tell us.'

All eyes moved to him.

'I think we might be poking at the wrong end of the loop-hole here.'

Twenty-Four

Jennifer Mendoza applied the flamenco-red lipstick to her lips and carefully used a paper tissue to kiss away the excess. That done, she gave her reflection a tentative smile.

The smile didn't linger, quickly morphing into a desolated look.

Jennifer came this close to reaching for the makeup remover bottle and wiping her face clean for the ninth time that evening.

'I look like a cheap, back-alley hooker,' she whispered to the mirror.

No, you don't, Jenny, the mirror whispered back. *'You're just not used to it anymore, that's all.'*

The mirror was right. Jennifer's makeup was subtle by any standards – just a little foundation, some eyeliner, light lipstick and a touch of blush – but it had been a very long time since Jennifer Mendoza had applied makeup to her face with the intention of going out on a date ... a real date. To her out-of-practice eyes, a mere contour of lipstick made her look like a circus clown. But a little makeup was better than no makeup at all, because her skin didn't feel or look like what it used to anymore.

Jennifer studied her reflection for a moment longer before breathing out and using the tips of her fingers to gently brush her fringe to one side. Her dark hair had been cut into a stylish and quite attractive bob, but she would be lying if she didn't admit that she missed her long hair.

In high school, due to her olive skin tone and how shiny her hair always was, her nickname had been Pocahontas, but Jennifer's hair, together with everything about her, especially her appearance, had fallen victim to her addiction, which began some twenty-two years ago, when Jennifer was only twenty years old.

Jennifer was born in Bellflower, a neighborhood of South Los Angeles. Her mother, Andrea Mendoza, was a drug addict who, to support her addiction, had turned to prostitution. There was no record of who Jennifer's father really was.

Not surprisingly, since her mother sometimes used their small apartment for business, Jennifer hated being at home, so she did most of her growing up in the streets of South LA, and she did it as an angry kid. She did go to school – first to Ritter Elementary and then to Jordan High, both public schools in Bellflower – but she never showed any real interest in completing her school education. Her grades were poor and her behavior was disruptive to say the least. Her teachers did try, but Jennifer simply didn't care and her mother cared even less. She didn't care if Jennifer went to school or not, got an education or not, graduated or not, as long as she was out of the apartment. At the age of seventeen, halfway through her sophomore year, Jennifer dropped out of school. That was just months before she became pregnant with her daughter, Tabatha.

Jennifer had promised herself that she would never end up like her mother, but she quickly learned that, unfortunately, life rarely turned out like most people expected, or hoped it would. The night after she turned eighteen, high on whatever drug people were passing around at the party, and having consumed enough alcohol to poison most fully developed livers, Jennifer ended up having sex inside a bathroom stall, in some B-rated nightclub in North Hollywood. The boy with whom she had sex, she had met that night. His name was Toby. She never got his last name. She never saw him again either.

Things got really tough after that night.

Jennifer's mother, Andrea, had recognized her daughter's reckless behavior months before her eighteenth birthday and had warned her that if she got pregnant, she'd be on her own. She couldn't afford to have a pregnant woman sitting in her apartment, scaring her clients away.

Andrea never backed down from her promise, sending a recently pregnant Jennifer to go live on the streets.

Jennifer did think about having an abortion, but her fear of what God would do to her in the 'afterlife' way outweighed her fear of becoming a mother. Nine months, almost to the day, after Jennifer had met Toby, she gave birth to Tabatha Mendoza, a stunning olive-skinned baby girl with midnight-black hair and sapphire-blue eyes.

While pregnant, Jennifer applied for several grants from the US Government that were specially allocated to single mothers. Because she was homeless, she was immediately approved for three separate programs. With that, she managed to secure shelter, food and clothing for Tabatha and herself, until she was able to work.

Jennifer tried hard to keep the promise that she had made to herself to not be like her mother ... to love and care for her daughter with every atom of her soul. And that was exactly how it was, at least for the first two years of Tabatha's life.

Just a couple of months shy of her daughter's second birthday, Jennifer managed to land a job at a food distributor warehouse in Culver City, where they lived at the time. With her new employment, she also succeeded in securing a new grant from the government – Daycare/Nursery Assistance. The grant guaranteed that Tabatha would be professionally looked after during the hours that Jennifer had to be at work.

One morning, as her three-month trial period was coming to an end, Jennifer was transferring and rearranging a few medium-sized boxes across a wide corridor, from one shelf unit to another. The boxes weren't as heavy as she thought they would be, so, to gain time and impress her boss, Jennifer began taking two boxes across at a time, instead of one. During one of her trips, she partially turned her body to check how many boxes were still left on the shelf behind her – a simple movement, one that should've offered no danger whatsoever – but that morning, maybe due to the awkward way in which she twisted at the hips together with her trying to use her chin to keep the top box from sliding off, something snapped in her lower back. The pain that shot up her spine was so excruciating, it felt as if her body had been severed in two. That was the end of her trial period.

Unfortunately for Jennifer, that was also the kind of injury whose fault fell totally with the employee, not the employer. Her instructions had been to carry one box at a time. It had been Jennifer's decision to try to gain time, coupled with her awkward body twist, that had caused her back to seize, not a lack of health-and-safety measures at the warehouse. What that meant was that Jennifer's injury had to be categorized as 'own short-term illness'.

In the USA, the federal government does not require employees to have access to paid sick-leave to address their own 'short-term' illnesses. It was up to the employer to decide if he would pay sick-leave or not, and Jennifer's employer wasn't about to pay a single penny to someone who wasn't putting in the hours. And if Jennifer didn't put in the hours, she wouldn't have a job.

That knowledge sent Jennifer into 'desperate' mode. She couldn't afford to lose that job. She needed to provide for her daughter and that was exactly what she told the 'pain management specialist', who she saw that same afternoon.

The year was 2002 and the 'specialist' was quick to prescribe the number one drug in the country at the time, used in the treatment of moderate to severe pain – OxyContin – a highly addictive, semi-synthetic opioid created and distributed by

Purdue Pharma. To be on the safe side, the 'specialist' decided to start her off on 20mg tablets instead of just 5mg, a practice known in the pharmaceutical industry as 'individual dosing'.

And boy, did it work.

For Jennifer, when it came to numbing her pain and allowing her to go back to work, those little round pink pills were like a miracle in tablet form and, under the guidance of her 'pain specialist', she took them freely and without restrictions. Soon, 20mg became 30mg, which quickly shot up to 40mg. Within only two months of her injury, Jennifer had become totally addicted to opioids. A week later, she lost her job.

Even with a legal prescription, OxyContin wasn't exactly a cheap drug. With no immediate income, there was absolutely no way that Jennifer could afford it anymore, but there were plenty of cheaper opioid alternatives out on the streets, and the cheapest of them all was also the worst of them all – heroin. The first time Jennifer stuck a needle in her arm, she wasn't even twenty-one years old.

From then on, her world simply collapsed on top of her. Her drug use intensified, she became a violent person, and her disregard for everything around her, including her daughter, grew exponentially.

By the age of twenty-two, Jennifer had essentially become the person that she despised the most in this world – her mother – exchanging sexual favors for money, or bottles of OxyContin, or little bags of heroin, sometimes even food . . . while her daughter was left alone to cry herself to sleep in the corner.

Jennifer knew that she needed help. She didn't want to be like her mother. She didn't want to be a user. She didn't want her daughter to hate her, but getting help at the height of what became known as the opioid crisis in America proved to be a lot harder than anyone would've imagined.

Just days after Tabatha's fourth birthday, Jennifer was arrested for soliciting, theft, and possession of narcotics. When she told the police that she had a young daughter sitting alone in her apartment in Culver City, social services were there in less than forty minutes, and what they found disgusted them – a neglected, bruised and crying Tabatha, who was immediately taken away and put into foster care.

In court, Jennifer pleaded guilty to all charges, including child neglect and cruelty, which, because she was a first-time offender, got her only four years inside – out in two, with good behavior.

But there was no good behavior.

In prison, Jennifer had to learn how to defend herself . . . how not to back down when being intimidated . . . and how to physically hurt others on purpose. And she learned quickly.

One night, after serving almost a full year of her initial sentence, three inmates tried to ambush Jennifer in her own cell over some silly argument that had happened in the courtyard a couple of days before. They bribed a guard to leave Jennifer's and their cells unlocked after 'lights out', but Jennifer had gotten word of the ambush and she was ready. As the three inmates entered her cell and lashed out at a dummy made out of rags and pillows on Jennifer's bed, Jennifer came out of the shadows behind them, carrying a shiv made out of a toothbrush. The fight didn't last long. Jennifer stabbed one of her attackers in her knee and another in her left eye – not deep enough to penetrate past the ocular globe and hit the brain, but deep enough to permanently blind the inmate in that eye. The third attacker tried to run, but Jennifer tripped her up and drove the heel of her right foot into her face, fracturing her nose. The incident earned Jennifer the kind of respect that prevented similar attacks against her from ever happening again, but it also got her an extra twelve years without the possibility of parole.

Jennifer Mendoza served all sixteen years of her sentence

without a break. She was released just over two years ago and since then she'd been nothing but a model citizen.

From prison, Jennifer wrote Tabatha a letter, sometimes two, every week, and she truly believed that her letters were being delivered and hopefully read. She knew that it would be years before Tabatha could read them by herself, so at first, she wrote several letters to Tabatha's foster parents – accepting her guilt for being such a terrible mother, thanking them for looking after her daughter and begging them to read her letters to Tabatha.

It never happened.

Not once.

Social services were delivering the letters as normal – at least most of them – and at first, Tabatha's foster parents were putting the letters aside for a later date, until Tabatha was old enough to understand what had happened ... but that was before they got word of Jennifer's second conviction – for the 'attack' and maiming of three inmates. With the new knowledge that Jennifer would spend at least the next fifteen years in prison, Tabatha's foster parents applied for 'permanent care', and they were quickly approved.

Not surprisingly, during her sixteen-year incarceration period, Jennifer never received a single letter back from Tabatha, let alone a visit, but she never gave up hope.

The first thing Jennifer did once she stepped out of prison was to try to locate Tabatha, but she had been unlucky, yet again. Jennifer was released from prison two years after Tabatha had turned eighteen – adulthood – according to California state law. What that meant was that Jennifer had no say in her daughter's life anymore. She didn't even have the right to know Tabatha's address, or if she was still alive. Nothing at all about Tabatha's life ... unless Tabatha wanted her to and, according to social services, she didn't, and there was a reason for that.

During her time in prison, Tabatha's foster parents hadn't

been kind about Jennifer, spinning horrible stories about her to Tabatha and doing away with every letter Jennifer had ever sent her daughter, making her believe that her birthmother never truly cared for her.

For the past two years, Jennifer had done everything in her power to try and locate Tabatha, to no avail.

But tonight wasn't about Tabatha. For the first time since Jennifer had left prison, tonight was all about Jennifer.

She checked herself in the mirror one last time.

Jenny, the mirror said, knowing what Jennifer was just about to do. *We're done here. You look great, girl. Go.*

Jennifer hesitated.

GO, already!

'OK . . . OK.' She turned off the bathroom lights, grabbed her handbag, and finally stepped out of her studio apartment in Van Nuys, San Fernando Valley.

Twenty-Five

Captain Blake hadn't exaggerated when she had told Hunter and Garcia that she had just come back from another ridiculously long and equally pointless budget meeting. She was exhausted, she couldn't wait to get home, and she desperately needed a large glass of wine. What she definitely didn't need was to try to decipher another one of Hunter's riddles.

'We might be poking at the wrong end of the loophole?' she asked Hunter, dipping her chin and using her right hand to slide her glasses to the tip of her nose.

Garcia also looked back at him a little uncertainly.

'We've only been talking about the medical side of the loophole,' Hunter began, indicating several photos as he spoke. 'The fact that the kind of injuries that this killer inflicts onto his victims prior to death can easily be mistaken for the sort of injuries that would've occurred had the accidents not been faked.'

'Yeah, well, you brought it up,' Captain Blake said.

'I did,' Hunter agreed. 'But like I said – that kind of information isn't too hard to come by.'

'So what are you talking about, Robert?' the captain asked, checking her watch. 'Which side should we be "poking" at?'

'The "unclaimed body" side of the loophole.' The answer came from Garcia. His gaze skipped over to Hunter, who nodded.

'Look,' Captain Blake said, as she used her thumb and

forefinger to slightly lift up her glasses so that she could pinch the bridge of her nose. She tried her best to keep her voice steady. 'It really has been a bitch of a long day. I'm tired. I want to go home. And I need a glass of wine like a baby needs a nipple, so can we all stop with the fucking conundrum and just get to the point here.' She allowed her glasses to slide back onto her nose before her piercing, magnified eyes looked back at Hunter and Garcia.

'This killer knows that if a body goes *unclaimed* for more than just one to two weeks . . .' Garcia got there before Hunter. 'The body is donated to medical studies, where only a small number of them end up in the hands of pathology students, and an even smaller number end up getting a full autopsy exam.'

Another nod from Hunter. 'No autopsy, no chance of finding out the inconsistencies.'

Captain Blake paused, her brain too tired to fully engage. 'So what does that actually mean?'

'It means that his victim selection isn't a random process, Captain,' Hunter replied. 'He doesn't pick just anyone off the streets . . . any passer-by. His victims are carefully selected.'

The captain took a step back, allowing her attention to return to the board for a long moment. 'So then his criteria would be what? That they're all loners? That they have no one who will claim their bodies once they're gone?'

'Bingo,' Garcia said, turning to face Hunter. 'Unless you've found out something very different from what I did.'

Hunter shook his head. 'It doesn't sound like I did.'

'You guys just lost me again,' Captain Blake said, sounding like she was about to give up.

Garcia quickly explained what he and Hunter had spent the afternoon doing.

'I had just got back from The Varnish when you popped up at the door, Captain,' he told her. 'We haven't had the chance to compare findings yet.'

'So what did you find out?' the captain asked.

'Not much.' Garcia went first. 'And exactly that – that Terry Wilford seemed to have been a bigger loner than we initially thought.' He walked over to his desk and grabbed his notepad. 'It's Tuesday, not the busiest of evenings for a cocktail bar, but I did talk to everyone who was at The Varnish tonight – the bartender, the waitresses, the owner, and the few customers who dripped through the door just as they opened.'

'Sabrina Davis?' Hunter asked.

'Yep,' Garcia confirmed. 'Talked to her the longest. She really was the only one who seemed to have known Terry Wilford on some sort of personal level, but even so, she knew very little about him.'

'Who's Sabrina Davis?' Captain Blake asked.

Once again, Garcia quickly explained. 'Honestly,' he said, flipping a page on the notepad, 'I could barely expand on what she'd already told Detective Cohen from MP. She'd only known Terry Wilford for eight months. That was when she started working at The Varnish. Her personal relationship with him started four months after that and it was – and I'm fully quoting her here – "Purely sexual, not romantic. We simply enjoyed each other's company and some nights, especially after some of the crazy shifts here at The Varn, we ended up in bed together. It was a great way of releasing stress. That was all. We were no Romeo and Juliet."' Garcia put down the notepad. 'She also told me that most of the time, they tended to use her place, instead of his.'

'Well, I'm no expert,' Captain Blake commented. 'But even a "purely sexual" relationship has got to have some sort of dialogue, doesn't it? They've got to talk about something before and after sex, don't they?'

'That was the same exact point that I put forward to Miss Davis,' Garcia confirmed. 'She said that yeah, they talked about stuff, just nothing serious, or too personal. He didn't ask about her life and she didn't ask about his.' He shrugged. 'To quote her again: "We just enjoyed fucking. We both knew that nothing serious would ever come from what we had."'

'How about everyone else at The Varnish?' Hunter asked.

'Exactly what we read in the Missing Persons file earlier today,' Garcia said, giving Hunter a very subtle headshake. 'According to everyone I spoke to, Terry Wilford was a polite and friendly person ... hard worker, never complained about his shifts, and he *kept himself to himself.*'

'I got the same at my end,' Hunter said.

'So did the people at Bar Chloe actually remember him?' Garcia sounded genuinely surprised.

'The bar manager.' Hunter nodded. 'He's been managing the place for nine years.'

'Terry Wilford worked at Bar Chloe in Santa Monica when he first moved to LA, five years ago,' Garcia explained, for the captain's benefit.

'I got pretty much a carbon copy of what you did,' Hunter clarified. 'Friendly, hard-working, polite ... and private.'

'So just like with the first victim,' Captain Blake asked, her head tilting in the direction of the board. 'We've got nothing to go on again?'

'Not exactly,' Hunter said, as he addressed Garcia. 'What did Luis Toledo have to say?'

'Nothing that could really help us,' Garcia replied, quickly retrieving his notepad from his desk once again. 'On Monday, July 1st, at around midnight, he and Randy Douglas were about halfway through cleaning wastewater discharged from the LA River canal, between the 7th Street Bridge and the 6th Street Viaduct, when they saw Terry Wilford up on the 7th Street Bridge, just about to jump.'

Captain Blake's eyes widened at her detective. 'Hold the fuck on. There were witnesses?'

Garcia nodded before continuing. 'He said that it all happened way too fast – just a matter of seconds, really. They saw him up on the bridge . . . they realized that he was about to jump . . . and that was it – he jumped. No hesitation. Mr. Toledo said that he tried. He ran as fast as he could, he yelled as loud as he could . . . but they were too far away from the bridge. Terry Wilford never even noticed them down there.'

'Did he say anything about Randy Douglas seeing something a little different from what he saw?' Hunter asked.

Garcia paused, his brow creasing. 'What do you mean?'

Hunter leaned against the edge of his desk. 'The first version of events I got from Mr. Douglas was quite similar to the one you got from Luis Toledo.'

'First version?' The question came from Captain Blake. 'How many versions did you get?'

'Two,' Hunter replied. 'In the first one, Mr. Douglas gave me a very similar run of events: it was just past midnight, they were about halfway through cleaning wastewater discharged from the canal and so on . . . when they spotted Terry Wilford up on the bridge. What I thought was intriguing was – why did only Luis Toledo run in the direction of the bridge and the jumper?'

'What?' Garcia, this time.

'Mr. Douglas told me that when he and Mr. Toledo realized that the guy on the bridge was about to jump,' Hunter clarified, '*Mr. Toledo* took off like a bullet, waving his arms, yelling at the top of his voice . . . all to try to stop Terry Wilford from jumping. So I asked Randy Douglas – what did he do? If Mr. Toledo ran toward the bridge to try to stop the jumper, why didn't he do the same? What did he do instead? Was he in shock? Scared? What happened? That was when Mr. Douglas broke eye contact with me, looking quite uncomfortable.'

'The whole story was a lie?' Captain Blake asked the same question that Garcia was just about to.

'No,' Hunter replied. 'I don't think so. I think that that was exactly what happened that night. Luis Toledo realized that Terry Wilford was about to jump and he tried to do all he could to stop him from allegedly killing himself.' He lifted his left hand at Garcia and Captain Blake. 'Now, there *is* a reason why Randy Douglas didn't do the same. As Terry Wilford leaped to his death, Mr. Douglas stood perfectly still because something else, up on the bridge, caught his eye.'

'Of course,' Garcia said, anticipating Hunter's explanation. 'There was someone else up there because Terry was already dead.'

Hunter drew in a deep breath as he nodded. 'Mr. Douglas could swear that Terry Wilford didn't jump from that bridge. He was thrown.'

Twenty-Six

As she stepped out of the bus, Jennifer spotted the restaurant just across the road from where she was standing – a very cute Italian-cantina-looking place, with outside tables decked with red-and-white checkered tablecloths. Most of the tables were already taken.

She knew that she was early. As the bus pulled into its stop, the digital clock at the front of it read 7:05 p.m. – twenty-five minutes before the arranged date time.

Jennifer's first thought was to quickly walk over to the restaurant and check their menu before her date arrived. Not to see if there was anything that she could eat – after sixteen years of prison food, Jennifer could eat half-fertilized chicken eggs, and she'd do it with a smile on her face and a song in her heart – no, she wanted to check what she could actually afford because, no matter what, she always paid her own way.

In prison, Jennifer had learned how to sew, and she was great at it – precise and fast in equal measure. Upon her release and with the help from an ex-inmate organization called One Stop Career Center, Jennifer secured a job as a sewing machine operator in Northridge, not that far from where she lived. Despite working long hours, the pay wasn't that great, which translated into almost no leftover money at the end of every week, which in turn translated into not being able to afford much – but Jennifer fought the urge to go check the menu and walked in the opposite direction. If things were too expensive, she could always use the 'I'm on a diet' excuse and just order a starter.

At the street corner, she lit up a cigarette and watched as the smoke from the burning tip danced in the air before her eyes. In prison, she used to pretend that she *was* the smoke, snaking up and away, flying over those walls and disappearing into freedom. As strange as it might sound, that odd smoke dance calmed her. It made her stronger. It gave her hope.

As she was finishing her second cigarette, she saw her date, Russell, walk round the opposite corner from where she was standing and enter the restaurant.

Her heart picked up speed inside her chest. She had to admit that she was nervous . . . very nervous.

Jennifer had met Russell just a little over four weeks ago, on the 233 bus from Northridge to Van Nuys. He had boarded the bus three stops after her, as she was returning home after another long day at work. The bus was almost full. The only seat left was the one next to Jennifer, but Russell surprised her with how polite he was.

'Is it all right if I take this seat?' Russell asked, in a voice that sounded just as tired as she felt.

'It's a public bus, isn't it?' Jennifer replied, without making eye contact with the stranger, her tone careless. 'Have at it.'

'It is, yes,' Russell agreed. 'But I understand that sometimes people just want to sit by themselves. Sometimes we just need a bit of space. If you do, I respect that and I don't mind standing up. It's really not a problem.'

This time, Jennifer looked up at the man standing by the empty seat next to her. He was about six-foot and well built. His thick dark hair was brushed off his high forehead and his beard was long enough to cover all of his jaw. His dark-brown eyes sat behind rimless glasses perched on a Greek nose, which gave him a somewhat intelligent demeanor, despite his dusty clothes. He was holding a workman's bag in his right hand, with his hard hat hooked onto its handle. He looked exhausted.

'It's OK,' Jennifer replied, her voice not so careless as a moment ago. 'You look like you could do with having a seat.'

'I look that bad, huh?'

'No. You just look tired.'

As Russell took the seat, Jennifer frowned at him for a second. 'Have I met you before?' she asked. 'Your face looks ... vaguely familiar.'

Russell looked back at Jennifer with an analytical stare before his eyebrows arched. 'If you travel this bus route frequently, you might've seen me around. I ride it into work early in the morning and back home at around this time most days, but I don't think we've ever actually met.'

Jennifer took a moment to think about it. 'Maybe,' she accepted.

'I'm Russell, by the way.' He offered her his hand.

'Jennifer,' she replied, accepting the gesture. 'But everyone calls me Jenny.'

That was the whole extent of their conversation for that evening. When Russell's stop came up, just a couple of stops before Jennifer's, he thanked her again for the seat and wished her a good night.

'I hope you get some rest,' Jennifer said.

'Thank you. You too.'

As soon as those words left his lips, Russell paused, realizing the double meaning of his sentence. His backpedaling was funny and cute at the same time.

'I didn't mean that you look bad ... or tired ... I just ... you know ... you know what I meant, right?'

Jennifer smiled, her chin jerking slightly forward.

'The door is gonna close. You better hurry.'

'Yeah . . .' He hesitated for an instant before grabbing his bag. 'OK, bye.'

Two whole weeks went by before they met again – same bus route, but this time there were no seats available. Russell stood a couple of seats ahead of Jennifer's. They recognized each other and exchanged a smile that seemed to carry more than just a simple 'hello'.

Three stops before Russell's, the lady that was sitting next to Jennifer got up and exited the bus. Russell stepped up, but before he was able to say anything, Jennifer nodded at the empty seat.

'Just sit down. No need to ask permission.'

Russell took the seat, with a renewed smile.

'I wasn't about to ask permission,' he whispered through the corner of his mouth. 'I was about to say that it's nice to see you again.'

Jennifer had to accept that Russell was pretty smooth.

This time they chatted until Russell's stop came up.

It wasn't until another whole week had gone by that they met again. This time, early in the morning, on their way to work. The bus was only half full, with loads of available seats, including the one next to Jennifer. Russell took it and their conversation was a lot more free-flowing than the previous time. Just before his stop came up, Russell took a deep breath and decided to try his luck.

'Listen, would you like to maybe go get a drink sometime after work . . . maybe even dinner . . . a coffee . . . something?'

Jennifer paused. It had been such a long time since anyone had asked her out, that the words sounded almost foreign to her.

'Umm . . . when?'

Russell's shrug was subtle but nervous. *When?* sounded hopeful. 'Umm . . . uh . . . whenever you're free, really.'

'I'm not sure when that will be.'

'OK . . .' Russell paused, before quickly reaching into his

workman's bag for a piece of paper and a pencil. 'Here.' He jotted
down his number. 'Just let me know when you're free, and we can
arrange something. How does that sound?'

Jennifer nodded in silence.

That had been a week ago.

Jennifer checked her watch. Russell had arrived exactly on time,
and he had clearly made an effort. He looked elegant, with a
button-up shirt and a blue tie under a well-fitting blazer jacket.

Jennifer looked down at her dress. It was a simple floral dress –
one that she had sewn herself just a few days ago, exclusively for
that night. She turned and checked her reflection in the dark shop
window she was standing next to.

'I look like a fucking bag lady,' she said to herself, with a
shake of the head. 'This was a mistake. I shouldn't be here. What
am I doing?'

Jennifer turned to walk away, but her reflection called her back.

Jenny, where the fuck are you going?

She paused. 'Back home, that's where I'm going. I should never
have said "yes" to a date. I should never have messaged him. This
was all a mistake.'

Her reflection tried to argue, but this time, Jennifer didn't want
to hear it. She stubbed out her cigarette and, with her head down,
quickly began making her way toward the bus stop.

'Jenny?' she heard Russell's voice calling from a distance. She
hadn't noticed that he had stepped back out of the restaurant just
seconds after she saw him entering it.

'Oh shit!' she whispered to herself, picking up the pace.

'Jenny,' he called again. 'Hey, it's here. Don Giovanni. You're
going the wrong way.'

Jennifer's heart was beating so loud, she was afraid that the
entire street could hear it. She took a breath, breathed it out and
turned to look back at Russell. He waved at her, displaying the

brightest smile she'd seen in a very long time. That was when she noticed that he had a red rose in his right hand.

Too late to walk away now.

'Sorry,' she lied, as she approached her date. 'For some reason I thought the restaurant was on the other side of the road.'

Russell handed her the rose. 'Cheesy, right?'

Jennifer smiled. 'Not at all. It's actually very sweet of you. Thank you.'

They turned and Russell led her into the restaurant.

Dinner went a lot better and smoother than Jennifer had expected. Not only because the restaurant wasn't too pricey, but Russell also proved to be a funny, respectful and very attentive person. When the check arrived, he tried to take care of it. His point was that he had been the one who had invited her out, but Jennifer was having none of it and insisted on paying her own way. Russell didn't argue. It was clear that he understood that it wasn't about money. It was about pride, and he totally appreciated that.

The time was approaching 9:30 p.m. when, just as they ordered coffee, Russell asked Jennifer if she would like to go for one last drink. He told her that he knew this Mexican bar, less than a block away, which served the best Mezcalita he'd ever had.

Jennifer had no idea what a Mezcalita was.

Russell explained that it was simply a Margarita made with Mezcal instead of tequila.

Jennifer looked back at him with the same blank stare. She clearly didn't know what Mezcal was either.

'Oh, you definitely need to try it then,' Russell insisted. 'It will change your world. Trust me. And please ...' His chin dipped down ever so slightly. 'Allow me to get it.' He immediately lifted a hand with his index finger pointing up before Jennifer could contest it. 'One drink ... let me buy you *one* drink, especially because you've never had a Mezcalita before, so you might not like it. It's unfair for me to ask you to spend money on something you don't know and might not enjoy.'

Jennifer pondered over Russell's words. She couldn't argue that he had a point. She got to her feet.

'Let me go to the bathroom and I'll think about it, OK?'

'Sounds fair,' Russell replied with a single nod.

Jennifer didn't really need the bathroom. She needed the mirror.

'What the hell do I do?' she asked her reflection, as she placed her hands under the cold tap.

You go and you get that drink with him, that's what you do.

'Why?'

Two reasons.

Jennifer waited.

One – you like him. He's probably the first man in forever who has treated you like a human being instead of a piece of meat.

No counterargument from Jennifer there. 'What's the second reason?'

You could do with some real sex tonight, you know what I'm saying?

'Fuck you!' Jennifer flipped the mirror off, dried her hands and returned to the table.

'OK, one drink,' she told Russell, the expression on her face telling him that she meant it. 'I have to work tomorrow morning.'

'That's a deal. One drink.' He quickly finished his coffee. 'If you like it, we can go back some other time for more, what do you say?'

Smooth, Jennifer thought, trying to curb a smile.

'*If* I like it,' she replied, as she too finished her coffee.

Russell grabbed his blazer jacket and, as she stood up, he held Jennifer's chair for her. They exited the restaurant and rounded the corner into a semi-deserted, badly lit street. As they did, Jennifer paused for a second. For a moment, she felt as if her legs had threatened to buckle under her weight.

'Are you all right?' Russell asked, gently holding on to her right arm. There was concern in his voice.

'Umm ...' Jennifer tried to gather herself. 'Just felt a little bit woozy, all of a sudden.'

'What, from that single glass of wine you had?'

'Probably.' She placed her left palm against a dark pickup truck parked just ahead of her and took in a deep breath.

The wooziness didn't go away. In fact, it came back with renewed strength.

Russell reached for the keys in his pocket and unlocked the truck.

Jennifer's eyelids fluttered at him.

'What ... what is happening?'

Russell rotated his head clockwise, then counterclockwise, trying to do away with the tension in his neck muscles. 'You're falling asleep.'

To Jennifer, his voice sounded different.

He pulled open the truck's back cabin door.

'I don't und—'

Before she could finish her sentence, Jennifer lost consciousness.

Russell grabbed her to break her fall and very quickly placed her on the back seat.

'I'll be dipped in shit!' he said to himself with a proud nod. 'That was just the perfect dosage.'

Twenty-Seven

Garcia paused at Hunter's words, frowned, then walked back to his desk to search for Terry Wilford's LAPD suicide incident report.

'It's not in there,' Hunter said.

'What?' Captain Blake's attention went from Hunter to Garcia, her palms facing up. 'How is it that an eyewitness's testimony saying that he'd just seen someone being *thrown from a bridge* isn't in the incident report?'

Garcia quickly skimmed through the file before handing it to his captain. There really was no mention of any of it.

'Because Randy Douglas never told the officer who questioned him that night,' Hunter replied, matter-of-factly, rounding his desk and taking a seat behind his computer. In his captain's eyes, he saw doubt and concern collide with each other.

'Luis Toledo convinced him not to,' Hunter explained. 'And it's easy to see why.'

'Oh, is it?' the captain asked. 'So please, help a blind woman here, because I can't see why at all.'

Hunter sat back on his chair. 'All you have to do is picture the scene – Luis Toledo and Randy Douglas are working away, mopping the concrete channel, chatting about last night's game or whatever, when one of them spots something up on the 7th Street Bridge, just ahead of them. Now let me point out that they are about seventy yards out, it's dark, and what they're witnessing is conveniently happening under the only lamppost up on the bridge that seems to be busted. It takes them a second to realize that what they are actually looking at is a jumper. Panic mode sort of kicks in and Mr. Toledo does what most of us would've done – he takes off toward the bridge to try to stop what's about to happen. Mr. Douglas is just about to do the same when something else up on the bridge catches his eye, just as Terry Wilford is "allegedly" leaping off the edge. So he pauses.'

'He sees someone else up on the bridge,' Garcia deducts. 'Just behind the jumper.'

Hunter points at his partner. 'That's what it looks like, but he can't be sure. So he stands still for an extra couple of seconds or so, trying ...' Hunter lifted his index finger to highlight his point '... through the darkness, and somewhere in between shock and panic, to make out something that is seventy yards ahead of him. Meanwhile, Terry hits the ground ... hard.' He clapped to emphasize the sound of the impact. 'Mr. Douglas hesitates for an extra second or two before he too does the inevitable and rushes toward the bridge. When he gets there, panic hits full-advance mode because they are both now staring at a total mess of broken bones and torn flesh, not to mention the blood.'

'So one of them calls the cops,' Garcia said, nodding at the report in the captain's hands.

'Luis Toledo,' she said, reading from the file.

Hunter got back on his feet and re-approached the board. 'While they're waiting for the ambulance and the LAPD – both of them in a pretty freaked-out state because you don't see something like that every day – Randy Douglas tries to tell Luis Toledo what he *thinks* he saw up on the bridge. Not just someone else with Terry Wilford – someone else pushing or throwing him off the bridge.'

Captain Blake breathed out in frustration. The rest was pretty self-explanatory.

'Even if Randy Douglas had told the attending officer what he saw that night,' Hunter continued, 'his partner, Luis Toledo, wouldn't be able to confirm it because he didn't see it. That would've immediately caused the officer to doubt Randy Douglas's testimony. It was dark, he was about seventy yards away, and he would've had about three to four seconds, tops, before Terry Wilford's body hit the concrete and desperation mode took hold. Even if he did see someone else up on the bridge with Mr. Wilford, the darkness, the distance, the panic ... all of it would've contributed to a very *unclear* picture. Who could really say that that second person wasn't trying to stop Terry Wilford from jumping? That person could've been moving toward Mr. Wilford to try to save him ... grab hold of him or something ... when Mr. Wilford stepped off the edge.' Hunter shrugged. 'From a distance and in the dark, it could've looked like that second person had pushed Terry Wilford, instead.' He paused to allow all that to sink in for a second. 'These are all facts that Luis Toledo pointed out when Randy Douglas told him what he saw.'

'The attending officer would've done the same,' Captain Blake agreed, now fully onboard with Hunter. 'It was a clear suicide scenario. Escalating it to a homicide would've meant at least double the work for everyone and, apart from Mr. Douglas's very skittish testimony, that officer would've had no real reason to suspect foul play and get homicide involved.' She shook her head. 'There's reasonable doubt all over that story.'

'And that's why there's no mention of any of it in the incident report,' Hunter confirmed.

'OK,' Captain Blake agreed, once again pinning Hunter down with magnified eyes. 'But if his partner dissuaded him from telling the attending officer that night his version of events, how come he decided to tell you today? He surely knew that you could've discredited his story in twenty seconds flat.'

'Repressed guilt,' Hunter explained. 'Randy Douglas told me that he just couldn't get the images from that night out of his head.'

'Understandable,' Garcia commented.

'And the more he thought about it,' Hunter carried on, 'the more certain he was of what he saw – Terry Wilford being pushed, or thrown, from the 7th Street Bridge.' He took a breathing pause. 'Randy Douglas didn't care if I believed his story or not, Captain. He just needed to tell someone, and by someone, I mean "the authorities". He needed to get it off his chest, do the right thing . . . clear his conscience. Whether we believe him or not isn't his problem. For him, the important thing is that the suffocating guilty feeling is gone – the information has been passed on.'

'Well,' Garcia said, walking back to his desk and grabbing his jacket from the back of his chair. 'Great story, Robert, but none of that really matters because we already knew that there had to be a second person up on that bridge. We already knew that Terry Wilford was dead before he "jumped". And we already knew that part of this killer's MO is to fake his victims' deaths.'

Hunter halted his partner with a subtle headshake. 'Well, not exactly, Carlos.'

Despite Garcia looking back at Hunter a little confused, it was Captain Blake who asked the question.

'Not exactly what, Robert? Not exactly that part of this killer's MO is to fake his victims' deaths?'

'No,' Hunter replied. 'Not exactly – none of that really matters – because that's not all I got from Randy Douglas.'

The room seemed to hold its breath in anticipation.

Garcia returned his jacket to his chair.

'What else did he give you?'

'It turns out,' Hunter began, 'that Mr. Douglas is sort of a pickup truck aficionado. He not only drives one, but he reads specialized mags, watches documentaries, goes to shows . . . the whole nine yards.'

'He saw the killer's pickup truck?' Garcia's mouth dropped half-open.

'Not exactly,' Hunter replied.

'Robert,' Captain Blake called, her tone half an octave lower, her voice forcibly steady. 'If you say "not exactly" one more time, I swear to God that tomorrow morning you'll be handing out parking tickets in Compton.'

'I was born in Compton, Captain.'

'Nuh-uh.' The captain shook her head in a way that Hunter and Garcia both knew meant she wasn't joking. 'Thin ice all around you, Robert. You better think hard about your next step.'

'Randy Douglas couldn't exactly see the pickup truck up on the bridge because it was too dark.' There was no play in Hunter's voice anymore. 'All he saw was a silhouette.'

Garcia's shoulders dropped.

'And that's where being an aficionado pays off,' Hunter said, reaching for his phone. 'He didn't have to see the truck. He recognized its shape, even just as a silhouette.' He tapped the screen on his phone a couple of times to call up a photograph. 'Our guy drives a twin-cab Dodge RAM, and it's either the 2500 or 3500 – one of the newer models.'

Garcia and Captain Blake stepped closer to have a look at Hunter's cellphone screen. The pickup truck shown in the photo was a large, twin-cabin model, with a spacious cargo bed. The truck also appeared to be a little higher off the ground than the average street truck.

'What do you mean by "one of the newer models"?' Garcia asked.

Hunter handed him the phone and reached for his notepad. 'Randy Douglas told me that the RAM 2500 and the 3500 got a small facelift in 2019. Nothing major, but the headlights and the front grill are different than earlier models. The grill is wider and a little higher, which forced a small modification to the edge of the hood. The truck looks meaner, according to Mr. Douglas. The problem is – the main differences between the 2500 and the 3500 models are all under the hood – the engines are different when talking horsepower, fuel consumption and so on, but look-wise, they're both basically identical. And Mr. Douglas was absolutely certain that the truck he saw up on the bridge that night was either the 2500 or the 3500, new model, Dodge RAM.'

Garcia's eyes stayed on the photo for a few seconds longer.

'The 3500,' Hunter continued, 'is Dodge's largest and most expensive RAM model to date. The 2500 is a little cheaper, but not by much, which indicates that our killer isn't a street bum. He is either employed, with a good, steady job, or he runs his own business, which is doing comfortably well.' He returned his notepad to his pocket. 'I'd say that he's probably somewhere in his mid-thirties to mid-forties. He is strong and well built. Terry Wilford weighed about two hundred pounds, and our killer managed to lift him over the bridge's guardrail. Fine,' Hunter accepted it. 'The 7th Street Bridge guardrail isn't that high, but still, our killer did it alone. Also, whatever job he does, it probably allows him plenty of free time.'

'Why do you say that?' Captain Blake asked, finally handing Hunter's cellphone back to him.

'We've already figured out that his victims are carefully chosen, right?' Hunter said. 'They're all essentially loners, but how does he know that?'

'Because he either knows his victims well enough,' Garcia replied. 'Or he studies them. He follows them around.'

'Exactly,' Hunter agreed. 'If instead of previously knowing his victim, he follows them around, then he does it for weeks ... months, maybe. It's the only way to make sure that his next victim is essentially a loner. You don't figure that out by following some-one for just a few days.'

'And you need a lot of free time to be able to do that,' Garcia commented.

Hunter nodded. 'But there's something else. Something that we don't yet know.'

'What something else?' the captain asked, once again checking her watch.

'His victim selection criteria,' Hunter explained. 'It cannot only be the fact that they are loners. If that was the case, in a city like LA . . .' He pointed at the window. 'He just needed to hit Skid Row and he'd be like a kid in a candy shop. Homeless and lonely people of all ages. People with no one in their lives who would miss them. No one who would've reported them missing either. That wasn't the case with either of the two victims we have here.' Hunter indicated the board. 'So yes, being a loner is probably part of this killer's victim selection criteria, but that's not why he chooses them. There's got to be something else. We just need to find out what that is.'

Twenty-Eight

The man who called himself Russell sat quietly at the corner of the room. His left leg was crossed over his right one and his hands were resting gently against his thigh, fingers interlaced, thumbs touching at their tips. His beard was gone. Shaved clean to show a squared and strong jawline. His dark brown eyes seemed full of mystery and anguish. He'd been sitting in that same exact position for several minutes . . . his breathing controlled . . . his gaze locked onto Jennifer, who was lying on the floor in a fetus position, just a few feet in front of him.

It had been around twelve hours since the cocktail of sedatives that he had poured into her coffee while she had gone into the bathroom had taken effect, and Jennifer still hadn't come to yet. But the man wasn't worried. In fact, he'd been expecting it. According to his calculations, the dosage that he had used would be wearing off at any minute now. That was why he was sitting in the room with her. He wanted to be there when Jennifer woke up, just like he had been there when all of them had woken up.

The man casually checked his watch before his eyes returned to his subject on the floor. He liked observing them. He liked watching as their chests rose and fell at odd rhythms and at different intensities. He liked watching their erratic breathing go from deep, to shallow, to almost no breathing at all, before repeating the whole cycle in its own randomized way. He liked watching their rapid eye movement pick up speed behind their heavy eyelids for almost a minute, only to slow down to total stillness in the space of a second. All of those symptoms – the odd chest movement, the erratic breathing, the crazy REM – they were all side effects of the drugs combo he had used.

He scratched the underside of his chin and, right at that moment, Jennifer jerked on the floor, as if she'd been kicked hard in her stomach.

The man had seen that before as well. His cocktail of sedatives were known to trigger a barrage of bad dreams. Nightmares so real that the subjects would sometimes jump, shake, twist, turn and scream in their sleep, but no matter how terrifying a nightmare they were having right then, it would all be a dream of angels when compared to what they would endure once they'd woken up.

On the floor, Jennifer jerked again, but this time the jerk came accompanied by a couple of short moans. Not the type associated with pleasure and the release of oxytocin. No, these were a sign of distress and an indication that Jennifer was about to regain consciousness.

The man calmly waited.

Jennifer jerked yet again – three times in rapid succession, as if three quick surges of electricity had just passed through her body. Each one followed by a new moan, gaining intensity as they progressed.

Here it comes, the man thought. *The Neo Burst.*

The 'Neo Burst' was what he had come to call the explosive waking-up process that all of his subjects inevitably went through. It reminded him of how Neo, in the film *The Matrix*, woke up in his pod after taking the red pill – just an explosive burst out of the dream world, back into the real one.

The man uncrossed his legs, leaned forward and rested his elbows on his knees. His hands were still together . . . his fingers still interlaced. His eyes settled back onto Jennifer's face. Despite everything that she had gone through in her life, she had somehow managed to keep at least some of her attractiveness from her younger days.

'What a waste,' Russell said under his breath.

Jennifer's rapid eye movement came back, but it was now somewhat different – a little slower perhaps – with her head moving from left to right in snatches.

The 'Neo Burst' was mere seconds away.

Russell didn't move an inch. He simply observed.

Three ...

Two ...

One ...

'Argh!'

Jennifer jolted awake with a gasp for air so desperate it sounded like a horror scream.

Russell said nothing.

As she finally broke free from her deep, twelve-hour-long sleep, Jennifer's lungs gulped oxygen as if they could drink it ... as if she'd been submerged in water until a millisecond away from drowning.

They all had reacted in a very similar way when they woke up – seemingly starving of oxygen. Russell began to wonder if, for some reason, they all had similar dreams as the drugs were just wearing off.

He had also dimmed the lights in the room they were in down to a comfortable level. He might've not known if his drugs induced his subjects to have the same dream, but he certainly knew that they would have caused Jennifer's pupils to dilate to about double their normal size. That effect would only wear off a few minutes after a subject had woken up. Not that he wanted her to be comfortable. Far from it, actually, but he already had quite a lot in store for Jennifer and, in all honesty, the dimming of the lights wasn't exactly for her benefit.

Russell watched as Jennifer's eyes blinked awake, but he could easily tell that her eyelids still felt heavy, as if they were telling her that they weren't done with sleep just yet. Still, Jennifer somehow found the strength to force them open.

She's a fighter, he thought. *No doubt about that.*

Another drug side effect that Russell knew for sure that Jennifer would experience was the brain numbing, leading to a slow understanding of what had happened to her.

First – the typical wooziness of waking up from a long slumber that had been chemically induced. For the first several seconds, maybe even minutes, nothing would make sense.

Second – she would notice that the air that she was so desperately gulping in felt musty and clammy, a clear indication that she was probably locked in a cramped room with bad ventilation.

Third – muscle and joint pains coming from just about everywhere, the consequence of spending so many hours asleep in a bad position on a hard floor.

And fourth – and this was where it all started to become fun for Russell – since her vision would still be blurred from her pupils' dilation, Jennifer would probably use her hands to feel around, her dizzy brain dying to understand what was happening. And she only needed to stretch out her arms in any direction for the first big surprise.

Russell waited.

'Where the fuck am I?' Jennifer whispered in a raspy voice that didn't sound like her own. 'What the hell is going on?'

No reply from Russell. He was waiting for her pupils to return to normal so her eyes could focus. Images would be more shocking than sounds.

Despite not being able to see much, Jennifer placed both of her palms against the floor and, with a painful-sounding moan, pushed herself into a sitting position. The effort, even though it was done slowly, nauseated Jennifer, causing her to dry-heave.

She immediately placed her left hand against her mouth, but not fast enough to stop a drop of bile from spitting off her lips.

'Argh . . . God!'

Russell watched as Jennifer tried to gather herself together, fighting the awful bitter-acidic taste he knew would have taken over her taste buds.

As he had predicted, Jennifer slowly extended her right arm out to her side, tentatively searching for something . . . anything that could help her identify where she was.

Russell sat back and crossed his arms over his chest. He couldn't wait to see Jennifer's reaction.

Just a little further, he thought, mentally urging her to carry on.

As Jennifer fully extended her right arm out, her fingertips finally reached something.

Russell held steady.

'What the . . .?' Jennifer paused, her eyes squinting at what she had touched, trying hard to focus. She opened her hand and allowed her fingers to wrap around something solid . . . something metal.

There was a second of hesitation before her left arm reached out to meet her right one. The fingers on her left hand wrapped around something identical to what she was already holding on to – two parallel metal bars.

'No!' The word came with an exasperated breath. Jennifer squinted again, but this time not so hard. Her vision was coming back to normal.

Devastating realization followed.

Russell waited, but he didn't have to wait long – half a second perhaps – until the expression on Jennifer's face changed from the stupor of confusion to utter desperation, her pleading eyes already filling up with tears. Still Jennifer hadn't noticed that she wasn't alone in that room.

'What the fuck is happening here?' she asked in a voice

strangled with emotions, as she shook the bars with all the strength that she had in her, which wasn't much.

Solid steel.

Jennifer looked up and Russell watched as the desperation that had cloaked her until then turned into core-shaking fear. The reason for that was because Jennifer saw more metal bars just above her head – two feet above her head. But Jennifer was sitting down, not standing up. That meant that Jennifer wasn't back in a cell, like she had clearly thought she was. She was locked inside something much worse. She was locked inside a cage – an animal cage.

Her body twisted left. Her left arm followed, reaching across to the other side. More solid metal bars.

For a couple of seconds Jennifer sat still, her arms stretched out in a crucified position, her fingers wrapped around metal bars to her left and right.

'No . . .' she whispered, clearly holding back tears. 'This can't be.' She once again tried shaking them.

Nothing . . . not even a squeak.

'No . . .' Her voice was starting to regain its strength. With each cry out she would yank at her cage, her body shaking with anger. 'No . . . no . . . nooooooooo.'

'I can see you're awake.' Russell finally broke his silence, his tone calm and controlled.

Jennifer's head immediately snapped up, her gaze moving to the dark corner directly in front of her, where Russell's voice had come from. Her breathing was shallow, and tears had run down her cheeks like thick raindrops. The look on her face was desperate . . . confused. It took her eyes a second or two to refocus and her brain a few more to identify the outline of a face, the contour of the nose, the shape of the eyes.

'Who . . . who are you?' Her tone was desperate and full of fear.

'You don't recognize me?' Russell asked.

Jennifer squinted and frowned at a face that triggered no memories at all.

Russell smiled, but there wasn't the slightest hint of human sympathy in it.

All of a sudden, Jennifer paused, her neck slowly craning forward. Not only had her pupils gone back to normal, but she was also getting used to the dim lighting in the room.

A new smile from Russell. He knew exactly what Jennifer was looking at . . . and it wasn't at him.

'Watch this,' he said, the smile never fading.

'Oh my God!' Jennifer felt fear envelop her like a suffocating blanket. Something pirouetted inside her stomach before rushing up through her throat and into her mouth.

This time, it wasn't just bile.

Twenty-Nine

For Hunter and Garcia, the next day began with a trip to Terry Wilford's apartment in East LA.

Late last night, Research had finally managed to get hold of Mr. Aldridge, Terry's landlord. Hunter and Garcia had been lucky. Mr. Aldridge had been away for thirteen days, dealing with tenants and a couple of properties just outside LA, which meant that Terry's apartment hadn't actually been touched. If Mr. Aldridge hadn't been away, upon hearing the news of Terry Wilford's death by suicide, he would've immediately boxed all of his personal belongings. Anything of value that he could've sold, he would've done it already, trying to recover some of the costs of at least two weeks' unpaid rent. Whatever was left, Mr. Aldridge would've stored, but not for long. The apartment itself would've been cleaned and with a property market that moved as fast as the one in Los Angeles, there was a great chance that a new tenant would've moved in already.

But none of that had happened yet. Mr. Aldridge hadn't been back to Terry's apartment since he had unlocked it almost three weeks ago, so that the Missing Persons detectives could have a look inside. He told the UVC Research team that he could meet the two homicide detectives at the property at 9:00 a.m., with the keys.

The building was a small, rectangular structure right on

the corner of Michigan Avenue and North Hicks Avenue, in Wellington Heights. It was only two stories high with a single, glass-door entrance lobby at its center. Long hot summers and tropical downpours had long ago caused the building's light-yellow coat of paint to crack and chip, and yellow wasn't yellow anymore. Due to everyday traffic pollution, the building's façade had acquired a bong-water brown hue to it. Clearly not the most attractive building on the street.

At 9:00 a.m. sharp, Mr. Aldridge opened the door to Terry Wilford's apartment for Hunter and Garcia and simply left them to it.

The front door led straight into a very male and restrained living room, which had been sparsely decorated with two black replica-leather armchairs, a black coffee table that was low to the ground, a TV set stuck at the center of a tall black wood module, and neutral art on the walls. One of the corners of the living room had been altered to create a small, open-plan kitchen, which contained a small stove, an old-looking fridge, a microwave and nothing else.

'I don't think we'll take long in here,' Garcia said, as he walked into the kitchen and checked the four cupboards in there – two under the sink and two on the wall. 'There isn't very much for us to check, is there?' In the cupboards he found a few pans, plates, cups, glasses and cleaning products.

Hunter didn't reply. Instead, he crossed the room in the direction of the door on the other side. It led directly into the bedroom – no hallway. The bedroom wasn't very spacious.

Garcia checked the fridge. 'He either didn't spend much time at home,' he called out, 'or he didn't really eat much. There's almost nothing in this fridge.'

Inside the bedroom, Hunter found a double bed with a single bedside table, a two-door wardrobe, a four-drawer compact chest and a fold-up chair resting against the side of the wardrobe. Just like in the living room, all the furniture was dark in color.

'Yeah,' Hunter finally called back. 'There isn't much in here either.'

'At least he was tidy,' Garcia commented.

Across the bedroom, on the other side of the bed, there was another door that Hunter knew would take him into the apartment's only bathroom. He went to check it.

In the living room, Garcia had walked over to the TV module, the only piece of furniture in there that offered any kind of storage – three cupboard-like doors directly underneath the TV set. Inside the first one, he found a couple of large folders filled with what looked to be bills and invoices. He tried the second door – more paperwork and documents. Terry Wilford wasn't only tidy with his apartment, he seemed to have been a very organized individual as well. Every document type had its own separate, color-coded folder.

Third and last door – pencils, pens, envelopes and a lidless box with some photographs. Garcia reached for it and flipped through the photos for an instant. There weren't that many – ten . . . twelve, maximum. The first few were of Terry behind the bar, posing with two different people. All three of them were in bartending uniforms. The lit neon sign high on the wall behind them read 'Winning Score Sports Bar' – one of the places that Terry had worked at back in Arizona. The next five or six photos showed Terry with a cocktail shaker in his hand, mid-mixing, or pouring colorful cocktails into nicely garnished glasses. In all of those photos, he sported a bright and friendly smile. The final two photos were of Terry's late wife, Joana, and their son, Joseph. In both photos, Joseph looked to be about ten or eleven years old.

Garcia put the box down and checked some of the document folders – bills, invoices, payment slips, receipts, etc. They would have to go over every slip of paper just in case, but there were too many for him to be able to check them right there and then. He placed everything on the coffee table and walked over to the bedroom. Hunter was standing by the wardrobe, which was wide open, his back to his partner. He looked to be holding something in his hands.

'Found anything?' Garcia asked, stepping into the room.

Hunter turned to face him. He was leafing through a large book. 'A family photo album.'

Garcia nodded. 'Yeah, I also found a few photographs in the living room. Nothing special, though, just Terry Wilford working as a bartender and a couple of his wife and kid, that's all. I also found his document folders – mostly bills and pay slips. We'll take everything with us.'

'No bartending photos in here,' Hunter said back, flipping another page on the album. 'Just him and his family, really.'

'Anything else of interest in that wardrobe?'

Hunter shook his head. 'Not really – clothes, shoes, a baseball glove and this.' He nodded at the album.

Garcia's eyebrows rose at Hunter, as he pointed to the door on the other side of the bed.

'Bathroom the size of a desk,' Hunter told him. 'Nothing in there either.'

'Chest of drawers?'

Hunter shook his head. 'I haven't checked it yet.'

'I'll do it.' Garcia walked over to it.

Hunter reached the end of the album and as he was about to place it on the bed, something in one of the last photographs caught his eye. He paused and stared at it for several seconds before flipping back a few pages. He studied a couple more photos on those previous pages before, once again, flipping back to the end of the album.

'Not much in here either,' Garcia said, closing the fourth and last drawer of the chest. 'More clothes, some bedding, some towels, a set of screwdrivers, and a few books on mixology. That's it.'

Hunter's attention was still on the photo album; the look in his eyes was something between concern and doubt.

Garcia paused. 'I know that look, Robert. What have you found?'

Hunter half tilted his head to one side in an unsure gesture, as he, yet again, flipped back a few pages. 'I'm not sure. Probably nothing. Probably just apophenia, which is what I do best.'

Garcia's nose crinkled at his partner. 'What is it that you do best?'

'You said that you found a few more photos in the living room, right?' Hunter asked. 'Where are they?'

'I'll go get them.' Five seconds later, Garcia was back with the box of photographs. He handed it to Hunter. 'So what the hell is apo ... whatever? The thing you said you do best.'

'Apophenia,' Hunter confirmed, as he flipped through all the photos in the box. Once he got to the final two, he paused. They were both of Terry's wife and kid.

Garcia was still waiting for his answer.

Hunter kept his full attention on the two photos.

'Robert,' Garcia called, his tone firm. 'I don't speak Gugguggle. What the hell is apophenia?'

'Maybe I should just show you.' Hunter handed the photo album to Garcia. 'Have a look at this photo.' He indicated the picture right at the end of the album. 'And then compare it to these ones.' He flipped back a couple of pages. 'Tell me if anything stands out.'

'All right,' Garcia took the album, using his right index finger as a marker on the page that Hunter had indicated. 'Am I looking for anything specific?'

'Not exactly. Just compare the photos and see if you can spot anything.'

Garcia began with the photos on the marked page.

Terry Wilford's wife, Joana, had been a stunningly pretty

woman, with a pixie face and large hazel eyes, framed by gorgeous dark-brown waves that went way past her shoulders. As a young kid, Joseph had been just a little on the chubby side, with a mop of luscious curly hair that he had clearly inherited from his mother. There were indications that he would possibly grow up to be a very attractive man.

Garcia flipped to the page at the end of the album.

Years had clearly gone by. Joseph looked to be in his early teens then. His chubby face had slimmed down, his hair had been cut shorter, and his features were starting to cash in on that promise of good looks.

'Well,' Garcia said, his unsure stare landing back on Hunter. 'His kid is certainly older from one page to the other.'

'Anything else?'

Garcia shrugged. 'Terry Wilford had a beard in the earlier photos. Their clothes are different . . . the location is different . . . and the photos were clearly taken years apart . . . that's it.'

'How many years, would you say?' Hunter asked.

Garcia twisted his lips to one side. 'I'm going to use the kid as a guide here because it's easier to guess the age change.'

'OK.'

'In these pictures,' Garcia said, indicating the ones on the marked page, 'the kid looks to be five . . . six, maybe.'

Hunter nodded his agreement.

'And in this one,' Garcia flipped to the end of the photo album. 'He looks about eight or nine years older. Definitely starting his teens, so I'll say – thirteen . . . fourteen?'

'And on this one?' Hunter handed Garcia one of the photos from the box. It was a photo of Joana and Joseph together.

'Umm . . .' Garcia waved his head from left to right. 'I'm going to guess that the kid is around ten . . . not older.'

'So easily at least a three-year gap from one photo to the other?' Hunter asked.

'I'd say that that's about right, yeah,' Garcia confirmed.

'And nothing made your mind wonder with questions?'

'No, not re ... What sort of questions?'

Instead of replying, Hunter's gaze went back to the album, which Garcia had placed on the bed when he took the loose photo.

Garcia waited, but he got nothing else from his partner. 'So are you going to tell me what the hell apophenia is, or was this it – comparing images and trying to figure out the time lapse between them?'

'In all honesty,' Hunter explained, collecting the album from the bed, 'apophenia is really just a fancy word for the tendency that humans have to find connections where they don't really exist – being either images, situations, words ... anything, really. Like kids finding shapes in clouds. And that was me right now – trying to see connections where no real connection exists.'

'So basically – overthinking,' Garcia said with a nod.

Hunter chuckled. 'That's one way of looking at it, yeah.' He reached for the loose photos, but Garcia halted him.

'Hold on a sec, Robert. That isn't what you do, though.'

Hunter frowned at him. 'What isn't what I do?'

'Find connections where they don't really exist,' Garcia replied. 'Or see patterns that aren't really there. For most of us – I'd agree. But not you. Not usually. What you do is find connections where others can't ... you see shapes that others have missed.' He indicated the album and the photo. 'So enough with the Gugguggle lesson and just tell me straight up – what is it that you think you saw in those photos?'

Thirty

Hunter began with the same photo that had first caught his eye – the one on the final page of the photo album. It was a picture of Joana and Joseph together, where Joseph looked to be around fourteen years old. The picture was taken on a bright sunny day. Joana was sitting on a patch of grass that had been recently mowed, with a large picnic basket by her side. She wore a spaghetti-strap floral dress and ankle-strap sandals. Joseph was standing just behind his mother, his arms by his sides, his eyes looking straight ahead; his smile was shy and it looked a little forced. The thorned name of the metal band across the front of his T-shirt was impossible to read.

'What caught my attention in this photo was Terry Wilford's son,' Hunter said. 'Joseph.'

Garcia repositioned himself and looked at the picture again.

'See his arms?' Hunter indicated.

'Yeah, what about his arms?'

'Right here.' Hunter tapped his index finger against the photo. 'Just below the elbow joint. His arms bend in very slightly at an odd angle, don't you think?'

Garcia squinted for better focus, as he brought the album closer to his face. 'Oh-kay.' He agreed. 'Very slightly, but isn't he holding his arms like that on purpose. You know, trying to look more muscular for the photo.' Garcia exaggerated the pose – arms down and flexed inward, pushing his chest out. 'Teenagers will do stuff like that.'

'That's not what he's doing.' Hunter indicated again. 'See, the bend isn't at the elbows, like you just did. It's a little below them.'

'Yeah, I see that now.'

Hunter flipped back a few pages on the album and indicated two different photographs. The first was a photo of Terry, Joana and Joseph together. All three of them were standing by a tall, lit Christmas tree. Joseph looked to be about five or six years old then. This time, he was standing right in front of his mother, while Terry stood to their left. Terry had stuck his tongue out and crossed his eyes for a silly and funny face. Joana had her arms over Joseph's shoulders, with her fingers clasped together over his chest. Both of them were laughing at Terry's silliness.

The second photo that Hunter indicated was a picture where Terry had a very happy five-year-old-looking Joseph sitting on his shoulders.

'Now have a look at these photos,' Hunter said. 'Or any other photo on this page. Can you see that same bend in the kid's arms?'

Garcia took his time.

'No,' he finally said. 'His arms don't seem to bend in at all here. In none of these photos.'

'That's because they don't,' Hunter confirmed.

Garcia looked back at his partner. 'So what does that mean? That he broke both of his arms at the same exact spot, just below the elbow?'

'Yes, that's exactly what it means,' Hunter agreed before his right eyebrow arched at Garcia. 'And here is where my brain began trying to make connections where they probably don't exist.' He pointed to the Christmas tree photo. 'No bend in the arm . . .' Then he flipped back to the photo at the end of the album. 'Bend in the arm – so Terry's kid, Joseph, broke both of his arms sometime between the ages of six and fourteen, right?'

'Yes,' Garcia nodded. 'OK.'

'And my guess is that he broke his arms when he was around ten years old,' Hunter said.

'How could you possibly know that, Robert?'

'I don't,' Hunter countered. 'That's why it's a guess.'

'Based on what?' Garcia pushed.

Hunter handed him the loose photograph from the box that Garcia had found in the living room – the one where Joseph looked to be around ten years of age. 'Have a look at this photo again.'

The photo showed Joseph and his mother standing by a small waterfall – a nature park of some sort. The sky behind them was completely cloudless and bright blue. Joana was wearing a red-and-white polka-dot summer dress, while Joseph had on a black, long-sleeved shirt. A few out-of-focus people could be seen in the background, enjoying the day. In the photo, Joana had bent down at the waist to give Joseph a kiss on the cheek. Joseph didn't look very comfortable. He didn't look like he was enjoying himself either.

This time, knowing what to look for, Garcia focused his attention straight onto Joseph's arms.

'I've got to say,' he finally commented. 'He must be hot.'

'Exactly,' Hunter agreed, as he indicated on the photo. 'It's a bright, sunny day ... in Arizona. His mother, plus everyone else you can see in the background, is wearing summer clothes – T-shirts, dresses, shorts, vests, and so on – Joseph is wearing a somewhat loose long-sleeved shirt. Why? He's a ten-year-old boy at a waterfall park.'

Garcia met Hunter's stare. 'Because he wants to hide his arms?'

Hunter waited.

'Because he wants to hide the casts.'

Hunter nodded at the photo before letting out a breath that was full of doubt. 'That's the problem, Carlos. I don't think he's got any on.'

'Any what, casts?'

Hunter nodded. 'How much do you know about human bones ... about their healing process?'

'Obviously not nearly as much as you.'

Hunter, once again, drew Garcia's attention to the picture at the end of the photo album. 'You see, what's interesting here is that what these slightly inward bends just below the elbows indicate is that neither of his arms healed properly ... not in the way they should have. That in itself is strange, because the bones of children are still growing, and their growth pattern can more easily accommodate broken or fractured bones.'

Garcia paused for an instant.

'Younger bones have far more periosteum than adult ones,' Hunter explained. 'And the significance of that is three-fold. One: younger bones are denser and stronger. Two: recovery and healing time is much quicker in younger bones. And three: if properly attended to, younger bones will heal back to perfection – even X-rays might struggle to identify an old fracture after the bone had fully healed, never mind naked-eye spotting it on a photo like we just did.'

Garcia picked up the photo album and flipped back to the picnic photo – no bend in Joseph's arms. He studied it again for a couple of seconds before reverting back to the picture on the last page. 'So you're saying that ...' He allowed the sentence to linger in the air.

'That Terry Wilford's son's broken arms were never professionally tended to,' Hunter clarified, as he shook his head. 'I don't think that he was ever taken to a hospital for those injuries, Carlos. The fractured bones were never correctly realigned and his arms were never properly immobilized. Maybe what he had on in this photo were some sort of homemade braces, if that, but I'm certain that that wasn't done in a hospital. The fractured bones in both of his arms mended, but at a slightly incorrect angle.'

This time, Garcia hesitated for a heartbeat. He'd seen similar scenarios before.

'The only reason why a parent wouldn't take a kid in need of medical attention to a hospital,' he said, his eyes still on the photo, 'is because they know that questions will be asked about how those injuries came to be. And if the doctors and nurses aren't fully convinced by the explanation, they'll call Child Protective Services.'

Hunter nodded. 'I know.'

Garcia handed the photo album back to Hunter. 'So you think that Terry Wilford – or his wife . . . or both of them – were violent toward their kid?'

Hunter shifted, his eyes sweeping the small bedroom before coming back to his partner. 'I'd say that that is a very good guess, but there's something else.'

Garcia questioned with a head movement.

Hunter once again indicated the photo on the last page. 'These inward curvatures on both of his arms indicate that these . . . were spiral fractures.'

Garcia coughed. 'The same type of fracture that Terry Wilford suffered before he died? While he was being tortured?'

'The exact same,' Hunter replied.

Garcia shook his head. 'No fucking way that this happened by chance.'

Thirty-One

'How old is this Joseph kid today?' Captain Blake asked, her eyes fixed on the picnic photo of Joseph and his mother.

They were all back inside the UVC Unit's office, standing in front of the picture board. Hunter and Garcia had just run her through the photos that they'd found inside Terry Wilford's apartment and what that could possibly mean for their investigation.

'Twenty-one,' Garcia replied, grabbing a freshly printed photograph from the printer tray and pinning it to the board. The printout was the most recent photo of Joseph Thomas Wilford that Garcia had pinched from his Facebook page. In the photo, Joseph was standing in front of a videogames shop called Fallout Games. He wore a black T-shirt, with another unreadable metal band name across its front, and faded blue jeans. This time, unlike most of the pictures in the photo album they'd found in his father's apartment, Joseph's smile didn't seem fake. From the last picture that Hunter and Garcia had seen of him – the picnic one – Joseph had grown at least another foot and he had clearly lost weight. Maybe too much weight, as he looked to be a little on the skinny side, but his skin had gained a bit of color and his brown curly hair, now dyed raven-black, had grown to just a fraction above his narrow shoulders.

'Quite a change from his teenage years,' the captain said,

studying the new photo. 'And has any of this been confirmed yet? Was he really being abused by his father . . . mother . . . whoever?'

'We don't know yet,' Hunter explained. 'I tried calling Joseph from his father's apartment, but the call went straight to his voice-mail. I left him as compelling a message as I could, but Joseph might not call back.'

'Yesterday we heard a recording that Missing Persons had made during a call between Detective Cohen and Joseph,' Garcia jumped in. 'There's no doubt that this kid hated his dad.' He nodded at the board. 'This might be the reason why. Joseph doesn't care about his father. He made that very clear in his conversation with Detective Cohen. He only called Missing Persons back to ask them to stop bothering him.'

'Joseph works at a carwash called Quick & Clean in Chandler,' Hunter said. 'There's no registered phone number for the car-wash. His cell number is all we've got.'

'We'll keep on trying, but . . .' Garcia shrugged.

'No other way that we can confirm if this kid was really phys-ically abused or not?' Captain Blake asked. 'Can Research help?'

'Unlikely,' Garcia replied. 'Who could they ask?'

Captain Blake knew that Garcia was right. Parental violence, especially against younger kids, was something that was always kept tightly under wraps for obvious reasons, where the injuries were always kept hidden from everyone at all costs – no doctors, no hospitals, no pharmacies, no hanging out with friends, no going out without a parent . . . nothing.

Garcia looked away for a second, his eyes lost, as a forgotten memory suddenly popped back into his head.

'When I was in seventh grade,' he said, 'there was this girl in my class, skinny and shy as hell. Never really talked to anyone much and she always had this terribly sad look on her face, you know?' He paused, pressed his lips together, then shook his head. 'Damn . . . I can't remember her name. Anyway, she would miss full weeks of school at a time, always with some really bad excuse, but she managed to finish seventh grade all right. After summer vacation, we started eighth grade and it was just a repeat of the previous year – sad, shy, skinny, quiet, missed classes all the time.' Another sad shake of the head. 'She never finished eighth grade. Never graduated from middle school. She died at home. An "accident", they said. Months later, as we were starting our freshman year, we heard that her parents had been arrested. I think her autopsy revealed the extent of the violence that she had been suffering at home, and none of us ever knew.' He breathed out in frustration. 'Damn, I can't believe that I can't remember her name.'

The captain's gaze moved to the aftermath photos of Terry's alleged suicide, taken at the scene, before skipping to the pictures from his post-mortem. The list of injuries that he had suffered during his torture phase was also pinned to the board.

'OK,' she finally said, without breaking eye contact with the board. 'So let's say that you got this right. Let's say that it confirms that this kid was being beaten up by his father when younger. What's the theory on these murders then? Because unless we got this all wrong from the beginning, I know that it can't be this Joseph kid. He can't be the one doing all this out of revenge.' She indicated the first half of the board, occupied by Shaun Daniels's photos. 'If that was the case, then how does the first victim fit into any of it? Why was Shaun Daniels taken, tortured and killed? And why was he taken first, even before the kid's father?' Captain Blake turned to face Hunter and Garcia. 'It just doesn't make sense. Then there's the fact that we've already agreed that if these murders are linked – if we're really talking about the same perp here – then this can't be the beginning. He must've been doing this for years because this simply cannot be the work of an inexperienced killer. It's too elaborate, too well planned . . . too knowledgeable.' She indicated Joseph's Facebook printout on the board. 'How does this child fit that profile? He's twenty-one years old.'

'He doesn't,' Hunter agreed, but before he could say anything else, the phone on his desk rang. The blinking light at the bottom-right edge of the receiver indicated that the call was coming from the Police Administration switchboard.

'Just a second, Captain.' Hunter pressed the blinking button.

'*Detective Hunter,*' the female operator's voice came through the tiny intercom speaker. '*I've got a Joe Thomas Suarez on line two for you.*'

Hunter's eyes moved first to Captain Blake then to Garcia.

'I'll be damned,' Garcia said, his eyebrows arching at Hunter. 'What sort of compelling message did you leave him?'

Hunter shrugged and pressed down on the intercom button. 'Please put him through.'

Thirty-Two

Outside the Police Administration Building, the sky was turning. Helped by the constant wind that blew in from the North Pacific, menacing dark clouds had started gathering over Downtown Los Angeles, making it look like either a solar eclipse or doomsday was just around the corner.

As Hunter told the switchboard operator to connect Joseph's call, Garcia and Captain Blake stepped closer to his desk, but as the operator patched the call through, all they got was a cracking/static sound, then nothing . . . just silence.

Hunter frowned at the phone. 'Hello . . .? Joe . . .?'

The line cracked again.

'Joseph . . .?'

And again.

'Are you there?'

Joseph's voice finally came through the intercom speaker.

'Hello? Is this Detective . . . Robert Hunter? Can anyone hear me?'

'Yes. It's a bad line,' Hunter replied. 'But I can hear you now. Joseph?'

'It's Joe,' the voice said, a sliver of annoyance already detectable in his tone. *'I don't use the name Joseph anymore.'*

'I apologize, Joe. And please, call me Robert.'

'I don't think that that will be necessary, Detective. This won't

*be a long call. All I wanted to do was ask the LAPD . . . again . . .
to stop calling me. And please, stop making up stuff just to get
me to call you back. I – don't – know – where Terry Wilford is.
And I don't care to know either. Can you guys please get that
through your heads?'*

'Making up stuff?' Garcia mouthed the words at Hunter.
'What did you say?'

Hunter gave Garcia a very subtle shake of the head. 'I'm sorry,
Joe, but what do you mean by "making up stuff"?'

'Are you joking?'

'Not at this moment, Joe, no.'

Hunter heard Joe breathe out an irritated breath.

*'All right, I'm going to explain this to you really slowly, in case
you are as dumb as the first detective who called me, OK?'*

Hunter glanced at Garcia and Captain Blake.

'About three weeks ago,' Joe began. *'I get my first call from a
Detective Cohen from the LAPD. He left me a message telling me
that Terry's gone missing, wanting to know if I knew where he
was.'* He chuckled a little nervously. *'As if I would know, or even
care about that man. I stupidly believed that my best move would
be to simply ignore the message, but the dude just wouldn't quit –
leaving message, after message, after message. I finally called him
back and very politely explained that I hadn't seen, talked to, or
even heard from Terry in five years. I did my best to make all of
that perfectly clear, including the fact that I – don't – care – what
happens to Terry. I thought that I had managed to get the message
through, but as it turned out – that wasn't the case.'*

There was another pause, and this time Hunter could hear
the sound of a cigarette lighter flicking, followed by a long drag.

*'Just over a week ago, I get a new message – Detective Cohen
again – telling me that Terry had taken his own life.'* Another
long drag. *'That was hard to believe, I'll tell you that. My luck
has never been that good, but hey, guilt and karma can be a real*

bitch sometimes, you know? Anyway, I really had nothing to say about that, so I never called back. Now imagine my surprise when this morning I wake up to a whole new message from the LAPD . . . a whole new version to this fucking soap opera – there was no suicide. Terry was murdered.' Joe laughed nervously. *'What's next? Abducted by aliens? Jesus, guys. So I'm calling to say this for the las—'*

'Joe,' Hunter cut him short. 'Please listen to me.'

'No, Detective. You listen to—'

'None of it was a lie.' Hunter tried to grab Joe's attention again, but the kid really didn't seem to care.

'Let it go, already, will you? I don't care—'

Hunter hated having to resort to shock tactics, but this wasn't going at all as he had envisaged it.

'I know what your father did to you, Joe,' he said, his tone non-aggressive . . . friendly even.

The stunned silence that followed didn't come only from Joe. Garcia and Captain Blake were both looking back at Hunter in disbelief.

Hunter's decision to refer to Terry Wilford as 'your father' was risky. He knew that, but he had a very good understanding of how emotions and the human brain worked, and he had seen Terry Wilford's family photo album – he'd seen the laughter that Terry had evoked in Joe and his mother with his silly face at Christmastime. He'd seen the smile on Joe's lips when Terry had carried him on his shoulders when he was a little boy. Despite how much Joe seemed to hate Terry Wilford at present, that sacred 'father/son' relationship had existed, at least for a while, and those were the sorts of emotions that very rarely fully disappeared without leaving any kind of residue behind. If Hunter could tap into just one happy 'father/son' memory, then maybe he had a chance of enlisting Joe's help.

'I can understand why you would feel the way you do toward

him,' Hunter continued. 'But please believe me, Joe – none of what you were told was made up. That was the exact sequence in which those events played out. Your father did go missing without a trace around June 21st. You are immediate family, so of course you had to be contacted. We had no way of knowing what kind of relationship you and your father had at present, so a reasonable assumption would be that he could've decided to go visit his son and didn't tell anyone.'

Another uneasy laugh from Joe. *'As if.'*

'Missing Persons did the best they could to try to track down your father,' Hunter explained. 'But unfortunately, they got nowhere ... until just over a week ago – on July 1st – when your father's body was found at the bottom of the 7th Street Bridge here in Los Angeles. All indicated to suicide.'

Hunter's pause was deliberate, analytical – not too short, not too long – but this time he got nothing back from Joe. No nervous chuckle, no annoyed deep breath, no quick retort ... just silence, and that was a good sign. No matter how much Joe disliked his father, the news of losing him in such a desperate way was always going to be shocking and emotional. Joe's silence could mean that memories were being accessed, taking him back to happier days.

'Again,' Hunter carried on. 'You being immediate family, you had to be informed of his passing. It was only during your father's post-mortem examination, two days ago, that suicide was ruled out. He didn't end his life, Joe. It was taken from him.'

The silence that followed before Joe said anything was tense ... anxious. When he finally spoke, the anger in his voice seemed to have lost most of its momentum.

'You said that you knew what my father had done to me. How could you possibly know any of that?'

This was the first time that Joe had referred to Terry Wilford as 'my father'. Part of that safety wall was starting to come down.

The look that Captain Blake gave Hunter spoke for itself: *You dug yourself into that hole. Now dig yourself out.*

'You're right,' Hunter accepted. 'I can't possibly know exactly how much hurt your father has brought into your life. And I apologize if what I said came across as patronizing. That wasn't my intention. But I do understand that he has physically and psychologically hurt you. The signs of which you'll carry for life, and I'm truly sorry for that.' Another breathing pause. 'But I'm going to be completely honest with you, Joe. The reason why I wanted to get in touch with you wasn't just to inform you of what was discovered during your father's post-mortem examination. I wanted to get in touch with you because we really need your help.'

The line cracked again.

'Joe . . .?' Hunter called. 'Are you still there?'

Another flick of the lighter. Another long cigarette drag.

'Yes, I'm still here. What kind of help are you talking about, Detective? I can't get my ass to LA, if that's what you mean. And I also don't have the means to provide for a funeral, you know?'

As he said the word 'funeral', Hunter heard Joe's voice slightly falter.

'The state will do that for you, Joe,' Hunter informed him. 'You don't have to worry. And no, that's not the sort of help I need.'

'So what, then?'

Hunter swiveled his chair to look at the picture board. 'These kinds of conversations are better to have face to face, but I understand that you can't make the trip to LA, so I propose that I either come to you in Chandler . . .'

Hunter saw a wide-eyed Captain Blake immediately lift her index finger at him and mouth the words: 'One word – budget – no chance.'

'Or we can just chat over the phone. It's your choice, Joe.'

'What exactly is it that you need from me, Detective?'

'Information.'

Joe seemed to hesitate. *'Information about what? I told you that I haven't seen or spoken to my father in five years. I know nothing about his life. Honestly, I didn't even know that he was in LA.'*

'No,' Hunter replied. 'That's not the sort of information I need. And I know that this is a very delicate subject, Joe, but what I need to know is a little more about the time that you were together as a family. I need to know how violent your father really was.'

The silence that followed was absolute, as if the line had gone dead. Hunter looked at Garcia and Captain Blake. Both of them shrugged back at him.

'Very,' Joe finally replied. *'That's your answer, Detective. He was very violent. Can I go now? Are we done here?'*

Hunter grimaced at the phone. 'I'm afraid I'm going to need you to be a little more specific, Joe.'

'No, *Detective.'* Some of the anger was back in Joe's voice. *'I've been trying to put all that behind me for five years now. I moved towns so that places and people wouldn't bring back memories . . . so that social services wouldn't take me because my father just upped and left after Mom died. I changed my name because I didn't want any part of him in my life. I've been trying to move on from all that hurt . . . all that pain . . . and I was doing all right until about a month ago, when I got the first call from you guys, telling me that Terry had gone missing.'* Joe sucked in a lumpy breath. *'And d'you know what, Detective? I – was – scared. I was scared that he was coming to find me, and just like that.'* He snapped his fingers. *'All the memories that I've been trying so hard to forget were back . . . the nightmares are all back. So yes, Detective, we're done here. Please don't call me again.'*

'Joe, wait.' Hunter's voice was urgent. 'He's not the only one.'

Silence came back to the line, but there was no dial tone. Joe hadn't disconnected yet.

'There are others, Joe.'

'*Others what?*'

'There are other victims,' Hunter said. 'The person who took your father's life ... it wasn't an accident. It wasn't over an argument in a bar, it wasn't in a street fight for some silly reason either. The person who took your father's life has killed before. He's been doing it for years, Joe. And if we don't stop him, he'll kill again. And he'll keep on killing. The information I'm asking for can help us stop him. Please, Joe.'

'*Hold on a second here,*' Joe came back. This time, there was a doubtful lilt to his tone. '*Are you trying to tell me that my father was murdered by a serial killer? Are you fucking kidding me?*'

'No, Joe, I'm not kidding you,' Hunter replied. 'And yes, like I've said, the person who took your father's life has killed before ... more than once, so, by definition, he falls into the category of a serial killer.'

'*Oh, c'mon! Really? So instead of the "alien abduction" scenario you decided to go with the "serial killer" one? Gimme a fucking break.*'

'Do you remember my name?' Hunter asked.

'*What?*'

'My name. I stated my name when I left you the message this morning. Do you remember it?'

'*Yeah – Detective Hunter ... Robert Hunter. So?*'

'My partner and I run a specialized unit for the LAPD Robbery Homicide Division called the Ultra Violent Crimes Unit,' Hunter explained. 'UVC Unit for short. Please Google it.'

'*What?*'

'Please,' Hunter urged Joe. 'Open the browser on your phone or on your laptop and Google "LAPD Ultra Violent Crimes Unit". We are one of only three police departments in the whole of America who run a UVC Unit. On the LAPD website, you'll find a link to our unit. Please have a look at it. It will describe the kind of crimes we investigate . . . the kind of criminals that we go after. We don't investigate everyday homicide, Joe. The Robbery Homicide Division does that.'

'*Are you for real?*'

'I am. Please, just Google it. I'll wait. You'll even get to see a picture of us.'

'*All right,*' Joe sounded defiant. '*I will.*'

Hunter muted his side of the call.

Captain Blake nodded at him. 'Good call.'

'I hate my picture on that webpage,' Garcia commented, turning to face the captain. 'Could we do something about that? Upload a new one, maybe?'

She looked at him over the rim of her glasses. 'It's the LAPD website, Carlos. Not Instagram. You're supposed to look like a donkey.'

Garcia's surprised eyes moved to his partner. 'I look like a donkey on that photo? Really?'

'We all do,' Hunter replied.

'Well, that can't be good.'

'*Why?*' Joe's voice came through the intercom speaker once again. The defiant tone was all but gone.

Hunter unmuted his side.

'*Why would a serial killer go after my dad?*'

Joe had just moved from 'my father' to 'my dad'. The fact that Hunter wasn't lying seemed to have knocked another chunk off Joe's safety wall.

'We don't know yet, Joe,' Hunter explained. 'But the information I need from you can help us figure that out too.'

Joe paused. Another good sign. Hunter jumped at the chance.

'Maybe I could try to make this a little easier for both of us,' he suggested. 'Instead of you telling me all that has happened back when you were a young kid, how about I ask you a few specific questions and you can just reply "yes" or "no"? It might make things a little easier. What do you think?'

Another prolonged silence.

'OK. *Let's try that.*'

Thirty-Three

Inside the UVC Unit's office, Captain Blake's lips pursed at Hunter, as she gave him an 'I'm impressed' look.

'Way of digging yourself out of a hole, Robert,' she whispered.

Hunter caught Garcia's attention with a gesture, before indicating the board and the list of injuries that Terry Wilford had suffered during his torture phase.

Garcia quickly retrieved it and placed it on Hunter's desk.

Before he could start, the sky outside cracked with thunder so loud that it sounded like a bomb had gone off just outside the PAB.

'What the hell was that?' Joe asked.

'Thunder,' Hunter replied. 'We're just about to get one of our famous tropical downpours over here.'

A second later, raindrops the size of rifle bullets began pelting down against their office window.

'And here it is,' Garcia whispered.

'OK, Joe, I'm ready. Can I start?' Hunter asked.

'I guess.' The reply came with an exhaled breath.

'You broke both of your arms when you were a young boy, am I right? Maybe when you were around ten or eleven years old?'

There was a pregnant pause, as if Joe hadn't heard the question properly. *'Umm.'* The doubtful lilt was back in his voice. *'Yeah, that's right. I fell off my bike.'*

Hunter and Garcia exchanged the same 'yeah, right' look.

Trauma, when instigated by fear, tended to embed its roots deeper into the human mind, making it harder to overcome. Most people, battling those types of traumas, would, more often than not, hold on to certain fears long after their threat was gone, allowing them to affect their lives for years to come . . . sometimes for life. Joe had run away from his father five years ago and he now knew that Terry Wilford was gone and would never be back, but it seemed that his mind was still holding on to the fear of being hurt . . . the fear of punishment. His mind was still holding on to an untruth, created to protect Terry, not Joe.

'Was that what your father told you to tell everyone?' Hunter asked. 'That your arm injuries were the result of you falling off a bike?'

Joe stayed quiet.

'Joe,' Hunter tried again. 'I understand why he would do that. I also understand how terribly difficult this is for you. I know that what I'm asking you to do right now is painful . . . the memories I'm asking you to tap into are tender and full of hurt . . . and if there was another way, believe me, I would've gone down that path, but there really isn't one, we've looked.' He paused for effect. 'The only way that this can work, Joe, is if you tell me the truth. There is no danger anymore.'

Another flicker of a lighter. Another long drag of a cigarette.

'*What do you wanna know, Detective?*'

Hunter drew in a deep, silent breath. 'Did your father do that to you? Did he *twist* your arms until they broke?'

Silence always had the magic power of stretching time, making it feel longer. The one that followed seemed to last an eternity.

'Just "yes" or "no" will do, Joe. I don't need any details.'

'*How could you possibly know that my father did that to me?*' Joe asked, his voice faltering again. '*I never told anyone what really happened. I didn't even go to the hospital back then. There's no record of it. And how do you know that he twisted them?*'

'Were you treated at home?'

'*Yes.*' Of all the emotions coming in and out of Joe's voice, anguish was the easiest one to detect. '*And because of that ... because I was treated at home, my arms aren't ... quite right.*'

'Thank you for being honest, Joe.' Hunter nodded at the phone, as his eyes moved down on the list. He knew that the faster he got through his questions, the better it was for everyone. 'How about ... cigarette burns? Did your father ever do that to you – burn you with the tip of a cigarette?'

Joe chuckled nervously again. '*Yeah ... he did. How do you know all this?*' he asked, clearly fighting back tears. '*How can you possibly know all this when no one else does?*'

'I don't,' Hunter replied, his tone calm and explanatory. 'I'm just trying to eliminate actions from a list, Joe. And you're doing great.' He chose to be less specific with the next question.

'With the cigarette burns – did your father target your hands, arms, feet, torso, legs ... could you tell me?'

Hunter used a pen to indicate on the list. During the torture phase, Terry Wilford had suffered cigarette burns in between his toes.

'*Feet.*' Joe's reply was almost a whisper. '*He burned my feet a few times ... between my toes ... so that Mom wouldn't see it.*'

Captain Blake brought a hand to her mouth. 'Fuck.' The word was muffled by her palm.

Hunter shifted on his chair. He debated if he should ask just one more question, or stop right then. He decided that he would ask a final question, but he would keep it as general as he possibly could.

'If it's OK with you, Joe,' he said, his eyes on the list. 'I'd like to ask you just one last question, and I truly only need a "yes" or "no" answer. You don't have to go into any details. Is that OK?'

'*Yeah.*' Joe sounded almost out of breath, as if he'd just finished a hundred-meter dash.

Once again, Hunter used his pen to indicate on the list.

Garcia and Captain Blake craned their necks to have a look.

Dr. Hove and her student had identified that the perpetrator had used something like diluted toilet bleach or some kind of soft detergent as eye drops on Terry Wilford. Something that would've caused considerable pain but wouldn't necessarily cause blindness.

'Did your father ever hurt your eyes in any way? Any way whatsoever?'

Silence.

'Just a ye—' Hunter tried to remind Joe, but he cut him short.

'*Yes, he did.*' Joe paused and Hunter had a feeling that it wasn't a final pause. Joe was debating if he should say anything else or just leave it at that. He decided to clarify. '*He got real angry one night. I was eleven ... twelve ... I can't fully remember, but after he beat me up, he held my head back, forced my eyes open, and dripped something into them that burned like fire. Pepper, alcohol, lime juice ... I don't know what it was. But I remember how much it burned.*'

Hunter was done with the physical punishment questions. There was no need to go through the entire list, but he still needed to clear a couple of points.

'When you were talking about your arms, Joe,' Hunter carried on, 'you said that you never told anyone what had really happened ... never went to the hospital either. Did you ever tell anyone at all about any of it ... at any time?'

'*About the beatings?*' Joe asked. '*About his temper?*'

'Yes,' Hunter confirmed. 'Did anyone know? A friend? A teacher? Another member of the family? Anyone at all?'

'*My mom knew ... at least about some of it, but ... she loved my father. She would always forgive him, no matter how drunk or violent he got.*' Joe paused, as if he was searching for the right words. '*You see, when my father was good, he was great, but when he was bad, it was like he was someone else . . . some angry, vicious monster out of control.'*

'Mood swings?'

Another nervous chuckle. *'Yeah, I guess you could say that. Super-violent one second, then remorseful the next.'*

Hunter noted that down. 'Was he also violent toward your mother?'

'Yes. Sometimes, but not always. I got the bulk of it.'

'Did anyone else other than your mom know? Any of her friends, maybe?'

A slightly hesitant pause. *'I can't be sure, but I don't think so. I never told anyone and I don't think Mom did either. Neither of us had many friends. I wasn't really allowed to play outside and my mom never went out without my father. He was also smart enough to hurt me mainly on my torso and legs. Parts always covered by clothes, so no one would see the bruises and start asking questions. My mom had to drop me off and pick me up from school every day. After some of the bad beatings, like the broken arms, I wouldn't go to school for weeks. No after-school activities either, but . . .'* Joe trailed off, as if lost in thought.

Hunter gave him a few seconds before pushing. 'Yes, Joe, but . . .?'

'But I think my sixth-grade teacher suspected it. She was always concerned, you know? Always asking me how things were at home . . . why I missed so many classes . . . why I always sat by myself at lunchtime . . . that sort of thing. She kept on telling me that I could tell her anything I wanted and she would keep it a secret. I never told her about any of it, but I think she knew. She was a really great teacher.'

'Do you remember that teacher's name?'

'Umm . . . yeah – Mrs. Broadhurst.'

Hunter wrote the name down.

'How about after you left Phoenix? After you moved away

from your father and the beatings? Have you mentioned any of it to anyone?'

'No. *I never told anyone. I don't want anyone to know. I came to Chandler to start a new life and leave everything behind, not to feel sorry for the life I had. I just want to move on.*'

Hunter nodded his understanding. 'How about writing down what was happening to you? A lot of kids keep diaries, or a journal, or something on those lines. Did you have anything like that back then? Did you ever make notes of the beatings?'

Joe snorted. '*No, why would I? Not something that I would like to keep a record of. And if I did and my father ever found out about it, it would've just earned me another severe beating, or worse.*'

Hunter took a second to scan through his notes. He had what he needed. He looked at Garcia and Captain Blake before using his hand in a cut-throat gesture.

'We're done here,' he whispered.

'Good,' Captain Blake whispered back.

Hunter thanked Joe for his help, but this time it was Joe who paused Hunter, just as he was about to disconnect.

'*Detective?*'

'Yes?'

They could all hear Joe's slightly restless breathing.

'*Where is he?*' he finally asked. '*Where is my father?*'

'His body is being kept at the Department of Medical Examiner-Coroner here in Los Angeles.'

Silence returned to the line, but once again, no dial tone. Hunter waited.

'*Is it true what you told me?*' Joe asked, sadness colliding with doubt in his tone. '*Will the state really provide for a funeral?*'

'Yes,' Hunter confirmed, under the nods from Garcia and Captain Blake. 'If the family cannot afford one, the state of California will provide for a dignified funeral or cremation.'

There was a long silence.

Hunter waited once again. He knew that Joe was still on the line.

'*If there is a funeral or a cremation ... could you please let me know?*'

'Of course, Joe,' Hunter replied. 'With plenty of time. You have my word.'

Thirty-Four

The rain over downtown LA had gotten heavier, the sky darker. The drumming of raindrops against the windows of the Police Administration Building sounded like a steamroller driving over endless sheets of industrial bubble wrap, but inside the UVC Unit's office, as Hunter put down the phone, the silence seemed absolute. For several long seconds, no one said a word, but all eyes were settled on the list of torture injuries that Terry Wilford had suffered.

Captain Blake was the first to speak.

'Just to confirm that we're all on the same page here.' She rounded Hunter's desk to face the picture board again. 'This is no crazy, once-in-a-lifetime coincidence, right? I mean – the injuries that Victim Two suffered during his torture phase being a carbon copy of the ones that he inflicted onto his own son years ago didn't just happen by chance, did it?'

'We all know that in our world,' Garcia said, gesturing first at their office then at the Robbery Homicide floor just outside their door, 'these kinds of coincidences simply don't exist, Captain.' He walked over to the picture board to join her.

'So this is the killer's motive.' Captain Blake phrased it as a conclusion, not a question. 'He's going after parents who used to abuse their kids, and he's paying them back in kind and with dividends. We're chasing another goddamn vigilante here.'

'Maybe,' Hunter said, his eyes moving to the phone on his desk, as if he were waiting for another call.

'Maybe?' the captain asked, her surprised gaze pinging to Garcia. 'Isn't it obvious?'

'Right now, Captain,' Garcia replied. 'We have a small problem with that vigilante theory.'

'Which is?'

Garcia indicated the first half of the board. 'Shaun Daniels. According to the info we have on him, he was never married . . . never had a kid. No steady girlfriend either. If this killer is going after parents who were violent toward their kids, he doesn't fit the victim profile . . . not at the moment.'

'At the moment?' Captain Blake looked truly confused.

'The info sheet we have on Shaun Daniels,' Hunter took over, 'is a very basic one. Research gathered it almost three weeks ago after we met with Dr. Hove about the inconsistencies found during his post-mortem.' He indicated on the sheet. 'Officially, he was never married—'

'But he might've lived with someone,' Captain Blake quickly caught up.

'That's what we're hoping for,' Hunter confirmed. 'After we found those photos in Terry Wilford's apartment earlier today, even before speaking to his son, Carlos and I discussed that same exact "vigilante" theory, Captain. We had no real idea of how long it would take us to get in touch with Joe, but neither of us wanted to wait.' He checked his watch. 'So on our way back to the PAB, about two hours ago, I called Shannon at Research with new instructions. They're already trying to find all they can on Shaun Daniels's love life. Maybe he wasn't always a loner. Maybe he did have a partner at some point . . . someone who had a kid.'

Captain Blake's attention moved back to the board, particularly to the list of pre-death injuries that Shaun Daniels's post-mortem examination had revealed.

- Missing toenails on his left foot.
- Broken fingers.
- Fractured ribs.
- Fractured eye orbit.
- Hypothermia.

'If we're right about this,' she said. 'If this killer really is mimicking the violence that parents inflicted on their kids, judging by the list of injuries that we have here, then we're talking about severely violent parents. If that's the case, keeping that sort of violence completely under the radar is almost impossible. Someone must know something.'

'If someone does,' Garcia offered, 'Research will find them.'

Thirty-Five

Once Captain Blake had left their office, Garcia leaned against the edge of his desk and faced Hunter.

'So what will the plan of action be here?' he asked, folding his arms in front of his chest. 'I mean, where do you want to start with all this?'

Hunter walked over to the coffee machine and poured himself a cup. 'Coffee?'

Garcia nodded.

Hunter poured a second cup and handed it to his partner.

'If we're right on this,' he began, 'then our main priority is to figure out who could have that knowledge ... and how did they get it.'

'Knowledge about the physical violence, you mean?'

'Yes. You heard what Joe said on the phone. He never told anyone about it. He never wrote it down, never kept a hidden journal, nothing ... and as far as he knows, neither did his mother. Maybe his sixth-grade teacher suspected it, but even if she had told anyone about her suspicions, and whoever she told wanted to act on it—'

'Why do it now?' Garcia picked up the thread. 'About ten years later.'

'Not only that,' Hunter added. 'But if Joe's teacher did tell anyone, chances are that whoever she told is from Phoenix, where they lived at the time, not LA. Considering that both of our victims were taken, tortured and murdered in LA, I don't think this killer is crossing state lines, Carlos. Whoever he is, he's based here.'

'Yeah, I agree.'

Hunter sipped his coffee. 'So here's our problem – how did this killer gain knowledge, not only of the fact that Joe Wilford had experienced severe physical violence at the hands of his father years ago and while living in Phoenix, Arizona ...' He lifted a finger for emphasis. 'But also of the *exact* type of injuries inflicted onto him? Those injuries didn't happen all at once, Carlos – the broken arms, the cigarette burns, the burning eye-drops, and whatever else – each of those injuries happened at different times, spread over several years. According to Joe, he never went to the hospital for his injuries, so there should be no official record. If Joe really never wrote any of it down, then how the hell did this killer get such detailed information?'

Garcia had a healthy sip of his coffee. 'Maybe his mother kept a diary.'

Hunter shook his head. 'And what? Somehow, ten years later, that diary ends up in the hands of a murderer here in LA, which so happens to be the exact same city that Terry Wilford moved to after he left Arizona? I don't think so.'

Garcia didn't argue. 'But someone has to have passed on that information.'

'True,' Hunter agreed. 'And by elimination, we're left with just one option. There's only one person left in the equation who knew about all the violence ... all the injuries.'

'Terry Wilford himself,' Garcia said, indicating a profile photo on the board.

'Yep.' Hunter finished his coffee and sat back on his chair.

'But wouldn't that make even less sense?' Garcia countered. 'He was the violent one. He was the one who lashed out against his wife and kid. Why would he tell anyone about his violent personality? It's not exactly a quality people would want exposed, Robert.'

'It might make a lot more sense than you think, Carlos.'

'Really? How?'

'Simple,' Hunter replied. 'Guilt. It takes a real special kind of psychopath to *not* know that what he was doing was wrong – the violence, the beatings ... all of it – especially when that violence was perpetrated against his own wife and kid. That knowledge almost always manifests itself as guilt, shame, or a combination of both. And that internal guilt would be the main player on the type of mood swings that Joe told us his father used to have.' Hunter tapped his notepad with the tip of his index finger. 'Going from being violent to being remorseful in no time. That guilt and shame, combined with violent mood swings that can't be controlled, can very easily push a person to *seek help*.'

Garcia paused for a beat. 'Are you talking about therapy?'

'Why not?' Hunter questioned back. 'When we're ill and we know we're ill, we seek help, don't we? We go to the doctor – it's normal behavior. I'm sure that Terry Wilford knew that his mood swings weren't right, and most of the battle against controlling anger is won by understanding where that anger is coming from. A therapist, or even an anger-management specialist, can help you do that.'

Garcia thought about it for a moment. 'But wouldn't it make more sense for him to seek help back in Arizona? While the violent mood swings were taking place?'

'And he might have,' Hunter replied. 'We don't know, but if he did and it helped – and therapy usually does help – he might've wanted to carry on with the sessions once he relocated. Maybe he feared that, without therapy, his violent behavior had a bigger chance of coming back. Maybe he started seeing signs of it again.'

Before Garcia could say anything back, the phone on Hunter's desk rang.

Hunter leaned forward and reached for it. It was Shannon Hatcher, the head of the Research team.

'Shannon,' Hunter said, as he switched the call to speaker-phone. 'Please tell me you've managed to find something.'

There clearly was a smile hanging on the corners of her words.

'*You can thank me later, Robert.*'

Thirty-Six

The new information that Shannon Hatcher had obtained on Shaun Daniels wasn't what she would call 'case breaking', but it did give Hunter and Garcia a brand-new lead.

They'd been right – Shaun Daniels hadn't always been a loner. Records indicated that nine years ago, and for a period of two years, Shaun had shared the same address with a Mexican American woman named Mariela Duron Esqueda. The information wasn't exactly cast-iron because there was a discrepancy with the records. It had been that discrepancy that had thrown Research off the right trail when they had gathered Shaun Daniels's basic information the first time around.

During the years of 2015 and 2016, the name Mariela Duron Esqueda appeared together with Shaun Daniels on a utility bill for a small property in Boyle Heights – a mainly Latinx neighborhood in Central LA, located just east of the Los Angeles River. What was interesting about that was that Mariela's name did not appear on any other official bill, including the city, local and district taxes.

That was a risky but fairly common tactic used by many Angelinos to obtain a 25 percent reduction on their local tax, due to single occupancy. The reason why that trick tended to work was because private utility providers and local government didn't exactly share information, but what really made Shannon believe that she was on the right track was the fact that Mariela had a son – Emiliano Esqueda – who in 2015 was thirteen years old.

Armed with that new information, Shannon was able to locate the school that Emiliano had attended during the years of 2015 and 2016 for his seventh and eighth grades – Hollenbeck Middle School on East 6th Street. After checking their records, she found out that Mariela Duron Esqueda wasn't the only name listed as a point of contact, should the school have ever needed to get in touch with Emiliano's parents. Mariela's partner's name was also listed as a guardian. That name was Shaun Daniels.

Bingo.

After 2016, it looked like Mariela and Shaun had parted ways. In 2021, Mariela relocated to San Jose, north California, but her son, Emiliano, who had just turned nineteen that year, had stayed in Los Angeles. And here came the biggest surprise of them all – in 2021, Emiliano Esqueda had joined the LAPD. He was still a first-grade police officer, assigned to the LAPD Southeast Community Police Station in Vermont Vista.

One final phone call and Shannon found out that that afternoon, Officer Emiliano Esqueda was policing the streets in Watts, South LA.

'What are the odds?' Garcia said, as he veered right to join South Alameda Street.

'Of the kid having joined the LAPD?' Hunter asked, rolling down the passenger window.

Garcia nodded.

Hunter sat back on his seat and observed the buildings flashing past until their car came to a halt at the traffic light on the junction of S. Alameda and 4th Street. Hunter's eyes then settled on the seven-story, boarded-up, white building to his right – the old 4th Street cold-storage facility building. Despite being boarded up, Hunter knew that it was far from unoccupied.

Just past the old cold-storage building was the beginning of the infamous Skid Row – a neighborhood of only 6.9 square miles, but with the largest, stable, homeless population in the whole USA. It was estimated that between ten and fifteen thousand homeless people lived in that single neighborhood at any one time.

Due to its size, the old cold-storage building had become a home, a leisure center, a drugs market . . . and a killing ground to many of the residents of one of the seediest and most dangerous neighborhoods in America.

Hunter couldn't even begin to imagine how many of those residents ended up on Skid Row as a consequence of having run away from home due to parental violence. Lives destroyed even before they had a proper chance to start.

'Joining the LAPD might've been Emiliano's way of staying off the streets, Carlos,' Hunter finally replied. 'And it could play to our advantage.'

Garcia chewed his bottom lip. 'Being with the LAPD might make him more inclined to help us out.'

'Let's hope it does,' Hunter agreed.

Minutes later, they finally entered the neighborhood of Watts.

The information they had was that Officer Esqueda was doing the regular street beat, together with a fresh-out-of-the-academy cadet, around Freedom Plaza – a medium-sized shopping mall just off the southern end of S. Alameda Street.

Garcia got to it and pulled into the mall's parking lot.

'I guess we're here.'

The mall was certainly larger than they had expected.

Hunter and Garcia exited the car and had begun making their way toward the main entrance when they spotted an LAPD officer leaning against a wall just outside Wingstop, smoking a cigarette.

Garcia checked his phone for the photo they had of Emiliano Esqueda. Since the photo had come directly from the LAPD Headquarters, it was pretty up to date.

'That doesn't look like him,' Garcia said, tilting his phone Hunter's way so that he could have a look at the photo.

Emiliano Esqueda was an average-looking man – black hair, round nose, dark-brown eyes and full lips under chubby cheeks. He seemed to have one of those non-memorable faces – a face that in a crowd would quickly blend in and fade into a nondescript blur.

'No, that's not him,' Hunter agreed. 'But he could be inside Wingstop getting some food.' He checked the time on the top left-hand corner of Garcia's cellphone – 12:47 p.m.

'Excuse me,' Garcia said, approaching the officer and quickly flashing his badge. 'Could you tell us where we could find Officer Esqueda? He's supposed to be working the beat around here.'

The officer, who looked young enough to still be in high school, dropped his cigarette and practically stood to attention.

'Umm ... yes, sir.' His eyes pinged from Garcia to Hunter. 'He should be at the other end of the mall, sir.' He indicated as he spoke. 'Just by Smart & Final, over there. I was just taking a quick cigarette break, but I'm all done.'

'Relax, kid,' Garcia chuckled. 'We're not the cigarette police. Enjoy your smoke, and thanks for your help.'

The two detectives made their way to where the officer had indicated. A minute later, they spotted Officer Esqueda just outside Smart & Final, helping a senior citizen load his car with groceries.

'To protect and to serve, I guess,' Garcia whispered before grabbing the officer's attention. 'Officer Esqueda?' he called. 'Officer Emiliano Esqueda?'

Emiliano placed the last of the grocery bags into the car's trunk before closing it and waving goodbye to the elderly gentleman. Only when the car had pulled away did he turn to face the two detectives.

'Who's asking?'

Hunter had been wrong. Emiliano Esqueda didn't actually have a non-memorable face. Up close, he had features that clearly stood out. His nose had a slight right bend to it ... his jaw was strong and squared ... and if you looked closely enough, you could see the shadow of a cleft chin, but the feature that really caught Hunter's attention was Emiliano's left profile. It did take some noticing, but it seemed that the outer edge of his left eye dipped in ever so slightly.

Hunter and Garcia showed him their credentials.

Emiliano frowned at their badges. 'Robbery Homicide UVC Unit? Are you sure you got the correct Officer Esqueda here?' His voice sounded like it was still making that transition from teenager to adult.

Garcia nodded. 'Is your mother's name Mariela Duron Esqueda?'

Emiliano's eyes widened at both detectives. 'Did something happen to my mom?'

'No,' Hunter was quick to try to calm him down. 'Nothing like that at all.'

'So why are homicide detectives asking me about my mother?'

'Just confirming that we're talking to the correct Officer Esqueda, like you asked,' Garcia said. 'That's all. We're not here about your mother.'

Emiliano let go of a breath so deep it was almost palpable. 'All right, so how can I he—'

They were interrupted by a piercing beeping sound coming from the front door to Smart & Final – someone had triggered their tag-alarm. As all three of them turned to see what the commotion was all about, they saw a tall man shoot out of the main door like a bullet train. The man wore white, high-top sneakers, blue jeans and a black hoodie jacket with the hoodie fully pulled over his head, hiding his face. He also had a dark-blue backpack strapped to his back.

A couple of seconds behind the man came two of Smart & Final's security officers.

'Stop!' the one in front called out. He already seemed to be out of breath. 'Stop!'

The second security officer was fitter than the first one, but not by much. It didn't take an expert to see that the cat-and-mouse chase was already lost. For every step the officers took, it seemed like the hooded man in front of them had taken three.

'Damn!' Emiliano said, with a subtle headshake. 'Not again.' A split second later, he turned on the balls of his feet and set off after the man in a mad sprint.

'Stop . . . LAPD.'

Hunter and Garcia glanced at each other.

'Seriously?' Garcia asked, as he watched Emiliano put some distance between them. 'A foot chase? In Watts?'

'To protect and to serve . . . I guess.' Hunter nodded at Garcia, looking down at his boots. They definitely weren't made for running.

'Fuck!' Garcia breathed out the word before both detectives took off in pursuit.

Thirty-Seven

The morning downpour had stopped hours earlier, but the intensity of it all was still reflected in the never-ending puddles and wet streets that could be seen just about everywhere in Downtown LA, and that included the parking lot to Freedom Plaza, in Watts.

Once the hooded man exited the front doors to Smart & Final, triggering its tag-alarms, he turned right and made a run for it. As he did, his high-tops smashed against a number of rainwater puddles that had formed just as the parking lot met the curb. Water splashed up like a kids' game, but that didn't slow the hooded man's pace. In fact, he seemed to be picking up speed – Aquaman style.

The two Smart & Final security guards were completely out of it even before the man had reached the end of the block, but Emiliano Esqueda was still pretty much in the game. And so were Hunter and Garcia. Despite their late start, all three of them had overtaken the two security guards within a dozen steps, but they still had some ground to make to get to their target.

The man cleared the last shop on the mall façade and veered hard right, taking East 99th Place, heading north.

More puddles.

More water splashing everywhere.

It was a short run to the end of E. 99th Place, which the man reached in no time. Once he got there, he took the next street along – East 97th – and quickly crossed it to the other side to reach an alleyway sandwiched between two shops.

Emiliano was a fast runner, there was no doubt about that, but with shoulder comms, a fully loaded police belt and officer shoes, he was making no significant gain on the hooded man. Hunter and Garcia on the other hand, despite the boots, were eating ground like two dragsters. They had just caught up with Emiliano when the man entered the alleyway.

'I'll try to cut him off,' Emiliano called out, swerving left and gesturing for Hunter and Garcia to carry on after the subject.

The two detectives crossed East 97th Street and proceeded into the alleyway. They were definitely gaining on the man.

'Stop,' Garcia shouted. 'LAPD.'

Instead of stopping, the man increased his pace.

'LAPD,' Garcia shouted again. 'Stop or I'll shoot.'

Hunter, who was just a couple of steps behind Garcia, knew that his partner wasn't about to shoot the man ahead of them, but those words tended to have the desired effect on most people. The man, however, didn't seem to care. Ahead of them, he splashed through another couple of puddles before swinging left, following the alleyway.

Hunter and Garcia were right on his tail.

The man finally emerged out of the alleyway and onto a residential road – Kalmia Street. Directly across the road from the alleyway exit was a communal basketball court and, since they were in LA, the home of the Lakers, no matter what time of day or night, someone would always be bouncing a ball and shooting hoops at a public blacktop court. That lunchtime, there were at least ten people on and around that court – four of them playing two-on-two, and the rest watching from the sidelines.

The man lost no time, quickly crossing the road to reach the gateless basketball court.

Using his right arm to point behind him, he shouted at the players and at everyone watching the game. 'Cops, cops.'

It was as if someone had pulled out a gun and fired a couple of rounds. The four kids in the two-on-two game took a quick peek in the direction that the hooded man had indicated. As they saw Hunter and Garcia emerge from the alleyway, they simply dropped the ball and ran.

The people on the sidelines also turned to look in the direction of the alleyway.

'Motherfucker!' one of them shouted, throwing the can of soda that he had in his hand Hunter and Garcia's way, before taking off like a rocket.

His move was immediately followed by a chorus of 'fuck' and 'shit'. Everyone scattered each-and-every way.

Despite the mad, ten-way split, Hunter and Garcia never lost sight of their target. They entered the court and crossed over to the other end in less than four seconds.

Ahead of them, the hooded man took a quick look behind him before getting to a small grassy park. He clearly saw that the two detectives were gaining on him fast because Hunter saw him practically spit out the word 'fuck'.

'LAPD,' Garcia tried again. 'Stop.'

The man, who showed no signs of slowing down, got to the end of the park and veered right, aiming for the entrance to another alleyway just ahead of him. Garcia, who was still a couple of paces in front of Hunter, was just about to catch up with the man when – BOOM.

Seemingly out of nowhere, Officer Emiliano Esqueda appeared on the man's left, flying through the air to tackle him down like a defensive guard smashing down on a quarterback. The man never saw Emiliano coming ... he never stood a chance.

Emiliano wasn't exactly a powerhouse when it came to his

physique, but he sure as hell had enough strength and momentum to send him and the man crashing to the ground.

As Emiliano collided with the subject, he grabbed hold
of him in an embrace that seemed watertight. They hit the
ground awkwardly, rolling as one because Emiliano simply
didn't let go.

The impact was hard enough to dislodge the man's backpack
clear off his back.

'Motherfucker,' Emiliano shouted, as they came to a halt just
inside the alleyway.

Behind them, Hunter and Garcia had also stopped running.
They were now bending forward, resting their hands on their
knees, trying to catch their breath.

Letting go of the man, Emiliano harshly rolled him over so that
his chest and face were pressed hard against the ground.

'You're under arrest, you motherfucker,' he said before grabbing both of the man's arms, twisting them behind his back, and
cuffing the man's wrists. As he did, he began reciting the Miranda
warning. 'You have the right to remain silent. Anything you say
can and will be used against you in a court of law . . .'

The man seemed to have already accepted his fate because he
didn't put up a fight.

While Emiliano recited the warning, Hunter collected the
man's backpack from the ground and unzipped it.

Garcia stood right next to him.

'OK,' Emiliano said, holding the man by the arms. 'Up . . . nice
and slowly.'

The man obliged.

Emiliano reached for the man's hoodie and slid it back from
his head, finally revealing his face.

It wasn't a man. It was a kid. Tall and skinny, but still just
a kid, who couldn't have been any older than eighteen. Black
hair, cut short, framing a round, childlike face where his cheeks

were covered in acne. He had a gap in his front teeth that could hold a toothpick. His eyes were as dark as his hair and, right then, the only thing in them seemed to be fear and sorrow . . . a lot of both. But his most distinct feature, at least at that time, was a black-and-blue left eye, where blood had recolored his sclera red, and a swollen bottom lip, showing a nasty cut at its right edge.

'I'm sorry, sir,' the kid said, tears welling up in his eyes. 'I'm really sorry.'

'Yeah, yeah, of course you are,' Emiliano said, reaching for his shoulder comms. 'Dispatch, this is PO 2842 in Watts. Respond.'

'Wait,' Hunter interrupted him. 'Don't radio it in.'

'What?'

'Don't radio it in yet.'

Both Emiliano and the kid looked back at Hunter in surprise.

'And why not?' Emiliano asked.

Hunter handed him the kid's backpack.

The radio on Emiliano's shoulder cracked once before a female voice came through.

'PO 2842, go ahead.'

Emiliano looked inside the bag before his eyes ping-ponged between Hunter and Garcia for a second. He reached for his comms.

'Dispatch, please stand by. I might need a 10-16 in response to a 484. Just checking now.'

'Ten-four, 2842. Standing by.'

Emiliano checked the bag again. 'Food?' he asked the kid. 'You were stealing food?'

The kid looked down at the floor, shame covering him like an ill-fitting coat. He was visibly shivering . . . and it wasn't from cold.

'And medicine,' Garcia said, nodding at the backpack.

Emiliano rummaged through it again. There was no alcohol, no money, no illegal drugs, no weapons . . . just food, water, two boxes of Band-Aids and a box of Ibuprofen. All of it from Smart & Final.

Emiliano shook his head at the detectives before reaching for his shoulder comms again.

'Dispatch, this is PO 2842 in Watts. Please disregard last comms. False alarm.'

'Ten-four, 2842.'

He turned to address the kid again. 'When was the last time you ate?'

The kid kept his eyes on the ground. 'Two days ago, sir.'

'What's your name, kid?' Garcia asked.

'Craig, sir,' the kid replied. 'Craig Thompson.'

Hunter picked up a slight drawl as the kid pronounced his last name.

'Where in Texas are you from, Craig?' he asked.

'Lubbock, sir. Northwest Texas.'

'And when did you get to LA?'

'Two days ago, sir.' Craig's eyes finally lifted from the ground to look at the three police officers around him. He was clearly struggling to hold back tears.

'How old are you, Craig?' Garcia, this time.

'I'm seventeen, sir.'

'Do you have any ID on you?' Emiliano asked.

Craig shook his head. 'I was robbed, sir. I'd been in this city for ... an hour, maybe two, and I got jumped. They took everything I had – my bag with all my clothes, my wallet, my phone ... everything.'

Garcia bobbed his head. 'Welcome to LA.'

'You've got nothing that can confirm that you are who you say you are?' Emiliano pushed.

Craig began shaking his head again, but paused mid-shake and nodded at his backpack. 'Umm ... on the outside pocket. My student card should still be there, sir.'

Emiliano checked the pocket and found the student card. The boy hadn't lied about anything. He showed the card to Hunter and Garcia – Coronado High School, Lubbock, Texas.

'Where are you staying, Craig?' Garcia asked.

Craig's reply was to look down at the ground again.

'Are your parents back in Lubbock?' Hunter asked.

'My mother is, sir, with her ... live-in boyfriend. My father died when I was nine, but I'm not going back to that house, sir. I'm not going back to Lubbock. I'd rather go to jail here. If you take me back, I'll just run away again.'

Hunter picked up more than just anger in Craig's words. He picked up fear as well.

'The beating to your face,' he asked. 'You didn't get that when you got jumped, did you?'

Craig stayed quiet.

'Your mother's partner?' Hunter pushed.

Not a word.

'Is that why you left Lubbock? To get away from him?'

'I just want a new life, sir. Any life but that one. I just can't take it anymore.'

Hunter's gaze moved to Emiliano. The officer seemed to be looking back at Craig, but his stare was distant, lost in a memory somewhere.

'Does your mother know about the beatings?' Hunter asked.

The boy nodded slowly, averting everyone's eyes. 'She doesn't really care.' His voice croaked.

'This isn't exactly the best way to start a new life, Craig,' Garcia said, once again nodding at the backpack. 'Have you ever been to prison?'

'No, sir. I've never been in trouble with the law. I'm not a thief, sir. I just ...' Tears began rolling down Craig's cheeks.

Hunter and Emiliano exchanged an understanding look.

'The detective is right,' Emiliano said, nodding at Garcia. 'If you want to start a new life in a different city, especially one like LA, this ain't it, Craig. Just for this . . .' He lifted the backpack. '. . . you could get six months in jail and a thousand-dollar fine. Do you have a thousand dollars?'

Craig shook his head.

'Do you want to spend your first six months in LA in hell? Because that's exactly how jail will seem to you, Craig – like absolute hell.'

Another headshake. 'I am sorry, sir. I was just hungry. And my face really hurts.' Craig leaned back against the wall in the alleyway, a little out of balance. His legs looked like they were about to give up under him. Clearly the crazy dash around the streets of Watts after two days without food had taken its toll on the boy.

'Are you all right?' Garcia asked.

'Yes, sir.' He took a deep breath and a moment. 'Just . . . a little dizzy. That's all.'

'OK.' Hunter took over, as he reached for the notebook in his pocket and began scribbling something down. 'So this is what we're going to do, Craig – we're going to go back to Smart & Final, you're going to pay for your groceries and I'm going to give you a list of addresses, OK?'

'I'm sorry, sir, but I can't pay for those groceries. I really don't have any money. Can I just give them back, instead? None of it's been opened. I'm sorry I took them.'

'I'll get these for you today,' Hunter said, earning him an intrigued look from Officer Emiliano and a tearful one from Craig. 'You do look like you could do with some food . . . and a shower . . . and some rest.' He finished scribbling down on his pad and tore off the page before giving Emiliano a nod.

The officer took a breath, nodded back and used his keys to free Craig's hands.

Hunter handed him the note. 'The first two addresses are soup kitchens. Neither of them are too far from here, and they can both provide you with at least one hot meal a day. The third address is a shelter that caters specifically for kids who have run away from violent and abusive households. They're good people there . . . friendly, caring . . . you'll see. The last address is a counseling service. You can talk to them about anything you like, but more importantly, they can help you find a job . . . get you started, you know?'

Craig looked back at Hunter with glassy eyes.

'We can drop you at the shelter on our way back,' Hunter offered. 'You can have a shower and they'll give you a bed to sleep in at night. At least for a few days. And the in-house nurse can have a look at your face, especially that eye.'

The law in the USA stipulated that parents were legally responsible for children in their care until the age of eighteen. The law also specified that a teenager had the right to leave home, without their parents' permission, at the age of sixteen. Since Craig was seventeen years old, the LAPD wasn't obliged by law to inform his parents of his whereabouts.

Craig went speechless for a moment. 'Thank you, sir,' he finally said back, wiping the tears from his face. 'Thank you so very much.'

Hunter simply nodded back, hoping that Craig Thompson wouldn't one day end up at the old cold-storage facility building on 4th Street.

Thirty-Eight

Less than fifteen minutes later, back at Freedom Plaza, Hunter and Garcia finally got to sit down with Officer Emiliano Esqueda.

Craig Thompson was sitting inside the same coffee shop, a couple of tables to their right, taking such large bites of the sandwich Hunter had bought him, he was risking snapping one of his fingers off.

'That was kind . . . what you did.' Emiliano addressed Hunter, nodding in Craig's direction. 'Most detectives I know are so sick and tired of excuses that they wouldn't hesitate in booking that kid in. "Save it for the judge," they'd say, and that would be it.'

'We all need a little help every now and then,' Hunter said.

Emiliano chuckled. 'I somehow get the impression that there's a little more to it than that.' He paused, as if considering his next words. 'Did you have problems when you were younger as well?'

Hunter noticed the way that Emiliano's eyes narrowed as he said the words 'as well'. He didn't seem to mean them as – 'Did you have problems when you were younger, just like Craig did?' He seemed to mean them as – 'Did you have problems when you were younger, just like I did?'

'Families can be difficult to deal with,' Hunter said, keeping his reply as general as possible. 'And unfortunately, we can't exactly choose our parents.'

Another chuckle from the officer. 'Yeah, you can say that

again.' He sipped his coffee and allowed his gaze to move over to Craig for a split second. 'Years ago, I found myself in a pretty similar situation. My mother and I moved in with her new boyfriend who . . .' He shook his head. 'Turned out to be a complete asshole.'

'Violent?' Hunter asked.

Emiliano looked away for a beat. 'Yeah, I guess you could say that.' Reflexively, his left hand moved up to his face and his index finger lightly brushed against the outer edge of his left eye, rubbing the gentle dip that Hunter had noticed earlier. It had been a subtle movement, one that Emiliano probably didn't even notice doing, but Hunter did. Some psychiatrists call it a telltale reflex . . . a subconscious giveaway – when a subject would unconsciously somehow drive attention to a part of the body associated with a memory, distressing or not.

Garcia seemed to have noticed it as well.

'Thankfully,' Emiliano continued, 'my mother was only with him for a couple of years.' His gaze became distant again – his mind clearly tapping into another undesirable memory for a quick second before he snapped out of it. 'Anyway.' He sat back on his chair. 'How about we jump back to the very beginning here.' His head jerked in Craig's direction. 'Before all this started. Why do detectives from the UVC Unit want to talk to me?'

'This boyfriend of your mother's,' Hunter questioned. 'The violent one . . . was his name Shaun Daniels?'

The mention of that name alone seemed to be enough to make Emiliano's body go rigid. His surprised eyes moved from Hunter, to Garcia, then back to Hunter. 'What is this? How do you know that?' He paused, his mind clearly racing through thoughts. 'Did he go after my mother again? After all these years? Is that why you mentioned her earlier today?'

'No, no . . . relax.' Garcia tried to calm him down again. 'Like I said before – this has absolutely nothing to do with your mother.' He sneaked a glance at Hunter. 'But it does have to do with Shaun Daniels.'

Emiliano half-opened his mouth, as if he was about to say something, but no words came out. His eyes kept on bouncing between both detectives.

'Shaun Daniels is dead,' Garcia finally revealed.

The half-opened mouth slowly closed.

The bouncing stare became a skeptical one.

'When?'

'Almost a month ago,' Garcia replied. 'His body was found on June 16th.'

Emiliano exhaled a heavy breath. 'I'll be goddamned.' The skeptical stare morphed again, this time into a thoughtful one. 'And the fact that two detectives from the LAPD Ultra Violent Crimes Unit are telling me this, clearly means three things. One – his death wasn't accidental. Two – he probably died in some horrific and quite violent way. And three – I made the POI list, right?'

Garcia gave him a sideways nod. 'You've got two out of three there.'

A half-frown from Emiliano.

'You're not a person-of-interest in the investigation,' Hunter informed him.

'Oh-kay, so why on earth are you telling me this?' He lifted both hands at the two detectives. 'Because I don't want to sound insensitive here, but seriously, I couldn't give a fuck about that asshole. And I'm sure that he deserved everything he got.'

'We're telling you this because we need your help,' Hunter clarified.

'My help?' Emiliano laughed. 'How?'

'Information.'

The bouncing stare came back. 'Information? Are you two kidding? Shaun Daniels was only with my mother for two years and that was what . . . eight, nine years ago? I haven't seen him since. And even during those two awful years, I would've moved heaven and earth to avoid that man. We didn't have a relationship. I hated the fucker.'

'We understand that,' Hunter said.

'Do you?' Emiliano countered. 'Because it really doesn't seem like you do.' He sat forward on his chair. 'Look, I knew nothing about that man back then and I know even less now. I didn't even know if he was still in LA, or not. How do you expect me to help you? I have no information on him, whatsoever.'

'The info we need . . .' Garcia, this time. '. . . isn't exactly about him . . . it's about you.'

'Me? I thought you said I wasn't a POI.'

'You're not.' Garcia took a breathing pause. 'What we really need to know is – what sort of violence did Shaun Daniels use against you and your mother?'

Emiliano looked at Hunter and Garcia as if he hadn't understood the question. 'What sort of violence? The violent kind. What other sort is there?'

'Sorry.' Garcia accepted the criticism, lifting his hands in surrender. 'Bad phrasing on my part. Let me be a little more specific and all you've got to do is say "yes" or "no", OK?'

Emiliano still looked like he was having trouble understanding exactly what to do, but Garcia knew that he would get it.

'Did Shaun Daniels ever use enough violence against either you or your mother to . . . maybe break a bone?'

The officer seemed to chew on that question for a couple of seconds. 'Yes,' he finally confirmed, his tone acquiring a somewhat angry edge to it. 'More than once.' He showed the two detectives his left hand. 'He broke two of my fingers when he slammed a door on my hand for no reason. He fractured one of my mom's ribs with a single punch because she refused to get him a beer from the fridge. And he fractured my left eye socket with an elbow slam.' He angled his head so that both detectives could see the dip in the outer edge of his left eye. 'The man was a fucking animal.'

Neither Hunter nor Garcia needed to note that down. They could both remember that broken fingers and fractured ribs were some of the injuries that Shaun Daniels had suffered during his torture phase, together with a fractured left eye orbit.

'And you've always lived here in LA?' Hunter asked.

'That's right. We used to live in Boyle Heights. After my mom finally got away from that monster, we stayed in BH for another year – different apartment, though – before moving to Gardena. My mom now lives in San Jose with her new partner, but this guy is different – kind, respectful . . . he's nothing like Shaun was.'

'I'm glad to hear that,' Hunter commented, and paused, knowing that his next question would sound strange, but it would also be the ultimate confirmation.

'And can you remember if he ever did anything that resulted in either you or your mother being cold? I mean . . . too cold?'

Emiliano's eyes widened at Hunter, as he held his breath for a confused moment. 'How could you possibly know something like that? Not even my mother knows about that night.'

And there it was – a confirmation even without a proper reply. Hunter was just about to thank Emiliano and end their conversation right there and then, but curiosity got the better of Garcia.

'What did he do?' he asked. 'I mean – this is LA. Even on a bad winter night, temperatures don't even get as low as forty degrees.'

Emiliano looked away for a beat. When he looked back at the two detectives, the focus in his eyes was undeniable – like a heavyweight champ's during a face-off just before the fight.

'For some extra cash,' he explained, 'two to three nights a week, Shaun drove a van for a food delivery company . . . a refrigerated van. One night, something happened. His shift got canceled, or something . . . I can't remember, but he came back home a lot earlier than he was supposed to. Mom was working at the diner that night, which so happened to be a very warm night. I thought that I'd be home alone, so me and a friend grabbed a couple of beers from the fridge and we're just chilling in the living room, smoking some pot, when Shaun came in through the door. He was already angry because he didn't get his night's pay. When he saw that we had grabbed a couple of his beers, he went ballistic. My friend bailed and I got taken for a ride in the back of the refrigerated van.'

'That's fucked up right there,' Garcia commented.

'That wasn't the end of it,' Emiliano continued, crossing his arms in front of his chest – another telltale reflex. 'I had no idea how long I'd been in the back of the van for – forty minutes, an hour ... I don't know – but I was fucking freezing. The van finally came to a stop and I thought that that was it. We were back home – punishment over, you know? But I should've known better.' He took a breathing pause. The focus in his eyes stayed exactly where it was. 'The back door to the van swung open and there he was – asshole Shaun – with a fucking water hose.'

This time, even Hunter cringed.

Emiliano shook his head. 'I got drenched from head to toe. Shaun slammed the door shut and we took off again. By the time we got back home, I could barely move. I couldn't feel my fingers. I couldn't feel my toes. My body was just beginning to show signs of hypothermia. I was ill for over a month after that – pneumonia.' He shrugged and the focus finally vanished from his eyes. 'How I didn't die that night, or in the days that followed, I have no idea. He told me that if I ever told my mother about that night, the consequences would be severe ... for both of us.'

'Did you ever tell anyone?' Garcia asked.

Emiliano's headshake was almost imperceptible. 'No one. Not even Lexy.'

'Lexy?'

'My friend who was drinking beer with me in the living room

when Shaun got home.' Emiliano shook the memory away with a head movement. 'So yes, Detectives, like I've said, that asshole deserved whatever he got. And I really hope that it was something nasty.'

Thirty-Nine

Once they left Watts, Hunter and Garcia dropped Craig off at the My Club Youth Center in Vermont – a charity shelter that offered help to abandoned children and runaway kids from abusive homes. The shelter was run by people who had suffered abuse themselves when young ... people who truly understood what Craig was going through.

Back in the car, Garcia sat still for a moment.

'I really hope that kid manages to make a life for himself in this city. He seems like a good kid.'

'He does,' Hunter agreed, his eyes back on the large, rectangular white building that was the youth center.

He hoped for the same, but he and Garcia both knew the harsh reality of Los Angeles – to a few, that city would truly become paradise on earth, but to so many who descended on the City of Light, full of hopes and dreams, searching for a new start, the City of Angels would turn out to be the exact opposite – the City of Broken Dreams, full of lost and desperate souls ... the place where innocence came to die and demons were born.

'So what's our next step?' Garcia asked, switching on the engine. 'Because the theory has definitely proved right, Robert – our killer *is* hunting down parents who were violent toward their kids and paying them back in kind and with dividends, like the captain put it, which can only mean that the killer himself suffered abuse in the form of excessive violence at the hands of his own parents, right?'

Hunter agreed with a nod. 'Enough to completely fracture his mind and transform him from an abused kid to a murderer, waging his own crusade on other parents.'

'So if his parents' violence is what broke him,' Garcia speculated. 'If that is really what put him on this crazy revenge path, then chances are that they were also his very first victims, right? This guy has probably murdered his own mother and father.'

Another firm nod from Hunter. 'He probably has. And that was the start of it all. That was the day that his mind fractured for good.' He lifted two fingers at Garcia. 'In theory, we get two kinds of homicidal fractured minds derived from abuse – explosive and composed. Explosive would be identical to what "temporary insanity" is, except it's not temporary.'

'So the person loses it and lashes out in a fit of rage,' Garcia said.

'In a fit of uncontrollable rage,' Hunter corrected him. 'The lashing out is usually exceptionally violent and very messy, and it happens suddenly – hence the term "explosive". The subject hits back and he won't stop hitting until all the bottled-up rage inside him has eased up. That's the fracture, right there, and it has the potential to completely erase the line between right and wrong from the subject's conscious mind.'

'So I'm assuming that what you called a composed, homicidal, fractured mind is the "hit back", but served cold.'

'Exactly,' Hunter confirmed. 'The mind fractures in the same way, the line between right and wrong is also blurred, but there's no explosion of rage. Instead, the revenge attack is planned out and the risks are calculated. These tend to be just as violent, but a lot tidier. And it usually involves torture. They are just as dangerous as the explosive types, but a hell of a lot harder to catch.'

'And of course,' Garcia nodded, 'that's the type that we're after. Why wouldn't it be?'

Forty

In Watts, before Hunter and Garcia parted ways with Officer Emiliano Esqueda, Hunter had asked him one last question, just to tie up a possible loose end. He asked him if he knew if Shaun Daniels had sought help for his drinking and/or anger problems when he was still together with Emiliano's mother. The officer's reply had been a resounding 'no chance'. He was very sure of it.

'So what's our next move, Robert?' Garcia asked, as they finally drove away from the youth center. 'Because I'm a little stuck. Our best theory here ... actually, our only theory here, is that our victims have sought help in the form of therapy, right? That's how the details of the physical violence they inflicted on their kids got revealed.'

Hunter looked to be in full thinking mode.

'The problem is,' Garcia continued, 'even if our theory is correct, it's not like we can just go and have a chat with every therapist and anger-management specialist in this city.' He laughed as he veered left to take South Alameda Street. 'We're talking about LA here, arguably the most neurotic city on the planet, where having therapy is as common as having a cup of coffee. The number of therapists, counselors, anger-management specialists, voodoo doctors ... whatever, in LA, must be in the hundreds, if not thousands.'

'The exercise would be pointless, anyway,' Hunter said. 'All of those professions have a code of conduct. None of them would disclose the names of their clients without a warrant, which we wouldn't be able to get. Plus, the killer could be the therapist, the psychologist, the counselor . . . whoever. In that case, if we turn up at their offices asking questions, all we'll do is warn the killer that we're on his trail.'

All Garcia could do was laugh. 'So basically, we're cooked, right? Case over.' He shrugged. 'We have no way of knowing if either of our victims did, in fact, talk to somebody about the violence they inflicted upon their kids. And even if we knew for sure that they had talked to someone, we then have no way of finding out who they actually talked to because there are no records.'

'Maybe there are,' Hunter came back.

Garcia's question was asked silently, with an odd eyebrow movement.

'You're right,' Hunter clarified. 'The number of therapists in LA must be in the hundreds, if not thousands, and the one thing that they all have in common is – they all charge for their time. What's the one thing that we found in both victims' houses?'

Garcia thought about it for just a heartbeat.

'Receipts.' A ghost of a smile graced his lips. 'Loads of them.'

Hunter smiled back. 'Both of our victims seem to have been pretty good in documenting their expenditures.'

'We need to go through them all again,' Garcia said. 'Including credit card records, but this time, we know what we're looking for.'

Hunter nodded. 'That's step one.'

Garcia frowned. 'Is there another step?'

'Therapy,' Hunter explained, 'of any kind . . . isn't exactly cheap, Carlos, and neither of our victims were exactly rich. On the contrary. From what I remember, Shaun Daniels was in and out of the red zone more often than we have lunch. And even if they'd found a therapist who charged a lot less than others, we'd still be talking about several sessions here, because no help is achieved with a single session. It's an escalation of trust, which needs to be built slowly. Cheap or not, those sessions add up.'

Garcia took in a deep, frustrated breath. 'OK. Any ideas?'

Hunter smiled. 'I have one.'

Forty-One

Once they got back to the UVC Unit's office, Hunter and Garcia immediately began going over the multitude of receipts they had found at both victims' apartments. Despite coming to the conclusion that paying for therapy sessions seemed to be a little out of reach for Shaun Daniels and Terry Wilford, they just didn't want to leave any stone unturned, but as far as they were concerned, the most important task was now with their Research team.

And that task was a very simple one – support groups.

Garcia hadn't exaggerated – Los Angeles was arguably the most neurotic city on the planet. Other than the City of Angels, LA was also known around the world as 'The Home to A-list Celebrities' – from TV and movie stars, to world-famous singers and musicians … from film directors and producers, to top sports personalities. There was no escaping the glitz and glam that surrounded that city, and with every mega-stardom came self-doubt, paranoia, neurosis and, of course, depression. Around the neighborhoods of Hollywood and Beverly Hills alone, therapists for the stars seemed to grow on trees. The problem was that any type of mental health issue didn't exclusively affect the rich and famous, but most of Los Angeles lived from paycheck to paycheck, barely able to put anything aside for a rainy day. Paying for a therapist, of any kind, was a dream too far for most Angelinos to reach. For that reason, free support groups, set up to try to help citizens battling against some of the most concerning mental health issues, could be found spread around the city and its outskirts.

Hunter was certain that in LA there wouldn't be a shortage of free support groups catering for parents who knew they had an anger or drinking problem . . . parents who were, or had been, violent toward their kids – and those groups were exactly what Hunter had asked the Research team to search for.

It was just past five in the afternoon when Garcia pushed himself back from his desk and rubbed his face with both hands.

'Damn, I need a googly-eyes break.' He blinked heavily a couple of times. 'Meaning – I'm getting googly eyes here from all these receipts. Have you come up with anything yet?'

Hunter also pushed himself away from his desk for a moment. Since they got back, he'd been going over every single receipt and invoice that they had found inside Shaun Daniels's apartment, totaling four and a half years. Garcia had been checking the ones from Terry Wilford's apartment – almost five years' worth of loose pieces of paper.

'Nothing that made me worry,' Hunter replied. 'A few unidentified receipts, but the amounts aren't large enough for a bulk therapy payment, and they don't repeat themselves, which they would do if he was paying for subsequent, individual sessions. You?'

'Pretty much the same.' Garcia got up to refill his coffee cup. 'Shaun Daniels was pretty tight with his budget. His therapy, if any, seemed to be booze and cigarettes.'

'Well, I still got a fair amount to go here.' Hunter nodded at the pile on his desk. 'But I could also do with a break.'

'Coffee?' Garcia offered.

'Please.' Hunter handed him his mug.

As Garcia was filling up both cups, the phone on Hunter's desk rang. Internal call. Research team.

Hunter took the call. 'Shannon, what have you found?'

'*Quite a bit.*'

Forty-Two

Hunter nodded at Garcia and immediately switched the call to speakerphone.

Shannon didn't miss a beat. *'I'm sending you an email right now with all the free and small-donations support groups we managed to find in LA. The number is actually astounding, Robert, and they cater for just about everything. Different groups also offer different types of therapies, as you will see. Not surprisingly, there's a large number of them that target excessive drinking and substance abuse – this is LA, after all. The list I'm sending you has been filtered down. It contains only the groups that deal specifically with the subjects you mentioned – alcohol and substance abuse, anger management, parenting and domestic violence. The domestic violence ones are divided into two types – abusive and abused – for people who are either perpetrating the violence, or at the receiving end it. Based on what you told me, I have flagged the "abusive" category as the most relevant. All of them meet once a week – evening time.'*

'Great job, Shannon. Thank you for this.'

'My pleasure. Just let me know if you need anything else.'

'Will do.'

Hunter disconnected and he and Garcia went back to their computers. Even though Shannon had filtered the list down to four main categories, the list contained 101 support groups. Of those, twenty-six dealt exclusively with anger management, and twenty-five with domestic violence – eleven catering to help perpetrators of the violence and fourteen catering to help those at the receiving end of it.

'Wow,' Garcia said, as he scanned the list. 'Shannon wasn't joking when she said that the number of groups was astounding, was she?'

'I guess not,' Hunter replied, already noting a few things down.

Garcia took a minute, reading the descriptions of some of the groups. 'So how do you want to go about this, Robert? I mean, since the killer could be anyone in the group, including the person who runs it, we can't just turn up and ask people if Terry Wilford or Shaun Daniels have ever taken part in any of their sessions. If we alert the killer that we're on his trail, he'll vanish.'

Hunter was still taking notes, but he gave Garcia a single nod.

'So what do you suggest we do?'

Hunter finally stopped writing and angled his body to the right, so that he could see his partner past his computer screen. 'Put ourselves in the killer's shoes.' He checked his notes for a heartbeat. 'If you were the killer, looking for victims – parents who are, or had been, violent toward their kids – and you decided that the best way to find them would be through support groups, how would you go about doing that from the very beginning?'

Garcia gave it a moment's thought before shrugging. 'I'd say I'd have two options. One – if I'm intelligent and patient enough, and we both know that our killer is – I'd get a certificate on anger management, counseling, therapy . . . whatever I needed to be able to *run* a group. That way I'd be sitting in on every session, meet every person who joins the group, and listen to all the stories they have to tell. That's how groups work, isn't it? People take turns telling the group their stories – things they've done . . . things they regret having done, and so on?'

'The dynamics might differ from group to group,' Hunter explained. 'But yes, that's the main gist of how group therapy works. And that's a good option. What's option two?'

Garcia tilted his head to one side. 'If I weren't running the group, then I'd simply join one and observe. Same principle as option one. I'm just not the leader.' He paused, considering something for a couple of beats. 'And if I'm being logical, option two would be a better call.'

Hunter didn't need to ask why. Putting himself in the killer's shoes for an instant, he would've also picked option two – just joining a group instead of running it – that way, he wouldn't need to stick with the same group all the time. He could jump around from group to group, maximizing his choices for a new victim and minimizing his exposure to the same group of eyes.

'OK,' Hunter agreed once again. 'But with both options, how would you choose your victim? Let's say that there are seven members in the group, including you, and for now let's say that you're running the group – so you have six possible choices for a victim. How would you pick? Or would you just take out everyone in the group over a period of time?'

'That would probably be a bad idea,' Garcia replied. 'Taking out every member of the group would certainly raise suspicions.'

'Remember that you're disguising the deaths as accidental, or suicide,' Hunter reminded him. 'People wouldn't actually know that they were being murdered.'

'Even so,' Garcia shook his head. 'If six members of the same support group all die from some sort of accident and/or suicide in the space of, let's say, a year, I don't think that that would go unnoticed, Robert. Unless I do it over several long years.'

'It is very possible,' Hunter conceded. 'Like you've said, our killer seems to be very patient, but let's forget about the timeframe for now and let me bring you back to the question of "choosing". Let's say you decide to take out only two members of the group.

How would you choose them out of the six? What would your criteria be?'

Garcia sipped his coffee while he thought about it. 'I guess I'd listen to their stories and I'd probably pick the two people who I thought had been the most violent toward their kids.'

'So your criteria would be "level of violence"?'

Garcia paused for a millisecond. 'For me, "level of violence" would definitely play a big part in picking my victims.'

'Would anything else play a part?'

Garcia nodded. 'Knowing what we already know, I'd say yes – risk management.'

'The "loner" factor, right?'

'For sure,' Garcia agreed. 'I don't think that it's a coincidence that the two victims we've discovered so far were both the quiet type, Robert – no partners, lived alone, very few friends, didn't go out much, didn't socialize with the neighbors, and all that. Shaun Daniels wasn't even reported as missing because no one knew . . . no one cared. So yes, I think that our killer minimizes his risk by factoring in the "loner" aspect.'

Hunter pinched his bottom lip, but said nothing.

'How would you pick?' Garcia queried.

'If I were being rational, probably in that exact same way – violent factor followed by the "loner" aspect.'

'*If* you were being rational? Why wouldn't you be?'

'Like you pointed out,' Hunter explained, 'our killer is clearly an intelligent person. Disguising murders as accidental deaths and/or suicide isn't an easy task and, as we know, our killer doesn't use the same method every time. That takes creativity and knowledge. But don't forget that he's also a broken person. The reason why he kills isn't because he's a born psychopath and his urge is out of control. It's because his mind has fractured as a consequence of the physical abuse he suffered when young. Fractured minds aren't always rational, Carlos.'

'So what other ways could he choose?' Garcia asked.

'There's no telling with a person who is that broken,' Hunter clarified. 'It could be something that makes sense only to him . . . something that only he sees.'

'Like what?' Garcia pushed.

'Anything. For example, one of the group members could physically remind the killer of the person who used to beat him up when he was young – father, mother, uncle, stepfather . . . whoever. Or maybe one of the stories he heard from a group member, despite not being the most violent, is similar to the kind of abuse our killer used to suffer.' Hunter shrugged. 'A member of the group could just dress like the person who used to perpetrate the abuse, or talk like them, or smell like them . . . his criteria is his own. The trigger can be something that only he understands and if that trigger is a direct reminder of the abuse he suffered, it will take precedence over everything else.'

'I didn't think of that, but regardless of what the trigger is, we both agree that our killer needs to be in the group, right? Sitting in on sessions to be able to pick his victims. There's no other way?'

'Absolu . . .' Hunter paused mid-word, his attention back on the list of support groups on his computer screen. Shannon and her team had done a great job in condensing the information on that list. It contained the name of the support group, the type of therapy or support it offered, a one-line explanation of its main mission, and the name of the person running it. It had been the name field that had caught Hunter's eyes.

'Shit!' Hunter whispered, but not quiet enough for it not to reach his partner's ears.

'What?' Garcia asked.

Hunter breathed out, leaned forward, rested his elbows on his desk and used the tips of his fingers to massage his temples.

'Maybe there's another way to pick the victims, Carlos. A way in which our killer doesn't even take part in the groups.'

'What? How?'

Hunter got to his feet. 'Let me ask you something first. Do you think that our killer could be a woman?'

Forty-Three

Despite Garcia having heard what Hunter had just asked, he angled his body around his computer screen to look back at his partner. 'What?'

'Do you think that our killer could—' Hunter began, but Garcia cut him short.

'I heard what you said, Robert. My "what" was purely meant as an expression of surprise.'

Hunter nodded, but still repeated the question. 'So do you think that our killer could be a woman?'

'No, I don't think so. This killer is definitely physically too strong, plus, according to Randy Douglas, the person he saw on the 7th Street Bridge, as Terry Wilford dropped to the ground, was male, driving a RAM truck, remember?'

Hunter nodded.

'Why?' Garcia asked. 'Do you think the killer could be a woman?'

Instead of replying, Hunter lifted a hand at Garcia and followed it up with a second question. He sounded angry with himself. 'How about revisiting a possibility that we've mentioned before, but for some stupid reason never went back to?'

'Which possibility are you talking about, Robert?'

'The possibility that this killer is working with someone else.'

Garcia hesitated for a heartbeat. 'And that someone else is a woman?'

Hunter nodded.

Garcia paused for an extra moment and his eyes skipped to the photos on the board.

Hunter waited.

Garcia caught up with the thought. 'Are you thinking something like brother and sister, maybe?'

Hunter's eyebrows arched at his partner. 'What if our killer wasn't an only child? Or what if we're talking about a foster kid, or something similar here? What if our killer didn't grow up alone in an abusive household?'

Garcia puffed out a shallow breath. 'You mean – he wasn't the only one suffering at the hands of his parents, or foster parents, or step-parents ... or whatever.'

'Not impossible,' Hunter commented.

'Then, *together*,' Garcia continued, 'brother and sister decided that they'd had enough and they finally hit back. Like the Menéndez brothers. Two minds fracture at the same time.'

Hunter nodded slowly.

'Fuck,' Garcia said, his attention moving back to the board. 'Give me a moment to try to process all this.'

'The reason I asked,' Hunter offered, 'is because out of the twenty-five support groups targeting domestic violence exclusively, sixteen of them are run by female therapists, or leaders ... and so are a large number of all the other ones.'

Garcia's eyes snapped back to the list on his computer screen.

'I did notice that,' Garcia replied. 'But I hadn't factored in the possibility of a second person, which now, thinking about it, is a very real one.'

Hunter checked his notes again.

'It would be an almost perfect way to divert suspicion, don't you think?' Garcia asked. 'The female partner of the "duo" runs the group, listening to their stories and collecting all the info on the members. When they've decided who to take ... who the new victim will be ... the male partner takes center stage.' He shrugged. 'If they're smart, all she has to do is be seen at some very public place on the night that the victim is abducted and job done – no way anyone can point a finger at her because she'll have a buffet of alibis.'

'Or ...' Hunter began, approaching the only window in their office. The sun was just starting to dip behind the horizon. 'Another way to minimize the risk of being noticed by other group members is – they could simply alternate attending the group sessions.'

'They could,' Garcia agreed.

'It's a good plan,' Hunter admitted.

'No, it's a *great* plan,' Garcia corrected him. 'But it's also very Hollywood blockbuster-like, isn't it?' He used his thumbs and index fingers on both hands to create two L-shapes in front of him, mimicking a movie screen. 'Brother and sister abused for years when kids until one day they finally crack and lash out, murdering their own parents in some grotesque way, thus starting their own revenge crusade on other abusive parents.' He put his hands down. 'It would make a great movie, Robert, but do you think something like that could be real?'

'Real life is much weirder than fiction, Carlos, you know that. But I don't know, I guess I was just ...'

'Apophenia?' Garcia said with a smile.

Hunter smiled back, surprised that Garcia had remembered the word. 'Always.'

Garcia exhaled as if they'd just come across another dead end. 'Single or double killer, Robert, sister or brother ... our problem is still the same. Without being able to ask anyone, how do we find out if Shaun Daniels and Terry Wilford did indeed take part in a support group, and if so, which ones?' He sat back on his chair. 'I understand that the idea here would be for the two of us to join a support group, or groups, pretending that we're abusive fathers ourselves, who are seeking help. Then we observe, right? We sit in on the sessions and we listen to the stories from other members, just like the killer must be doing, but how do we pick him out? That's problem one. Problem two is – without being able to ask anyone . . . and with the groups meeting only once a week, we could be doing this for months, Robert, years even, before we get any sort of breakthrough . . . if we do.'

Outside their office window, down on the street below, Hunter watched a young mother cross the road pushing a two-baby stroller. His eyes stayed on the two babies for a quick moment before he turned and looked back at Garcia.

'Maybe there's a way,' he said, quickly walking back to his desk.

'Maybe there's a way for what?'

'Maybe there's a way that we can ask the people who are running the groups if Shaun Daniels and/or Terry Wilford have ever taken part in a session.'

'Umm . . .' Garcia shook his head, as if waking up from a dream. 'How? We've already been through this. Bad idea, in case the killer, or an accomplice, is running the group.'

Hunter couldn't believe he hadn't thought of this earlier. 'Our Research team are experts in backtracking a person's life, remember?' he reminded Garcia, nodding at the list on his computer screen. 'And we have the names of every group leader – therapist or not.'

Garcia's gaze skirted to Hunter, darted away, darted back. 'We can ask them to backtrack all group leaders – male and female – starting with the domestic violence groups.'

Hunter nodded. 'In theory, Research should be able to backtrack them all the way to their childhood, right? They should be able to find out who their parents were, where they went to school, where they obtained their certificates and so on. A whole personal history.'

'They should, yeah,' Garcia confirmed.

'But if we're right about the fact that our killer's first ever victims were probably his own parents,' Hunter continued, 'then chances are that after they were murdered, the killer, or killers, have had a name-change before starting their killing crusade.'

Garcia thought about it for a moment. 'That's what I would've done, but if they didn't, it's probably because they also disguised their own parents' deaths as accidental. Maybe that's what gave them the idea in the first place.'

Another nod from Hunter. 'Either way – if our killer, or an accomplice, is running any of these support groups, Research's backtrack should do one of two things.' He lifted a finger at Garcia. 'If they had a name-change and created a name out of thin air, the backtracking will halt all of a sudden – no history past a certain point because the name is false.'

'Which would be a big red flag,' Garcia jumped in. 'If the name isn't false, if they stole the name from someone else, then the backtracking will come up against a very odd jump – from one life to a completely different one. Another big red flag.'

'Correct,' Hunter agreed, before raising finger number two. 'If our killer decided not to have a name-change because his parents' murder was well hidden as accidental, then Research's backtrack will find two deceased parents, where both of them died in the same event.'

'And we're back to a red flag,' Garcia said.

'So no red flags against a support-group leader,' Hunter concluded, 'means that we'll be OK to approach him/her and ask about Shaun Daniels and Terry Wilford.'

Garcia smiled. 'That should work ... and save us a hell of a lot of time.'

Hunter reached for the phone on his desk once again, but before he could connect to Research, a knock came on their office door.

'Come in,' Garcia called.

The door was pushed open by Detective Brighton from Homicide. 'Hey, guys, are you coming now, or later?'

Both Hunter and Garcia just looked back at him with blank stares.

'You guys forgot, didn't you?' The question was clearly a rhetorical one. 'Detective Jenkins's surprise birthday party? We're all gathering at the Library Bar just around the corner?'

'Of course,' Garcia said, jumping to his feet and stealing a peek at Hunter. 'What time is she getting there again?'

Detective Loretta Jenkins had been with the LAPD Robbery Homicide Division for just over four years, after working her ass off as an officer for nearly ten. She was smart, fearless, friendly and vicious when she needed to be. Inside the RH Division, Loretta Jenkins was well liked and very well respected. She could also drink most of the division under the table.

Brighton checked his watch. 'In about an hour.'

Hunter gave him a firm nod. 'Sure, we'll be ...' Instead of finishing his sentence, his gaze moved to a floating spot in the air and it simply stayed there. He said nothing else.

Garcia also stayed quiet.

'Are you OK there?' Brighton asked Hunter, but got no reply.

'Is he OK?' he directed the question at Garcia.

'Yeah, yeah,' Garcia came back. 'We're fine.'

Brighton's stare returned to Hunter before he gave the room a subtle headshake. 'You two are a fucking weird unit, you know that? You guys need a vacation, or something.'

'We'll be there,' Garcia reassured him.

As Brighton closed the door behind him, Garcia's attention turned to Hunter, who had put down the phone without making the call to Research.

'I know that look, Robert. What did you just think of now?'

Hunter didn't reply. Instead he went back to his computer.

'Robert, what are you looking for?'

'The Missing Persons Report for Terry Wilford that we got from Detective Cohen.'

Garcia frowned. 'I've got it here.' He checked the pile of files on his desk. 'I printed it out earlier. I find it easier that way. Why? What do you need?'

'When I read through the file,' Hunter replied. 'I remember it mentioning that Terry worked almost every night at The Varnish, with the exception of one night – a night that he had off every week for years. What night was that?'

Garcia's eyes lit up. 'Holy shit! The support-group sessions, they're all in the evenings.'

Hunter nodded.

Garcia flipped through the report until he found what he was looking for. 'Here we go – Tuesdays. Terry Wilford always had Tuesdays off.

Hunter reached for the phone on his desk once again. This time, he did talk to Shannon in Research.

Forty-Four

The task that Hunter had given Shannon and the Research team wasn't exactly a difficult one, but it was certainly laborious. Backtracking a person's life could easily be done from behind a computer keyboard, especially if the researcher had access to information that was restricted to the general public, like police files, traffic accident documentation, school records and so on, but for a thorough backtracking job, the researcher would also need to spend time on the phone – talking to doctors, teachers, relatives ... whoever they needed to, depending on the case, to get the kind of personal history they were looking for. And what Shannon and her team were looking for in this particular instance were 'no red flags'.

There were twenty-five names on the initial list that Hunter had given Research, and that would no doubt take time, but Hunter and Garcia didn't need all the information at once. Research could trickle it through, a name at a time, and the two names right at the top of that list were Keri Liftridge and Roberto De Souza. Both of them were career therapists, and both of them ran two of the eleven domestic violence support groups that catered specifically to help those perpetrating the violence. And their support groups met on Tuesday evenings – Terry Wilford's only night off during the week.

It took Research almost a full day to backtrack Keri Liftridge's life to a 'no red flags' status. They were able to track back on her personal history all the way to her birth. Her parents were still alive and living in Connecticut. Shannon herself had spoken to both of them on the phone.

Due to the fact that Roberto De Souza's family was all back in Puerto Rico, his backtracking was taking a little longer than the team expected, but all indications were that he would also make the 'no red flags' list.

'So what do you want to do?' Garcia asked, as he walked back into the UVC Unit's office, holding an unopened can of Dr. Pepper in his right hand. 'It's Thursday today, neither Keri Liftridge's or Roberto De Souza's support group meet until Tuesday, but we don't need to wait until then to go talk to either of them.' He cracked open the can. 'Though Mrs. Liftridge's support group meets in Monterey Park, her regular consulting office is in North Hollywood.'

'Yeah,' Hunter replied. 'I saw that.'

'Roberto De Souza doesn't have a private office,' Garcia continued. 'During the day he's a school psychologist at Morningside High School in Inglewood.'

Hunter checked his watch – 4:20 p.m. 'Well, school is out. So just turning up at Morningside High could turn out to be a wasted journey.'

Garcia knew that, whenever possible, Hunter preferred to turn up unannounced. It gave them the upper hand.

'School might be out, but we can still drop by Keri Liftridge's office in North Hollywood. It'll take us less than half an hour to get there.'

'We can,' Hunter agreed. 'But I don't want to do that together.'

'Why not? She's a "no red flags".'

'Still,' Hunter explained. 'Regardless of finding out if any of our victims had attended any of these support groups, we'll still have to sit in on all of them.'

Garcia nodded, picking up on what Hunter had meant. 'And it's better if they don't know that there's a cop sitting in on their session.'

'Much better,' Hunter agreed.

'So with the groups that you talk to the leader, I sit in on their sessions.'

'And vice-versa,' Hunter agreed.

'So who's going to drop in on Keri Liftridge today?'

'I can do it,' Hunter said, already reaching for his jacket. 'You can take the sessions.'

'Fair enough. Tomorrow I'll talk to Roberto De Souza and you'll take the sessions.'

Hunter smiled. It seemed like they finally had a workable plan of action.

Forty-Five

Loud, heavy, screaming metal music blasted through the ceiling speakers once again, sending Jennifer's body into another sudden-awake jolt, and immediately bringing back the final boss of headaches. Her terrified and already full-of-tears eyes shot open in a fright. Nothing made sense anymore. Her brain was too tired, her body too weak for her to be able to keep her grip on reality. Time had become nothing but a blur ... an unreadable smudge on the fabric of her life, or whatever was left of it.

Jennifer had no real idea of how long it had been since Russell had drugged her that night at the restaurant before taking her captive. At first, she tried to keep track of time by relying on her body clock, which she knew was as precise as it could be. That precision came courtesy of sixteen years behind bars, when every single day was regimented down to the minute, forcing her body to grow so used to routine, it became an addiction.

Jennifer knew that no matter what, she would get hungry three times a day, because for sixteen years, she was only fed three times a day, and at the exact same time every single day, with very few exceptions. That meant that her stomach would first signal hunger at 6:30 a.m., then again at midday, and one last time at 6:30 p.m. – never before, never after. Those were three different internal alarms that seemed to have embedded themselves into her DNA. The fourth and final alarm came at ten o'clock at night – lights out – that was when her eyelids would show the first signs of becoming heavy.

What that all meant was that in normal circumstances, Jennifer didn't need a clock to be able to tell the time. Her body would give her a pretty good idea of what time of the day it was, but these weren't normal circumstances . . . far from it . . . because since she'd been taken, her body and mind had been deprived of four of the most important elements for survival.

Light – darkness surrounded Jennifer twenty-four hours a day, except when Russell was in the room with her. Every time that happened, Russell would use a different light intensity – from candlelight shadows to retina-melting bright – tricking and disorienting her visual cortex.

Food and water – both came at her captor's own discretion – sometimes once a day, sometimes not at all – causing havoc with her metabolism and keeping her energy levels at a bare minimum.

And finally sleep – rest had become a luxury that Jennifer could just about kill or die for. Russell would keep her awake either by blasting fast, screaming, metal music at her for as long as twenty hours a day, or by surprising Jennifer with a jet of freezing water that would keep her clothes wet and her shivering for hours.

And that was how a military wear-down tactic called 'destructive conditioning of morale' worked, because despite feeling exhausted . . . despite getting just three hours of sleep in the past thirty, Jennifer was actually grateful that this time she had been awoken by loud music instead of freezing water. On 'freezing water' days, she would always wake up locked inside a five-foot by five-foot animal cage – no space to stand up, no space to move around, no space to extend her legs. When ear-piercing, shrieking metal music was used, Jennifer would wake up inside a solid concrete-walled room. Still a prison cell, but at least she could stretch her legs.

And stretch her legs was exactly what she did, but without

standing up. She felt too tired ... her legs too weak to support even her measly 120 pounds. But even if her legs could hold her weight, she wouldn't be able to stand up because by now, the soles of her feet were nothing but raw flesh – another weapon in Russell's torture arsenal. Every day, at least once a day, he would tie her down and spank the soles of her feet with a long and thin bamboo cane until they bled. The pain was excruciating, but Jennifer wasn't tied down, which meant that she wasn't getting her feet tortured again ... at least not for now.

She slowly forced herself into a sitting position and rested her back against the concrete wall. Reflexively, her skin-and-bone hands moved to the side of her head and rested over her ears, but it made no difference. The music was so loud that she could feel her ribcage and sternum rattling inside her.

Then, just like that, the room went eerily silent. Jennifer felt so disoriented, she couldn't even tell if the loud music had been playing for five minutes, or five hours. She opened her eyes and they instinctively tried to sweep the room, moving from left to right, but there was no light anywhere. All that surrounded her was darkness and stale air. She didn't want to cry anymore, but tears were already gathering around the lower rims of her eyes, threatening to spill out at any second, because deep inside, Jennifer knew that she was never getting out of that room. At least not alive. She knew that there was no one coming for her, but worst of all, she knew that she would never see her daughter again and that she would never be able to tell her how sorry she was for all the mistakes she'd made.

Despite all the horrors that came with sixteen years of prison, it was right there, sitting alone with her back against the wall of a pitch-black, godforsaken torture room, that Jennifer finally lost all hope. She didn't want to fight anymore.

'Please ...' she said to no one, her voice shaky and barely audible. 'Just kill me and be done with this.'

'What do you think he's doing?' a voice asked from one of the dark corners of the room.

'ARGH!' Jennifer screamed, her skeleton practically jumping out of her skin. She pressed her spine tighter against the wall behind her.

'He *is* killing you. He's just doing it slowly.'

Those words crawled along Jennifer's skin, sticking to the sweat that had slicked into the grooves of her palms, and slipping into her nostrils as they flared with her uneven breathing. It wasn't the fact that she wasn't alone in that room that had most disturbed her. It was the fact that the voice that had replied to her plea didn't belong to Russell.

It belonged to a woman.

Forty-Six

Keri Liftridge's practicing psychology office was located in North Hollywood, right on Victory Boulevard, on the third floor of a dark-glass-fronted building that could easily be mistaken for a private bank. Hunter got there just as the clock struck five in the afternoon.

At the building's reception lobby, he cleared security with a quick flash of his credentials before taking the stairs up to the third and topmost floor. The door to the psychology office was closed, with a sign that read, 'Please ring for admittance', followed by an arrow pointing to an intercom unit mounted on the wall to the right of the door. There was a camera built into the intercom.

Hunter pressed the button and waited. It took only a couple of seconds for someone to reply.

'Yes, how may I help you this afternoon?' The female voice that came through the tiny intercom speaker was gentle, with a somewhat soothing quality to it.

'Is this Mrs. Liftridge?' Hunter asked.

'No. Mrs. Liftridge is with a client at the moment. Do you have an appointment for today?'

'Not exactly,' Hunter replied, lifting up his credentials so that the camera could pick it up. 'But if possible, I'd like to have a quick word with her. It really won't take long.'

'*Umm ...*'

'It really is important,' Hunter pushed, sensing the hesitation.

There was a quick moment of indecision before the door buzzed open. '*Of course. Please come in.*'

The door opened into a small reception room, where the only pieces of furniture were a filing cabinet and an office desk, behind which sat a lady so petite that Hunter had to angle his body to one side to be able to see her past her computer monitor. She looked to be in her mid-forties with dark, straight hair that had been cut short – fringe-bob style – dark eyes and a smile so well rehearsed it looked natural.

'Please come in, Detective ...?'

'Hunter. Robert Hunter.'

'I'm Janice,' she said, without standing up. 'It's nice to meet you, Detective Hunter. Unfortunately, I can't interrupt Mrs. Liftridge's session.' She indicated the door to her right and Hunter's left. 'But you're welcome to take a seat in the waiting room if you like, and I'll let Keri know that you're here as soon as her session is over.' She quickly checked the clock on her screen. 'Which will be in about ten minutes' time. I can't guarantee that she'll be able to see you today, but I can try.'

'Does she have another appointment after this one?'

'No. This is her last session for the day.'

'Thank you, Janice. I appreciate it. I'll wait.' Hunter turned the handle on the door to the waiting room and pushed it open.

On average, therapists' sessions were usually between forty-five minutes and an hour long, and they were always by appointment, no walk-ins. There was never more than one client waiting at a time. It wasn't like going to the dentist. For that reason, therapists' waiting rooms tended to be compact, but not too cramped, in case the client struggled with claustrophobia. The decoration was always placid – not too many colors or extravagant furniture, with the lighting warm and calm. The room that Hunter found himself in was no different. It had been minimally furnished, with just one armchair and a low coffee table. The armchair – an oxblood, Chesterfield club chair – faced a wall that displayed two framed prints – both very tranquil images. On the coffee table, there were a few magazines spread out like a deck of cards. Across the room, by the door that led into Keri Liftridge's office, there was a twin-tap water dispenser.

Hunter chose not to take a seat. Instead, he studied the two framed images – the first one showed a deserted beach, with snow-white sand and baby-blue waters. The second was a photograph of a sunset somewhere, where the sky had turned orange-red, silhouetting the mountains on the horizon. Hunter had to admit that the prints had an almost hypnotic effect.

He was just about to pick up one of the magazines when he heard the sound of a door closing, coming from inside Keri Liftridge's office. That probably meant her session had ended and that her client her left through the office exit door. That was another common feature in therapists' offices – a client never exited through the waiting room. Client crossing client was a big no-no in the therapy world. There was always a private exit door. A few seconds later, Hunter heard a phone ring inside Keri's office. The conversation didn't last long. Seconds after that, Keri Liftridge opened the door to her office and stepped into the waiting room.

'Detective Hunter?' she said, offering a delicate and well-manicured hand. 'I'm Keri Liftridge. You wish to speak with me?'

Hunter shook her hand, as he introduced himself.

'LAPD Homicide?' Keri's eyes narrowed at Hunter. Her voice became tense. 'What is this concerning? Has something happened to one of my clients?'

Keri Liftridge was almost a whole foot shorter than Hunter, with reddish-blonde hair that was neatly tied back into a slick bun. Her makeup was minimal, but done in a way that perfectly

Chris Carter

accentuated her dark eyes and her high cheekbones. She was dressed very professionally, in a light-blue suit, white blouse and short black heels. The sleeves of her suit jacket were rolled up to expose her forearms, but what most impressed Hunter about Keri was that everything about her exuded confidence – her posture, her movements, the way she spoke, her tone of voice . . . everything.

'Do you mind if we talk in your office?' Hunter asked.

Keri hesitated for a split second, her eyes showing concern. 'Yes, of course.' She turned to indicate the door. 'Please, come in.'

Hunter followed Keri into a room that felt just as tranquil as the waiting room that they were in, but at least double its size. It was nicely decorated, without coming across as presumptuous, comfortably lit and very cozy. Apart from Keri's antique pedestal desk, there were two armchairs, identical to the one in the waiting room, a Chesterfield three-seater couch and a typical therapist's chaise longue.

'Please take a seat, Detective,' Keri said, broadly gesturing at the room. 'Anywhere you like.'

'I'm OK standing, if you don't mind.'

Hunter's reply seemed to worry Keri even more. He picked up on it and quickly clarified.

'This shouldn't take long.'

Keri studied Hunter for a couple of seconds longer than he expected before finally nodding. 'Whatever you prefer,' she said, leaning back against the edge of her desk. Her arms stayed relaxed and by her sides.

Hunter lost no time in explaining the reason for his visit, without revealing too many details.

'So basically,' Keri said, once Hunter was done. 'You need me to confirm, or deny, if any of these people that you're talking about have ever attended any of my domestic violence support-group sessions?'

'That's all I need,' Hunter confirmed.

Keri nodded slowly. 'And since you're a homicide detective, it's safe to assume that they're either suspects in an investigation, or they're the victims.'

'That's also correct.'

Keri crossed her arms in front of her. 'OK. So who are they?'

Hunter handed her a photo of Terry Wilford. 'His name is Terry. Terry Wilford.' He was careful to use the verb in its present tense. 'Please bear in mind that if he did attend any of your group sessions, it could've been a while back, as opposed to recently.'

Keri took the photo from Hunter's hand and studied it for a few seconds before nodding confidently. 'Yeah, I remember him. He did use to come to my sessions on Tuesday evenings, and you're right – it was a while back.'

Hunter felt his stomach drop, as his brain caught up with what Keri's confirmation truly meant for their investigation. 'How long is a while back, can you remember?' He kept his voice as steady as he could.

Keri took another moment. 'It's hard to be exact, but I'd say at least six months, probably longer, but ...' Her stare got lost somewhere in the space between her and Hunter.

'But?' Hunter pushed.

'But I'm sure that Terry isn't the name he used at the sessions.' She immediately lifted a hand at Hunter. 'Which is no surprise. It's a tough group, Detective. The people who attend it are climbing a huge mountain – they're accepting that what they've been doing is wrong ... they're accepting that they need to do better ... and they're accepting that they need help. That means that in one way or another, they're ashamed of their actions ... of what they've done. To face a group of complete strangers and admit to that takes courage, of course it does, but they're still ashamed. It's not surprising that many of them keep their names private.'

'Of course,' Hunter agreed. 'Just out of curiosity, can you remember which name he used?'

Keri's attention went back to the photo. She chewed her bottom lip for several long seconds before shaking her head. 'I'm not one hundred percent sure, but I think it was something easy to remember. John, or Paul, or something like that.'

Hunter nodded before handing her the second photo. 'This is the second individual that I'm interested in.' This time, Hunter didn't use Shaun Daniels's name. 'Can you remember him from any of your sessions?'

Keri placed Terry's photo on her desk before taking the new image from Hunter's hand. As she studied the picture, Hunter studied her. Her eyes narrowed a touch as they moved around the photograph. Her lips pursed and twisted left before she, once again, bit her bottom one. There were no signs of recognition anywhere. Hunter knew the answer even before she spoke.

'No. I've never seen him before. He never attended any of my group sessions. His face doesn't look familiar at all.'

Hunter didn't need to ask if Keri was sure. He knew she was. And that had to mean that their killer had clearly maximized his options. He didn't stick to a single support group. Why would he? The more he moved around, the more stories he would hear. The more stories he heard, the more potential victims he would meet. But that wasn't the only advantage of jumping from group to group. There was also the risk management side – the less that he was seen in a group ... the less people tended to remember his face.

'So we're talking about victims here,' Keri said, returning the photo to Hunter. Her tone was calm and confident.

Hunter locked eyes with her.

Keri gave him a subtle shrug. 'What are the odds of two different murderers attending domestic violence support groups at the same time?'

Hunter couldn't fault her logic. He nodded once. It was pointless denying.

Keri's attention went back to the photo that she had placed on her desk.

'What was his real name again?'

'Terry Wilford.'

She shook her head at the photo and the look in her eyes turned sad. 'Poor guy. He really was working hard to tackle his problem. He was trying to change. I remember how emotional he got at times. How much he regretted what he had done.' She returned the photo to Hunter. 'I really hope he had a chance to make things right, or at least a chance to say that he was sorry.'

'Was he very vocal in the group?' Hunter asked.

'I encourage everyone to talk,' Keri explained. 'It's the only way that group therapy works. People have to talk ... they have to let things out. When they do, we all listen.'

'I understand that, but I also know that some group members would need more encouraging than others, while some would be less shy to come forward with what they have to say.'

Keri nodded, as if she'd just picked up on Hunter's drift. 'You've been through group therapy before.'

Hunter found it easier to simply agree with a head gesture.

'You're right,' she said. 'Some group members do need a little more encouraging than others.' There was a thoughtful pause before Keri scratched the skin between her professionally plucked eyebrows. 'If my memory serves me right, he was what I'd call an average member. Since you've been to group therapy, you understand the dynamics of it, right? We go around in the circle, taking turns sharing experiences, and those experiences don't necessarily need to deal directly with domestic abuse or violence. People might want to share something about their past, or about their childhood, or their parents, or school, or work environment ... whatever they feel like sharing. Some choose to pass when their turn comes, so we skip to the next member – no judging . . . no pressure. Terry wasn't a "passer". Like I've said, he was really trying hard to tackle his problem, and the only way to do that is by talking . . . by sharing . . . and he did so.'

'And do you remember seeing him chatting to other group members either before the sessions, after, or during a break?'

Keri's eyes settled on Hunter's face and they stayed there for a few analyzing seconds. 'You're starting to worry me a little, Detective Hunter.'

Hunter said nothing because he could already guess what Keri's deduction had been.

'If you're here asking about two possible members of my support group,' she continued, 'who have become murder victims in the same investigation, and the follow-up questions are about who they might've been talking to before, during or after the sessions, it can only mean one thing – you suspect that the killer was also a support-group member.' Keri paused, thought about it, then corrected herself. 'Or worse even – *is* also a support-group member – because he hasn't been caught yet.'

Keri Liftridge was clearly intelligent and a very quick thinker. Hunter knew from experience that trying to bullshit a person like her was rarely a good idea.

'We're trying to track back as much of Mr. Wilford's life as we possibly can,' he explained. 'It's standard investigative procedure. Every human connection he had is a possible suspect – from someone he met in a support group to a homeless guy he chatted to every now and then on the streets. We're just trying to identify other people who could maybe give us more information on him. Every little piece matters, but yes, Mr. Wilford's murderer could've been a member of your support group. Right now, he could be anyone.'

Keri seemed to appreciate Hunter's honesty. He picked up on that and quickly brought the question back to her.

'So do you know if he became friends with anyone in the group? Or was there someone who he chatted to more often than others?'

Keri shook her head, as she thought about it. 'It really is hard to remember. Like I said, it was a while back and the sessions are only once a week ...' She paused and squinted at nothing at all, while lifting an index finger at Hunter, who craned his neck in her direction. 'Hold on a second. I think there was someone. Yes, Terry always sat by the same person, and I think they did get talking. In fact, I'm sure they did.'

'Do you remember who that person was?' Hunter asked. 'Does he/she still come to group sessions?'

'He,' Keri confirmed, before hesitating for another short moment. 'And funny that you've asked, because yeah, he's been coming to sessions for a few years now, I think.'

Hunter felt the hairs on the back of his neck stand on end.

'But it's on and off,' Keri explained. 'All group therapy members are like that. People join a group for a few sessions then disappear for one reason or another. Some try other groups ... some fail to see any benefits from the sessions and quit ... whatever the reason is. Since the sessions are government-funded, meaning free for all members, there's no commitment, no specific number of sessions they need to attend either. No one has to cancel their appointments, or explain the reason why they'll stop coming. Some come back weeks or even months later, attend a few more sessions, and then disappear again. That's just the way it goes.'

'Has he been to any recent sessions?'

Keri shook her head. 'No, not for a while.'

'A while?'

'Several months. At least.'

'Can you remember his name?' Hunter asked, then immediately corrected himself. 'Or the name he used in the group?'

'Umm ...' Keri looked down at the floor, as if searching

for something. 'Michael,' she replied before nodding firmly at Hunter. 'The name he gave us was Michael.'

Of course he would use a common name, Hunter thought. *A name that's easy to remember and equally easy to forget.*

'How do new members join?' he asked. 'Is there a roster . . . an attendance sheet . . . anything?'

'Not really. People who'd like to come and join the group for the first time can either call or send an email via a web form. Both services have an automated reply with the location, the rules and the starting time. These are people looking for help, so no one is turned down. There's no screening either. Sometimes we can have as many as twelve to fifteen people in a session.' She shrugged. 'Sometimes only two or three. Whenever people want to come back, all they have to do is turn up on the night. That's it.'

'And you're sure that this Michael was the person who sat next to Terry Wilford during the sessions he attended . . . the person he talked to?'

'Yes, I'm pretty sure.'

'Can you maybe describe him for me?'

Keri's head tilted sideways.

'Whatever you can remember,' Hunter pushed. 'Height . . . body type . . . anything you can recall.'

'Umm . . .' Keri thought about it for an instant. 'He's tall, maybe just a couple of inches shorter than you. He's also . . . athletic? I'd say. Clean-shaven . . . short dark hair . . . dark eyes.' She shrugged. 'That's it, really.'

'Do you have a ballpark age?'

'I'd say somewhere in his late thirties . . . maybe very early forties.'

'How about any distinctive marks? Tattoos? Scars? Anything?'

Keri's bottom lip pursed forward as she tried to remember. 'Umm . . . yeah, actually.' She snapped her fingers before pointing at Hunter. 'A couple of his fingers are a little . . . odd-shaped.'

'His fingers?'

'Yeah, on one of his hands, but I can't be sure which. It's not exactly noticeable, but I remember them because I've handed him a cup of coffee a few times at session breaks and they caught my attention.'

'Oddly shaped in what way?' Hunter asked.

Another shrug. 'Just curved a little awkwardly at the knuckles. As if maybe they were broken when he was younger and didn't heal in the way they should have. I remember thinking that that must've been one of the reasons why he had become violent toward his children or wife. The reason why he had joined our group. He probably suffered constant violent physical abuse when he was younger, which can, in time, lead to modeling behavior. That's when—'

'Children imitate their parents,' Hunter said with a nod. 'Or anyone they look up to. If the abuse was constant, the brain can misinterpret that as normal. Once they grow up, they can easily model that same behavior. Like father, like son, kind of thing.'

'Exactly,' Keri agreed. 'Sixty to seventy percent of parents who become abusive toward their children and/or partners have, in fact, grown up in an abusive household themselves.' Her expression became thoughtful once again. Hunter noticed it and pushed.

'Something else you remember?'

'Yeah,' Keri nodded. 'Just now we were talking about being a "passer" during the group sessions, remember? Michael was one of those – definitely the quiet type – didn't talk much, shy, passed often when his turn came . . . but he was very attentive to others and their accounts.'

A little voice inside Hunter's head whispered: *But of course he was.*

Forty-Seven

The next day, Garcia took a trip to Morningside High School in Inglewood, to talk to Roberto De Souza – the psychologist who ran the second domestic violence support group that met on Tuesday evenings.

By the morning, Research had managed to finally fully back-track De Souza's life, adding him to the 'no red flags' list. He'd been living in LA since the age of eighteen, when he relocated from Puerto Rico on a full UCLA academic scholarship. He majored in Counseling Psychology and, in addition to being the senior counselor at Morningside, he ran four free therapy support groups around Los Angeles – domestic violence, self-harming, depression and anger management.

At Morningside High, Garcia's lunchtime meeting with De Souza ran smoothly, but with no reward. Garcia showed him a couple of photos of Shaun Daniels but, despite taking his time studying both photographs, De Souza didn't recognize him at all. He had been running the Westmont domestic violence support group for the past five years, and he was positive that Shaun Daniels had never been to any of their sessions. In fact, he was positive that he'd never seen Shaun in any session from any of his other three support groups either.

In the morning, Hunter had briefed Garcia on the results of his meeting with Keri Liftridge the night before. Just like they had anticipated, there was now a very good chance that their killer didn't stick to just one support group. He bounced around, maximizing his victim choice. And if the killer could do it, so could anyone else.

Different groups offered different types of support . . . different types of feedback, but more than that – many people struggled with more than just one type of problem, and some problems were directly related to each other: for example, domestic violence and anger management, depression and anxiety, or substance use and addiction. It wasn't uncommon for a person to take part in more than one type of therapy, or attend more than one support group at a time. Terry Wilford could've easily been such a person. He could've also been alternating between both Tuesday evenings' domestic violence support groups, or even trying different ones on different nights, whenever he managed to get the night off. For that reason, Garcia also showed De Souza a photo of Terry, but De Souza had never seen him before either.

'Just one last question before I go, if I may?' Garcia said, getting to his feet. He'd been sitting before De Souza's desk in his small office in Building C, inside the school campus.

'Of course,' De Souza replied, using both hands to tuck two loose locks of his longish black hair behind his ears.

'Do you happen to have a member called Michael in your Tuesday evening support group at the moment?'

'Michael?' De Souza's voice was naturally quiet, just a notch above a whisper.

Garcia nodded. 'He's the silent, observant type. Tends to take a pass when his turn comes to share with the group, but pays a lot of attention when others are speaking.'

De Souza sat back on his chair while he searched his memory.

'Tall, almost six-foot,' Garcia added. 'Dark hair . . . athletic build? When he was young he broke a couple of his fingers in one of his hands and they didn't exactly heal properly, so they seem a little odd . . . a little curved at the knuckles. Maybe you noticed something like that with one of your members?'

De Souza was still searching.

'Please bear in mind that he doesn't have to be a current member. Maybe he attended a few group sessions a while back, and I mean *any* of your groups, not necessarily just your domestic violence one.'

De Souza poked the inside of his left cheek with his tongue.

'Umm . . .' He adjusted his glasses on his wavy nose. 'Now that you mention it, I think I did have someone like that in a group.'

Garcia's eyebrows lifted up. 'Really? When?'

More tongue rolling against the inner cheek. 'Not that long ago, actually. Maybe four . . . five weeks. Like you've said – quiet guy, quite shy, didn't speak much . . . very observant.' He lifted his right hand at Garcia. 'But many are when they just join a support group. They're always hesitant because the admittance of guilt isn't easy, so instead of talking, they just observe.'

'The fingers?' Garcia asked.

De Souza nodded. 'Yeah. On his left hand, you mean?'

'I can't be sure.'

De Souza took an extra moment. 'Neither can I, but I did notice them a couple of times. It's one of the things I do a lot in my sessions. As a member is speaking, I tend to observe the rest of the group. You can learn a lot from their reactions to other people's accounts – their expressions . . . their movements.'

'Anything else you noticed about him?' Garcia asked. 'Anything kind of memorable? Tattoos? Scars? Anything?'

De Souza went back to thinking mode.

'No,' he said after several long seconds. 'Nothing comes to mind, but . . .' There was a headshake.

'But?'

'But like you've said, he wasn't in my domestic violence support group.'

'No?'

'No,' De Souza confirmed. 'He came to a few of my anger management group sessions. And . . .'

Garcia waited.

'I'm sure that the name he used wasn't Michael, which isn't surprising. Most group members don't use their real names.'

'Can you remember the name he used?'

De Souza tried, but gave up after a while. 'No, I'm sorry.'

Garcia thanked him, but just as he was about to exit the office, De Souza stopped him.

'Russell,' he called out.

Garcia turned to look back at the psychologist. 'I'm sorry?'

'The name he used.' De Souza nodded with conviction. 'It just came back to me. It wasn't Michael. It was Russell.'

Forty-Eight

The next couple of days seemed to ooze by in a heap of frustration. Research did an outstanding job with their 'no red flags' list, because even with some names taking a lot longer than others to be fully backtracked, they managed to clear all twenty-five domestic violence support-group leaders by lunchtime on Monday, 15 July – just five days after they'd started their backtracking marathon.

'So whoever this killer is,' Garcia breathed out, as he read the email they'd just received from Research, 'he's not running any of the domestic violence support groups.'

'I know,' Hunter agreed from behind his desk. 'But that's something that we were already expecting, Carlos. Jumping from support group to support group maximizes his choices for a victim and minimizes the risk of him being noticed. Plus, if our killer really turns out to be this Michael, or Russell, or whatever name he wants to use, then we already know that he attends the group meetings instead of running them.'

'Yeah, I know,' Garcia said, as he approached the coffee machine. 'Would you like a refill?

'No, I'm OK for now, thanks.'

Garcia poured himself another large cup of coffee and immediately had a healthy sip. He never failed to impress Hunter with how he could drink boiling-hot coffee as if it were just lukewarm. Asbestos mouth, Hunter called it.

'I just wish we had a little more to go on before we start drop-ping in on the group sessions,' Garcia continued, returning to his desk. 'All we have are two names, which are obviously false, a physical description that matches half of the male population in this city, and a small detail – fingers awkwardly curved at the knuckles – which, according to the info we have, aren't even that noticeable. That's it. Nothing else.' He chuckled. 'It's like chasing a fart in a hurricane, Robert. And the fart doesn't even smell that bad to give us a hint.'

'I agree it isn't much, but it's a hell of a lot more than we had a week ago, Carlos.'

'I'm not going to argue that.' Garcia lifted both hands at Hunter. 'It's certainly progress, but like I said, I just wish we had a little more to go on, because all we can really look for, as we sit in on these sessions, is the fingers detail.' He gave Hunter a single-shoulder shrug. 'So I thought that maybe, as I join a new group, I could go around shaking hands with everyone, but that's not really how support-group introductions are done, right?'

Hunter firmly shook his head. 'Definitely no handshaking. You do that and you might as well show everyone your badge.'

Garcia slouched his hips forward on his chair, his head back over the backrest so that he was staring straight at the ceiling. 'So tonight I'll take the group in Westchester and you the one in Carson, right?'

'Yep,' Hunter agreed. 'The session starts at seven-thirty. Don't be late for yours.'

'I won't.'

'And remember – don't be too talkative, either,' Hunter reminded him. 'Act shy . . . as if you were still uncertain you want to be there.' He leaned forward on his desk. 'Leave your gun and badge in the car, and whatever you do, Carlos, please refrain from making jokes. They really don't go down well when we're talking therapy. Especially your sarcastic ones.'

'Yes, I know,' Garcia replied. 'We've been through all this before.'

'Also,' Hunter reminded his partner. 'Keep your eyes peeled for anyone who seems to be in disguise – wig, hats ... that sort of thing.'

'Disguise?'

'This killer is very cautious, Carlos. He goes to great lengths to stage his murders as accidents. He figured out a loophole in the system. He uses different names with different groups. It wouldn't surprise me if he also completely changed his appearance to match that name-change. Risk management, and our killer is very good at it.'

'OK,' Garcia accepted. 'I'll be on the lookout.'

'And don't forget to dress down.'

Garcia sat up straight. 'Shall I go get a white wife-beater?' He sounded enthusiastic. 'I can wear it under an unbuttoned, lumberjack, long-sleeve shirt. That will give me the look, won't it?'

'Too stereotypical. The trick is to *not* call attention to yourself.

Garcia laughed. 'Relax, Dad. I was joking. I know what I'm doing, all right?' He clicked his tongue as he gave Hunter a sideways wink. 'I'll just wear the unbuttoned lumberjack shirt with a few finger-thick gold chains over my manly chest.'

Forty-Nine

That night, both support-group sessions started at 7:30 p.m. sharp. To give most group members a chance to speak, if they wanted to, the sessions lasted, on average, ninety minutes, with a coffee break roughly halfway through it. There was no attendance sheet . . . no roll call . . . no name check.

For his session, Garcia did dress down – faded blue jeans, oldish black T-shirt, white sneakers and hair in a not-so-tidy manbun. He acted shy, kept his eyes low and didn't utter a single joke or sarcastic comment throughout the entire session.

Garcia had never been to a group therapy session before and, when taking into account that these were all people who had been, or still were, violent toward their children and/or partners inside their household, he was surprised with how calm and considerate everyone really was. There were eight people in his group, including himself – five men and three women – no Michaels . . . no Russells. The moderator – in other words, the person who ran the group – was a very sweet lady in her early fifties, who reminded Garcia of his middle school principal, Mrs. Dorset.

The group therapy dynamic was very simple. It started with a little introduction by the moderator, quickly explaining the group's mission and the few rules. The first rule they already knew – all cellphones were to be left in a box by the entrance and they all had to be either switched off or set to flight mode. Once everyone was seated, the moderator would then ask each person to introduce themselves, adding a quick line explaining why they had joined the group, regardless of them being a returning member or not. The third and final rule was simply to be considerate. That was it. From there, whoever wanted to share an experience with the group – and those experiences didn't necessarily need to deal directly with domestic violence or abuse – would simply raise their hand and the moderator would call on them. There was no time limit and listening members were asked not to interrupt. At the end of the account, the member was asked if they were open to suggestions or comments from the other group members. If 'yes', the moderator would ask the group if anyone wanted to offer a comment or a suggestion. If 'no', the moderator would move to the next group member who wanted to share an experience with the rest of the group and the process would start again.

That evening, only four out of the eight members shared accounts with the group – three men and one woman. The accounts were always told in the third person, just like Hunter had told Garcia that they would be. The reason for that was because if phrased wrongly, a member could be, in essence, confessing to the crime of assault, or worse. For that reason, as if this was some kind of tacitly recognized disclaimer, every single account began with the words 'This happened to a friend of mine . . .'

Garcia listened to what everyone had to say in complete silence. He found it easier to focus his gaze on the floor, allowing his eyes to every now and then quickly move up and search the hands of a particular group member at a time. He used that technique throughout the entire session and he was sure that no one had noticed him doing it. But despite how expertly Garcia had peeked at everyone's hands and fingers, he didn't spot any abnormality.

When his turn to share something with the group came up, Garcia did exactly what he and Hunter had rehearsed.

'Brian,' the moderator asked. Her voice was velvety and

tranquil. 'Would you like to share anything with the group at this time?'

Garcia clasped his hands together between his thighs. His eyes stayed on his thumbs for a moment before he looked up and gave the group a shy nod.

'OK.' He took a deep breath and held it for a second. 'My name is Brian and I . . .' He looked to his left, as if he were just allowing his eyes to wander aimlessly. 'I have trouble controlling my temper sometimes. Sometimes the smallest of things makes me angry a lot more than it should, you know? And I . . . just don't know what I'm doing. Rage just takes over . . . I see red and . . .' The pause was deliberate.

'Can you give us an example?' the moderator asked. 'It helps us understand the sort of rage that you're talking about.'

Garcia quickly searched the faces of the other group members – three of them were looking directly at him. Two other members were looking down at the floor, and the last two had their eyes closed, but they were still paying attention to his words.

'Sure,' he finally replied. 'This happened to a friend of mine.'

Every member of the group nodded back at him – an unspoken acknowledgment of the well-worn disclaimer.

'His wife had bought this toy piano for their son,' Garcia began. 'And that day – it was a Sunday, I'm sure – my friend and his son were sitting in the living room and his son just wouldn't stop hitting the keys on that damn thing. Not playing them . . . no . . . just hitting them – ping, ping, ping, ping.' He demonstrated with his hands. 'My friend asked him to stop many times . . . but the kid just carried on – ping, ping, ping, ping. My friend could've got up and left the room . . . he could've gone sit outside or something, but instead, he simply lost his temper with his son . . . and . . .' Garcia's eyes wandered right.

'Take your time, Brian,' the moderator said, nodding at him. 'There's no rush. Just take a deep breath. The first time is always the hardest. Just remember that no one is here to judge, OK? We're all here to help.'

Garcia had to swallow the smile that threatened to stretch his lips because Hunter had, once again, hit the nail on the head. He had told Garcia that if he got the pauses between words right, stalling at the right moment, and following it up with a guilty look, either the moderator or a group member would encourage him to carry on, stating something like – 'there's no judging in this group', or 'we're all here to help', or something similar.

Garcia nodded slowly, took another flaky attempt at a deep breath and proceeded with his rehearsed story.

'And my friend just remembers losing it completely and grabbing his son by his hands. After that – nothing. It's like a void . . . some sort of blackout, you know? It's like chunks just disappeared from his memory.' Another forced pause. He saw a couple of members nodding at him.

'What's the next thing your friend remembers, Brian?' the moderator asked.

Garcia blinked then looked up. This, Hunter had told him, was their trump card.

'The next thing he remembers,' Garcia said, 'was his son screaming in pain.' His gaze moved left and right, scanning the group. 'Because somehow, a couple of his fingers were broken.'

No one's reaction caught Garcia's attention – no one seemed too shocked, or disgusted, or angry, or anything. They all just seemed gloomy, as if they all completely understood where Garcia was coming from.

Hunter had explained that if the killer was sitting in on the session, at the mention of physical violence that either matched or was very similar to the type of violence that he had suffered as a kid, there was a very high possibility of a telltale reflex, just like Emiliano had displayed when they were sitting in that coffee shop in Watts. Maybe the subject would allow his eyes to drop to his hand, the one with the fingers that hadn't healed properly ... or lightly rub it, as if there was some pain there ... or even momentarily hide it by crossing his arms or tucking his hand inside his pocket. It would be something subtle ... something that even the subject wouldn't notice that he was doing. But Garcia saw nothing – no gazing at the hands, no rubbing, no hiding ... nothing. If the killer was sitting in on his session, he had, over the years, become an expert in keeping his cool.

When Garcia was asked if he was open to suggestions or comments from the other members, his reply was simple.

'Maybe next time.'

Once the session had ended, Garcia hung around outside for a few minutes, pretending to smoke a cigarette. Hunter would do the same at the end of his session.

The cigarette stunt was also part of the plan. Due to the fact that Garcia had declined comments and suggestions from the other group members after he'd shared his story, hanging out outside, alone, would give anyone an open chance to approach him in a more private way. It could be anything, from deep words of support to something as subtle as 'Well done tonight, Brian, I'll see you next week' – anything that could signal an attempt at a possible beginning of a friendship. But no one approached Garcia. As the other group members exited the building, they all went their own separate ways in total silence. And just like that, the night was over.

Fifty

In his first support-group session, Hunter had also drawn a blank. He had used the name Jonathan instead of Brian and the story that he had told his group was pretty similar to the one Garcia had used. The main difference was that, in Hunter's story, his friend had broken his daughter's fingers, not his son's.

In their original list, Research had discovered twenty-five domestic violence support groups scattered around LA – eleven catering to help those who perpetrated the violence, and fourteen catering to help those at the receiving end of it. The eleven that catered to help those who perpetrated the violence all met in the evenings, spread throughout six of the seven days in the week – two on Mondays, two on Tuesdays, one on Wednesdays, one on Thursdays, four on Fridays and one on Sundays. Hunter and Garcia divided the workload as equally as possible, with Hunter attending six of the eleven meetings and Garcia the remaining five. Two of the Friday meetings would have to wait for the following week.

With every support-group meeting, Hunter and Garcia used different names for different sessions, but their tactics stayed the same – act shy, eyes low and do your best to get a look at everyone's hands and fingers. In every group meeting, they used the same story, told in the exact same way. When asked, they both declined the option to have other group members comment or suggest something. At the end of every session, both of them would hang out alone outside, pretending to smoke a cigarette, while all the other members left. But despite playing their roles to near Oscar-winning performances, the rest of Hunter and Garcia's week had been a carbon copy of their first night – no fingers oddly bent at the knuckles, no telltale reflexes from anyone at the mention of the angry outburst against the imaginary kids ... and no one approaching either of them once the meeting was over.

As the following week began, Hunter and Garcia were faced with a dilemma – stay with the eleven 'abusive' domestic violence support groups for a second week, or move on to the fourteen 'abused' ones. They discussed it for a moment and they both agreed that a single week with the abusive groups wasn't nearly enough. They had to keep trying, so on Monday evening, Hunter and Garcia went back to the same support groups they had attended the week before. In Garcia's group, he got almost the exact same group of people as the week before, with the exception of an overweight man who didn't turn up, but this time Garcia passed when his turn to share came up.

In Hunter's case, a new member had joined, while two from the previous week were missing. The new member was a woman in her late twenties, who had apparently been physically abusing her husband for quite a while.

Tuesday, Wednesday and Thursday were exactly the same, with both of them going back to the same support groups they had attended the week before. The faces were pretty much the same throughout, with the exception of one new member in Garcia's Tuesday evening group, and one in Hunter's Thursday evening one. Neither of the new members gave either Hunter or Garcia reason to worry.

Friday was the only evening with four different support groups, which meant that, in their second week, both Hunter and Garcia would be attending brand-new groups on their Friday visits.

With all eleven 'abusive' domestic violence support groups, the rules were exactly the same – no cellphones allowed, no interrupting when another member was sharing an account, and be courteous; everyone was there for the same reason – to try to better themselves. But with every new group they attended, their frustration grew another notch.

Sure, after almost two full weeks and eleven support groups, with an average of six to twelve members per group, of course there were a few members who had caught either Hunter's or Garcia's attention. Some of them had looked up when either detective had shared their made-up stories. Some of them had shaken their heads, or widened their eyes, or even rubbed their hands at the mention of the broken fingers, but none of them had fingers that bent awkwardly at the knuckles, none of them fit the basic physical description they already had, and absolutely no one had approached either Hunter or Garcia as they hung out alone outside the group-meeting venues . . .

. . . until that last Friday.

Fifty-One

That Friday evening, both Hunter and Garcia got to their respective support groups with ten minutes to spare. Hunter's support group met in North Long Beach. Garcia's group met eight miles northwest of that location, in Watts – the same neighborhood where they met Officer Emiliano Esqueda. Garcia's meeting for that evening was scheduled to start at 7:30 p.m., just like most of his previous support-group meetings, but Hunter's one, due to it being a little further outside central LA, started forty-five minutes later, at 8:15 p.m.

In Watts, the meeting was being held in a classroom on the second floor of a public high school building and, once again, the few rules given out by the group's moderator at the start of the meeting were simple – no phones, don't interrupt, and be courteous.

Garcia switched his cellphone to 'flight mode' and placed it inside a basket before taking a seat next to a tall African American man, with droopy eyelids and sad eyes. People were still arriving, while a few were already at the refreshment table, pouring themselves coffees, teas, and digging into the cookie jar. Just a minute after Garcia took his seat, a dark-haired man with a short ponytail, whose eyebrows looked like savage caterpillars, took the chair to his left.

'Would you like one,' he said, offering Garcia one of the oatmeal cookies he had brought back from the table with him.

'No, thank you,' Garcia gave the man a shy smile. 'I just had dinner.' He lied.

Tessa, the moderator, a petite lady in her early thirties who looked to be of Korean descent, welcomed everyone with a pleasant smile and a few comforting words, but just as she was about to start proceedings, a tall and well-built man came to the door. He had clearly run up the stairs to get to the classroom in time.

'Is it still OK if I join?' he asked, as he caught his breath, his tone uncertain, his voice pleading.

'Of course,' Tessa said, ushering him inside before indicating the pile of chairs in the corner. 'Please grab a chair and join the circle. Sit anywhere you like.'

The man reached for his cellphone, tapped its screen a couple of times and placed it inside the phone basket. This clearly wasn't his first support-group session. He then grabbed a chair from the pile that Tessa had indicated and slotted it between two of the four women in the group, three seats to Garcia's right.

Garcia was the second out of the ten attending members to introduce himself, and this time, he went with the name 'Jack'.

Introductions done, Tessa asked if anyone would like to be the first to share something with the group.

The caterpillar-eyebrows man to Garcia's left lifted a shy hand.

'I can go first,' he said. His name was Trevor.

Just as with all the members' accounts in all previous group meetings that Garcia had attended, the stories were told in the third person, and every single one of them started with the phrase, 'This happened to a friend of mine'. As they introduced themselves, every group member was sure to emphasize the fact that they were trying their best to do better ... that they knew they had a problem ... and that they were willing to work on it. But despite all their excuses and verbal 'disclaimers', Garcia knew that many of them would never do better, and at times he really had to level himself not to blow his cover.

In the past two weeks, Garcia had heard over thirty-five accounts from people who had physically hurt either their kids, their partners or both. Reading between the lines of all the 'this happened to my friend' stories, Garcia knew that he had sat face to face with individuals who had physically hurt the very people who they were supposed to love, and they had hurt them in some of the most horrific ways: from flesh-cutting, where a scar would forever live, to scalding their skin until it'd blistered; from knocking them unconscious with a fist punch, to bone-breaking. Right from his first ever group meeting, Garcia knew that Hunter had been right. If this killer really was after parents who had physically hurt their kids, these support-group meetings were a treasure chest.

That evening, seven out of the ten group members shared stories. The late arrival, who had introduced himself as George, was one of the three who passed when his turn came up, but right from the very first account, the one shared by caterpillar-eyebrows Trevor, Garcia noticed how attentive George was to every story being told. He seemed to be eagerly taking in every word as if at the end of the meeting the moderator would quiz the group. That immediately put Garcia on alert, so for the first forty-five minutes of the meeting – until they reached the coffee break – Garcia tried his best to get a good look at George's hands and fingers, but in doing that he encountered two problems. The first was that the angle at which they were sitting in relation to each other was an awkward one, because droopy-eyelids man, sitting to Garcia's right, took at least 70 percent of his line of vision. To peek at George, Garcia had to lean forward a fair amount and twice, in the many times that Garcia had repeated the movement, George had caught him doing it. Their eyes locked for a fraction of a second and all that Garcia could do to try to play it down was pretend that he was just stretching his stiff neck.

The 'play down' move might've worked the first time around,

but as Garcia's and George's eyes met for the second time, Garcia saw how oddly George looked back at him. He clearly wasn't buying the stiff-neck excuse anymore.

The second problem that Garcia had encountered was that from the instant that he'd sat down, George kept his arms crossed in front of his chest, with his hands conveniently tucked under his armpits. If he did uncross them even once during the entire meeting, it had been when Garcia wasn't looking.

At the 45-minute interval, Garcia saw George leave the classroom, probably going for a bathroom break, like a few were doing. He waited ten seconds, so as not to be too obvious, and casually followed the group outside.

George was nowhere to be seen.

But Garcia already knew from when he'd arrived that the closest bathroom was just down the corridor and around to his left. As he rounded the corner, he saw the bathroom door closing. Garcia chose not to wait, in case George had decided to split before the meeting resumed.

This was an all-girls' school, so there were no urinals in the bathroom. Five toilet stalls lined the south wall, with three washbasins positioned directly across the room from them, on the opposite wall. George wasn't washing his hands. Garcia turned to face the stalls. Only one of them was occupied. He looked left then right to make sure that he was alone, before bending down a little to peek under the stall door, but the gap wasn't wide enough and he couldn't quite make out the person's feet. For him to get a proper look, he would have to kneel down and bring his face to just an inch or so from the floor. He paused and gave it a moment's thought.

If he tried properly looking under the stall door, there was a chance that someone could walk in on him, or worse, George, if he really was the person inside the stall, could all of a sudden open the door and catch Garcia as a peeping Tom – definitely not a good look. But all Garcia really wanted to do was to take a peek at George's hands and fingers, not have an intimate conversation with him – and what better way to do that than being right at the next washbasin, while George washed his hands?

Garcia quickly decided on a plan of action. He would wait at the second washbasin – the one in the middle – pretending to be checking his reflection in the mirror. Once George left the stall, he would only have two choices – both of them right by Garcia's side.

So Garcia did exactly that – stood facing the mirror, pretending to be checking something in his right eye, for almost two minutes before he finally heard the stall door behind him unlock. But the person who'd been locked inside the toilet stall wasn't George. It was droopy-eyelids man, who gave Garcia a half-embarrassed nod.

They both quickly washed their hands and returned to the support-group meeting. George was sitting back between the two women, arms crossed in front of his chest, hands tucked away under his armpits.

Where the hell did he go? Garcia wondered, as he got back to his seat.

When Garcia's turn to share came up, he gave them the story that, by then, sounded so natural coming out of his lips, he felt he could ace a polygraph. As he delivered his tale, his sad tone of voice and seemingly aimless head and eye movement were nothing short of perfect, and he made absolutely sure that at the exact moment that he said the words – 'the next thing that my friend remembers was the sound of his son screaming in pain because, somehow, a couple of his fingers were broken' – he had casually leaned forward, resting his elbows on his knees, and his gaze had panned right, in the general direction of George.

That was when he saw it.

Not George's hands and fingers, but the look in his eyes . . . the muscle that involuntarily twitched on his lower jaw . . . the way in which his crossed arms clearly tightened their grip on his chest, as if to hide his hands even more.

Garcia wasn't sure if George had noticed that Garcia had picked up on how discomforted he looked, but this time, it was George's eyes that darted away a little awkwardly.

Garcia felt a lump come to his throat.

Once he finished telling his story, Garcia sat back on his chair and made no new attempt to peek at George's hands and fingers again.

He didn't need to.

His gut was telling him that he was right.

Fifty-Two

At the end of the meeting, as everyone was leaving the classroom, Garcia quickened his pace to get to the parking lot before everyone else. The plan was the same as it had been from the start – hang out outside in plain sight, giving other group members a chance to approach him, if they so wished. But as Garcia exited the back gates onto the school parking lot, he paused, his eyes narrowing at something that he hadn't noticed before – a truck that was parked about four spaces to the left of his Honda Civic – a dark-colored, twin-cab, Dodge RAM pickup truck. The reason why he hadn't noticed the truck before was because it wasn't there when he'd arrived, ten minutes before the support-group meeting was supposed to start. Whoever was driving that truck had gotten to the meeting after he did.

Garcia turned to look behind him – no one else was coming out of the school building yet. He got to the truck as fast as he could and rounded it to check the model badge at the back of it. He needed to be sure.

Garcia's heart stuttered.

He was looking at a black Dodge RAM 3500 pickup truck – just like the one that Randy Douglas had seen up on the 7th Street Bridge on the night that they saw Terry Wilford's body drop to the ground.

Garcia looked up to check the school building again. A couple of people had just come down the stairs, but neither seemed to be making their way toward the pickup truck. One of them had paused to light up a cigarette, while the other had turned left, tucked his hands into his pockets and disappeared down an alleyway. Due to the poor lighting at the parking lot and the fact that Garcia was looking at them from behind the truck and through its twin-cabin, he couldn't tell exactly who either of them was, but Garcia didn't panic. After all, his car was parked just there. It wasn't as if he was about to get caught red-handed, as he snooped around somewhere he didn't belong. He straightened his body, casually walked over to his vehicle and got inside.

Every evening, for the past two weeks, as they were both done with their support-group meetings, Hunter and Garcia would either text or call each other, just to let each other know how their meeting had gone. Their texts, though in plain English, read like some sketchy drug-dealers' code – 'no juice tonight, see you tomorrow' or 'no oddly shaped fingers all night. Catch you in the morning'.

Garcia wasn't one hundred percent sure if George, or whatever his name really was, had fully noticed the kind of attention that Garcia was paying him throughout the meeting, but the one thing that Garcia knew for sure was that people spooked easily . . . and guilty people spooked even easier. Right then, Garcia had a feeling that if George left that meeting without Garcia tailing him, neither he nor Hunter would ever see him again.

Garcia was just about to type out a message to Hunter, quickly explaining that he needed to tail a suspect, when he sensed a presence just outside his driver's door.

Garcia never saw him coming – as if that tall figure had just materialized out of nowhere, spawning right out of the dark shadows to be by Garcia's car, giving him no time to react.

Buzz.

Garcia felt a sharp sting at the base of his neck, immediately followed by a jolt of electricity so powerful he felt as if his flesh was being cooked right under his skin. Garcia's body jerked violently in place. His cellphone flew up from his hands, hitting the windshield and the dashboard, before landing on the passenger seat. His head slammed backward against the headrest hard, and just as he was about to pass out – just as his eyes rolled up and into his head – Garcia heard the man outside his car say:

'Looking for me?'

Fifty-Three

In North Long Beach, Hunter's final domestic violence support-group meeting went just like every other meeting that he'd attended in the past two weeks – no oddly shaped fingers, no telltale reflexes as he delivered his made-up story and no one approaching him at the end of the meeting for a friendly chat. As he finally stubbed out his cigarette and got back into his car, he rested his head on the steering wheel and breathed out.

'This is just crazy,' he told himself with a shake of the head.

Hunter was used to frustration. It was part of the job. Most murder investigations moved forward slowly, a small piece at a time, while some would drag behind at a snail's pace. Sometimes, the whole investigation would just grind to a halt due to the lack of evidence or clues ... and that, Hunter knew, was exactly what was happening to this case.

With over one hundred different support groups scattered around LA that catered to help people who could easily fall into the category of abusive parents, he and Garcia could be doing this every night for a whole year and never identify a single suspect, but Hunter didn't know what else to do. They had no crime scene to investigate, no new forensics report to study in the hope of new clues ... and no other avenue to pursue other than the one they'd already been going down for the past two weeks.

He and Garcia needed to regroup and rethink.

Hunter reached into his jacket pocket for his cellphone and began typing one last 'sketchy drug-dealers' text message.

Yet again, no crooked fingers or shady reactions tonight. Need to re-evaluate our approach.

But before he pressed the 'send' button, Hunter paused.

There was no message from Garcia.

He checked the time – 9:58 p.m.

Garcia's support-group meeting was supposed to have ended an hour ago. There should've been some sort of message by now. They always texted each other within five to ten minutes of their meetings ending.

Hunter dialed his voicemail service – no new messages either.

Something wasn't right.

Hunter didn't believe in premonition, sixth sense, divination, omens ... whatever name people called it these days. But he had always trusted his gut. It had guided him down the right path and saved his life more times than he could remember, and right then, his gut was screaming at him that something had gone wrong.

He quickly dialed his partner's number. The call went straight to voicemail. The message he left was simple and to the point: *Carlos, where the hell are you? Call me back.*

Hunter disconnected and dialed Dispatch, asking them to track Garcia's cellphone location.

While he waited, he deleted the original message that he had typed and typed a brand new one, identical to the voicemail he'd just left. Five seconds after pressing 'send', his phone rang in his hand.

'*Detective Hunter?*' the young male voice at the other end of the line asked, as Hunter took the call. '*My name is Milton, I'm with the LAPD COMPSTAT. We've just tracked Detective Garcia's cellphone location, like you've requested. His GPS and tracking chip are pinging normally, but he's not answering his calls. We've also tried to contact him via PD radio, since he's got a unit in his car, but we got no response either.'*

'So where is it?' Hunter asked. 'His cellphone. Where did you track it to?'

'To a high school car park in Watts.'

'Thomas Riley High School?' Hunter asked, remembering the name of the school where Garcia had said that his support-group meeting was taking place that evening.

'That's exactly the one,' Milton replied.

'And you're sure that his cellphone is showing at the car park, not inside a school building.'

'I'm sure,' Milton confirmed before explaining. *'Without any high-structure interference, regular GPS tracking systems are accurate to within a radius of about sixteen feet, but LAPD detectives' cellphones are equipped with a tracking chip, which is accurate to within three feet. His cellphone is definitely in the parking lot, not in a school building.'*

Hunter knew that meant Garcia's cellphone wasn't inside the phone basket that is passed around before the meetings start.

'Are you still tracking the phone? I mean, right now?'

'Yes, we are.'

'Is it moving, or stationary?'

'Stationary. It's been stationary since we acquired its location, a couple of minutes ago.' There was a half-hesitant pause. *'What it looks like, Detective, if you'll allow me an opinion, is that Detective Garcia simply left his cellphone inside his car. Maybe he's just watching a high school basketball game, or something.'*

'No, that's not it,' Hunter replied. 'He didn't forget his phone inside his car.' He switched on his engine. 'OK. I need you to do me two favors, Milton. First, I need you to send me the exact location of his cellphone.'

'Give me a second ... done.'

Hunter heard a ping coming from his cellphone.

'Second, I need you to call Dispatch and ask them to send a black-and-white to that location, right now – possible officer in distress.'

'*On it.*'

'Thank you, and keep on tracking his cellphone until I get there. I'm on my way now.'

'*Not a problem,*' Milton replied. '*I'll keep you posted if there's any status change.*'

Hunter disconnected and put his car in gear.

If his gut feeling was screaming at him before, it was now playing a full-blown metal concert through a wall of sound – something had definitely gone wrong.

Fifty-Four

Garcia blinked himself awake, or at least he thought he did. His eyes felt like they were open, but he could see nothing other than absolute darkness.

But this wasn't a dream, this wasn't a nightmare – God knew he'd had plenty of those and in none of them had he ever felt physical pain, which was the only thing that he could feel right then ... sickening, debilitating pain.

The back of his neck felt like it was on fire – as if a lit charcoal stone was just sitting against his skin, scorching and blistering it, as it burned through onto the flesh beneath. That agonizing feeling had forced his neck muscles to tighten to the point of spasms, sending shards of pain traveling down his spine until they hit its base, at which point they would break out in every direction.

Right then, the phrase 'everything hurts' had never felt so real.

Zing.

There it was again – another explosive stab of pain coming from his neck, like fireworks shooting into every corner of his body, seemingly ripping through tendons and muscles to finally sear every nerve-ending he possessed, and some he wasn't even aware existed.

Reflexively, his hand tried to move up to the source of the pain, but it didn't get far. In fact, it didn't move at all, because both of his arms were bound at the wrist to something solid.

'What the fuck?'

It seemed like the intense pain had shot its shards into his brain as well because Garcia couldn't remember much.

Where the hell was he and why was he there?

Every time he tried to think, it felt as if he had activated a kaleidoscope of sharp razors inside his skull.

Zing.

More fireworks, forcing him to clench his jaw and his body to convulse in place, but still, Garcia pushed his brain through what he could of the pain to try to remember. If he could remember what had happened, he would probably stand a better chance ... of what exactly, he had no idea.

Think, man ... think, he urged himself.

The kaleidoscope inside his head rotated again.

The sharp razors dropped like confetti.

More pain.

More convulsing.

But finally, through all the jaw clenching, fragments of something began to come back to him. And they came back fast – the school classroom ... the support group ... the late arrival who called himself George ... the parking lot outside ... the black pickup truck ... sitting inside his car ... and then nothing ... until he woke up in this dark hell.

That gap in Garcia's memory, Hunter had explained to him once, was called 'selective amnesia'. It was usually brought on by some sort of traumatic event. To try to shield the person from the kind of psychological fractures that the traumatic event could cause, the brain would then choose to forget just part of an event. That's why he could remember the entire night until just before the attack that had rendered him unconscious. All that was missing from his recollection was the attack itself – the most traumatic part of the event.

Garcia tried to move his hands again. As he did, he felt

something dig at his wrists, but the pain already moving around his body was so intense that the digging at the wrists felt like a summer breeze.

Since Garcia couldn't bring his hands to his body, he simply moved them in place, using his fingers to feel around, trying to better understand his predicament. Judging by how tight and how thin the ligatures to his wrists were, he guessed that they were zip ties. What his wrists were bound to was hard and cylindrical in shape, like a metal tube, or something similar.

Garcia could also feel that he was in a lying-down position, with his legs stretched out under him and his ankles secured in place, probably by another pair of zip ties. The only conclusion he could come to was that he had been tied down to some sort of hospital bed or gurney.

Using all the strength that he could muster, Garcia pushed from the hips to jerk his body upward. The effort sent another spray of pain up and down his spine, but he was able to figure out something else as well. Only his body jerked. The bed that he was bound to didn't move an inch, which told him that it was either a very heavy bed, or it was bolted to the ground.

Flash.

All of a sudden, the lights came on.

Finally, confirmation that his eyes were really open, because as the light traveled through his pupils and reached his retinas, it felt like a needle had punctured his cornea and it was now scraping at his ocular globe. A whole new dimension of pain was created – and with the pain came a crazy explosion of colors, blurring his vision.

Instinctively, Garcia shut his eyes as tight as he could, but it made no difference. The pain was already traveling through his nerves and the colors just kept on coming.

He grimaced and winced, which only served to stretch his neck muscles even more, as if they were about to snap.

'Is it too bright for you?'

The male voice caught Garcia by surprise, but he resisted the urge to look and kept his eyes firmly shut. He knew that if he opened them up right then, he wouldn't be able to see anything anyway. He'd been in darkness for God-knew-how-long, so even if he hadn't been sedated, which he was sure that he had been, his pupils would be naturally dilated. All that would happen would be that his eyes would devour the light in the room, and light would just add fuel to the already all-consuming fire of pain.

Instead, Garcia breathed in through his nose and tried to concentrate on the voice.

'Would you like me to dim them down for you?'

Garcia had heard that voice before. He knew he had.

Still keeping his eyes closed, he nodded his reply.

Through the thin skin of his eyelids, Garcia sensed the lights dimming.

'Take your time,' the voice said. 'Don't be too eager. Your pupils will soon adjust.'

Of course Garcia had heard that voice before. They had been sitting in the same support-group meeting – George, the late arrival, right?

Garcia began trying to open his eyes again. First just a hair ... then a fraction ... then halfway.

'That's it,' the voice encouraged him. 'Do it slowly, or the light will feel like a thunderbolt from hell.'

Garcia finally managed to get his eyes fully open. As he did, the man standing by the light switch rotated it back to full power, bathing the room in such brightness, it could've given Garcia a suntan.

'Fuck!' Garcia shouted, immediately slamming his eyelids shut again, but it was all too late. Pain exploded behind his eyes, enveloping his brain and compressing it in a vice grip before expanding like a tsunami throughout every atom of his body.

'Really?' The man laughed. 'You think I'm here to make this a more pleasant experience for you? Would you like a fucking massage as well? I'm good at those.'

Garcia heard steps coming closer. A couple of seconds later, the man spoke again, but this time, his voice was right by Garcia's ear.

'You better savor that little pain that you're feeling right now – and that is *little* pain – because what's coming your way will make your soul want to abandon ship and leave your body here to rot. Do you understand what I'm saying?'

The pain was so intense that Garcia felt dizzy ... too dizzy, actually. He was passing out again, but there had been a delay ... a hesitation between him opening his eyes and the man at the light switch bringing it back to full power again. It had been just a tiny gap, but a gap that had allowed Garcia to lock eyes with the other person in that room, and that was when he realized that he had been wrong.

The person he saw standing just a few feet from him wasn't George, the late arrival at the support-group meeting. It was Trevor, the caterpillar-eyebrows man.

Fifty-Five

Splash.

The bucket of freezing water did exactly what it needed to do – woke Garcia back up again.

This time, not surprisingly, he woke up in a fright, desperately gasping for air. His heart pounded inside his chest with such intensity that he thought it would break through his ribcage and land on his lap. His eyes, bloodshot, blinked frantically as they tried to regain focus.

It wasn't exactly the 'Neo Burst' that the man was used to, but Garcia also wasn't exactly the kind of victim that he would have down in his cellar. But just like the saying went – there was a first time for everything.

'And there you are.' The man's voice echoed through the room.

Still unsure of what was really happening, caught somewhere between the stupor of a chemically induced sleep and the rude freezing-water-to-the-face awakening, Garcia's brain was doing all it could to catch up.

Once again, Garcia found himself in a dark room, but this time the room wasn't nearly as dark as the one that he was in the first time that he came to. Still, his eyes had to fight the dim light for a moment before they were able to start refocusing.

The first thing that Garcia realized was that he wasn't in a lying-down position anymore. He was sitting down. His wrists and ankles were still tightly restricted, probably tied to the legs and arms of the chair that he was in, but this time, so was his head, which had been slotted in between two thick wooden sticks that protruded out of the chair's high backrest. A thin strap of something, which Garcia guessed was another zip tie, wrapped itself around his forehead, pressing his head back, completely immobilizing it in place. There was no way that he could turn or move his head in any direction. All that Garcia could do at that specific point in time was to try not to panic.

As his pupils slowly began getting used to the low light, the darkness around him began to disassemble itself into different shapes. His eyes moved left and right to try to identify his surroundings, but without any head movement, his field of vision was extremely limited – mostly just straight ahead, and straight ahead all he could see was a man standing several feet in front of him.

'Welcome back,' the man said, leaning against something that looked to be a table.

Garcia first took in his entire figure – tall and well built, with broad shoulders – before allowing his eyes to settle on his face. There was something familiar about it, but Garcia couldn't recognize any of the details – small nose, low cheekbones, shaved head, light-brown eyes, and no eyebrows, which simply made his whole face look odd.

Garcia concentrated, his brain trying hard to place him against the image at the forefront of his memory, because he was sure that the man he'd seen standing by the light switch earlier, just before he'd passed out again, had been caterpillar-eyebrows Trevor.

The man read Garcia like an open book.

'Concentrate on my voice,' he said, folding his arms in front of himself and sounding exactly like Trevor. 'The face is too different for you to be able to properly place me.' He paused and it looked like if he'd had eyebrows, they would've arched upward, widening his eyes, but since there was absolutely nothing where his eyebrows should've been, his facial movement simply made his already odd face look either comical, or frightening. Garcia couldn't tell which.

'Plus,' the man continued, his voice calm, 'I used a trick called "feature attention displacement". Do you know what that is?'

Garcia took a deep breath. That had been something else that Hunter had explained to him years ago, when they were chasing a criminal called Lucien Folter.

Feature attention displacement was when someone would create a disguise and overemphasize one or two aspects of that disguise, to the point of making it look unusual – very thick eyebrows, extra-bushy moustache, a scar, a limp ... something out of the ordinary. What that did, in reality, was push others to concentrate their attention on the odd feature. When that happened, their brains would, more often than not, disregard everything else. If anything went wrong and a witness was called upon to give the authorities a description of the person in question, their memories would keep on going back to the odd feature, practically unable to remember anything else.

'And I fell for it like an amateur,' Garcia replied, his voice barely a whisper. 'The caterpillar eyebrows, right?' The words hurt his throat as they caught like broken glass against the vulnerable tissue there. But the pain that he was experiencing then felt like nothing compared to the kind of pain he'd felt earlier. The neck spasms had ended ... the fireworks of pain had dissipated ... the kaleidoscope of razors behind his eyes had vanished.

The man laughed and nodded. 'The caterpillar eyebrows. That's pretty much all you can remember from Trevor, isn't it?'

Garcia felt like an idiot because the man was right. All that his memory had retained from Trevor's face had been the caterpillar eyebrows.

'Yeah, you look much better now.' Garcia made no effort to strip the comment of sarcasm. 'The boiled-egg look suits you.'

The man looked back at him and smiled – another facial expression that didn't match the lack of eyebrows.

Frightening, Garcia had decided. Not comical.

'So what's your name?' Garcia ventured a question, his voice beginning to regain some of its strength. 'I mean your real name. Because I'm sure it isn't Trevor ... or Michael ... or Russell.'

The man was clearly taken aback. He wasn't expecting Garcia to know any of that.

'I'm impressed.' The man unfolded his arms and took a step to his right. 'You know more than I would ever have given you credit for.'

As the man stepped right, the light reflected off different objects that had been placed on the table he'd been leaning against.

The only two objects that Garcia recognized from where he was sitting were a pistol and a bottle of water.

The man used his left hand and reached for one of the objects on the table. Not the pistol. Instead, he chose a seven-inch stainless-steel blade.

'To be honest,' he said, moving the blade around in front of his eyes, as if he was inspecting it. 'I don't even know anymore, but it doesn't really matter, does it?'

As the man moved the blade around, Garcia finally saw it. His left index and middle fingers both curved outward slightly, bending from the first knuckle. Subtle, but still noticeable.

The man put down the blade before picking up a new one – this time, a large stainless-steel meat cleaver. 'A name is just a name, isn't it?' He now looked like he was staring at his own reflection in the cleaver. 'I am who I need to be ... and that changes from time to time. Michael ... Russell ... Trevor ... *Carlos* ... whoever. In the end, I'm just the one who gives them what they deserve.' The man's eyes moved from the cleaver to Garcia. 'I am the bringer of retribution.'

'Cute,' Garcia said back. 'Did you come up with that name yourself?'

The man smiled again.

Garcia held the man's stare for an instant. 'I'm sorry, but is the blade swapping and the stare-down supposed to scare me?'

The man shrugged. 'I don't know. Is it scaring you?'

'No, not really.' Garcia paused, his eyebrows lifting ever so slightly. 'Well, maybe just a little bit. But that's probably because without any eyebrows, your forehead seems to go on for weeks. Do you actually know where it starts and where it ends?'

The man put down the cleaver. 'Have you ever heard the saying – sarcasm is the lowest form of wit?' He reached for something else on the table – a kitchen blowtorch.

'Of course I have,' Garcia replied. 'But that thought is incomplete. What it truly says is, sarcasm is the lowest form of wit, but the highest form of intelligence – Oscar Wilde said that.'

'Oh.' The man tried to sound impressed. 'An educated cop. That's surprising.'

'Really? You should meet my partner, then, Trevor. Can I call you Trevor, or do you prefer one of the other names? I'd rather have a name than not.'

'Russell.'

'WHOA!'

The whispered name caught Garcia totally by surprise, making him jump in place. It hadn't come from the man in front of him. It came from somewhere to his right. And it scared him stiff.

Reflexively, he tried to turn his head in that direction, but it just wouldn't move. His eyes, on the other hand, darted hard right, but whoever had spoken was hidden in the dark shadows and way out of his field of vision. Despite his feebleness, Garcia could clearly identify the voice as being female.

'Who's there?' he asked.

No reply.

Garcia's eyes moved back to the man ahead of him. 'Who's there? Who's in here with me, Trevor?'

'Russell,' the female voice said again.

'Who are you?' Garcia asked.

The man put down the blowtorch. 'Who is she?' He sounded confused. 'I thought that you were here for her.'

Garcia's heart sank until it was nothing but a lead weight at the bottom of his stomach. The man could only be talking about a new victim. Someone that he'd already been torturing for days.

'But you're not here for her, are you?'

'Listen,' Garcia said, addressing whomever else was in the room with him and trying his best to sound confident. 'Everything will be all right, OK? I'm a detective with the LAPD. We'll get you out of here.'

Russell laughed. 'Are you sure about that, Mr. Highest Form of Intelligence, LAPD Detective? Because from where I'm standing, it doesn't look too good for you.'

Garcia kept his eyes on Russell.

'You have no idea who she is, do you?' Russell asked.

Garcia stayed quiet.

'OK. Let me show you.'

Russell walked over to where Garcia was sitting and rounded his chair.

'What are you doing?' Garcia asked.

Instead of answering him, Russell unlocked the wheels and swerved the whole chair ninety degrees to its right.

There was nothing there but darkness.

'Hello?' Garcia called out tentatively.

Russell moved right and flicked on a new wall switch.

A dim light sprang to life, illuminating a spot about six feet in front of Garcia.

His eyes widened at what he saw. At the same time, he felt a pit open up in his stomach.

Garcia was looking at an animal cage that couldn't be any larger than five feet by five feet. Inside it was what could only be described as the crumbs of a woman. Even if Garcia knew who she was, he doubted he'd be able to recognize her. It really did seem that she had no flesh on her anymore, only skin and bones, some of which looked to be about to rip through her thin skin and protrude out. She was lying on the floor, which was caked with blood, curled up into an ugly ball. Her eyes seemed almost loose inside their sockets ... her cheeks had sunk into her mouth ... and her lips seemed to have disappeared completely, substituted by a thin, colorless line. The way in which the light reflected off her saggy skin served only to accentuate her dark veins, making her look like a zombie straight out of a Hollywood blockbuster production. Due to the position that she was in, Garcia could see the soles of her feet, which were nothing but a combination of raw flesh and caked blood.

She was dying. There was no question about that.

'You monstrous sonofabitch,' Garcia said, his gaze on the stick-thin figure inside the animal cage.

'What?' Russell said from behind him. 'No sarcastic joke this time? What's the matter, Mr. LAPD Detective? Not funny enough for you?'

The woman on the floor tried to look up at Garcia, but she was so weak that her head just collapsed back to the ground.

Garcia felt his throat constrict.

How evil could one person be?

Russell rotated Garcia's chair back to its original position, locked the wheels and returned to the table of instruments. As he did, he picked up the handheld blowtorch again.

'I'm going to ask you a few questions,' Russell said, taking two steps toward Garcia and lighting up the blowtorch. 'How close this fire gets to your skin will depend on your answers.'

Silence.

'How did you find us?' Russell asked.

Garcia's skin turned into gooseflesh. *Us*. How did you find 'us' . . . not 'me'. Was he referring to himself and the woman in the cage, or himself and an accomplice?

'Us?' Garcia tried his luck. 'Who is us?'

Russell frowned at Garcia, which once again made his face look alien without any eyebrows. 'You really ain't got a clue about anything, do you?' He walked back to where the table was and returned the blowtorch to it before reaching for another light switch on the other side. This one ignited a bulb several feet to the left of the table, its weak light just falling into Garcia's field of vision.

'Jesus!' Garcia gasped, his heart now beating at the bottom of his throat. He truly couldn't believe what he was actually looking at.

He and Hunter had been wrong.

There weren't two of them.

There were three.

Fifty-Six

At that time at night and with sirens blasting, Hunter covered the eight miles that separated North Long Beach from Watts in just under ten minutes. The GPS coordinates that Milton had simultaneously sent to his cellphone and car satnav system took Hunter to Firth Boulevard and the entrance to the Thomas Riley High School car park.

The whole parking lot sat in semi-darkness, with only two lampposts operating. The first was located on the boulevard, just outside the car-park entrance gates. The second was by one of the school buildings, all the way on the other side of the lot. Garcia's car was parked about halfway between the two lampposts, practically hidden in the shadows. Parked directly behind it was an LAPD black-and-white unit. Its flashing lights were on and Hunter could see two uniformed officers outside their vehicle. They seemed to be checking Garcia's Honda Civic.

Hunter parked by the police cruiser and immediately stepped out of his car. As he did, the officer standing by the Honda's driver's door turned to face him.

'You've got to be kidding me, right?' the officer said, his eyes widening at Hunter, as the beam of his flashlight moved over to the detective.

It was only then that Hunter realized that the officer was Emiliano Esqueda.

'What's going on here?' Emiliano asked, his gaze firmly on Hunter.

The second officer, who had been peeking into Garcia's car through the passenger window, straightened his body and adjusted his cap on his head.

'That's Detective Garcia's car,' Hunter replied, nodding at it. 'You remember him, right?'

Emiliano nodded back.

'How long have you been here for?' Hunter asked.

'We just got here.' Emiliano glanced at the other officer.

'About a minute before you,' he confirmed.

'We got a radio in from Dispatch for a possible officer in distress,' Emiliano explained, giving Hunter a shrug and broadly gesturing at the car park. 'None of that here, except this lonely vehicle. We were just checking it, when you arrived.'

Hunter approached Garcia's car. The driver's window was wide open, but he saw no signs of a break-in or a struggle. There was no blood on the door . . . no blood on the seats . . . no blood on the ground outside the car either. On the passenger seat, Hunter saw his partner's cellphone.

'Have you checked the trunk yet?' Hunter asked.

'Like I've said,' Emiliano replied. 'We just got here. We were just about to check the car when you arrived. We haven't touched anything yet.'

'Good,' Hunter said, walking back to his car to collect three pairs of latex gloves. 'This is possibly the scene of an officer's abduction. So be very careful with whatever you touch.' He handed them each a pair of gloves.

'An officer's abduction?' Emiliano asked, his eyes bouncing from Hunter to the second officer, then back to Hunter. 'From here?'

Hunter rounded the car and pulled open the passenger door. 'Detective Garcia was attending a support-group meeting at this school earlier this evening.' He reached for Garcia's cellphone. 'He was supposed to message me once the meeting was over, which happened over an hour ago. He didn't.'

'A support-group meeting?' Emiliano turned to look back at the school building. 'What kind of support group?'

'It's part of an ongoing investigation,' Hunter explained. 'We were both attending meetings undercover.'

Hunter pressed a side button on Garcia's cellphone to wake it up and tapped its screen. He and Garcia had long ago shared their cellphone and computer login passwords, just in case something like this ever happened.

'So you think that someone who was also at the meeting took him?' the second officer asked.

'That would be the logical deduction.' Hunter nodded.

On Garcia's cellphone, he navigated to the text application that they always used and checked the last message Garcia had sent him. It was a message from the previous evening, after Garcia's support-group meeting had ended – *And again . . . nope . . . nothing tonight. See you in the morning.*

Hunter checked the last call out. It had been made to Anna, Garcia's wife, that evening, at 7:09 p.m.

Hunter had just placed Garcia's cellphone into his pocket when a short and stumpy, Indian American man exited the school building and made his way to where they were standing.

'Is there some sort of problem here?' he asked, as he got nearer.

'Who are you?' Hunter asked in return.

'I'm Pakesh, the school caretaker,' the man replied, his gaze rounding the group, his index finger pointing back at the school building. 'I was coming over to lock the gate to the parking lot when I saw the police lights.'

'Are there any CCTV cameras on this parking lot, Pakesh?' Hunter asked, not holding out much hope. From where he was standing, he couldn't see any.

'No, nothing here,' the caretaker replied. 'This is a very quiet school.'

'Women only, right?' Emiliano said, with a nod.

'That's right,' Pakesh confirmed. 'It's a special school for pregnant minors and teen mothers – part of the LA Unified School District. We have a few CCTV cameras in the building, down a few of its corridors, but that's all.'

Hunter breathed out as he pressed the release button for the glove compartment in Garcia's car. In there, he found his partner's weapon and badge.

This was bad – whoever had taken Garcia had clearly taken him by surprise because he didn't even have a chance to reach for his gun. The perpetrator was also intelligent enough to leave Garcia's cellphone and the car behind. Now, there was no way that they could GPS-track him.

'Did you know that there was a support-group meeting happening at the school tonight?' Hunter asked Pakesh.

'Yes,' Pakesh nodded. 'That's Mrs. Kimura's support group. Teresa Kimura, but she likes to be called Tessa. She's a very nice lady. Been running the group here every Friday evening for years.'

'Do you know which classroom they used for the meeting tonight?' Hunter asked.

'Yes,' Pakesh replied, turning to face the school building once again. 'Classroom 233, right in that building, over there.'

'Any CCTV cameras on that corridor?' Hunter again.

'Yes, but it's switched off.'

'What's the point of a security camera if it's switched off?' Emiliano asked.

'Tessa's request,' Pakesh replied. 'For the anonymity of her members.'

'What support group is it?' Emiliano again. 'Who is it supporting?'

'It's a group to help people struggling with domestic violence,' Pakesh confirmed.

Emiliano's eyes darted toward Hunter, who calmly turned to address Pakesh again.

'As the group was leaving the meeting earlier this evening, did you happen to see anything out of the ordinary?'

'Out of the ordinary?' Pakesh looked unsure.

'Anything strange,' Emiliano tried to clarify. 'An argument, maybe? Some kind of altercation between two or more of the group members? A fight here in the parking lot? Loud shouting? Anything?'

The caretaker shook his head, yet again. 'I didn't even see the group leaving tonight. I was in the other building, fixing a few desks.' He shrugged it off. 'I'm good with things like that, you know? DIY stuff.'

Hunter straightened his body and looked around the empty parking lot, his mind racing through the few options he had.

He could get in touch with the support-group moderator, Teresa Kimura, but how could she help? Just like with every support group that he and Garcia had attended in the past two weeks, Hunter was sure that Teresa Kimura didn't keep an attendance sheet. There was no roll call and no name-checking. Even if she remembered everyone who had been at her group meeting that evening, how would that help? What could she do? Give a sketch artist six, eight . . . ten different sketches? And how long would it take the LAPD to track them all down?

Hunter shook his head at himself. The best he could do was to get a forensics team to that parking lot as fast as he could and hope that they could lift something from Garcia's car – maybe a fingerprint from one of the doors, or a hair follicle from somewhere inside the vehicle, but that too was a shot in the dark.

Garcia took good care of his car, but Hunter knew that he hadn't had time to have it washed in at least a couple of weeks.

Forensics could come up with tens of different fingerprints and/
or DNA profiles. And all of that took time ... a lot more time
than Garcia had.

From experience, Hunter knew that when a perp took a police
officer hostage, there were basically only two reasons for that.
Either the perp would use the officer as a bargaining chip, if he
found himself pressed into a corner, or that officer would be murdered. And since this perp wasn't being pressed into any corners,
why would he use Garcia as a bargaining chip?

Fifty-Seven

Despite the dim light, Garcia could clearly see the two people to the left of where Russell was standing. They were both sitting down, both in wheelchairs ... just like Garcia was, but neither of them seemed to be tied down to their chairs. They were just sitting there, quietly observing what was happening in the room.

'What the fuck?' Those words rode on a deflated breath.

Garcia was staring back at a man and a woman. Both of them appeared to be somewhere in their eighties, but Garcia could easily be wrong. It was impossible to tell for sure because they both looked almost mummified. Their scaly skin clung oddly to whatever flesh they still had left on their bodies. Their faces looked sunk-in and ghostly white, as if they hadn't seen the sun in years. There were odd scratches all around their almost cloudy eyes, and the stare in them seemed completely lost ... catatonic, even. Their lips were cracked, their fingernails were broken, their skeletal-looking hands were covered in liver spots, and their teeth and gums were dark ... possibly rotting. The man had already lost all of his hair and the skin on his head was blotchy and flaky. The woman wasn't doing much better, with only a few unraveled strands left on her head.

As the dim ceiling spotlight shone down on them, they blinked a couple of times. The man winced once, as if the light hurt his eyes. These two clearly weren't Russell's accomplices, like Hunter and Garcia had suspected ... they were his victims.

'Let me introduce you to my mom and dad,' Russell said, gesturing at the old couple.

Garcia's gaze shot to him, followed by a long moment of hesitation.

'These ... are your parents?' he asked, eyes wide, brow furrowed.

'One and the same,' Russell said in reply. 'You can thank them if you like.'

Garcia's expression gave away his confusion.

'A moment ago you called me a monstrous sonofabitch,' Russell explained, as he shrugged. 'Well, everything I am ... everything I became, I owe it to them. They created me.' He smiled at the old couple. 'And I do mean *created*.' He started to slowly unbutton his shirt.

Garcia wasn't quite sure of what was really happening right then.

'Do you actually have any kids, Detective?' Russell asked.

'No, I don't.'

'But you understand the premise of being a parent, right?' Russell didn't wait for a reply. 'As they say, it's supposed to be a labor of love. Your parents bring you into this crazy fucking world and they are supposed to be the first people you come into contact with ... your first experience with another human life on this planet. They are the ones who are supposed to bring you up and care for you ... the ones by whose side you are supposed to feel safe, protected from harm ... the ones who are supposed to be there for you ... to support and defend you, regardless.' He undid the last button on his shirt. 'In essence, you're a part of them ... an extension of who they are. You share the same flesh ... the same DNA ... the same blood. *Family*. That sacred word that's supposed to mean so much.'

His stare moved back to Garcia and Garcia could swear that he saw fire burn in his eyes.

'They're supposed to love you *unconditionally*.' Russell stepped into the light so Garcia could better see him. 'Well ... let me show you how much my parents loved their only child, Detective. How much the word "family" meant to them.' He took off his shirt, allowing it to drop to the floor.

Garcia's eyes widened, as his jaw dropped open. It was hard to make sense of what he was looking at.

It looked as if Russell was made of scars – thick, ugly, leathery scars that covered most of his torso – from the base of his neck, down to his lower abdomen: small scars, large scars, scars over scars, scars crisscrossing scars. His body was a tapestry of cruelty. Some of them – the larger ones – had been stitched up, as the stitch scars were clearly visible, but it was easy to see that the stitches had been crudely applied by an amateur. There was no symmetry in them, no precision ... just a crude 'this will do' kind of job. Under his belly-button, Garcia could see what looked like cigarette-burn scars, and his right nipple seemed to be missing. In its place, all that Garcia could see was a leathery and corrugated patch of skin, clearly scorched by fire.

Russell turned around so that Garcia could see his back.

'Jesus fucking Christ!'

More scars – tens of them. Just above his hips, two of the scars dipped into his flesh, almost like bullet wounds, but not as deep.

Russell indicated his torso. 'Three of my ribs have been fractured.' He lifted his left hand. 'Two of my fingers broken.' He pointed to his feet. 'As well as four of my toes.' He pointed to his left ear. 'A punctured eardrum and a fractured orbital bone.' He bent down to pick up his shirt. 'No, I was never in the military and I've never been to war. My war was fought in here.' He broadly gestured at the house. 'And in here.' He pointed to his head. 'I was beat up, almost every day, from a very early age. I can't actually remember when it all started, but I was still a little boy – all the way to the age of eighteen.' Russell began re-buttoning his shirt.

'I wasn't allowed to have any friends. I wasn't allowed to go out. If I ever did anything that they didn't agree with – spoke without being spoken to first . . . had a drink of water without having their permission . . . fell asleep at the table because they never allowed me to sleep more than six hours per night – anything I did that they didn't agree with, was a reason for a beating. *Discipline*, they called it. Any situation, no matter how gentle, no matter how innocent – a different tone of voice, a smile that they thought to be out of context – could trigger a rage attack that I could never understand. And there was no escaping from them. I tried at first. I would run and hide – under the bed . . . behind the sofa . . . inside a cupboard . . .' He shook his head, as he remembered. 'I would pray that monsters that hid under beds really did exist, and that they would take me instead of me having to face another beating.'

Garcia had also been an only child, but he couldn't even begin to envisage what Russell's childhood would've been like. Just a little boy, locked inside a horror house, bursting with anxiety and absolutely petrified of both of his parents. A kid forced to keep all his fears, all his pain, locked inside because he had no one to tell . . . no one who would listen.

Russell turned to face his parents before continuing.

'And that was how I learned that monsters – the ones that can really hurt you – do exist.' His tone was so placid, it sounded like he was reading a story out of a children's book. 'But they aren't shadows lurking behind your clothes, at the back of the wardrobe. They don't hide under beds, or in cupboards, or in the woods. They don't spring out of your nightmares, and they don't only come out at night. No. Real monsters – the ones that can really hurt you . . . the ones that can truly scare you – are a lot closer than we think. They're all around us. And in my case, those monsters turned out to be the very same people I came to call "Mom" and "Dad".'

No reaction from Russell's parents.

He turned to face Garcia again. 'As a little boy, I was only hand-spanked, but it soon moved to belts, wooden sticks, shoes.' He shrugged. 'As I grew older, the beatings got more severe – whips, chains, wire cords . . . anything that could break skin and create another beautiful scar, as if they were sculpting me to look like this. So if you're wondering, Detective, yes, I already looked like a freakshow by the age of eighteen. Every time my parents left the house, they would lock me down here . . . chained to a wall. Sometimes I'd be here for days.'

There was so much pain in Russell's words that even Garcia got goosebumps, but he wasn't surprised. He understood that we, as human beings, begin developing our personalities at a very early age – while we are still babies, actually . . . before real memories are formed – and that personality is heavily influenced and shaped by our relationships with others . . . the people closest to us: namely, our parents. In Russell's case, from what Garcia had heard, that would've been a total catastrophe from the get-go. The psychological devastation that he received as a child clearly manifested itself as severe trauma in his adult life. In short – if a person grows up surrounded by monsters, there's nothing else that that person can turn out to be, but a monster.

'But all that ended when I turned eighteen,' Russell continued, a smirk finding its way to his lips. 'That was when, for all intents and purposes, my parents passed away, conveniently leaving me this house, complete with my dad's secret cellar.'

So that's where we are, Garcia thought. *Locked inside the cellar under Russell's house.*

As Russell mentioned the passing of his parents, Garcia saw the lady in the wheelchair, Russell's mother, turn her head to look at him. If Garcia had seen fire burn inside Russell's eyes just a moment ago, in hers, he saw nothing but pure, unadulterated sadness. His father, on the other hand, didn't move a muscle.

'So,' Russell continued. 'Like I've said, they created me . . . they made me the person I am today. So if you think I'm a monster, Detective, you can thank them for that, because I am a made monster. I am the monster they created.' He spread his arms wide – crucified position – and turned to face his parents. 'Aren't you proud of me, Mom and Dad? Aren't you proud of your son? Wasn't this what you wanted me to become? Like father, like son, hey, Dad?'

Russell's mother looked away from her son, her stare settling back on Garcia.

Russell breathed out and walked back to the table of instruments. 'It was a good thing that my dad had his own business and worked from home. My mother never worked a day in her life. She'd always been a lazy bitch.'

No reaction from Russell's mother.

'Neither of them ever had many friends, so the story of their death wasn't that hard to weave.'

'You've kept your parents alive,' Garcia asked, 'and locked in your cellar since you were eighteen years old?'

'Seventeen years.' Russell practically sang that last word.

'Holy shit!' Garcia whispered. It was impossible to comprehend the amount of anger, the dedication that it took to keep your own parents as prisoners for seventeen years. This was the kind of hatred that just wouldn't dissipate, no matter how much time had passed. This was the kind of hatred that left no room for remorse, no room for mercy, no room for regrets. Russell was thirty-five years old and it seemed that he'd never – not even once in his life – experienced love . . . from anyone. If his body showed that many scars, there was no telling how truly fractured his mind really was.

Coming from his right, Garcia heard the woman in the animal cage cough a breath. She too had been listening to Russell's accounts, as if they were attending another support-group meeting.

'Hold on, Detective.' Russell lifted his hands. 'I'm not that cruel, if that's what you're thinking. I've kept them locked in here, yes, but I've never once touched them. I've never hit my father, or my mother. After all, they're my *family*. And family is sacred, remember?'

A bead of sweat pearled on the back of Garcia's neck before slipping down along his spine.

'At first, I thought I would,' Russell revealed. 'Physically hurt them, that is. I thought that when I finally got them down here, I'd chain them to the walls, like they did to me, and beat the shit out of them. Make them pay for every little scar they gave me ... every nightmare that haunts me ... every tear I cried ... every lost day of my life.' He paused, his gaze distant, clearly taking him back to years ago. 'It took me years to build up the courage to finally do something. I used to be so terrified of them, so scared of fighting back, that there was a time when I believed that I would never be able to break free ... I would never get out of this house.' The pause came with a smile. 'But I did that night. The night before my eighteenth birthday.' Russell turned to face his parents. 'Do you remember that night?'

Once again, there was no reply from Russell's mother, but Garcia saw tears beginning to well up in her eyes.

'They always had a drink before going to bed,' Russell explained. 'So it was easy ... a lot easier than I had imagined. Just a few drops in each glass and that was it. When they fell asleep, I dragged them down here and chained them to the walls, but when it came to hurting them ... I lost my nerve. I just couldn't do it. They were still my father and mother.' Russell took a breathing pause. 'So instead of hurting them, I went out. I just wanted to get out of this house ... out of the hell that I had lived in for so long. I walked for hours, until the sun came up. In the morning, I sat in a park somewhere and just watched people walk by, not knowing what the hell I would do ... trying to dig deep inside myself to find something ... some hope, maybe. Hope that things would get better. Hope that I wasn't too fucked up already.' Russell shrugged. 'But there was no hope inside of me. There was no love, no compassion ... no feelings at all. All I really had locked inside was sadness and what I was given by my parents. The one true thing that I found down in this cellar. Do you know what that is, Detective?'

'Anger?' Garcia ventured.

'Darkness,' Russell corrected him. 'All I could find inside of me was darkness. A darkness so deep that I felt like I was drowning in it. So, on the morning of my eighteenth birthday, sitting alone in that park, I decided that that was exactly what I would do – drown. I decided that I wouldn't come back to this house ever again ... that I would just leave my parents chained to the walls in this godforsaken cellar, and that I would get up from that bench and go see the ocean.'

The question inside Garcia's eyes didn't go unnoticed.

'I'd never seen it before,' Russell explained. 'I was eighteen years old. I'd lived all those years in a city where there are several different beaches. And I'd never once seen the ocean. My parents never took me to the beach.'

Garcia's gaze scooted over to Russell's parents, but there was no reaction from either of them.

'So I decided that as my last act in this life,' Russell carried on, 'my own eighteenth birthday present to myself, I would go see the ocean and then simply walk into it. For someone who was already drowning in darkness, the ocean sounded like a much better option.'

'But you didn't,' Garcia prodded. He had no escape plan, but he knew that he had to somehow keep Russell talking until he thought of something ... if he thought of something.

Russell shook his head. 'No, I didn't. Thanks to a little girl and her father.'

Fifty-Eight

Russell said nothing else after mentioning the little girl and her father. Instead, he turned to face the instruments table again, which Garcia quickly figured out wasn't a good move ... at least not for him.

'A little girl?' he asked. *Keep him talking ... just keep him talking.* 'Which little girl?'

Russell studied the instruments on the table, trying to decide which one to take this time.

'Her name was Nancy,' he replied. 'But I didn't know that at the time. I'd never seen her before. Like I said, I was never allowed out of this house. I was just in the park, trying to figure out what to do, getting my head wrapped around the idea that I was just about to leave my parents chained to a basement wall and go drown myself, when I saw this little girl and her father walk by. He was dragging her by the arm so firmly, she looked like a ragdoll. The poor girl was in tears ... her tiny little legs trying so hard to keep up with how fast her father was dragging her. As they walked past the bench I was sitting on, he yelled at her and pulled on her arm harder. Her shirt hiked up a little at the back. That was when I saw the bruises. Right then, the little girl lifted her head and looked straight at me.' Russell nodded at nothing at all. 'There was so much sadness and pain inside her tiny little eyes. The kind of sadness and pain that I understood. The kind of sadness and pain that I knew so, so well. She didn't have to say a word. One look and I knew exactly what her life was like.' His gaze met Garcia's. 'Right then, I understood that I wasn't alone. I wasn't the only one going through the kind of hell that I had been going through. There were others ... thousands of others. That was when I realized that the darkness that I'd been given by my parents – the darkness that lived deep inside me – didn't have to be a curse. I could make it into a gift – an eighteenth birthday gift.'

'So you decided to become a vigilante?' Garcia asked. 'At the age of eighteen?'

'No,' Russell replied. 'I decided to help them. I decided to help people like me ... people whose *family* was never a family ... people made of scars ... just like I was. So instead of drowning myself, I came back to this house and started to re-plan my life. There was no mortgage on this house anymore. It had all been paid off by then, and my father had enough savings for me to live off for a few years.' A humorless chuckle. 'At last my father had done something right.'

Garcia finally saw movement coming from Russell's father. He slowly turned his head to look at his son and some dormant muscle on his lower jaw twitched once.

Russell saw it too, but he didn't seem to care.

'So,' he continued, 'I used those years of savings to learn and train. I needed to get strong because at the age of eighteen, I had the body of a ten-year-old.' He gave Garcia a matter-of-fact shrug. 'Gaining muscle was hard. It took me a long time and a lot of effort, but learning ...' He shook his head while pursing his lips. 'That was a different ballgame altogether. It turns out that I have a very logical and analytical mind, which means I learn fast. Certain subjects make more sense to me than others, like programming, medicine and anything to do with numbers, like the stock market. So I read – book, after book, after book – until I got good at all three. It took me a few years, especially to get good at medicine. For you to do that you need to practice.' He smiled. 'Lucky for me that I already had a pretty well-equipped surgical room in my cellar. All I needed were practice subjects. Would you like to guess who my first practice subject was?'

Garcia blinked a thought. 'The little girl's father.'

Russell's non-existing eyebrows arched again.

'You followed them home that morning,' Garcia deduced.

Russell nodded. 'I did, but this was four, almost five years later. I was just about to turn twenty-three at that time. I didn't know if they'd still be living in the same house or not.' He angled his head to one side. 'He was. She wasn't.'

Garcia waited.

'Her mother,' Russell explained, 'his wife, had finally had enough and gathered the courage to walk away. It turned out that she was also being beaten up by him. He was a drunk. So I simply approached him at a bar one night, bought him a couple of drinks, and slipped a sedative into one of them. Once I got him down here, I hurt him in the exact same ways he'd hurt his little girl and his wife. And I did it slowly. Just one injury at a time. Until he was gone. It took him almost two months to die. But he was the one who gave me the idea of how to find others just like him.'

'Support groups,' Garcia said.

Russell rubbed his nose. 'On his first night down here, as he pleaded for mercy, screaming in pain, he told me that he knew that he had a problem . . . that he was trying to get better . . . and that he was attending support-group meetings. I hadn't thought of that by then, but it was so logical. I didn't have to go looking for them. They would come to me. All I needed to do was sit and wait . . . pay attention to what they were saying and *ta-da* – the practice subjects would, as if by magic, show themselves. It was perfect because we're talking about people who want to stay anonymous. They use fake names at the meetings, which doesn't actually matter because these types of support groups don't keep a record of who has attended their meetings. We are as anonymous as anonymous can be, and members tend to be the loner type too, just like my parents were – no friends . . . no real family that could give a fuck. They really aren't the type of people who are dearly missed, if you know what I'm saying.' Russell's face twisted into a new expression but, without eyebrows, Garcia couldn't quite decipher it. 'Plus, disguising their deaths as accidental is a genius move, wouldn't you agree, Detective? I could hurt them in every imaginable way and still get away with it.'

The woman in the animal cage coughed again and Garcia's eyes moved hard right, but to no avail.

Russell used her cough as a cue. 'Take her, for example.' He nodded at the cage. 'Real name – Jennifer Mendoza – a fucking worthless junkie who kept her four-year-old daughter locked in a cage in her living room, while she fucked men for drug-money in the bedroom. Once she got high, she wouldn't feed her daughter for days. And for some fuck-knows-why reason, she would also smack her daughter on the soles of her feet. She was *four years old*.' He turned to address Jennifer in the cage. 'How does all that feel now, Jennifer? Good?'

'I . . . love . . . my . . . daughter.' It sounded like it had taken Jennifer the strength of gods to utter those four words.

'But of course you do,' Russell said in reply. 'I love *my* parents.'

'How many?' Garcia asked, the hairs on the back of his neck standing on end because he dreaded the answer. 'You just told me that you claimed your first victim at the age of twenty-three – that's twelve years ago. How many have you killed in those twelve years?'

There it was again – the eyebrow movement without any eyebrows. 'I prefer the word *punished*.'

'How many have you punished?' Garcia rephrased the question.

A careless shrug. 'I don't do what I do for numbers, Detective. I do it because these people deserve a dose of their own medicine.

The things that they do to their own sons and daughters ... you wouldn't believe.' Russell, once again, indicated the scars on his torso. 'From scarring, to disfigurement, to breaking bones, to death. And I'm not even going to mention the mental health destruction that it causes. They bring a kid into this world, ideally, through an act of love. But that's not what they give out ... that's not what we get. What we get is hate ... and anger ... and whiskey breaths ... and mood swings ... and punishment, for the simple fact that we exist ... for the simple fact that we are *here*. But guess what, Mom and Dad?' With his arms opened wide, Russell turned to face his parents again. The next sentence was delivered through gritted teeth. 'I didn't ask to be here. I didn't ask to look like a freak. I didn't ask for all this hurt ... all this pain.' He smiled at them. 'But you did.'

'How many have you punished?' Garcia asked again, interrupting Russell's outburst at his parents.

'Sixty-three.'

The reply caught everyone by surprise because it didn't come from Russell.

It came from his mother.

Fifty-Nine

Despite being frail, Russell's mother's voice echoed throughout the room that they were in like a gunshot, dragging Garcia's and Russell's eyes straight to her.

'Is that so, Mom?' Russell asked, his tone firm.

'Sixty-three,' she repeated. Her eyes didn't meet her son's. 'Twelve years.'

Her husband slowly looked at her and nodded his confirmation.

There was something that went beyond chilling in the way that Russell's mother had replied, and in the way that her husband had agreed. It was as if they were both proud of their son's achievements.

Garcia's stomach knotted inside of him. He was looking at a serial killer who'd been operating under the radar and in their own backyard for twelve years. A killer who had possibly claimed sixty-three victims – certainly one of the most prolific serial killers that he and Hunter had ever come across – and they knew nothing about it. How was that even possible? It had to be a mistake.

'How do they know?' Garcia asked. 'How do your parents know that there were sixty-three victims?'

'Because he makes us watch.' Once again, Russell's mother beat him to the punch. Her voice was just a little steadier than moments ago. 'If we refuse, he uses an eye speculum to force our eyes open.'

Garcia breathed out. That was the reason for the odd scratches around their eyes.

'*Watch this,*' she continued. 'That's the command he uses when he wants us to watch – *watch this*.'

Garcia's surprised and questioning eyes shot to her before rolling over to Russell. 'You . . . force them to watch, while you torture and kill people?'

Russell looked back at him sideways. 'It's only fair, don't you think, Detective? Give them back at least some of the psychological damage they gave me?'

Garcia's stare intensified.

'Like I told you.' Russell made it sound trivial. 'I'm a made monster. I am what I am because of what they were. Don't you think that it's only fair for them to see what they created? To watch what I'm capable of simply because I'm their son?' He finally picked up an instrument from the table – a surgical scalpel. 'I'm their own artwork, Detective – darkness sculpted out of deeper darkness, if you like. I'm their own flesh . . . their own blood . . . their own DNA. I'm their legacy, so I think that it's only fair that I allow them to witness the fruits of their labor of love.' He pointed at himself. '*Me.*'

Garcia saw tears roll down Russell's father's cheeks, but he didn't move. Instead, his wife leaned over and used the tips of her fingers to wipe them from his cheeks.

Russell saw it too, but all he did was snort before walking over to Garcia again. 'Now that the sad stories are over, Detective, I'd like to finally go back to my question.' He grabbed Garcia by the shirt.

Garcia laughed. 'You should drop the scaring act. I already told you that. It's not working. You're not going to hurt me.' He truly hoped that, out loud, he sounded more confident than he did in his head.

Russell looked to be frowning back at him. 'Is that so, Detective? How do you figure?'

'Because you're not stupid,' Garcia replied. 'I'm a homicide detective with the LAPD, investigating a case ... your case. Do you think that I've been doing this all by myself?' He paused, even though he knew that Russell wouldn't answer his question. 'It's an official LAPD investigation. There are notes, files, reports ... a whole map of discoveries that led me to you.' Garcia shrugged. 'All of a sudden, on the night that I attend a support-group meeting as part of the investigation, I disappear. What do you think is going to happen? My team is just going to go on as if everything was peachy?'

Russell let go of Garcia's shirt and smiled. He was so close that Garcia could smell his acrid breath.

'The LAPD doesn't take too kindly to one of their own going missing. They'll come after you with everything they've got – SWAT teams ... SIS ... cops ... the works. How long do you think it will be before they come knocking?'

This time, Garcia paused for effect.

'It's over, Russell ... Michael ... Trevor ... whatever name you want to use. You know it, and I know it. Right now, my whole team is going over all of my notes ... all of my investigation files, following the same trail I did to get to you. I'm surprised they haven't kicked your door in yet.'

Russell straightened up his body.

'Your best bet is to put down the scalpel, cut me loose ... and hand yourself in. Do that, and I can guarantee that they won't shoot you dead. You'll spend the rest of your life in prison, there's no doubt about that, but at least you'll be alive.'

Russell pretended to be thinking about it before sending a politician smile Garcia's way.

'You're a good bullshitter, Detective,' he said, as he began pacing in front of Garcia. 'But not good enough.'

'Is that so?' Garcia came back. 'How do *you* figure?'

'How long do you think you've been down here for, Detective?' Russell asked.

Garcia hesitated. 'I don't know. You tell me.'

'I've kept you sedated for days,' Russell revealed. 'Observing . . . waiting . . . checking the news . . . and nothing. My door is still there . . . unkicked.' He licked his lips slowly, while maintaining heavy eye contact with Garcia. 'There's no way anyone can track you, Detective, least of all back to me. I left your car at the school parking lot. Your gun and badge stayed in the glove compartment. Your phone, I left exactly where it landed. And before you try some new lie, I know that you didn't text or call anyone after you checked my truck out because I was observing you.'

Garcia tried thinking of something to say back, but he had nothing.

'There were no CCTV cameras on that school parking lot,' Russell continued. 'No recording of what happened . . . no one to witness me grabbing you. There's no attendance sheet for the meetings. No names. No addresses. Nothing. So you see, Detective – no one can get to you because no one knows where you are. No one can get to me because no one knows who I am, and I've left nothing behind for anyone to track.' He indicated his shaved head and eyebrows. 'No hairs.' He stepped closer and showed Garcia the tips of his fingers. The skin on them had been completely scarred by fire. 'No fingerprints.' He took a deep breath and closed his eyes for just a second. 'I'm a ghost, Detective. They can't get to a ghost.'

'Well, I got to you, didn't I?' Garcia tried arguing back.

This time, Russell threw his head back and laughed loudly. 'You had no clue who I was. In either of the two meetings.'

Two meetings? Garcia thought. *What the hell is he talking about?*

Garcia didn't hide his surprise too well, because Russell picked up on it.

'You still have no clue, do you?' The pause that followed was anxious. 'Well, allow me to enlighten you.'

Sixty

Before continuing, Russell walked back to the table of instruments and reached for the bottle of water. He undid its cap and took a swig straight from the bottle.

'Thirsty?' he asked Garcia.

'Not anymore,' Garcia replied.

'Suit yourself.' Russell shrugged and took another swig before finally explaining. 'Monday evening support group in Westchester, a week ago. You were wearing blue jeans, a black T-shirt and white sneakers. I was sitting two chairs to your left. I was the second person to share with the group.'

That had been Garcia's first ever support-group meeting.

He searched his memory and what he found baffled him because he remembered it well – only four out of the eight members had shared accounts with the group that evening – three men and one woman. The second person to share had been a tall and overweight man, with long scraggly hair, thin eyebrows and plump cheeks. He looked absolutely nothing like Russell, or Trevor.

Right then, Garcia couldn't believe how stupid he had been. Hunter had warned him about the possibility of the killer disguising himself as he moved from group to group.

Once again, Russell read the surprise in Garcia's eyes.

'Don't blame yourself, Detective,' he said, his tone proud.

'Over the years, I've become somewhat of an expert when it comes to disguises.' A pause, followed by a sideways look. 'That night, I spotted you. I noticed the peculiar way in which you were looking at others. You looked to be paying particular attention to their arms ... or hands – as if you were searching for something. That got me thinking. You could've been there for different reasons – maybe you had started dating someone who had been beaten up by her ex-husband, or father, or stepfather, or whatever ... and you had decided to find him and teach him a lesson. Or maybe you could've been a watered-down version of me ... of what I was doing – just looking to punish some of those freaks. I couldn't really be sure, but I knew that you weren't there seeking help. What it really looked like was that you were there searching for someone in particular ... someone with some identifiable physical characteristic, like a tattoo ... a birthmark ...' Russell swapped the scalpel from his left hand to his right one, so that he could wave the fingers of his left hand at Garcia. '... or oddly shaped fingers.'

Garcia did his best to show no reaction.

'Then, once the meeting was over,' Russell continued, 'I saw you hanging out outside. There was definitely something a little weird about you, but then again, most people who attend those meetings are weird. It was when I saw you at the meeting in Watts that bells really started ringing. I kept my eyes on you the whole time. Very similar behavior to our first encounter, but you seemed to have taken quite an interest in the guy who came in late – George, that was what he said his name was, right?'

Anger began quickly gathering momentum inside Garcia. Anger at himself because he hadn't noticed any of that.

'But things really took a turn when I saw you outside,' Russell confessed. 'Checking out my truck, and I knew that you were there looking for me, but I gathered that you still didn't quite know who I was. All you probably had were a few minor details – male, possibly attending domestic violence, or anger management support groups, a dark pickup truck, and crooked fingers. And then it dawned on me.' He shook the scalpel at Garcia. 'Of course crooked fingers. It matched your bullshit story about breaking your son's fingers, didn't it? You were probably looking for some sort of telltale reflex from someone in the group, right?'

Garcia was impressed. Russell wasn't only an intelligent person with an analytical mind. He was also very perceptive.

Garcia stayed quiet.

Russell paused directly in front of him. 'There's no one coming for you, Detective.' His voice was chilling. The scalpel returned to his left hand. 'Just like no one came for any of them . . . ever . . . because no one knows who I am. Just like you didn't. You were just lucky to spot my truck. That was all. You didn't even know who was driving it.'

There was a long pause, where their heartbeats seemed to stutter together with anxiety.

'The way I see it, all I really need to do is get rid of my truck and give the support groups in LA a break.' He smiled. 'But there are support groups outside LA as well, did you know that?' Sarcasm dripped off Russell's words. He walked over to Garcia and placed the scalpel against the detective's neck. 'But you were right, Detective. It *is* over. For you.'

Sixty-One

Garcia wasn't the type who scared easily, but what he saw burning inside Russell's eyes as he quickly moved up to where Garcia was sitting sent fear spreading throughout his body like pumped blood. He was losing this game – he knew that – and this was the final whistle.

'Wait,' Garcia called out, his voice not as steady as he would've liked. 'What are you doing?'

In one quick and smooth movement, Russell moved the blade from Garcia's neck to his chest, pulled his shirt away from it and drove the surgical scalpel through the shirt, slicing it open from top to bottom to expose the detective's torso.

'I'm doing what I do best,' he replied, placing the scalpel in his back pocket, returning to the table and, once again, retrieving the kitchen blowtorch before his chin jerked in the direction of his parents. 'I'm making them watch.' He addressed his parents. 'Watch this.'

As if hypnotized, the old couple immediately set their unblinking eyes forward, looking directly at Garcia. Russell's command practically turned them into robots.

Garcia felt a panic attack coil just beneath his sternum, as every muscle in his body tensed.

Russell lit up the blowtorch and walked back to where Garcia was. 'I'm only going to ask these questions once, Detective. If you don't reply, or if you lie to me . . .'

Garcia locked eyes with Russell.

'What was the information that you had on my truck?'

Garcia saw no point in lying.

'Pretty much what you just said – a dark Dodge RAM pickup truck – either a 2500 or 3500 model. That was it. That was all we knew.'

'And how did you come across that information?'

'Your truck was spotted at the 7th Street Bridge,' Garcia replied. 'The night you dropped Terry Wilford from it.'

Russell studied Garcia's expression for a moment before deciding that he didn't like that answer.

'Bullshit.' He brought the torch fire to Garcia's torso – left side, just between the sixth and seventh ribs.

Garcia felt the fire immediately blister, then rip his skin clean off the flesh. For some reason, there was a two-second delay between what he felt and the guttural scream that he let out. A scream so primal that it could've woken the dead. His body jerked violently on his chair, as he tried to deal with the kind of pain that he'd never felt before.

'Motherfucker,' he yelled at the top of his voice. A split second later, his nostrils picked up the smell of burned human flesh, which Garcia knew from experience was a distinctively different smell from burned animal flesh. 'What the fuck? I answered your question. Arghhhhhhhh, fuck, that hurts!'

'No,' Russell came back. 'You gave me a bullshit answer, that's what you did. There was no one at the bridge that night. Do you think I didn't check?'

'Not on the bridge,' Garcia replied through gritted teeth, his voice whizzing. The pain was so intense it distorted his vision and sucked the air right out of his lungs. 'Under it, you sanctimonious prick. Two LASAN workers were cleaning the concrete channel that evening. They were the ones who spotted your truck.'

Russell studied Garcia's face once again, but there was nothing else there other than the expression of pure agony and pain.

He didn't like that answer either.

'More bullshit.'

This time, Russell brought the fire to the center of Garcia's chest and, in a slow, up–down movement, scorched a three-inch patch of skin right between his pectoral muscles. He kept the flame there for at least three seconds longer than he did when burning at Garcia's ribs.

White-hot pain exploded from that spot, traveling at lightning speed through every nerve in Garcia's body before meeting up again in his brain, where it blew up like a nuclear bomb. He let out another feral scream that sounded alien. This one was enveloped in spit, which flew off Garcia's mouth in every direction. Every muscle in his body tensed so tightly he began getting cramps in his shins and fore-arms. He convulsed, and carried on convulsing for seconds, even after Russell had dragged the flame away from Garcia's blistered and charcoal-black skin – the flesh beneath it red-raw and moist.

The disgusting, almost putrid smell of scorched flesh hit Garcia's nostrils in no time, traveling even faster into his stomach, where it collected whatever it could find there before erupting back up his esophagus.

Garcia's vision blurred and he puked.

Russell knew that that was coming and moved out of the way in time.

Vomit spilled down Garcia's chin and down to his chest, where it found the freshly burned piece of moist flesh. As acrid bile came into contact with the open wound, a new, gigantic octopus of pain spread its tentacles up, down, and sideways, grabbing and squeezing every nerve it touched. The room began spinning around Garcia.

'There's no way that anyone standing on the concrete channel under the 7th Street Bridge could have identified my truck to that degree. The night before I had blown out a lamppost on the bridge. That's where I stopped. There just wasn't enough light. Superman himself couldn't have spotted a black Dodge RAM 3500 up on the bridge from that distance.'

Garcia felt as if his whole body was on fire. Cold and hot sweat spilled out of his pores, making his skin glisten as if he'd just come out of a shower.

'One of the workers,' Garcia finally replied, his breath catching on his throat, 'is a truck aficionado. Can tell a truck just by its silhouette.' He managed to regain his breath, but not his balance. The room was still spinning around him. 'The 2500 and 3500 have a very distinct design.'

Garcia knew that he couldn't take another burn. He would pass out if he did.

Russell paused, analyzing Garcia's words one more time. *Too plausible a reply for someone to come up with on the spot and under so much pain like Garcia was.* He decided to accept it.

'All right, how about the fingers? How did you find out about that? And think before you reply, Detective, because if I suspect that you're lying, the next thing that I'll burn ...' This time Russell paused for dramatic effect. 'Will be one of your fucking eyeballs. Are we clear, Detective?'

That was when Russell heard a voice come from where his parents were sitting.

'Somehow ... I really don't fucking think so.'

Sixty-Two

Despite the unidentified voice catching him completely by surprise, Russell's reaction was a combination of being startled and prepared in equal measures. He did jump in place, but at the same time, in one smooth and quick movement, he dropped the handheld blow-torch that he was holding, swung his body around and reached for the surgical scalpel that he had placed in his back pocket.

The scalpel ended up at Garcia's neck and Russell ended up directly behind the chair that Garcia was in. The whole move took just a second, as if Russell had rehearsed it many times before.

His eyes quickly found the uninvited guest.

Hunter had his weapon trained on Russell, but as he finally stepped into that crazy torture chamber, his eyes caught sight of yet another person in that room besides Garcia, the perp and the old couple in the wheelchairs, who he had already spotted from the door, before entering the room.

Across from where Hunter was standing, level with the perp and Garcia, but a few feet to their left, Hunter saw another figure that, just like the almost mummified couple to his right, didn't seem human – a woman, on the floor, inside an animal cage. She was nothing but skin and bones, her feet were a bloody mess, and she wasn't moving.

Hunter's aim moved to her for a split second before he decided that she wasn't a threat.

Weapon back to the perp.

'Easy there,' the man with the scalpel to Garcia's neck said, surprise and anger burning inside his eyes. 'You wouldn't want me to slice your friend's neck open like a turkey on Thanksgiving, would you?'

Hunter blinked at him. Whoever he was, he looked a little alien, with a completely shaved head and no eyebrows.

This cellar, Hunter thought, *is proving to be a complete freakshow.*

'Carlos,' Hunter called, his aim unflinching. 'You good?'

Garcia seemed to finally have regained his breath. 'I'm barbe-cued, that's for sure.'

'Yeah, I can smell that.' Hunter nodded. 'Ma'am . . . Sir . . .' he addressed the old couple on the wheelchairs to his right, though his eyes never left the man behind Garcia's chair. 'You two OK?'

There was no vocal reply, but through the corner of his eye, Hunter saw both of them slowly nod.

He knew that it would be pointless asking the lady in the animal cage if she was OK. If she wasn't already dead, she was certainly knocking on death's door.

'Why don't you put the scalpel down?' Hunter said, giving the shaven-headed man a firm nod.

'That's not gonna happen,' the man said back. 'What will happen is – you're going to put your gun down and kick it over here.'

Garcia tried to smile, but it came out a grimace. 'Let me intro-duce you to my team,' he said, addressing Russell.

Hunter's eyes moved to him, with a very clear question in them. *Your team?*

Garcia ground his teeth in pain. 'Robert, meet Russell . . . or Trevor . . . or Michael . . . just take your pick.'

'Well, Robert,' Russell said, his chin jerking in Hunter's

direction. 'Did you hear what I just said? Put down your fucking gun and kick it over here.' He pressed the scalpel tighter against Garcia's throat.

Garcia winced and Hunter saw a drop of blood appear at the tip of the scalpel before running down his partner's neck.

'Yeah.' Hunter's eyebrows lifted ever so slightly. 'That's also not going to happen.'

Russell chuckled. 'Do you honestly want to test me?' He brought his lips to about an inch from Garcia's left ear. 'You better convince *your team* to drop his weapon, Detective, or the next sound you're going to hear will be you gagging on your own blood.'

'He's not going to do that,' Garcia said back, his eyes on Hunter.

'Really?' Russell asked, as he drew the blade a little deeper into Garcia's flesh. A mini blood waterfall began cascading down his neck. 'Just a little bit deeper and I'll hit your jugular. When I do, it's game over. You know that, right?'

'It's already game over,' Hunter said from across the room.

Russell's attention skipped to him.

'You're not getting out of this, and you know it,' Hunter explained. 'The house is probably already surrounded by LAPD officers, who will be coming down this hellhole of a cellar any minute now – and they'll come down here with itchy trigger fingers and loaded weapons. Your only chance of coming out of this cellar alive is to put down that scalpel and hand yourself in. You do that, you live. You don't . . .' Hunter nodded. 'I'm pretty sure that they'll shoot you dead.'

'Yeah, bullshit,' Russell replied. 'There's no one else coming. You came after your friend here alone, didn't you?'

'I did,' Hunter agreed. 'But do you really think that once I found that secret trapdoor in your kitchen, leading down to a concealed cellar, inside a *multiple-homicide suspect's house*, I didn't call for backup?' A subtle shake of the head. 'This isn't a Hollywood movie. In real life, we sense danger, we don't take chances – we call the cavalry. No one is playing games here.'

'Even if you did,' Russell replied, 'no one's gonna do anything. Unless you'd like your friend back with a gushing neck and lifeless.'

Hunter shrugged. 'He's a cop ... an LAPD detective. When we signed up for this job, the risks were all pretty well explained. Many of us lose our lives in the line of duty. That's just the way it is and we're all OK with it. If you wanted a bargaining chip, you should've taken a civilian.'

Garcia's facial expression told Hunter that he really hoped that Hunter was just bluffing.

'Thanks for the tip.' Russell gave Hunter an odd smile. 'Lucky for me that I have one of those right here.' His head jerked right to indicate Jennifer inside the animal cage.

Hunter peeked at her before his attention returned to Russell. Through the corner of his eye he could see that the couple in the wheelchairs hadn't moved a muscle yet. 'I'd say that she's about six feet away from you,' he told Russell. 'Quite a gap. Do you think you can get to her before my bullet gets to you?'

Hunter saw the woman inside the cage try her best to lift her head and look at him. The effort exhausted her and she allowed her head to go back to the floor.

Another smile from Russell. 'I can ... if I bring your friend with me.' He used his foot to unlock the wheels on Garcia's chair. 'Because I know that you won't shoot, despite all that "dying in the line of duty" bullshit speech.'

As Russell pulled the wheelchair back a couple of feet so that he could angle it right, he kept the scalpel against Garcia's neck. 'So,' he said, defiantly, as he began inching the wheelchair toward Jennifer's cage. 'Do you trust your aim enough to take a shot in this dim light? You might hit your friend here.'

Hunter's and Russell's gazes were locked – Hunter's analytical . . . Russell's challenging.

'See,' Russell said, the wheelchair getting ever closer to Jennifer's cage. 'All bullshit . . . like I said. You ain't gonna take a fucking shot.'

Right then, Hunter saw Garcia smile at him.

Hunter smiled back.

'Don't mind if I do.'

He squeezed the trigger once.

Sixty-Three

The smile was the signal.

Garcia knew that his partner was an expert marksman. At a distance of twenty-five feet, Hunter could put a bullet through a donut hole as it swung on a piece of string. To inch Garcia's wheelchair toward Jennifer's cage, Russell needed to use his right hand to push the chair. That meant that the pressure that he was applying to the scalpel with his left one had to be greatly reduced. In doing so, he relaxed his posture just enough to better expose his arm. When Garcia felt the blade relax against his skin, he gave Hunter the signal.

The shot was inch-perfect, hitting Russell right at the top of his left shoulder blade. The bullet ruptured his subdeltoid bursa before shattering the humerus head and exiting at the back. Blood splattered up in the air in a crimson cloud, spitting droplets all over Russell's and Garcia's faces.

At such a close distance, the bullet/shoulder impact was powerful enough to propel Russell backward, throwing him to the ground. His arm went immediately limp and he had no other option but to drop the scalpel. As he did, he let out a guttural grunt of pain and anger. There was no way that he was using that arm anytime soon.

'Motherfucker!' he shouted, his right hand moving quickly to the fresh wound, as blood gushed out of it.

Hunter knew that he would hit his target, so he started running almost at the same time as he squeezed his trigger, covering the distance between him and Russell in the blink of an eye.

'Don't you dare move,' he said, his weapon now inches away from Russell's face. 'How're you doing, Carlos?' he called, glancing at his partner. 'Is that vomit on you?'

'No, it's barbecue sauce. We were just about to start a party when you showed up.'

With his weapon still trained on Russell, Hunter bent over and from the floor, retrieved the scalpel, which had fallen just behind Garcia's wheelchair.

'Is Anna OK? How long have I been missing for? How many days?'

'Days?' Hunter said, as he used the scalpel to cut Garcia's right hand loose before handing the blade to him. 'You've been missing for about three, three and a half hours, give or take.'

Garcia quickly sliced through the zip tie shackling his left hand before finally freeing his head from the chair's backrest. A deep skin-groove from the zip tie crossed his forehead from one end to the other. He looked at Russell. 'You lying motherfucker.'

'What?' Hunter asked.

'I'll explain later,' Garcia said, freeing his feet. 'So what took you so long? I left you clear instructions.'

'The photo?' Hunter asked.

'Yeah, the photo,' Garcia replied. 'What else? Clear as daylight.'

Sixty-Four

A few hours earlier – Thomas Riley High School car park

Hunter leaned back against the hood of his car and checked his watch – 10:32 p.m. He had called forensics about five minutes ago and asked them to urgently dispatch a team to the parking lot of the Thomas Riley High School in Watts.

'Detective,' Officer Emiliano called, as he joined Hunter at the front of his car. 'Do you need us to stay around? Is there anything that you'd like us to do?'

Hunter didn't see the point. What could they do? Help him wait?

Hunter shook his head. 'No, you guys can go. There's nothing else to do here but wait for the forensics team to arrive.'

Emiliano nodded, his eyes studying the detective in front of him. 'OK,' he finally said, reaching for his pen and pad. 'I'm just coming off my shift now, but if you need any help with anything.' He scribbled down his number. 'Even after hours . . . off duty . . . it don't matter.' He tore the page off and handed it to Hunter. 'Give me a holler, all right? I'd love to help, if I can.'

Hunter took the piece of paper and thanked Emiliano.

As the officer walked back to his black-and-white unit, Hunter checked his watch again – two minutes had gone by since the last time he checked. He folded the piece of paper that Emiliano had given him and placed it inside his jacket pocket. As he did, his fingers brushed against Garcia's cellphone that he'd put there just minutes earlier. He retrieved it, feeling its weight in his hands for a couple of seconds before waking up the screen and typing in Garcia's password.

The phone sprang to life.

Hunter stared at its home screen for a moment. He knew that Garcia hadn't sent him a message. He'd already checked. But just like someone who had misplaced his keys and kept on checking the same pocket, over and over again, Hunter tapped the text message application icon and navigated back to the last message that Garcia had sent him. Nothing had changed. It was still the message that Garcia had sent him the night before: *And again ... nope ... nothing tonight. See you in the morning.*

'Fuck!' Hunter rubbed his forehead with the heel of his left hand.

He checked the call log one more time – nothing had changed there either – last call out at 7:09 p.m., to Anna.

'Fuck ... fuck ... fuck!'

Whoever took him, Hunter thought, *got to him pretty damn fast.*

Not knowing what else to do, Hunter tapped the photo gallery icon on Garcia's cellphone, bringing up a screen titled 'My Albums'. The screen showed a collection of thumbnails, each representing a different photo album stored in the phone. The first album in Garcia's cellphone – top left-hand corner – was titled 'camera', and the thumbnail image for it immediately caught Hunter's attention. It wasn't a very clear photo, but it seemed to be the thumbnail of a pickup truck.

'What the fuck?'

Hunter quickly tapped the thumbnail and the screen refreshed to show the contents of the camera album. He, once again, tapped the thumbnail in the top left-hand corner – the photo of the pickup truck, the most recent photo added to that particular album. The full image loaded onto the screen and Hunter felt his core freeze.

The photo had been taken from about fifteen yards away and showed a black Dodge RAM pickup truck parked about four spaces to the left of Garcia's blue Honda Civic. The lighting was terrible, but both vehicles were still easily identifiable, and there was no doubt that the photo had been taken in that same school parking lot.

Hunter looked up, his eyes searching his surroundings. The photo showed both vehicles from the front. Garcia had taken it from the school gates, as he exited the building to get to his car, and before anyone else had gotten to the parking lot.

That, Hunter thought, *was a very smart move.*

Sixty-Five

It took Shannon less than two minutes to get back to Hunter with an address for the license plate number that he'd given her. That address took him to a cul-de-sac, high in Hollywood Hills.

The first thing that Hunter noticed as he switched off his headlights and turned right into the isolated road was that there were only five houses on that street, with plenty of trees in between them. Two of the houses seemed to be vacant, with a 'For Sale' sign on the front lawn. The one that he was looking for was the very last property at the top of the cul-de-sac.

The two-story house looked spacious enough, with three large front windows – two on the bottom floor and one on the top one – a gable roof, a patchy front lawn and a ranch-style front porch. The iron fence that surrounded the house was there for aesthetic reasons, not security, which allowed Hunter to breach it with ease.

He could see no lights on anywhere.

To the right of the house there was a two-car garage. The driveway that led up to it was made up of poorly laid-out and uneven concrete slabs, most of which were cracked and warped, with grass and weeds having sprung out along the joints. The garage door was closed and there was no vehicle parked either on the driveway or in front of the house.

Hunter quickly walked up to the garage and tried the door. To his surprise, it was unlocked. Hoping that the hinges wouldn't squeak too loudly, he carefully lifted the door, but only enough for him to be able to stoop under it.

The hinges didn't scream at all.

Inside the garage, Hunter found two vehicles parked side by side – a 2020 Cajun Red Chevrolet Impala, and a 2021 Dodge RAM 3500 pickup truck – the same Dodge RAM pickup truck that he'd asked Shannon to locate just a little while ago. Both vehicles were locked and clearly alarmed.

Hunter exited the garage and walked back to the house. Despite the curtains that covered both front windows being drawn shut, he could still tell that there was no light coming from behind them.

He tried the front door – locked.

He tried the windows – locked.

Hunter rounded the property as far as he could, before a hedge fence, by the back of the house, stopped him from going any further. On the way, he passed two other windows – curtains drawn ... no lights ... both locked.

Just a few feet from the hedge fence, on the right side of the house, there was a glass-panel door. Hunter used his flashlight against one of the panels to peek inside. The door led into what appeared to be a large utilities room. From outside, Hunter couldn't see much, just a washing machine, a tumble dryer, several shelves packed with what seemed to be canned food, and several stacked-up cardboard boxes.

He tried the handle on the door – locked.

Police protocol dictated that he should first ring the doorbell and talk to whomever came to the door ... if anyone did. But if he was at the right place – and his gut feeling was telling him that he was – then ringing the doorbell would only serve to alert whomever was inside, and Hunter wasn't about to do that.

According to California state law, an officer needed a warrant to enter a private property without the consent of the owner. But, like with every law, there were exceptions. One of those exceptions was if the officer had reason to believe that a life could be in danger inside the property.

Hunter used his elbow to give one of the glass panels a firm knock. It smashed without too much noise, as the glass pieces fell onto a doormat on the inside. He cleared away the remaining glass shards and carefully unlocked the door.

No alarm.

Weapon and flashlight in hand, Hunter pulled the door open and finally entered the house.

Sixty-Six

Hunter had been right – the glass-panel door led into a large but relatively empty utilities room. From outside the house, before stepping into the room, Hunter checked the ceiling corners for motion monitors – there were none. He quickly crossed the room to get to the door on the other side, just past a stack of empty cardboard boxes. This new door was made of solid wood – no glass panels. Hunter put his ear against the door and listened for a moment – no sound. He tried the handle – unlocked.

The next room along was the kitchen, which was impressively large, with an asymmetrically designed, black-and-white-checkered floor and plenty of cupboards, both high and low. Once again, before stepping into the room, Hunter checked the ceiling corners for motion monitors and, once again, he found none. The kitchen smelled clean. There was no smell of cooked food, or anything gone out of date.

On the dish rack, Hunter could see only one plate, one glass and one set of cutlery.

The door at the other end of the kitchen was already open – no light beyond it. Hunter got to it and paused, listening from its edge for any sounds coming from the next room, or from deeper inside the house. He got nothing but stillness and silence. No motion monitors again.

The door led into a dining room, with a small four-seater table, a tall, glass-door display unit, an empty drinks cart and not much else. The window on its west wall was one of the two windows at the front of the house. Once again, Hunter cleared the room quickly to get to the next door, to the right of the drinks cart. This door was closed. He placed his ear against it and listened for several long seconds. He couldn't hear a sound. He tried the handle – unlocked.

The dining room linked directly to a sparsely furnished living room, which made the room seem even larger than it already was.

No motion monitors either.

Hunter stepped into the room and allowed his eyes to carefully sweep the space ... the shadows ... the corners ... the hiding spots ... for signs of someone else there. He found none. On the east wall, just behind a three-seater sofa, there was a set of French doors that opened onto the back garden and the pool area. The pool was completely empty of water and there didn't seem to be a pool house, or a utilities shed, anywhere. From the sofa, looking back into the room, Hunter could see three doors. The one to his left was the door that he had come in through from the dining room. The door in front of him was already open and he could see that it would take him to the house's entry lobby and give him access to the staircase, leading to the top floor. The door to his right was closed. He tried that one next.

Ear to the door – not a peep.

Door handle – unlocked.

Ceiling corners – no motion monitors.

Hunter stepped into a comfortable office/study room, with a desk that faced a window on the south wall. On the desk, Hunter could see an impressive computer setup, with a triple-monitor.

Hunter walked up to the computer on the desk and pressed down on the space-bar key. All three monitors came alive, displaying different graphics and stock charts – not CCTV camera footage – which was what Hunter was hoping for.

The window on the west wall was the second front-of-the-house window. The other two walls were lined from top to bottom with books in computer programming, economics and trading, and medicine.

Hunter was about to move back into the living room and go try his luck upstairs when he paused . . . something about that house didn't feel quite right.

Murderers who abducted their victims so they could torture them for days before taking their lives needed a place to do exactly that – keep their victims captive while torturing them for days – and Hunter knew from experience that those types of murderers didn't do that in their bedrooms, regardless of them living alone or not. This killer had probably been taking victims into captivity for years, maybe even decades. From what they'd gathered so far, he was organized and meticulous. Someone like that would have at least a secure room . . . a room from which his victims would have no chance of escaping . . . a room in which he could torture them to his heart's content and no one would be able to hear a sound. Such rooms were almost always created either underground or on the ground floor. They rarely existed on higher levels due to logistics.

Sure, Hunter also knew that in the majority of cases where such rooms were found, they existed in remote locations – a cabin in the woods, a hut high on the mountains, a bunker hidden in a forest, a disused warehouse on the outskirts of a town . . . some-where isolated enough to give the perp some peace of mind based solely on location. And of course Hunter knew that that could be where this killer was keeping Garcia. But Hunter had to work with what he had, and what he had was the photo in Garcia's cellphone – the black Dodge RAM 3500 that was parked in the garage just outside.

The logical assumption was that that had been the same pickup truck that the perp had used to transport Garcia from the school parking lot, where he was rendered unconscious, to wherever he was being held captive. If Garcia was being held at any other isolated location, how come the 3500 pickup truck was parked in the garage?

Hunter *had* to work with what he had, and what he had was a horrible gut feeling that he was missing something, and whatever it was that he was missing wouldn't be upstairs. So, in his mind, that left him with only one option – a secret room somewhere.

Since there was no pool house or utilities shed in the house's backyard, Hunter figured that if that house hid a secret room, it would be inside – either behind a wall, or under it – not outside.

Two of the walls in the room that he was in had windows, so they were automatically discarded. The other two were lined from top to bottom with books – very possible – but the east wall, the one with the smaller of the two bookcases, also had the door that he had come in through from the living room. There was no secret room behind that wall. That, once again, left Hunter with only one possibility – the bookcase against the north wall. He approached it and immediately saw a problem – the bookcase wasn't built into the wall. It was built from wooden modules – the build-it-yourself type – probably purchased from some flat-pack, DIY store. Those weren't the type of bookshelves that could hide a Murphy door.

That was when it dawned on Hunter.

The oddly designed kitchen floor.

The kitchen floor resembled a typical, old-style, Italian, black-and-white checkered floor, but its squares were asymmetric – not only in size, but in orientation as well – creating an almost psychedelic effect. Why would anyone want a psychedelic floor in their kitchen?

To hide a trapdoor. That was the first answer that came to Hunter's mind.

He quickly made his way back through the house and into the kitchen.

In there, he stood still for a long while, listening as carefully as he could, while his eyes attentively followed the beam of his flashlight on the floor, slowly moving around like a spotlight following a solo ballerina on stage.

Nothing.

Hunter couldn't hear a sound, and no matter how hard he looked, he also couldn't see any indications of a secret floor panel that could lead him to a secret, underground room.

But just because he couldn't see it, it didn't mean that it wasn't there. Hunter knew that only too well.

After so many years investigating ultra-violent crimes, Hunter had come across a few Murphy doors that had led him into secret rooms. Some were badly built, hidden inside a wardrobe or under a staircase, and were relatively easy to spot, but some had been so expertly created that they were practically impossible to find unless they'd been activated.

Murphy doors were usually activated either by pressing a button that had been hidden somewhere or by pushing a lever; in that kitchen, there were plenty of places to hide both.

Walking over to the high cupboards on the north wall, Hunter used his flashlight to look under them, while feeling the edges and corners with the tips of his fingers. There were five cupboards built against that wall, but Hunter found nothing under them – no button, no lever, no false panel.

Next, he simply opened all the cupboards, took a step back, and paused. Four of them had several items in each – pans, pots, cups, plates, jars, glasses, kitchen utensils, kitchen supplies – all the normal items that he would expect to find in most kitchens – but in one of the cupboards, the first one on the far right, there were only two cans of tuna on the lower shelf. That was it. Nothing else.

Hunter thought about it for a millisecond.

If he had to constantly activate a secret mechanism to release some kind of trapdoor somewhere, he would want quick access to it. If the release mechanism was hidden inside a cupboard, he wouldn't fill that cupboard with stuff, otherwise he would have to move all the stuff out of the way first before getting to the mechanism. Once activated, he would have to move everything back to its original place. And he would have to do that every time he wanted to access his secret room. Not exactly practical.

Hunter returned to the first cupboard and pushed the two cans of tuna to one side.

He couldn't see anything.

Holding his flashlight with his left hand, he used his right one to feel the back panel inside the cupboard.

He pressed its edges, searching for a click-spring mechanism – the most used mechanism for concealed false panels.

He pressed the top edge – nothing.

Bottom edge – nothing.

Center – click.

The panel dislodged.

Hunter's heart stuttered.

He pulled it open to find a lever.

'Bingo,' he whispered, as he reached for the lever and flipped it down. As he did, he heard a new clicking noise come from behind him. Hunter directed the beam of his flashlight back to the floor and searched, but nothing seemed to have changed. No secret door had sprung open ... no black or white square had clicked out of place.

But he had definitely heard a new clicking sound once he flipped the lever.

Must've been another false back panel somewhere.

Behind him, all the cupboards there were located under the sink.

Hunter got down on his knees and opened them all. It took

him just a couple of seconds to find it. He was right – a second false panel had sprung open – this one revealing a round, metal button. Hunter pressed it and heard the thump of a lock opening just a few feet to his right.

And there it was.

A secret, heavy and steady floor door, leading down to what Hunter knew would be the killer's torture chamber.

He took a deep breath, checked his weapon and took the stairs down.

Sixty-Seven

Hunter took the cement steps going down to the house's cellar as cautiously as he possibly could, counting each step as he took them, and he was immediately surprised. This was a deep, deep cellar. It took him eighteen steps to get to solid ground. And it was pitch-black and cold down there.

As Hunter climbed down the last step onto the adobe floor, he paused, the beam of his flashlight circling the room that he was in, while his eyes took in everything they could.

That first room was rectangular in shape and not very spacious. The walls were crude and seemed to be made of solid concrete blocks. At the center of the ceiling, a single light bulb sat inside a heavy-duty metal mesh box. Ventilation was provided via a makeshift system, where a thick PVC tube, sporting unevenly spaced holes, ran along the edges of the ceiling before disappearing out the only door in that room . . . a door that led deeper into that hell cave. No wonder the air down there felt heavy and stale.

Pushed up against one of the walls, Hunter saw a large-capacity, solid-lid, chest freezer with a thick padlock hanging from the lid latch.

The padlock was unlocked.

Hunter walked over to the freezer and lifted its lid – empty and unplugged – but what made Hunter's heart drop to the bottom of his stomach were the scratches and blood smears that he saw on the inside of the lid and along all four internal walls. The freezer that he was looking at wasn't used to keep food from perishing. It was used as a human-freezing container.

Shaun Daniels had frozen to death inside that box. Hunter had no doubt of that.

Just like he'd done upstairs, before entering a different room, Hunter paused by the door and listened for sounds coming from deeper inside that cave, but all he could hear was the low humming of the makeshift ventilation system in operation.

The door, which was more of a passageway because it had no physical door, led into a corridor that L-shaped itself to the left at the end, but not before passing two more doors – both also on the left. No motion monitors again.

How big is this fucking cellar? Hunter wondered. He truly hoped that it wasn't as large as the whole of the house's ground floor. If it were, this place would be massive, and that was never a good thing.

Weapon and flashlight in hand, Hunter entered the corridor and carefully approached the first of the two doors. It was open and, just like the room that Hunter had come from, it was pitch-black in there.

He stopped at the doorway and circled the room with the beam of his flashlight.

It wasn't a room. It was a holding cell – square in shape and no larger than seven foot long by seven foot wide. The air inside it was saturated with the smell of feces, urine, vomit and bitter human sweat.

On the floor, pushed up against the cell's back wall, was a filthy, bloodstained, single-person mattress. No pillows ... no blankets. At both ends of the mattress, chains with wrist and ankle shackles sprang out of the walls. To Hunter's right, in one of the corners of the room, there was a dirty plastic bucket with a metal lid on it. Hunter didn't have to check it to know that that bucket was the cell's latrine. On the ceiling, inside another metal-mesh box, instead of motion monitors, Hunter could see speakers.

The walls to that holding cell seemed to have been sound-proofed, which Hunter thought was pointless. They were so deep under the house that someone could've been lying with their ear pressed hard against the kitchen floor upstairs and they wouldn't be able to hear a gunshot if it had come from behind a regular closed door down in that death cellar, let alone a human scream.

Hunter returned to the corridor and moved on to the next door along.

Another holding cell, but this one was larger than the one Hunter had just come from. Once again, the walls seemed to have been soundproofed. The single mattress pushed up against the back wall was in much better condition than the one in the previous cell – no bloodstains – and here, there was a pillow and a blanket. Identical chains with wrist and ankle shackles also sprang out of the walls, but the latrine, to the right of the door, wasn't just a simple plastic bucket with a metal lid. It was a proper, heavy-duty, portable toilet, with a removable waste tank.

Compared to the previous cell, that one was a Presidential Suite.

That new cell was also saturated with the same smells as the previous one, but there was a new scent lingering in the air – a scent that was hard to describe because it was one of the oddest combinations of aromas that Hunter had ever inhaled: bitter ... sweat ... sour ... pungent ... consistent but scarce ... heavy but light ... all rolled up into one. Even though it was hard to describe, Hunter knew exactly what that smell was because he had come across it before ... way too many times.

That, Hunter knew, was the smell of human fear.

Hunter got to where the corridor L-shaped itself to the left and paused by the edge of the wall, once again listening for any sounds, and once again he heard nothing, which wasn't exactly surprising, now that he knew that the rooms down in that hellhole were soundproofed.

Carefully, Hunter rounded the corner to find yet another two holding cells – these ones on the right wall – and they were pretty much a replica of the two cells he'd seen in the previous corridor. The first one was smaller and squalid when compared to the second one.

What the fuck? Hunter thought, as the beam of his flashlight searched the space again. *What does this killer do? Upgrade his victims to better captivity conditions depending on good behavior?*

The next door that Hunter came to wasn't on the walls to his left or right, it was directly in front of him and it had been left ajar. Hunter tiptoed to it and paused. There was no light coming from behind the door – no sounds either.

Hunter pulled the door open and stepped into a new space. This was a large room – larger than the living room upstairs.

Once again, his flashlight searched the spaces ... the corners ... the hiding spots ... for signs of someone else there. There were none, but the room chilled Hunter to the core because he knew this room. He'd been inside similar ones before ... plenty of times.

Holy shit!

Hunter was standing at the door to an operation hall ... a surgical room that could very easily double as an autopsy theater. That room, Hunter had no doubt, was used for torturing victims. In there, the odd scent of human fear was simply overwhelming, but it collided with those of cleaning agents, antiseptics and disinfectants.

'Arghhhhhhh!'

The faint scream reached Hunter's ears like a lover's whisper, catching him completely by surprise and making him shiver in place. His heart picked up speed inside his chest like a jet plane at takeoff, but his eyes held steady, following his flashlight, which shot in the direction of where the dim sound seemed to have come from.

Another door – all the way across the room from where Hunter was standing and a little to his left.

This time, Hunter didn't search the spaces, the corners or the hiding spots. Despite being muffled and sounding like a whisper, Hunter could easily tell that that scream had come from Garcia.

As stealthily and as quickly as he could, Hunter got to the new door and tried the handle – unlocked. He carefully pulled it open just enough to dislodge the door from its frame. As he did, he also saw light come from inside the next room.

'*One of the workers,*' Hunter heard Garcia say, but his voice was labored and heavy, and full of pain. He sounded like he was fighting for breath with every word. '*. . . is a truck aficionado. Can tell a truck just by its silhouette.*'

Hunter peeked through the door opening, but he couldn't see anything. The door opened onto what looked to be a five-foot-long walled strip of nothing – like a mini entry corridor before the main room, which was located to the left, and that was lucky. That meant that Hunter could pull the door fully open and step into the room, but he would still be protected by the wall.

And that was exactly what he did – quickly and silently.

Once inside the room, Hunter flatbacked his body against the wall at the edge of the mini entry corridor, looked left and took the quickest of peeks.

What he saw shocked him.

Just past the corridor, a few feet to the right, he could see a couple in wheelchairs. They looked old – really old – but Hunter could be mistaken because, truthfully, they both looked to be at the brink of death ... mummified even. Their gazes were unblinking and straight ahead, as if they were either hypnotized or watching something they just couldn't tear their eyes from.

Whoever they were, Hunter knew that they couldn't have been the ones who had taken Garcia. So who the hell were they?

The conclusion that Hunter came to was that they had to be captive victims, just waiting to die.

To the left of the couple, Hunter caught a glimpse of a table of instruments covered in weapons – most of them blades of some sort.

'*All right.*' Hunter heard a new voice that came from deeper inside the room. The voice was male, strong and threatening. '*How about the fingers? How did you find out about that? And think before you reply, Detective, because if I suspect that you're lying, the next thing that I'll burn . . . will be one of your fucking eyeballs.*'

Time to act.

From his flatback position, Hunter rotated his body left, 180 degrees, landing him at the opening to the room. The old couple in the wheelchairs were just a little to his right and a couple of feet ahead of him – just at the edge of his field of vision. Hunter's arms were stretched out, double-gripping his weapon. His eyes were ready to search left, right and center for his target, but they didn't need to. The target was about twenty-five feet directly in front of him, a little bent over in front of a terrified-looking and shirtless Garcia, who had been tied to a high-back chair.

'*Are we clear, Detective?*'

Hunter aimed his weapon at the man's back. 'Somehow . . . I really don't fucking think so.'

Sixty-Eight

Back inside the torture chamber, Garcia was still waiting for an answer from Hunter.

'So,' he asked again. 'What took you so long? Mr. GrillChef over here was just about to turn me into a burger.'

'You do know that if he had taken your phone with him,' Hunter countered, 'or destroyed it right there on that parking lot, I would've never found you, right?'

From the floor, Russell looked back at Hunter with pure hate in his eyes.

'Hands behind your back,' Hunter commanded, getting down on one knee and using his left hand to roll Russell over – face to the ground ... back toward Hunter. The movement wasn't a delicate one.

'Arghhhhhh! Fuck you!' Russell shouted, as Garcia helped Hunter on the ground, pressing Russell's face hard against the concrete floor, while Hunter cuffed Russell's wrists behind his back.

With a shattered humerus head, the behind-the-back arm twist would've felt like the shoulder joint was rolling on barbed wire. Russell screamed and kicked, with spit flying off his lips, bouncing against the floor, and returning to his blood-splattered face – the nose, the eyes, the mouth ... everywhere.

Hunter holstered his weapon, grabbed Russell by the back of his shirt and hoisted him up into a sitting position against the back wall.

He was about to go check on Jennifer, when he and Garcia heard a new voice coming from just behind them.

'James.'

In a blink of an eye, Hunter and Garcia swung around to find Russell's father standing by the instruments table.

While their attention had been on securing Russell and cuffing his hands, neither of them noticed Russell's father get up from his wheelchair and approach the weapons on the table.

He chose the pistol, which he had firmly in his grip, aiming directly at the two detectives before him. The weapon looked enormous in his frail hands.

'Sir ...' Hunter said, his hands up, palms facing forward in a 'surrender' gesture. 'Please, put the gun down.'

'His real name is James,' the old man said. 'James Richard Whitely. Not Russell ... not Trevor ... not Michael ... James.'

'Sir,' Hunter tried again. 'Please ...'

But James's father didn't seem to be listening. The determination in his eyes seemed unflinching.

'And you shot him ... you shot my son.'

Your son? Hunter thought, but, despite his total surprise, neither his voice nor his expression gave anything away. 'Sir,' he tried again. 'I know how bad this looks, but ...'

'I know what you're thinking,' James's father continued, ignoring every word Hunter said. 'That I'm too old ... too weak to be able to use a gun, right?' He didn't give the detectives a chance to reply. 'Well, I guess we're just about to find out.'

'Shoot them, Dad,' James called from behind Hunter. 'Shoot them.'

'Sir, you don't want to do that.' Hunter's voice was calm but firm. 'Believe me. You really don't.'

The old man's gaze moved to his wife for a fraction of a second before returning to Hunter. 'You think so. *Watch this.*'

He squeezed the trigger.

Twice.

Sixty-Nine

For Garcia, time seemed to slow down as if he could control it. He heard James's father say the words 'watch this', then pull the trigger on the gun for the first time, and he could swear that he saw the bullet leave the barrel of the gun and travel through the air, inch by inch, gaining on its target fast, until it finally came into contact with soft tissue.

Perfect shot.

Game over.

The projectile disappeared into the target's head, only to come out on the other side, bringing with it bone fragments, soft tissue, gray matter, blood, hair, and the end of life.

Just as he said the words 'watch this', James's father had swung his arm right, aimed his gun at his own wife, and pulled the trigger.

Time had slowed down to such a degree that Garcia saw her looking back at him with a smile on her lips, as if they had planned this all along.

Her head practically shattered on impact.

As soon as James's father squeezed the trigger, he pulled his arm back toward himself fast and, before anyone could even blink, placed the barrel of the gun inside his mouth and gave that trigger another firm tug.

The back of his head simply exploded, creating a wet mist of blood that was littered with brain and skull debris. That heavy ball of human carnage kept on traveling upward, until it splattered itself against the ceiling above him.

While his wife's lifeless body tumbled over on her wheelchair, his collapsed to the ground like a puppet with severed strings. Blood began pooling on the floor fast, creating a dark scarlet rug that was quickly enveloping both of their bodies.

'Noooooo!' James shouted from the opposite wall. He tried to get up, but Garcia stopped him with a hand to the shoulder . . . the left shoulder.

'Arghhhhhh! You fuck!'

James crumpled back to the floor, his eyes wide, the pain so intense he looked like he was about to pass out.

'Jesus!' Garcia said, his stare pinging to Hunter. 'What the fuck just happened here?'

Hunter's full attention was on the old, lifeless couple on the floor. His heart was beating way out of synch with his thinking because he knew that he and Garcia should be dead. 'They finally found a way out,' he replied.

'What?' Garcia asked.

'I don't know the story here,' Hunter explained. 'But if I had to guess, I'd say that they've been kept captive down in this cellar by their own son for I don't know how long.'

'Seventeen years,' Garcia said.

Hunter's eyes almost popped out of their sockets as he looked back at Garcia.

Garcia nodded. 'Seventeen years they've been locked down here.'

It took Hunter a couple of seconds to process that.

'It looks like they were kept separate from each other,' Hunter continued, his chin jerking in the direction of the door that led back into the cellar of horrors. 'Each in their own cell, where I'm guessing they were either kept shackled to the walls at all times, or heavily sedated, so that they wouldn't end their own lives.' He turned to look at James on the floor. 'This was the first opportunity they got . . . and they took it.'

'Fuck you,' James seethed, before spitting up at Hunter. It hit Hunter's trousers.

Hunter didn't move. His eyes stayed on James, but he addressed Garcia. 'I have a feeling that what he said just before pulling the trigger – "watch this" – wasn't meant for us.'

Garcia shook his head confidently. 'No, it wasn't.' But before he could explain the meaning of that command, they all heard a new noise coming from the door to the room.

In a flash, Hunter pulled out his semi-automatic pistol and aimed forward. A split second later, Officer Emiliano Esqueda appeared behind the dead couple, weapon in hand . . . eyes wide.

'LAPD,' he shouted, and was immediately cut off by Hunter and Garcia.

'Easy . . . easy,' they both shouted in unison.

'It's us,' Hunter called out. 'It's just us. Take a deep breath and put down the gun, Emiliano. It's just us.'

The kid was visibly shaking, his breathing heavy, his eyes full of fear.

'What . . . the fuck?'

Emiliano gulped in air. He was still holding his weapon in a double grip, aiming forward, but his stare was all over the place, clearly trying to understand what it was that he had just walked in on.

'What the fuck happened here?' he asked again. 'What is this fucking place? Who are all these people?'

That was when it dawned on Garcia.

He turned to face Hunter.

'He's the cavalry?' he asked, his eyes narrowing to slits.

Hunter looked back at him. 'What?'

'The cavalry,' Garcia repeated it. 'You said that this wasn't a Hollywood movie and that after you found the trapdoor in the kitchen, you called the cavalry.' Garcia tilted his head in Emiliano's direction, while arching his eyebrows at Hunter. 'He is it? The cavalry?'

Hunter shrugged. 'He was willing to help.'

Garcia breathed out despair.

Seventy

Two days later
Police Administration Building – 4:00 p.m.

'Sixty-three victims?' Captain Blake asked, as she entered Hunter and Garcia's office, carrying the report that she'd just read. 'Twelve years and sixty-three victims?' Her gaze bounced between her detectives. 'Do we have any proof of this?'

'Not yet,' Garcia replied, with a shake of the head. He was sitting at his desk, his shirt unbuttoned halfway, staring down at the huge bandage job on his chest. 'Forensics is still at the house, Captain,' he explained. 'And with that cellar, they'll probably still be there a week from now – probably longer – but so far they've come across no records: no box full of drivers' licenses, no photographs of bodies or victims captive in those cells, no video recordings, no schematics or drawn-out plans on how to take any of his victims, no list of names, no victim trophy chest . . . nothing. If James Richard Whitely has a list of all the victims he took over the past twelve years, we haven't found it yet.'

'They won't find anything like that,' Hunter informed them.

'How can you be so sure?' the captain asked.

Hunter shrugged before clarifying. 'Because James Whitely is a *made* psychopath, Captain – not a born one. His desire to torture and kill didn't come from some inexplicable urge deep within him. It came from a sense of duty. He believed that he was doing the right thing, and that was – punishing parents who had been violent toward their kids. He had no desire to keep records of his victims. He's not the type of killer who, after the murder act, would keep going back to images or mementos so that he could relive the whole act again. On the contrary, what he wanted to do was get rid of them. There was no narcissistic side to his murders . . . no posing of the bodies to show them off . . . no attention-calling to any aspect of what he did. He didn't even have a "signature" per se, except for the fact that he disguised his murders as accidents, and that was done to protect himself. He had no preferred way of killing either. He simply did to them what they did to others.' Hunter shook his head confidently. 'He won't have a list of names, or a treasure chest, or mementos, or anything. His victims weren't trophies . . . they were his job.'

'So that number,' Captain Blake said, putting the report down on Hunter's desk, 'is purely based on his mother's account. A woman who was kept locked down in a cellar, chained to the walls, for seventeen years. A woman whose brain was probably already mush before her husband blew it off her skull.'

'That's right,' Garcia agreed, finally lifting his eyes to look back at his captain. 'But I don't think that she got that number wrong, Captain.'

'She probably didn't,' Hunter agreed, indicating the file on his desk. 'You read the report, Captain. From his first ever victim, James made his parents watch, and he tortured each victim for days . . . weeks . . . months, even. They couldn't look away . . . they couldn't close their eyes.' He lifted his hands at her. 'It's true that memories can't exactly be trusted – they warp, they shatter . . . and they're put back together in ways that look nothing like the original – but in this case, James's mother had nothing to warp and shatter her memories with. They were locked in that cellar in an endless loop of nothingness and darkness. All she ever saw, for the past twelve years, was her son torturing others. Just think about that for a minute. Those kinds of memories are hard to forget, Captain. They're hard to warp . . . and they don't shatter.'

'Well, whatever happens from now on,' Garcia said, jumping in, 'it's got nothing to do with us anymore. We've done our job. The ball is now totally in the DA's court.'

Captain Blake chuckled. 'Yeah, like they'll convince him to talk, right?' She shook her head. 'This is going to be another war fought inside a courtroom.'

'He's not walking away from this, Captain,' Hunter told her. 'But he's just as much a victim in this as anyone else. His parents ended his life even before it began – all that violence and abuse . . . never loved – he had nothing to grow into, except for a monster. He needs help, not incarceration. Even the DA understands that. James Whitely will serve a prison sentence for the rest of his life, I have no doubt of that, but it won't be in a regular prison. The district attorney will probably recommend that he be sent to DSH Patton – the most secure psychiatric hospital in California, and one of the best in the land. He'll have a better chance of getting help there than anywhere else.'

'Talking about victims,' Captain Blake asked, 'how is Miss Mendoza doing?'

'Very weak,' Hunter replied. 'But she's fighting. The doctors said that she was entering the last stages of starvation. That's when the body starts consuming its own muscles for protein – including the heart. As a result of lacking every nutrient possible, she has developed anemia and is showing the initial symptoms of beriberi.' Hunter nodded. 'But she's a fighter, even her doctors are saying so. All we can do is wait and hope for the best.'

Captain Blake's gaze settled on the report on Hunter's desk one last time.

'You know,' she said, her voice a little quieter than normal. 'There's no doubt that James Whitely was a monster. But he was a monster who was going after worse monsters. Some of the people he took, probably deserved what they got.'

'Well, I didn't,' Garcia said, indicating the bandaging on his chest.

'How is that going, by the way?' Blake asked.

'Like a Texan ribeye steak that's been left on the grill for too long. That's how it's going. And get this, right? These were my wife's exact words, as she changed my bandages this morning.' Garcia put on a silly voice. '"About time you got a few manly scars, isn't it?"' Garcia shook his head at the room. 'I mean – what the hell?' He lifted his hands, showing Hunter and Captain Blake the deep scars in his palms from his very first investigation with the UVC Unit. 'What does she think these are? Birth marks?'

They all broke out laughing.

Hunter got up and reached for his jacket.

Garcia did the same.

'We were just about to go get some lunch, Captain,' Hunter said. 'Want to come along?'

'Where are you guys going?'

Hunter glanced at his partner. 'I'm thinking somewhere where we can get a nice Texan ribeye steak ... medium rare.'

'Oh, you've got jokes now, do you?' Garcia said.

Captain Blake smiled. 'How about we go to a Brazilian barbecue house, instead? I know a great one called "Down in the Basement".'

Garcia threw his hands up in the air as they all walked out of the UVC Unit's office. 'Great, everyone is a comedian today.' He pushed ahead. 'And wherever we're going ... we're all just having salad.'

Acknowledgements

As always, my heartfelt thanks go to a few special people, who for so many years now have been a big part of my professional life – my agent, Darley Anderson, for being the best agent an author could have. And Mary Darby, Georgia Fuller, Salma Zarugh, Rebeka Finch, Francesca Edwards and the whole team at the agency, for simply being able to create magic. My editor at Simon & Schuster – Katherine Armstrong – for always improving my manuscripts tenfold. My editor at Ullstein, Germany – Monika Boese – for all her incredible work and support.

A huge thanks also goes to Richard Vlietstra, Harriett Collins and the whole team at Simon & Schuster. Thank you so much for still believing in me. You guys are amazing.

FIND OUT MORE ABOUT
CHRIS CARTER

Chris Carter writes highly addictive thrillers
featuring Detective Robert Hunter

To find out more about Chris and his writing,
visit his website at

www.chriscarterbooks.com

or follow Chris on

 @ChrisCarterBooksOfficial

All of Chris Carter's novels are available
in print and eBook, and are available to
download in eAudio